Book 2 of the "Demon of the Deep" series

AF603697

Splinter Heart

Briar Belmont

This is a work of fiction. All names, characters, events, places, organizations, and incidents portrayed in this novel are either products of the author's imagination or are used fictitiously. No identification with actual persons (living or deceased), places, buildings, and products is intended or should be inferred.

SPLINTER HEART

Copyright © 2026 by Briar Belmont

All rights reserved.

No part of this book may be reproduced in any form or by any electronic or mechanical means, including information storage and retrieval systems, without written permission from the author, except for the use of brief quotations in a book review.

NO AI TRAINING: Without in any way limiting the author's [and publisher's] exclusive rights under copyright, any use of this publication to "train" generative artificial intelligence (AI) technologies to generate text is expressly prohibited.

Cover Art by: María Arteta https://marosar.carrd.co/

Typography and Illustrations by Amphi https://www.books-amphi.studio/

Map By: Isaac Jordan

ISBN 979-8-9905007-4-7 (hardcover)

ISBN 979-8-9905007-3-0 (paperback)

ISBN 979-8-9905007-5-4 (ebook)

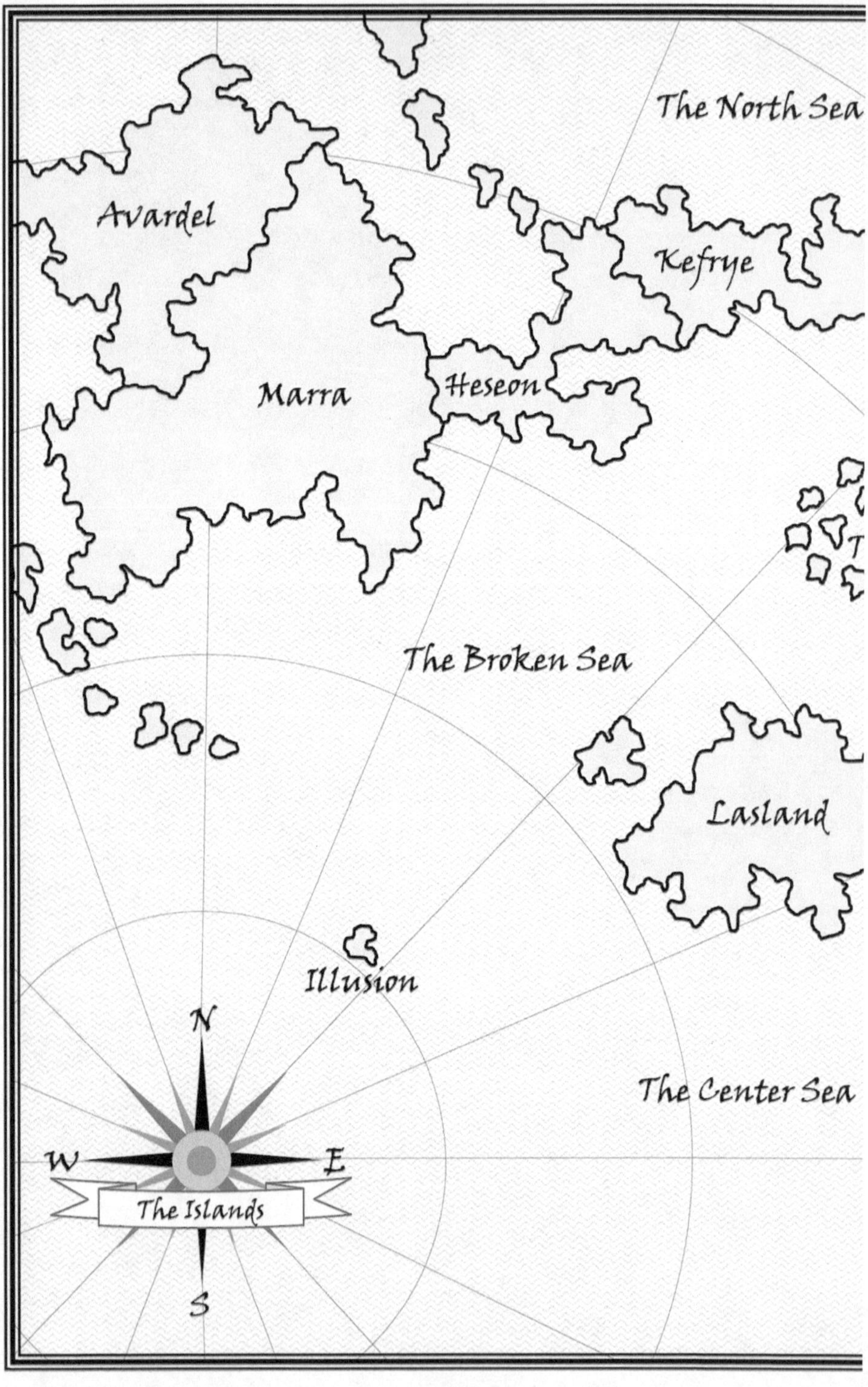

The North Sea

Avardel

Kefrye

Marra

Heseon

The Broken Sea

Lasland

Illusion

N

W

E

The Islands

S

The Center Sea

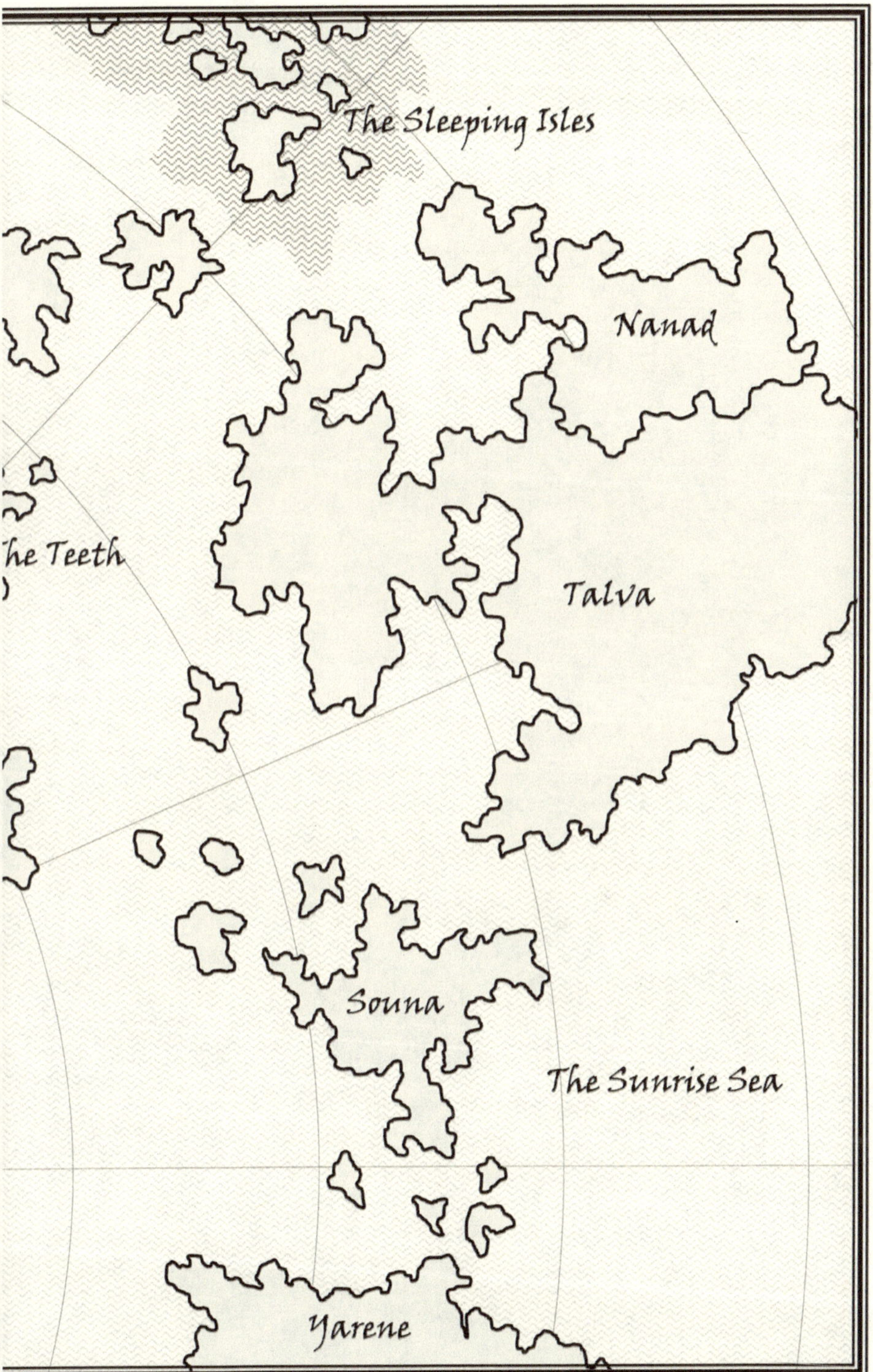

The Sleeping Isles

Nanad

he Teeth

Talva

Souna

The Sunrise Sea

Yarene

AUTHOR'S NOTE

For the sake of my own sanity and the vibes of this book, please suspend your disbelief about a few key factors for this world. STIs don't exist, and these pirates all bathe regularly.
Agreed? Agreed.

Please see the back of the book or follow the QR code for content warnings.

ALSO BY BRIAR BELMONT

Demon of the Deep Series

#0.5 Undefined Tides

#1 Demon of the Deep

#1.5 (To Be Announced)

#2 Splinter Heart

#3 (To Be Announced)

To Dessa,
Besties till the end.

Part 1

The Teeth

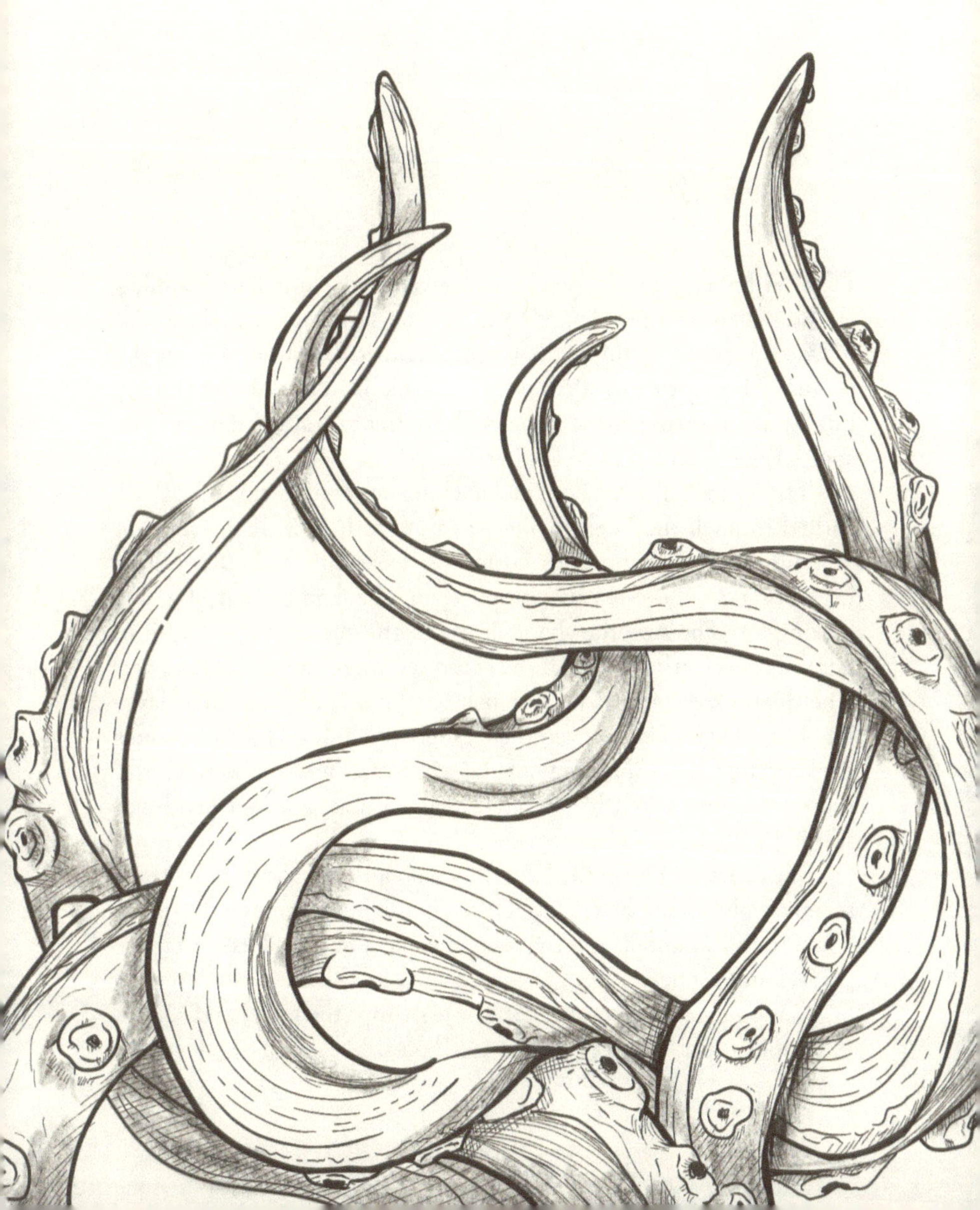

CHAPTER 1

MAY 1ST, 1668

The scent of old metal and seawater hit Zanta like a familiar slap as she stepped into the dockside salvage shop. All manner of things that could, and had, washed up on the shores of Roseforte crowded every available inch of the small space, but for a worn path just wide enough for her to venture deeper. She spotted a bucket of old keys and waded to it.

The grime of tarnished metal clung to Zanta's fingers as she carded through the bucket. She was used to it now. After years of searching in every antiquities, curiosities, locksmith, and salvage shop in every port the *Monsoon* stopped in, she knew what she was looking for. The size, the shape of the teeth—she could picture it in her mind so clearly. It was all she could see when she closed her eyes. The dream she focused on to block out the nightmares. That large brass key that had hung from the leather cord around Silver Stroud's neck, nestled in his thick gray chest hair. Sometimes she wondered if she even remembered it correctly, or if the image in her head had warped with the passage of time.

She drew out one of the keys. It was about the right size; the teeth seemed right. Zanta held it up to the light fighting through the grimy window and squinted, as if that would make it reveal all its secrets.

Was it the one?

"Oi, you gonna buy something or just grope the merchandise?"

Zanta nearly jumped out of her boots. She hadn't noticed the grizzled shop owner perched on a stool in the corner, looking just as old and washed up as his merchandise. He struggled up from his seat and shuffled through the jumble of wares toward her. Once he was stationary again, he swayed slightly on his feet and wiped his red nose on the back of his hand. A bottle of something strong-smelling sloshing, but not spilling.

"I'm still looking," Zanta said flatly. She set the key aside and continued digging through the bucket.

"Well hurry up."

Zanta glared at him out of the corner of her eye. "You got somewhere to be?" She was in no mood for this today, the anniversary of Silver Stroud's death.

The anniversary of the day she'd driven a piece of his own beloved ship through his heart, and lost the most precious thing in her life.

The shopkeeper pointedly sloshed the bottle's contents around. Zanta sighed and held up the key before his bleary eyes.

"How much for this?"

The old man rolled his eyes as if selling the junk in his shop was the greatest burden of his life.

"Five copper tals," he said.

"Two," Zanta countered.

"Four."

"I thought you wanted me out?" Zanta raised her eyebrows.

He scratched his belly beneath his stained shirt.

"Three."

Zanta was over it. She dug the coins out of her pocket, dropped them into his waiting hand, and left before he could make it back to his stool in the corner.

She scowled as the door thudded shut behind her and shoved the newly acquired piece of her collection into her pocket in place of the coins. Gorgeous spring weather graced the Roseforte rooftops, but the clear blue sky and warm breeze did nothing to lift her mood. In fact, it would have been better if rain, gloom, and cold wrapped the city. At least then she could focus on her current misery instead of the past.

She would have liked to look for more keys in the shop. It was the only thing that soothed her when she got antsy like this, and she'd never been to Roseforte before. It was a fresh hunting ground.

Zanta retrieved her hat from her pack and shoved it onto her head over her braids. It was a floppy-brimmed thing to keep the sun out of her eyes, instead of her usual black tricorn with red ostrich plumes. That one was too distinctively Splinter Zanta, and she didn't exactly want to advertise her presence here.

Zanta and her crew had snuck into Talva's southernmost mainland port on board the *Monsoon*, disguised with a painted-over name and forged papers of a Yarenen merchant. All of that wasn't strictly necessary. They could have found some hidden cove down the coast and snuck in on foot instead. But what was the fun in that?

Not that she was having any fun now.

Her bootheels thudded on the cobblestones as she made her way down the sunny street. She had things to do. The cold war between Marra and Talva seemed quiet as of late, and that meant one or both of them were moving pieces in secret, ramping up for something big. What piece would they move next? Both had exhausted the islands that were easy pickings. Marra had a firm hold on its colonies. Talva was in the midst of putting down an uprising in Nanad, but from what she'd heard, it would be over by the end of the year. Only powerful allies remained, and neither could risk invading those without direct retaliation from the other.

Zanta shouldn't worry herself over all of that. Besides causing trouble for them when the opportunity arose, there was nothing she could do. She had other things on her mind, namely that stirrings and rumors about Silver Stroud's treasure had resurfaced again. Talk of what and where the treasure could be had led her here to Roseforte. But, as expected, she'd hit a dead end. Her leads had come up short—just the same old sailors spouting nonsense for clout. So she was back to digging keys out of shop bins and hoping.

Because Zanta knew where the treasure was, she just didn't have the means to open it.

Now she had only one more errand to complete before the *Monsoon* could set sail. Zanta looked up in time to see the other thing she was looking for, the Swan Inn. The sign over the inn's door depicted a white swan with a pink rose tucked into its wing. It seemed respectable, up the hill a bit from the harbor and nestled between an apothecary and a bakery. The street rang with the sound of a blacksmith's hammer, and the scent of baking bread and freshly cut flowers almost overpowered the salty harbor breeze. This must be the place Logan Crowder, first mate of the *Siren Song*, had told her about.

She paused on the threshold to let her eyes adjust to the dim interior. The sun had begun to sink from its midday height, and the inn's main tavern room was quiet, only a few stragglers picking at fish and leek pies and sipping the dregs of their ale. Zanta spotted a plump older man wiping down a table near the back.

"I'm looking for a woman named Nia," Zanta said to him without preamble, trying not to let her lingering annoyance at the drunken shopkeeper and this day in general come through in her voice. "I was told she works here?"

The man looked at her over a pair of spectacles that balanced at the tip of his blotchy nose.

"She does. Who's askin'?"

"Well I have—"

"She's busy," a woman Zanta assumed to be the proprietress interrupted curtly, stepping out of the kitchen at the back. "If you're one of her lovers, you'll just have to wait till she's done with that other one." She stomped back into the kitchen, leaving both Zanta and the bespectacled man in stunned silence.

"Excuse my wife's poor manners, please, young lady," the man said after a moment. "She's just cross because Nia left her with the tail end of the midday rush. Can't say I blame 'er though, that young man was a might handsome." He seemed to realize what he'd said, and before Zanta could correct him, tried to backtrack. "Not that you're not a handsome gal yourself, dear. It's just that...I mean...I'm sure Nia—"

"That's not what I'm here for." Zanta finally cut off his flustered rambling. The man visibly relaxed, and dabbed his sweaty brow with the rag he'd previously been wiping the table with.

"So what can I do for you?" he asked, obviously relieved not to have found himself in the middle of a jealous lover's squabble.

"I'm delivering something for a friend."

"Well, don't know how long she'll be. You can leave it with me if you'd like." He eyed the pack on her back curiously.

"I'm to deliver it into her hands only, unfortunately," Zanta answered. She supposed she could always lie and tell Logan she'd given the package directly to Nia. She didn't actually know him that well, but he'd paid her, and she was generally a woman of her word, despite being a pirate.

The man frowned. "Well, like I said, don't know when she'll be down. You're welcome to wait if you buy a meal or a drink."

Zanta sighed. She'd really hoped to be on her way back to the *Monsoon* by now. If they didn't catch the tides tonight, it would be tedious trying to sail out of the harbor tomorrow with everyone else. She supposed she could kill an hour or so searching for keys at nearby shops, but she really should get back to prepare for departure. How long could this girl entertain a handsome young man anyway?

As if reading her mind, the man leaned over to whisper, "Might be a while if I'm honest. Astounding stamina, our Nia."

In that case there was no use waiting around.

"I'm leaving with the tide tonight," Zanta said. "Please tell her to meet me at berth forty-four at the docks if she'd like to collect the package. She should ask for Sarah." With that, she turned on her heel and left.

CHAPTER 2

MAY 1ST, 1668

Nia collapsed onto her back on the mattress, breathless and sweaty. The man beside her wrapped an arm around her waist and planted a kiss on her shoulder. Even though they'd literally just finished having sex, the gesture felt a little too forward. She didn't even know his name for gods' sake. Didn't know what to moan during the act. She blinked slowly up at the timbered ceiling of her attic room and bit her lip.

She was coming down from the post-coital bliss too fast. It wasn't that the sex was bad, far from it, but it hadn't been enough to banish pressing thoughts from her mind.

She placed a hand on the man's warm chest, admiring the handsome nose and strong jaw that had attracted her in the first place.

"When do you sail?" she asked, injecting the expected dreaminess into her voice.

He was a sailor on a merchant ship out of Souna. But down in the tavern, she'd overheard him bragging that he used to have a place on the ship of Silver Stroud.

"Tomorrow morning," the man answered sleepily.

Nia propped herself up on her elbow, tracing lazy circles through his chest hair.

"I heard you say something about Silver Stroud," she cooed, like a lovestruck girl enraptured by the idea that the man in bed with her was once a dangerous pirate.

The man gave a wry smile, and Nia internally rolled her eyes. The ego of a man like this was so easy to read, but often got in the way of the truth. She'd chased down so many leads like this, only to have them turn out to be baseless bragging. This man looked too straightlaced to have been a pirate, but then again, no sailor was truly upstanding.

"Did you know him?" Nia asked. "What was he like?" She honestly didn't care. She knew the answer already, but she couldn't jump straight in with her real questions.

Nia only half listened as he glancingly answered her question, instead regaling her with a tale of his own supposed swashbuckling adventures. She kept an interested look on her face, and her fingertips continued circling over his chest.

"—he always carried that damn key around," the man was saying. Nia perked up. This was something true. Maybe this sailor *had* actually known Stroud.

"What was the key for?" Nia feigned a gasp of realization. "It couldn't be the famed missing treasure?" Her hand pressed flat on his chest now, and she leaned forward eagerly, hoping the gesture made her seem like an impressionable girl, and not a woman probing for information.

"Could be." The man chuckled. He pulled her against him and smoothed her ginger hair back from her face. "Perhaps I have a piece of the treasure with me."

Nia's stomach performed a painful flip. A piece of the treasure? It was not something that should be separated into pieces like a collection of useless baubles. Either this man was lying, or the treasure had been cut apart. If it truly had been, her life was over.

Nia's heart raced.

"C-can I see it?" The question came out shaky with dread and hope, but he didn't seem to notice.

"You'll have to promise not to tell anyone," the man said with a wink. He released her and rolled to the edge of the bed to fish for his trousers. His hand slipped into the pocket, and Nia knew even before he withdrew the object that he was a liar.

He rolled back toward her and held up a broach.

A broach, as if that could even come close to the value of the true treasure. She wanted to slap him for wasting her time. Then again, she'd had an ulterior motive in sleeping with him in the first place, so could she really blame him for being a liar too?

He smiled at her charmingly, expecting her to melt with how impressed she was.

"You know...you can have it if you want. A pretty girl deserves pretty things." Indeed, she did deserve pretty things; she had a whole box of trinkets from men just like him under the bed.

He took her hand and placed the broach in her palm. It was surprisingly light, definitely tin instead of silver. She peered more closely at it, and tried very hard to hide her disdain. The inlaid gems were clearly glass.

Nia forced down the anger that threatened to boil up. Not only was he a liar, but he didn't even have the grace to lie with convincing props. Perhaps she had laid on the simpering barmaid act a little too thick.

"How lovely!" she exclaimed. Her voice sounded strained to her own ears, anger and disappointment warring in her stomach. Her skin felt like it was crawling off her body. She glanced at the small round window tucked up under the roof gable and clapped her free hand over her mouth as if shocked.

"Oh my, it's getting late. I must get back before dinner, or I'll be scolded."

The man frowned, but got the hint.

Once he was gone, she leaned against the wall of the kitchen, trying to calm herself.

Another dead end. Another day that she was trapped here on the Talvan mainland with a box of useless trinkets under her bed instead of the one thing she really wanted.

Because the treasure did not belong to Stroud—it was hers, and it was her only chance at freedom.

"Nia!" Madame Durand's sharp voice startled her out of her bitter thoughts, and she spun to face the proprietress of the Swan Inn.

"Yes ma'am?" They both knew her good girl act was just that, an act. But Nia saw it as a fun little game between them. Nia did what she wanted and Madame Durand pretended to be angry, when really, they both knew Nia was the best employee the inn had ever had. The Durands would never fire her, even if she skipped out occasionally to sleep with handsome strangers in search of treasure.

Not that the Durands knew about the treasure, they just thought she was a slut.

Madame Durand was red-faced and scowling. Nia felt a twinge of guilt over leaving her alone with the tail end of the midday rush.

"You had a visitor while you were away," Madame said. "A young woman—"

Monsieur Durand chose that moment to enter the kitchen, hitting his wife on the ass with the door as it swung inward.

"Nia!" Monsieur Durand greeted her cheerfully, ignoring his wife as she swatted him on the arm in retaliation. "A young woman came with a package for you."

"A package?" Nia wracked her brain for what it could be. She wasn't expecting anything, but she had many acquaintances and many lovers, any of whom might send her something. "Where is it?" She didn't see anything sitting around the kitchen.

"Well she said she could only deliver it to you directly. But she couldn't stay while you were, ah...busy."

"So is she coming back?" Who could the woman be? Most of her flings were men. They were easier to get information out of, but the occasional woman did pass through her bedchamber. Perhaps one was inclined to give her a gift?

"She said she was leaving with the tide tonight, and to meet her at berth forty-four if you want it," Monsieur Durand replied. His wife glared at him, but he seemed delighted by the whole thing. "And to ask for Sarah."

The bitterness was fading now, replaced by curiosity over the identity of the woman and the contents of the package. She didn't know any Sarah. But she was never one to turn down a gift, or a chance to get out of work. She thanked Monsieur Durand and moved to leave through the back door before Madame Durand stopped her, still scowling.

"You'll not abandon me for dinner as well," she snapped. "You can go after."

"But they might—"

"No buts, we pay you to help us around here. We feed and lodge you. You can't go gallivanting off after every pretty thing that catches your eye."

Nia sighed. Of course she wasn't going to get away with shirking her duty twice in one day. The Durands saw her the same as everyone else did—a frivolous girl who slept around and liked the glittering trinkets her various paramours gifted her. She'd done nothing to correct them. She bought herself pretty dresses with the money she saved by living in the attic. She wore the glass-gemmed, tin broaches like the one she'd gotten today. She preened in front of the cracked mirror in the hall and took sailors to bed.

What the Durands didn't see was her drawing information out of her sex-sated partners and flirtatious patrons alike. Not just about Stroud's treasure, which she'd been searching for since before she arrived in Roseforte, but any intriguing information she could sell on to the right people.

It wasn't completely a ruse. She did like the sex, and the pretty dresses. They made her feel connected to her body, adorned the way she wanted to be. Using her body for pleasure instead of work made her feel better about being trapped, and stilled that itching incompleteness that plagued her day by day. But still, she'd rather be home, if home would have her. She'd rather not hide anymore.

"Yes, ma'am."

It quickly became clear after the dinner rush that Madame Durand had no intention of letting Nia pick up the mysterious package in time, and it was past dark when Nia managed to escape her duties. Maybe it was revenge for leaving her with all the work earlier that day. Maybe she had just forgotten her promise. Eventually Monsieur Durand took pity and helped Nia sneak out while his wife's attention was elsewhere.

"Take Bruno with you, he should be done with work," Monsieur Durand whispered to her at the back door. "I don't want you going to the docks by yourself."

Nia nodded and stepped over to the bakery next door where the apprentice, a bulky youth named Bruno, was just hanging up his apron.

"Care to take a walk? I have errands at the docks," Nia said.

Bruno wiped the sweat from his brow and nodded. Monsieur Durand, fatherly as he was, often asked Bruno to walk the other tavern maids home at night for safety. Going down to the docks with Nia would be no different. They said nothing as they hurried down the street, the night air almost as stifling as the busy tavern had been.

There were many things she hated in this life, but she hated sweating most of all. It was her eternal struggle that both her job and her favorite pastime involved a lot of it. She couldn't imagine how it must have felt for Bruno to stand by the roaring bread ovens all day.

Bruno's large hand touched her waist to keep her from stepping in the path of a wagon as they came within sight of the harbor. His fingertips pressed to the links of the silver waist chain through her bodice only briefly. When his hand retreated, Nia touched the same spot. It was a habit now, double-checking the waist chain was still there even though it had no reason not to be. She never went anywhere without it and its tiny silver key, her most prized possession.

Salty wind off the harbor lifted her spirits as they approached berth forty-four. Visiting the docks usually made her melancholy. She wished she could throw herself into the surf and swim away back to her old life. Merely touching the water would have dire consequences now. So she avoided going near it if she could. It was too tempting. Even the sea breeze wafting up to the inn made the longing so unbearable some days that she considered just walking inland until the sea was nothing but a distant memory of the one thing she could no longer have.

But today, the promise of a reward kept those feelings at bay. She stepped confidently onto the wooden dock over the lapping waves, with the hulking and silent form of Bruno trailing behind. This would take but a moment. She would be back on solid ground again before anything could happen.

The docks were busy with the first arrivals of spring after a long and arduous winter. Out at anchor, several ships sat with their decks shrouded beneath white canvas tents, no doubt repairing damage from the last dregs of winter storms that had rolled through only a week before. There was no sign of those now; the fickle weather had decided to skip its usual gentle spring blush in favor of full summer heat.

A small, Yarenen style ship sat at anchor in berth forty-four. Its fanlike sails unfurled, and the crew bustled over the deck, preparing for departure.

Bruno hung back, looking uncharacteristically nervous as Nia hailed one of the sailors.

"I'm here to see Sarah. I was told she has a delivery for me."

The man told her to wait, then disappeared belowdecks. Presently, he returned with a tall, dark-skinned Yarenen woman carrying a wooden box. She strode down the gangway and stopped before Nia.

"You're Nia?" The woman's brown eyes swept her from head to toe.

"I am." Nia did the same, letting her eyes wander over this stranger. The woman stood on the end of the gangplank, furthering the gap between their heights. She was generously proportioned—not as curvy as Nia herself, but more muscled from her life at sea. Loose red trousers were tucked into knee-high black boots, and a sleeveless white top showed off both her generous cleavage and muscle-corded arms. A small gold ring studded one nostril, matching the ones in her ears. She held herself with a self-assurance that spoke to both power and confidence.

This was not a simple Yarenen merchant as she seemed. This was a pirate.

Nia smiled up at her. No wonder the Durands had both thought this woman was another of Nia's paramours. She was gorgeous, and Nia had a penchant for rogues.

"I hear you have a package for me."

The woman handed over the light colored wooden box with peach blossoms carved into the lid. A piece of parchment tied to the latch with a pink ribbon fluttered in the warm breeze. Nia tucked the box under her arm and flipped the card over.

Open alone
-JL

JL? Nia bit her lip, riffling through her memory for a fling with those initials, but came up empty.

"Who's JL?" she asked the pirate, who watched her closely.

The pirate's lips parted to answer, but a shout interrupted. A unit of Talvan navy soldiers sprinted down the docks.

"Shit," the pirate said under her breath. "You better go before—"

BOOM!

Every ship in the harbor shivered with the force of the explosion. Nia ducked instinctively, bringing the beautiful box over her head as a shield. An old, familiar panic spiked through her gut, but she forced herself to look out to the harbor, trying to parse the source of the threat. The tent-shrouded ships, which she had assumed were undergoing repair, had abandoned their coverings to reveal wooden catapults, their flaming payloads lighting the night like a meteor shower.

Was Roseforte under attack? It was Talva's best stronghold in the south, one of the main ports the Talvan Empire used to deploy ships to Souna and the Sunrise Sea. Who would dare attack them? The soldiers from earlier hadn't been coming for the pirates; they'd seen something wrong before the first projectiles flew. Now the docks swarmed with soldiers and sailors deploying navy ships from their resting places around the sides of the harbor.

The attacking ships weren't large enough to be warships, and if they flew any colors, Nia couldn't see them in the dark. Marra wouldn't have sent ships to attack Talva directly, would they? Nia didn't know much about politics, but even she knew a direct attack between the two empires would ignite the cold war they'd been locked in for decades. They preferred to play out their wars with the game pieces of their colonies. They didn't put their own mainland citizens in danger, only those they had subjugated. Maybe the Nanadie rebels had finally gathered enough resources to launch a proper rebellion?

"We're under attack!" a soldier yelled, dislodging Nia from her reverie. They'd made it to berth forty-four, half of them splitting off toward the next ship along the dock. Another flaming projectile arched through the night, trailing embers and crashing into a ship anchored not far away.

The docks sprang into action like a kicked anthill, soldiers and civilians alike either arming themselves, or running for safety in the direction of the fort that crowned the hill. Nia scrambled a few feet toward solid ground, Bruno already turning to flee, intending to run like the rest of them. She had to make it back to the inn and warn the Durands to get to the fort where they could hunker down and wait it out. Distantly, she heard shouts of "Get down!" along the pier, but the meaning didn't register until the world exploded around her.

Breath punched out of her as she hit the dock hard. The force of the explosion quaked the pier as rock and fire crashed down at the entrance to berth forty-four, obliterating the soldiers and the dock beneath them. Despite the damp, the wood caught immediately, blazing between her and safety. Nia sat up, still clutching the box to her chest. Where was Bruno? She couldn't see him past the columns of thick black smoke already engulfing the docks.

A hand closed around her upper arm, and she looked up in a daze to see the pirate woman. The pirate said something, but Nia couldn't make it out over the ringing in her ears. The pirate shouted louder, then hooked her arms beneath Nia's armpits and hauled her toward the ship.

"Wait," Nia gasped, struggling out of the pirate's grip and nearly falling as her own full weight threatened the integrity of her shaking legs.

"We gotta go!" the pirate shouted over the roar of fire and the ringing in Nia's ears. Tongues of flame crept along the wooden planks between them and solid ground.

"But..." She had to get to the Durands; she had to find Bruno and make sure he was alright. She *could not* set foot on a ship. Even now, she already felt the creep of imminent death along her skin from where seawater had splattered her.

"Don't be stupid," the pirate growled. Behind her, the crew cast away the lines securing their ship to the docks. One of the crew shouted something at them. "What are you gonna do? Swim for it?" The pirate grabbed Nia's arm again. "We'll drop you off at the next port, I promise."

That wasn't really the problem. She could hold her own with sailors, even pirates. The problem was the sea. She couldn't leave the mainland.

When Nia just stared at her dumbly, the pirate let out an exasperated growl and began pulling her up the gangplank.

"Wait," Nia gasped. "I can't, I..." The pirate ignored her, hauled Nia onto the ship with little ceremony, and began issuing orders as pirates pulled up the gangplank behind them.

Nia's eyes filled with tears. So this was it. This was how she was going to die, killed by the thing she loved the most, the sea she couldn't even touch.

The pirate shoved her into a corner by the rail where she would be out of the way. Her peach-colored skirts puffed up around her, and Nia curled into a ball around the mysterious box.

It would start with heart palpitations, and she would get dizzy, then...She hoped she would pass out before the pain started. Before the prickle of a thousand needles made her feel like she was being flayed alive. Maybe it would be like dying in her sleep.

How long would it take? Minutes? Hours? She didn't know. She'd only witnessed the slow death that she was destined to succumb to in a few years, as her mother had. It had taken ten years for her mother to die that way, never returning to the sea. While she didn't know how quick this way would be, it would certainly be quicker than that.

A brief flash of pity entered her mind for whomever was going to find her body if they managed to escape the harbor.

She looked over the dark water to where the Talvan navy ships rushed out to meet the attackers. It was all so pointless. These greedy bastards continued to take lands and people that weren't theirs, racing each other to see who could consume the most the fastest. Yet she couldn't even get the one thing that truly belonged to her, the thing that would let her return to the sea. Her treasure.

The pirate ship banked away from the battle toward the shallower side of the harbor mouth that couldn't accommodate the deeper-keeled ships. Well underway now. So close to the open sea.

Nia closed her eyes and waited for the end. Was the pounding of her heart due to fear or her imminent demise? She couldn't tell. She'd always been so careful to stay away from the water. The Swan Inn was just far enough away from shore to hold the constant, low grade nausea at bay. Night after night she'd lay in bed, whether alone or with a companion, mentally cataloging her body for signs of the same slow fade her mother had endured for a decade before her ultimate death. She'd always thought fading away would be better than the pain she'd experience if she returned to the water.

But maybe it was better this way, dying on the sea instead of on land. Determination gripped her suddenly. She was definitely going to die, whether from the battle or the curse of her existence, so why shouldn't she be reunited with the sea one last time? The dark, dirty waters of the harbor were nothing compared to the blue waves of her home, but at least she would feel the sea on her skin again.

She tucked the box safely against the rail. Her swishing skirts made not a sound beneath the barrage as she climbed up on the rail, rough rope scraping her palms. Dark choppy water gazed back up at her, and she imagined it weighing down her skirts and pulling her under, closing over her head, salt invading her nostrils.

She dangled one foot over the edge, her shoe dropping into the darkness and quickly sinking, as she would do soon enough. She sucked in one last breath of air and let go of the ropes.

Strong arms seized her waist and yanked her back. She and her savior tumbled to the deck in a heap of skirts and swearing. Nia struggled, trying to crawl back toward her inevitable death. She could choose this. She was going to die one way or another, so it might as well be her way.

The pirate woman tackled her to the deck again, straddling her hips and forcing her flailing arms up beside her head. Her brown eyes were wide, teeth bared in both anger and fear.

"Are you fucking crazy?" The pirate shouted over the cacophony of cannon fire. "You'll drown!"

She would. She shouldn't be able to drown, but in this form it was inevitable.

"Let me go!" Nia struggled again, but the pirate didn't budge. The pins in Nia's hair dug into the back of her scalp. They were almost out of the harbor now, slipping between a series of small islands into the night. Soon they would be in the open sea.

"You'll die," the pirate repeated, as if Nia was a panic-addled little girl.

"Let me," Nia growled. The pirate blinked at her, fingers slackening slightly with shock. Nia pressed her advantage, bucking her hips up and dislodging the pirate. She only made it one step before the pirate caught her again. She grunted as Nia elbowed her in the side but held on, dragging Nia toward a hatch in the deck.

"Open it!" the pirate ordered a crew member. Then she dumped Nia unceremoniously into a dark hold full of crates and baskets. Nia scrambled to her feet. The hold was shallow enough that her head poked out of the hatch. The pirate woman leaned over the opening to look down at her, head framed by stars and the light of distant flames.

"No one dies on my ship without my permission," the pirate said forcefully, before closing the hatch over Nia's head, leaving her in darkness.

With a frustrated growl Nia pounded on the hatch but it didn't budge. Her heart sank. Soon the symptoms would start, and she'd die alone here in the dark without ever being able to taste the sea again.

She slumped against a basket full of cloth, drawing her knees up to her chest and resting her forehead against the silky fabric of her skirt. All the fight fled her body. She'd avoided the sea for years, always wondering when it would finally claim her. And now she had to spend the last moments of her short life in the dark. The sounds of battle slowly faded behind them. They must be properly at sea now, leaving everything behind. She waited.

And waited.

After what seemed like hours, with no heart palpitations or anything else, she raised her head.

She was at sea, and she wasn't dead.

Her treasure was here.

CHAPTER 3

MAY 2ND, 1668

Rowan grinned as he perched on the rail of the *Siren Song*, one hand gripping the ropes, and leaned out over the sparkling blue waters of the Broken Sea. Wind whistled between his teeth, the sun slowly baking his skin. This was the life he'd fought for. The freedom he would never give up, not even for love.

So it was a good thing his beloved was the Deep Water Demon.

Ahead, their quarry, the *Sweet Lettie*, sped over the waves, the promise of violence and riches scenting the air in her wake. She was a beautiful two-masted ship sailing south from Kefrye, a bit smaller than the *Siren Song* and painted with feathery white detailing along her sides.

It wouldn't be long now until Rowan had her in his clutches.

They'd spent days chasing the spry little ship, bearing down then backing off, steering her toward the Teeth where her doom waited. Despite their closeness in size, the *Siren* could have caught the *Sweet Lettie* a dozen times over by now. But it was all a part of the little game Rowan and Yves liked to play.

Last year, during the first summer of their marriage, the Ghost Hawk and the Deep Water Demon had struggled to balance their insatiable desire to be near each other with their need for freedom on the sea. Wanderlust had been the only thing that kept Rowan in thrall before he met Yves, and they'd experienced the inevitable growing pains of two people who were fiercely independent, yet unhealthily possessive of one another. So they'd devised this game. From spring to fall, the peak pirating season, they moved independently of one another, free to go about their business as they pleased. But on a prearranged date and location, one of them would lie in wait, and the other would bring him a little treat. A bit of foreplay to whet the appetite.

It allowed them to see each other regularly while still operating independently. But more importantly, it made the sex hotter.

Anticipation kindled in Rowan's gut, knowing Yves waited for him somewhere among the Teeth. To make up for the time Yves had missed last spring repairing the *Kraken* after the battle of Wave Harbor, they'd gotten an early start on the season this year. It would be the first time they'd seen each other in the nearly two months since departing their home island of Illusion at the spring thaw.

Sometimes Rowan felt like a cat bringing half-dead rodents to its master. Usually Yves gobbled up whatever Rowan deigned to bring him, but this time Yves had requested the *Sweet Lettie* specifically, and refused to reveal why. The ship had been easy enough to find, and now they were almost to the arranged destination. They were almost together again.

Ahead, the *Sweet Lettie* banked starboard toward the Teeth. No doubt her captain intended to lose their pursuers within the shallow, labyrinthine channels between the rocky white islands. Rowan had used a similar tactic before, which ultimately resulted in his eye being stabbed out. Unfortunately for the *Sweet Lettie*, the same Teeth that made pursuit near impossible also held a myriad of places to hide a ship. She would find no salvation between those white shores.

It was time to turn up the heat, and scare those soft merchant fools so bad that they wouldn't see the *Kraken's Fury* lurking until it was too late.

Rowan jumped down from the rail, pleated Kefryean skirt fluttering around his calves, and strode up to the quarterdeck, where his first mate, Logan, waited.

"It's time."

Logan smiled wryly beneath the fringe of wavy blond hair smushed down by his hat. He always seemed simultaneously amused and exasperated at times like this. He was the voice of reason most days, the anchor that kept the Ghost Hawk from flying too close to the sun.

Logan signaled to the crew members in the rigging.

"Let's put on some speed! It's time to catch us a ship!"

The crew shouted back in excitement, jumping to adjust the sails to more efficiently catch the wind. The canvases filled, and the *Siren* immediately picked up speed.

They caught up to the *Sweet Lettie* quickly, and soon Rowan could hear the panicked shouts of the *Lettie*'s crew carrying over the water. His own crew now worked in practiced silence, and though he had trained them to do so himself, it always surprised him how in tune each crew member was with the others, moving as if in a natural dance.

Rowan set the spyglass to his good eye, searching the *Sweet Lettie*'s deck for anything that might give the *Siren Song* an advantage. A merchant ship, especially a Kefryean one, wouldn't have many guns. Kefrye had fallen to Marra's might years ago, and they were kept minimally armed to prevent the people from rising up against their much more powerful oppressors. Hence why they were such easy prey for pirates.

Rowan wondered once again why Yves would ask him to retrieve this ship specifically. Was there something on board he desired? A particular piece of treasure or an important person they could ransom? Rowan knew that Marra had recently installed a new governor in Kefrye, and dignitaries typically flocked to things like that. The *Sweet Lettie* was quite a fancy little ship, perhaps one that important people would book passage on.

Rowan's gaze raked the deck of the ship. The crew seemed frantic, unprepared. They had bet their survival on the *Lettie*'s quickness and ability to maneuver through the shallow waters of the Teeth. Unfortunately for them, they were being chased by the one pirate ship that could catch anyone.

The *Sweet Lettie* banked to starboard, passing behind the first of the jagged white islands. Rowan lost sight of her for a moment, only the top half of the masts visible over the debris-strewn rocks. He lowered the spyglass and whistled.

Nephele, his gray hunting hawk, chirruped in answer and took off from one of the yardarms above, gliding down and landing on the scarred leather encasing his shoulder. Rowan fed her a treat from the pouch on his belt and scratched at the soft speckled feathers on her chest.

"Wanna go visit Yves?" Rowan cooed at her. Nephele swallowed the treat almost whole and cocked her head at him, fixing him in her golden gaze. The hawk was none too fond of Yves, but she mostly tolerated his presence. She leaned over and nibbled at a strand of Rowan's light blond ponytail. "He'll have a treat for you," Rowan wheedled. Nephele was a sucker for treats, especially the expensive cuts of meat Yves bribed her with. Rowan was quite sure he'd fed her a piece of a human once, but chose not to think about it too closely. Nephele shifted on Rowan's shoulder as the *Siren* finally banked around the edge of the island, her claws digging into the leather.

"Oh, fine." Rowan took out another treat and showed it to her. She snapped her beak, the hawkish equivalent of licking her lips. "Go tell Yves we're almost there," Rowan told her, then tossed the treat high over the water. Nephele took off, swooping over the rail and catching the tasty morsel midair. Her wings beat a few times, rising up to circle the *Siren* once before flying off toward where the *Kraken* lay in wait.

The *Siren* quickly gained on her prey now, cutting through the water like Nephele through the sky. "Try to nudge them toward the Canine," Rowan said to Logan, his eye still trained on the ship ahead of them. The Canine was the tall, slightly pointed island the *Kraken* would be hiding behind. It resided on the other side of the Teeth, and the *Siren* would need to carefully herd the other ship toward it in order for their plan to work. The *Kraken* was much larger than both the *Siren* and *Lettie*, and wouldn't be able to navigate the more shallow channels near the interior of the islands. If the crew of the *Lettie* caught on that they were being herded in a specific direction and veered off course, the *Siren* would be on her own to take down their prey, ruining the game.

"Aye, Captain," Logan replied.

Rowan looked back toward the *Lettie*, then flipped up his eyepatch and squinted at it. It had become a habit of his since discovering the green stone sphere nestled in his eye socket allowed him to see things beyond the norm. Nothing changed, no flickers of color or shadow. Satisfied, he flipped the eyepatch back down, hiding the jade eye again.

The *Siren* banked to starboard, as if she was trying to come up on the *Lettie*'s side. The *Lettie* turned down another channel, and the *Siren* quickly corrected course to follow. They dogged the other ship, always staying just far enough away to pretend that they couldn't catch up. Always nudging the unsuspecting merchant further and further into their trap at the Canine. The closer they drew, the faster Rowan's heart beat. Not because battle was imminent, but because every fathom of water the two ships gobbled up drew him ever closer to reuniting with his beloved.

Finally, the Canine appeared ahead. Logan deftly steered the *Siren* around a jut of rock that hid beneath the waves, and Rowan set the spyglass back to his eye as the rest of the crew prepared for battle in silence. He searched the skies for Nephele's sleek form and found her wheeling through the air currents around the Canine's white peak over a hundred feet above. Plenty of height to hide even the *Kraken*'s impressive masts.

A spike of anxiety lodged in Rowan's gut, as it always did. Worry that this time the *Kraken* wouldn't be there. That fate had found some way to wrench Yves from him.

A shout sounded from up ahead, and Rowan lowered the glass. They were gaining on the *Sweet Lettie*, tightening the noose. Rowan could see the sailors' faces now, but not the fear that no doubt marred them. A creature crept from its hiding place behind the Canine, its great glass and wood tentacles glimmering in the harsh sunlight. The sharp anxiety dulled as the bow of the *Kraken* pulled out from behind the white rocks. Seeing the other ship always filled his heart with elation. Her deep blue sails full of wind and the Deep Water Demon's flag with its tentacled skull and hourglass snapping in the breeze. She surged through the water, sure as a predator, blocking the *Sweet Lettie*'s path.

Panicked shouts echoed across the water as the merchant sailors realized they were trapped between the unyielding force of the *Kraken* and the sharp talons of the *Siren*. They knew exactly who they faced, exactly the reputation of the pirates who now held their fates in their bloodstained hands.

"Prepare to board!" Rowan ordered. The *Lettie* dodged left, attempting to sneak between the *Kraken's* bow and the island, which would leave the *Siren* trapped behind her ally's bulk. The *Kraken* fired a warning shot off her bow.

All at once the fight seemed to go out of the merchant ship, and the *Siren* finally allowed herself to catch up, pulling up to the starboard side and trapping the ship between not only the two pirates, but the shallows next to the island as well. Nephele screeched high above, scenting impending violence in the air.

Rowan bounded down to the main deck as the crew threw grappling hooks across the water. Fox and Gaël appeared at his side, Fox grinning and Gaël stoic as always. He and Fox had become Rowan's de facto bodyguards in battle. The captain's elite force for cutting through the enemy, getting him to wherever he needed to go, and guarding his blind side.

"Not too much bloodshed," Rowan ordered, his voice low so only his boarding party could hear. They nodded. Gaël flipped one of his axes across the back of his hand and caught it again.

"What's our goal here, Captain?" he asked.

Rowan wasn't quite sure. He didn't know what Yves wanted with the pretty little ship but judging by the fact that the *Kraken* had fired a warning shot and not just straight up obliterated the *Lettie*, Rowan suspected Yves had plans that required her to stay intact. So there were two ways they could go about capturing this ship without a drawn out, bloody battle. Intimidate them into surrender, or kill those in charge.

"Capture the captain, and secure the ship," Rowan ordered.

Rowan leapt over the shrunken gap as the crew hauled the ships together, landing on the pristine deck of the *Sweet Lettie*. He leveled his pistol at the first terrified crewman he saw and fired, not looking to kill. The bullet caught the man in the arm, and he screamed, clutching at the wound as it poured crimson onto the deck. Thumps sounded behind Rowan as the rest of his boarding party landed on deck. It bolstered him.

"Bring me your captain!" Rowan barked, his voice ringing off the cliffs. Across the water, the *Kraken* maneuvered closer. The crew of the *Sweet Lettie* was in a frenzy, but a group broke off and charged toward Rowan's landing party, yelling a frightened battle cry. Rowan holstered his pistol and drew his cutlass just in time to stab the first man in the gut. Blood gushed over his hands as he yanked the blade back out and let the man fall at his feet. Rowan's crew charged around him like a rushing tide, clashing with the sailors with a whoop. Rowan stalked forward, eye scanning for the captain or first mate, anyone with the authority to surrender the ship to him.

"There." Fox pointed the tip of his knife toward the other side of the deck, where a rotund man in a fashionable, curled wig frantically tried to release a landing boat from its moorings.

"Let's go."

They began to cut a swath across the deck. But more sailors were surrendering than fighting, and the rest of Rowan's crew rounded them up with ease. Rowan and his two shadows had made it halfway across the deck when the bewigged man reeled back with a scream of terror. But it wasn't Rowan he was afraid of. He stumbled away from the half-released boat as three figures prowled over the rail like horrors from the deep, dripping wet from their swim across the short distance from the *Kraken*.

Rowan let out a startled laugh as his one blue eye met Yves's dark, demonic ones. Yves dispatched the captain with a knife across the throat, arterial blood spraying across his beautiful face. He didn't even spare a glance for the man whose life he'd just taken.

So it wasn't the captain that Yves was after, even though he looked like a rich man whose family would pay a hefty ransom. But Rowan couldn't think of that now. He was drawn across the deck toward Yves like a moth to a flame, and Yves likewise seemed transfixed by him. Everything else fell away as they drifted together like a pair of dreamers.

Face-to-face once again after so long apart. Every moment without Yves had felt muffled, but now that he was only feet away, the world brightened again, even as the chaos around them slowed. Rowan smiled, tasting blood, but Yves didn't smile back. He crossed the remaining distance between them in a few long strides, looking murderous.

"Are you hurt? Where?"

Rowan let Yves fumble with his bloodstained clothes for a moment, searching for an injury that wasn't there.

"People are watching," Rowan said, low and warning, side-eyeing the captured sailors who now stared at them. None of the pirates cared. They were used to it by now.

Rowan caught Yves's wrists.

"I'm not hurt," he reassured him.

The murderous worry in Yves's eyes dimmed, replaced by a sultry expression that suited his beautiful face much better.

"They're watching, are they?" he purred.

Yves grabbed Rowan by the neck, leaving finger marks in the blood spatter, and pulled him into a hard kiss. Rowan tried not to visibly melt into his arms as Yves's tongue snaked into his mouth.

In the year since their marriage, they had taken many ships, hunting both together and separately. And they'd fucked like rabbits each time they reunited. But they'd never, *never* so much as touched in front of outsiders. Never kissed. Never given any hint that their relationship went beyond business. They couldn't risk the authorities finding out and using them against each other. Not again. Not after Rowan had lost his eye and been used to lure Yves into a trap that had resulted in his death and the near wreck of the *Kraken*.

This felt like meeting for the first time all over again. Defiant. The tension as palpable as salt in the wind. Except this time Rowan already knew the addicting taste of Yves's lips. The heady sting of being full of him. The passion creeping like a shadow beneath his skin.

The contours of Yves's twisted soul.

And now he was in Yves's arms on the deck of the *Sweet Lettie* with blood on their faces and what felt like the whole world looking on.

Either Yves was planning to kill them all, or something had changed and he no longer cared to keep the nature of their relationship a secret.

Either way, Rowan could never refuse him.

He wrapped his arms around the back of Yves's neck, rising on his toes to deepen the kiss. He felt more than heard Yves groan deep in his throat.

When the kiss broke, lightheadedness feathered Rowan's vision, and he let Yves take his bloody hand and drag him toward the door beneath the quarterdeck.

"Nothing to see here," Yves barked over his shoulder.

"Eyes down," Gaël ordered the prisoners, but many of them continued staring. They knew exactly who Yves and Rowan were. They'd just witnessed the two most infamously ruthless pirates on the seas making out in broad daylight.

Yves shoved Rowan up against the door as it slammed shut behind them, lips and hands almost frantic, as if he could not stand to be apart from Rowan a moment longer. His kiss tasted of blood, and burned coppery on Rowan's tongue. The blood from his shirt soaked into Yves's immaculately expensive clothes, but neither of them cared. The question of why Yves had chosen to reveal their relationship to outsiders pushed to the back of Rowan's mind in the onslaught of physical sensation. Rowan couldn't help the moan that escaped his lips.

Yves broke the kiss, but kept Rowan pinned against the door. One hand cupped the side of Rowan's face, the pad of his thumb swiping through the blood on his cheek. They leaned their foreheads together, breathing heavily.

"I missed you," Yves said simply, black hair falling into his eyes. A joyous warmth spread through Rowan's stomach, mingling with the heat of desire. Being apart was always painful, but with the tension between the empires heating up, the seas were more dangerous than ever, and though Yves could come back from death, Rowan had no such privilege. He was always grateful to find his way home to Yves.

"Missed you too," Rowan murmured back. He wanted to stay this way forever.

Yves's thumb continued stroking Rowan's cheek, even as his lips strayed across the other. His tongue lingered on the spots of blood, lapping them up like sweet nectar from Rowan's flushed skin. Rowan tilted his head back against the door, and Yves's mouth trailed down his throat, eliciting another moan.

"You must stay quiet, darling," Yves warned. "You wouldn't want those poor doomed sailors to hear." A smirk twisted his lips as he moved the collar of Rowan's shirt aside and pressed a kiss to Rowan's collarbone.

"So they are doomed, then," Rowan said breathlessly.

"That all depends on you." One of Yves's hands braced against the door beside Rowan's head, the other moved from his cheek down to his waist. He began slowly untucking Rowan's shirt. Rowan could tell Yves was barely keeping himself restrained. If they were alone on the ship, Rowan would already be naked and stuffed full of Yves's cock. But there were witnesses, so Yves took his time.

"Me?" Rowan almost squeaked as Yves's fingers skimmed beneath the waistband of his skirt.

"If you're a good boy and keep quiet, I might have a better plan for them."

"What pla—" Rowan's words cut off with a gasp as Yves palmed his aching cock. Two months was much too long to be without him.

"A plan where they don't die, darling. I know how softhearted you can be."

Rowan's protest turned into a moan as Yves squeezed his cock through the fabric. Yves tsk-ed and nipped Rowan's collarbone again.

"You just killed one of those poor sailors with your lack of self-control."

"You can't be serious."

"Do you want to take that chance?"

Rowan clamped his lips shut around the next moan. They were both killers, there was no doubt about that, but that didn't mean Rowan was bloodthirsty. It didn't mean he could let those men die needlessly if Yves was willing to spare them.

Let the game begin.

He grabbed Yves by the front of his blood and seawater-soaked shirt and yanked him up so they were face-to-face again.

"And what if you make a noise?" he asked. "How do I get to punish you then?"

Yves blinked at him for a moment before his eyes darkened.

"That won't happen," he said with surety.

Rowan locked eyes with Yves, bit his lip, and bucked his hips forward, pushing his cock into Yves's hand. The friction sent heady pleasure straight to his head, all the sweeter for their lengthy separation. But he didn't make a sound.

Yves captured his lips in a hard kiss, hands delving up beneath Rowan's skirt to skim his thighs. He stripped Rowan's underpants down his hips and stroked lightly down the length of Rowan's shaft. Rowan shivered, but wouldn't fold so easily.

Yves's lips roamed freely over Rowan's exposed skin as he stroked until Rowan was a quivering mess, brought to the edge of completion only to be denied at the last moment. Still Rowan remained silent, his bottom lip dented and bloody with the effort of keeping his sounds of pleasure contained.

"Not going to crack easily, I see." Yves grinned and pulled his hand away, denying Rowan again. Rowan bit back a whimper, instead letting it come out as a huff of frustration and hopeless arousal.

Yves wiped the precum from his palm into Rowan's hair, fingers threading through the blond locks.

"If you're not going to give in, you might as well put that pretty mouth to good use." Yves pushed Rowan's head down, and Rowan obeyed eagerly. He fell to his knees as Yves released his own cock. Yves had become much more comfortable with receiving pleasure this way in the year they'd been married. He enjoyed it so long as he was the one in control, and he always was.

The velvety tip of Yves's cock pressed to Rowan's bloody lips. Yves pushed the back of Rowan's head, breaching Rowan's mouth slowly, savoring every inch of slide into the soft interior. Rowan let his teeth lightly graze along the shaft, sending a shiver through Yves's body. His cock hit the back of Rowan's throat, and Rowan looked up to meet Yves's eyes. Rowan still wore his eyepatch, so the demon part of his husband was hidden. But he sensed the darkness lurking just beneath, and it both thrilled and terrified him.

Rowan swirled his tongue along the underside of Yves's shaft as Yves withdrew and thrust in again. He braced his hand against the door, leaning over Rowan's kneeling form. Rowan opened up his throat as much as he could, but as always, the limitations of his mortal body proved no match for Yves's size and length. No matter how much he practiced, he simply could not accommodate Yves fully.

Rowan wrapped his fingers around the base to compensate, pumping in time with Yves's thrusts. Yves moved faster, clutching Rowan's hair to keep his head in place. It was strange, doing this in complete silence, but somehow it also heightened everything. Every small sound they *did* make felt all the more alluring for its rarity.

Rowan let his mouth be used, his own cock twitching with lack of attention. He stroked it with his other hand, trying to find some release in his own touch. Yves growled low in his throat and nudged his hand away, trapping it between the floor and the silver-capped toe of Yves's boot.

The next thrust into his mouth was hard and deep. A strangled whimper escaped Rowan's throat, and Yves pulled his head back. He released Yves's cock reluctantly, a string of saliva still connecting the tip to Rowan's bloody lip.

Yves pulled Rowan to his feet by his hair and produced a metal vial from his coat pocket.

"Turn around," he ordered roughly. Rowan obeyed, facing the door and feeling suddenly exposed with nothing under his skirt in this unfamiliar ship. Yves's fingers trailed up the back of Rowan's thigh to his ample ass. The cork of the vial popped open, a familiar coconut scent wafting toward him as Yves spread the lube over his fingers. He leaned close against Rowan's back, his tall, foreboding presence crowding Rowan against the door. He kissed the side of Rowan's neck as he rucked up Rowan's skirt and pressed his fingers between Rowan's cheeks, finding his neglected hole.

Rowan held his breath.

"Don't forget our deal," Yves murmured, "not a sound."

Before Rowan could even nod, Yves slipped one finger in up to the knuckle. Rowan pressed his forehead to the wood, trying his hardest to suppress the moan that bubbled up. He succeeded just barely. Yves curled his finger, stroking Rowan's insides in a wavelike motion. It was too much and yet not enough. He wanted Yves to take him, ravage him like the pirate he was. He wanted Yves to lose control and show him how much he'd missed him.

But they both held themselves stupidly in check for the sake of this game of silence.

When he was loose enough, Yves slipped in another finger and began to open Rowan up in earnest. His breath wafted hot against Rowan's skin, and Rowan bucked his hips back to take Yves's fingers in deeper. They'd been apart for so long that he thought he would burst with every touch. The only sound that permeated the room was their heavy breath and the faint squelch of Yves's slick fingers.

Yves pressed his nimble fingertips to Rowan's prostate, and lightning raced up his spine.

"Please..." The word left his mouth before he could stop it. It was more of a moan than a word but he was too far gone to care.

"Please just fuck me," Rowan begged, as Yves's fingers circled the bundle of nerves again.

"You're not ready yet," Yves growled. His fingers moved faster, seemingly on the brink of giving in to Rowan's begging. Rowan pushed his hips back against Yves's fingers again and felt Yves's hard length pressing against his ass cheek.

"I've been waiting long enough," Rowan panted. Yves gripped his jaw and turned Rowan's head to kiss the corner of his lips. The slick fingers of his other hand withdrew reluctantly and Rowan held back a whine at the sudden emptiness.

"If that is your desire, how can I refuse?" Yves spun Rowan to face him and lifted him into his arms, slamming him back against the door so hard it rattled in its frame. Rowan wrapped his legs around Yves's waist and buried his hands in Yves's onyx hair.

Yves kissed him desperately, long tongue swirling through Rowan's mouth, tasting the iron of his sluggishly bleeding lip. Yves rolled his hips, cock rubbing between Rowan's cheeks. He must have slicked it up while Rowan's back was turned. He broke the kiss and tilted Rowan's hips away from the door, leaving his upper back pressed to the wood. His fingers tightened on Rowan's thighs, and even without being able to see them, Rowan thought he felt a few of the tentacles wrap around his back to stabilize him.

Yves met Rowan's gaze, eyes blazing with lust. He positioned himself at Rowan's entrance and slammed home. The door rattled again and Rowan moaned, forgetting for a moment that lives depended on his silence. Pain lanced briefly up his back as he stretched around Yves's girth, but it was nothing compared to the ecstasy of being stuffed full of him at last.

Yves smirked at Rowan's slipup, drawing back and snapping his hips forward again, sending a jolt of pleasure through Rowan's body. He choked back another moan, remembering what was at stake. Yves remained staunchly silent, but with every hard thrust, Rowan could see him losing more and more control, even as he pushed Rowan closer to the edge. He tugged at the roots of Yves's hair, eliciting a hiss in response. Yves's fingers pressed harder into Rowan's flesh, and he increased the pace.

Rowan was beyond pain now, riding the tide of unbelievable pleasure. He gritted his teeth, breath coming out ragged as he fought to keep quiet. He wanted to scream, howl, profess his love, and moan Yves's name over and over again until he lost his voice. The veins in his neck stood out with the strain of keeping it all inside. His legs shook as divine lightning arced between his bones and suffused his muscles.

"Let it out, darling," Yves purred. "You know you want to."

Rowan pressed his lips shut, determined not to give in, despite the pleasure taking him apart at the seams.

One particularly deep stroke hit every sweet spot, sending a wave of fire through his nerves so hot that he almost broke. His back arched, body shuddering in Yves's arms. His teeth sank into his bottom lip again. Blood burst on his tongue.

The tentacles pushed at Rowan's back. Yves lifted him from the door and, still seated inside, took a few strides to deposit Rowan on his back upon the sturdy captain's desk, not even bothering to clear it of the piled charts and maps. Parchment crinkled as Yves braced his hands against the desk, leaving small red smears of blood over the thick border lines between Talva and Nanad.

He bent low to capture Rowan's bloody mouth. His hips rutted in shallow pulses as his tongue swiped across Rowan's bottom lip. Rowan squeezed his shivering legs around Yves's waist. He could feel every inch of Yves's length, every throb of Yves's heartbeat inside his body.

They belonged here. They belonged together.

Yves broke the kiss and smiled down at Rowan, his own lips and pale cheeks smeared with Rowan's blood and that of their enemies. Rowan moved his hands from Yves's now disheveled hair to cup his face between his palms. He was the most beautiful thing Rowan had ever laid eyes on. Rowan's thumbs smoothed over his high cheekbones, black lashes kissing his fingertips. Sometimes he still couldn't believe this perfect, otherworldly man was all his.

For a moment, Yves was captured in his loving, blissful gaze.

Then the curl of his lips turned vicious. He kissed Rowan's palm as he pulled back so only the tip of his cock remained inside. His eyes locked onto Rowan's again and he thrust in hard, causing the desk to scrape across the wooden floor and sending a jolt up Rowan's spine.

Yves licked the blood from his own lips. He bottomed out with every thrust, sending wave upon wave of euphoria through Rowan's body, clouding his mind and pushing him ever closer to the edge. Tears brimmed in his eyes, and he couldn't take his gaze away from Yves's gorgeous face. His dark hair was mussed and falling into his eyes, and harsh breath rasped between his parted lips.

A sheaf of parchments fell to the floor as Yves moved one of his hands to wrap around Rowan's cock. Rowan bit back a sob of relief that came out as a pathetic whimper. Yves's strokes grew sloppy.

Rowan's sore back arched off the desk, head tilting back and mouth gaping open in a silent scream. Pleasure pulsed through his nerves in waves as Yves pushed him over the edge into a chasm of bliss.

Rowan's cum spurted between Yves's fingers, dripping onto the rucked up hem of his shirt. He wrenched Yves down into a kiss to muffle the filthy moan that bubbled up in his throat. Yves released Rowan's cock and wrapped his arm around the small of Rowan's back, lifting him further up the desk and climbing on after him. Their mouths moved in tandem, breathing each other in. Rowan's fingers dug into Yves's scalp, and Yves's arm tightened around him. Yves's thrusts quickened, chasing his own release now. He growled low in his throat as Rowan's body quivered with aftershocks, his insides clenching and pulsing around Yves's cock. He returned Yves's kisses with all the passion of their long absence.

A few more strokes and Yves spilled hot and hard into Rowan's clenching insides. Rowan's legs tightened around Yves's waist to keep him inside. His mouth opened wider to deepen the kiss. Yves's tongue lazily played with his, both of them coming down slowly from their euphoria.

Finally they broke the kiss, resting their sweaty foreheads together, basking in the afterglow. Rowan ran his thumb down the length of Yves's nose, admiring every line of him. They could forget the outside world for this moment and only be here in each other's arms.

When their breathing and heartbeats had slowed, Rowan unwound his legs, and Yves unseated himself from inside him. He climbed off the desk and helped Rowan sit up on the edge. He smoothed the white-blond hair back from Rowan's face and kissed the tip of his petite nose.

"You lost," Yves said simply.

The reality of the situation came rushing back, and Rowan blushed fiercely. He'd tried his best to be quiet. But between the errant moan, the rattling door, and the desk scraping across the floor, there was no way their crew and the prisoners hadn't heard exactly what they were doing. Rowan caught Yves's hand.

"They shouldn't die because I couldn't control myself," he said urgently. "Besides, you made noise too."

Yves smirked, and hauled him to his feet. Rowan's lower back ached, and Yves caught him around the waist and drew him close as his legs went a little wobbly.

"I like when you can't control yourself," he chuckled. "You actually did much better than I expected."

"So..."

"So you'll see what I have in store soon enough."

In only a few minutes, they had both sufficiently recovered. Rowan stepped out of the circle of Yves's arms. There would be time enough later to bask in each other's presence. Right now, they had to go back to real life and do what they came here to do. Rowan's mind whirled through the possibilities of what Yves had planned. But as well as he knew him, Rowan also knew better than to try to predict his husband's next move.

Yves snatched him back around the waist, cradling Rowan in his arms so Rowan's back was pressed to his broad chest. Rowan had never quite gotten used to how petite and protected he felt in Yves's arms.

Yves bent to nuzzle the crook of Rowan's neck.

"Just another minute," he murmured.

Rowan chuckled, reaching up to smooth his lover's hair.

"What's gotten into you?"

Yves wasn't typically so clingy, even after a long time apart. Usually they were able to wait until all the pirating business was done before giving in to their carnal desires. But not this time. What had changed?

Yves's dark eyes flashed with mischief.

"It doesn't matter right now. I have a gift for you. If you accept it, perhaps I'll have mercy on those poor sods you couldn't even be quiet enough to protect." He pulled a small silver object from his coat pocket. It was smooth and smaller than his palm, shaped like a tulip bulb with a piece at the bottom that flared out. Rowan had never seen anything like it before.

"W-what is that?"

From the wicked tilt of Yves's smile, it couldn't be anything good.

Yves's eyelids dipped low. The fingers of his other hand trailed over Rowan's stomach beneath his shirt.

"Would you like me to show you?" Yves licked his lips. Predatory. Rowan found himself trapped in his hunter's gaze, unable to look away.

"Yes," he breathed.

He watched, morbidly fascinated, as Yves retrieved the vial of lube from his pocket and spread a generous amount over the object's sleek form.

"Bend over," Yves ordered.

Yves pushed him forward so his hands were flat on the map-strewn desk. He brushed Rowan's skirt aside and angled his hips so that his ass stuck out. By now Rowan had a pretty good idea of what the object must be for, but it still sent a shiver up his spine when the cold tip of the metal pressed to his still loose and cum-filled hole.

Yves leaned close, lips brushing his ear.

"I'm going to put this inside you." His voice was silky smooth. He gripped Rowan's jaw in one long-fingered hand as he squirmed. The other pressed the object forward ever so slightly so the rounded tip breached Rowan's hole. "Don't worry. It won't get lost. I had it specially made just for you." The plug—Rowan understood fully what it was now—entered him further. Stretching. Yves's tongue ran down the shell of Rowan's ear, over the line of silver earrings.

"This is going to keep you ready for later. And it's going to keep my cum nice and safe inside you."

The plug advanced further, and Rowan whimpered.

"Once it's in, we're going to dress and go back out there in front of our loyal crews who just heard me fuck you senseless. And with every step, you'll feel it inside you, slick with my cum. And you're going to think about what I just did to you and what I'll do later. You're going to know you're mine."

The plug slid home and Rowan moaned. He shifted uncomfortably, the plug pressing at his insides with every movement. How was he meant to face his crew with this thing inside him? He was already sore, and the rounded silver tip barely brushed his prostate. Teasing. Torturing.

"Can you do that for me, darling?"

Rowan licked his parched lips and nodded.

"Say yes," Yves commanded.

"Y-yes..."

Yves released his jaw and stepped away, all smiles and charm once again.

"Now, we'd best return. We've kept our guests waiting long enough."

. . .

Rowan had adjusted slightly by the time they stepped back out onto the deck. He was still a bit disheveled, but Yves—seemingly by some demonic magic Rowan had yet to discover—was clean and perfect. Not a hair out of place, but still a bit blood-soaked. Rowan realized some of the bloody smudges on Yves's clothes and face were distinctly finger-shaped, and hoped no one else noticed.

Every eye on deck swiveled to the two captains the moment they emerged. The prisoners stared in both awe and fright. The pirates looked on with a knowing gleam. Fox was outright grinning, and he looked Rowan up and down as if he *knew* about the plug.

Rowan vowed to make him scrape barnacles later.

The two pirate captains crossed the deck side by side. Every few steps the plug brushed Rowan's prostate, sending a jolt through his nerves. He bit the inside of his cheek, trying his damnedest to walk normally and not blush.

They stopped in front of the group of kneeling prisoners. There were fewer than two dozen of them left. Fewer than Rowan remembered. Had Yves ordered them killed with every noise Rowan made? Surely not. Rowan must have been misremembering. Yves might be a bloodthirsty bastard, but he didn't lie to Rowan, not anymore.

John stepped up beside his captain as Rowan and Yves surveyed the prisoners. Rowan could tell at a glance that they were a green bunch. Not to the point that they would be useless as sailors, but not as highly experienced and trained as the two pirate crews.

Rowan's mind turned back to Yves's mysterious machinations. This ship was a relatively small fish compared to the rich bounty they usually hunted together. It hadn't been much of a challenge. But Yves had asked for the *Sweet Lettie,* and that's what Rowan had delivered. Rowan's gaze flicked to the side, trying to gauge Yves's expression.

"Some of you already know me," Yves began, his voice carrying over the deck. He paced a few steps down the row. Rowan blinked, and looked closer at prisoners' faces. One was vaguely familiar, but in his distracted state, he couldn't place him.

"Some of you know us only by reputation, but if you don't..." He sketched a gallant bow, the huge ruby in his earlobe flashing in the sun. "I am the Deep Water Demon, and this is the Ghost Hawk.

Whatever you have heard, I assure you it's tamer than the truth." This earned a few chuckles from the pirates. Rowan didn't react, except to shift his stance in an effort to relieve the pressure on his insides.

"Before you lies an opportunity." Yves paced back to Rowan and drew one of the pistols from Rowan's brace, gracing him with a manic wink before turning back to his audience. "The *Sweet Lettie* belongs to us now. Normally we'd rob and abandon you. But you've simply seen too much." He cocked the pistol and the prisoners cringed. A few looked like they were about to cry. Surely Yves wasn't planning on actually killing all of them. He'd said he would reconsider if Rowan agreed to accept his gift, which wasn't the only reason Rowan currently had a silver plug up his ass, but that had certainly been a factor. If Rowan had to step in and stop him, neither of them would be pleased.

"My loyal first mate deserves a reward for all his hard work over the years. So I am gifting the *Sweet Lettie* to him."

John's head snapped toward his captain, sharp eyes darting between Yves, Rowan, and the prisoners. It seemed not even the loyal and devoted first mate was privy to his captain's plans. Yves ignored the reaction. His eyes remained trained on the prisoners.

"So I present you fine sailors with a choice." Yves leveled the pistol at them. "Join us, or die."

CHAPTER 4

MAY 2ND, 1668

Zanta picked up the last key, brass warming quickly in her hand as she tried to fit it into the lock. It slid in halfway before the mismatched teeth caught on the tumblers. She jiggled it a little, but it was no use. With a frustrated sigh, she tossed it into the small pile of nearly identical keys beside the iron chest. It clinked as it slid down, coming to rest on the wooden floor.

Zanta sat back against the side of her bed, popping a ginger candy into her mouth before massaging feeling back into her legs. She'd been unable to sleep after the *Monsoon* escaped Roseforte Harbor, and did what she always had when insomnia gripped her. She sat on the floor before the iron chest that contained Silver Stroud's treasure and tried key after key, even the ones she'd tried a hundred times before.

It had become a sort of meditative habit over the years, a ritual to soothe her troubled mind. And like every time before, none of the keys fit.

She shoved the chest away with her foot. It barely budged, but the dull thud of her boot against its side was satisfying.

It was a pretty thing, an iron chest with a flat lid, about the length of her forearm on all sides. The top and sides were decorated with swirls of polished filigree reminiscent of waves, now marred by the dents and scratches of Zanta's and a dozen locksmiths' many attempts to break into it. A small section of filigree was currently pushed to the side to expose the keyhole. Empty and taunting. Ever since she'd first laid eyes on it, Zanta had been fascinated by the chest that Silver Stroud so closely guarded and considered as his greatest treasure. Even Emilie, his first mate and Zanta's late fiancée, had never seen its contents.

Now both of them were gone, and Zanta was left with a locked chest and an aching heart.

Morning light streamed in from the windows at her back, reminding her that she hadn't slept yet. It wasn't just the residual adrenaline of escaping Roseforte, or even that the fifth anniversary of Stroud's and Emilie's deaths had come and gone and she had nothing to show for it besides grief that returned again and again, no matter how many times she pushed it away.

It was that woman.

Zanta groaned and leaned her head back against the edge of the mattress. That woman. Nia. She'd gone mad and tried to jump overboard as soon as the *Monsoon* set sail. Was she suicidal? She'd seemed completely fine up until she'd been dragged onto the ship. Then again, from Nia's perspective, it probably seemed like she was being kidnapped, and sailors weren't exactly known for treating women well.

Let me.

Zanta closed her eyes, Nia's tearful, determined face from the night before rising fresh in her mind's eye. Nia had wanted to die, longed for it even. Zanta could hear the despair so clearly in her voice. She understood. She'd been the same after Emilie's death, but she'd never gotten far enough to give in to that darkness.

Zanta hadn't had the energy to deal with it all last night, so she'd left Nia in the storeroom. She supposed now that it was morning she would have to let Nia out and chart a course for the nearest Talvan port to drop her at.

She groaned as she got to her feet. She hoped Nia hadn't suffered too much in the stuffy storeroom. She seemed like a nice enough woman. Maybe she'd found something soft to sleep on in the baskets and crates.

The baskets that Zanta suddenly remembered were full of rope, and other things Nia could use to achieve her goals.

Zanta sprinted onto the deck, startling the morning watch. Skidding to a stop next to the hatch, she wrenched the bar open, dreading what she might find within. The hatch opened with a squeal, and she reluctantly peered in.

The sight that met her was not the one she'd dreaded. Nia's generous form lay curled in peaceful slumber on a pile of cloth she'd taken from various parts of the storeroom and formed into a makeshift nest. She lay on her side, peachy skirts tucked around her feet and one pale, manicured hand pressed to her lips. Her chest rose and fell with the even breath of sleep.

Zanta sat back on her heels, relief washing through her.

Nia stirred when the light from the open hatch touched her face. Her eyelids fluttered open, and she wiped a bit of drool from her lip with the back of her hand. She sat up slowly, taking stock of her surroundings before looking up.

Zanta had expected fear on Nia's face, maybe even lingering despair. What she did not expect was cheerfulness.

"Good morning!" Nia exclaimed, a bright smile spreading across her lips. "Have you come to let me out?"

Her pale face shone peachy in the morning light, matching her skirt. She'd taken her ginger hair out of its pins and it now tumbled around her shoulders in soft waves like calm waters at dawn.

"Um, yes. As long as you don't try anything," Zanta said warily. Was this an act? A ploy to lower Zanta's guard then fling herself into the sea the first chance she got?

"Oh, I'm over it," Nia replied brightly.

What a strange woman she was. Zanta would be happy to be rid of her as soon as they reached land.

She reached down to help Nia out of the storeroom, watching, ready to catch Nia and lock her back up if she tried to make a break for the rail. But Nia patted the dust from her skirts, then threw her head back to let the sun shine on her face. After a few moments, her peridot eyes cut to Zanta. Zanta tensed.

"I'm not going to jump," Nia said lightly. "I told you I'm over it. No need to look at me like that."

"And I told you, no one dies on my ship unless I say so," Zanta replied firmly, but her muscles relaxed.

"Well I wouldn't have been on your ship. I'd have been in the water." Her words were flippant. Then, seeing Zanta's horrified expression, she added, "What? Aren't you a pirate? You've seen people die before."

"Why would you think I'm a pirate?" Zanta crossed her arms.

Nia gave her a look that said *come on, be reasonable*, and decisively did not answer her question. Instead she asked one of her own. "What's your name anyway? It's not Sarah. I've never heard of a pirate captain by that name."

So not only had she clocked Zanta and her crew as pirates, but rightly guessed Zanta was the captain. Well, she supposed there was no use keeping up the charade of being merchants now that they'd left Roseforte.

"Zanta."

Nia's pretty freckled face went through a range of indecipherable emotions in a split second before settling once more into a pleasant smile. But strain lined its edges. Nia's fingers flexed at her side, half hidden by her skirts.

"You're the one who killed Silver Stroud," she said, voice flat.

"That's me." Zanta was always flippant about it. Most people thought her an ambitious mutineer. They didn't know how much she'd lost.

Another flicker of something Zanta couldn't decipher.

"Splinter Zanta. I should have known. They say you're the prettiest pirate this side of Souna." Her eyes roved over Zanta's form. "Looks like they're right."

Zanta frowned, hoping that would dispel the butterflies that had suddenly decided to escape her stomach by way of her throat.

"Yes, Splinter Zanta. And you are Nia...I didn't catch your surname."

"Oh. I don't have one. I'm an orphan," Nia said, the smile not leaving her face. Zanta herself had chosen to cast aside her family name when she became captain, to protect her family from potential connection. She couldn't imagine never having had a family name at all, no history to cling to.

"Well, regardless. I assure you that you're in no danger on my ship. We will drop you off at the next port and—"

"That won't be necessary." Nia cut her off, sidling closer. Both her hair and skirts swished in the breeze. "I'm staying."

"Staying?" It only took a moment to regain her composure. "I'm afraid that's not possi—"

"Anything is possible; you're the captain," Nia interrupted again. Zanta's fear over her potential death was quickly becoming annoyance. "What do you need? A cook? Someone to clean? I can do anything I set my hand to."

"Why would you want to stay on a pirate ship?" Zanta asked. She could feel her brow doing that thing Emilie had always said would give her wrinkles.

Nia spread her hands, encompassing the sea surrounding them and all that had happened last night.

"Where would I go? Roseforte is sure to be in shambles. I have no money or possessions to my name. If you drop me off at a random port I'll be destitute, and on the streets before you even sail over the horizon. Besides..." Nia stepped boldly into Zanta's space, eyelids lowering flirtatiously. She ran the back of her index finger down Zanta's cheek, and Zanta flinched. "...You have something I want."

The moment was broken by the clang of the aft bell calling the first shift to work. Nia lowered her hand and stepped away. Her eyes landed on the wooden box, still tucked next to the rail where she'd left it. She scooped it up.

"Show me where I'll be sleeping."

Captain Zanta deposited Nia in yet another storeroom. Thankfully this one was much larger, and had an actual door. Apparently the crew quarters were full, but this suited Nia just fine. She liked privacy.

She strung the hammock Zanta had given her between the rafters. Zanta had told her to see her first mate, Sabriye, about her new duties "only till we make port." But Nia was tired from her night on the floor and wanted a nap. She had no intention of being dropped off on land again, not when she could feel her treasure so close at hand.

Nia had spent most of the night wondering over the presence of the treasure here. But now she knew the reason. This wasn't Stroud's old ship, the *Silverfin*. That ship was as familiar to her as her own body. But it was the ship of Splinter Zanta, the woman who had killed Silver Stroud by driving a piece of his own ship through his heart, if the stories were to be believed. Of course Zanta would have Stroud's belongings. Now the question was, where would Zanta keep the chest?

Had she been able to open it? Nia figured not, since it was still here and held little value to anyone but Nia. Zanta must think it was valuable beyond measure if Stroud had guarded it as jealously during Zanta's tenure in his crew as he had when Nia was still on the *Silverfin*. She'd keep it somewhere safe. A smuggler's hold perhaps, or the captain's quarters.

Zanta obviously wasn't going to just hand it over. Nor would she trust Nia enough to show her secret holds or let her unsupervised into her room. But that was no matter.

Nia knew exactly how she was going to get it.

She thought of Zanta's smooth skin beneath her fingers. The way her lips had parted in surprise when Nia flirted with her. She rubbed her knuckles against her own cheek. Zanta's reaction today had proved she was susceptible to Nia's charms.

Nia smiled to herself and sat on her new hammock, swinging gently. Her fingers ran over the peach-blossom carvings of the box in her lap. She flipped the tag over and read it again.

Who was JL? Perhaps the box's contents would provide an answer.

She lifted the lid, and discovered exactly who the box was from.

Nestled in a bed of pink velvet were four beautifully carved and polished wooden cocks of varying sizes, shapes, and colors. Her gaze landed on the thickest one, and her smile broadened even more. She recognized it instantly, the cock that had given her a week of pure, unadulterated bliss more than a year before, and again last fall. She would never forget a cock like that, or the man attached to it.

John Hakon.

Which meant the cock two down, carved of blond wood and slightly curved to the left was...Logan.

John and Logan. JL.

The lining of the lid popped open under her fingers to reveal a soft velvet harness with a variety of metal rings matching the girths of her new collection.

Life was about to get very interesting indeed.

CHAPTER 5

MAY 2ND, 1668

The infirmary on board the *Siren* was quiet as Henri carefully threaded a sterilized needle and placed it in Robin's waiting hand. Robin graced him with that familiar gentle smile before bending over Fox to begin stitching the cut across his thigh. The *Siren*'s crew had come out of the battle with the *Sweet Lettie* relatively unscathed, and Fox was their last patient of the day. He winced as the needle pierced his skin, but otherwise gave no reaction. He was busy flicking through one of Henri's penny novels. Henri was fairly sure that Fox still couldn't read, but this particular novel featured a few somewhat creative illustrations that he seemed amused by.

Robin closed up the wound with meticulously even stitches, his tongue tucked into the corner of his mouth in concentration. Henri couldn't help the way his heart softened as he watched his boyfriend work. In the almost two years they'd known each other, he'd learned a lot from Robin. Since Henri had been hobbled by his broken leg for so long, Robin had pressed him into service and somehow Henri had become his informal apprentice.

The infirmary door opened, and Logan ushered in four of the new recruits from the *Sweet Lettie*.

"These men need medical attention," Logan said. He looked a bit frazzled, probably because he was stuck watching after the new unwilling crew members Captain Rowan and the Demon had sprung on them.

Robin's concentration didn't waver from his task, so Henri smiled in the recruits' direction, hoping to put them at ease.

"Leave them to us."

Logan simply nodded and left the recruits standing warily just past the threshold, too nervous to venture further. Robin tied off the last of the stitches and stood, wiping his hands on a clean cloth.

"We'll see the most serious injuries first. Lighter cases can—"

"Robin!"

Robin froze as a tall young man who looked to be in his early twenties pushed through the others. His right sleeve was bloodied and a streak of his sandy blond mop of hair was stained crimson from a gash above his ear. He rushed to Robin. Henri jolted from his seat, but the young man got there first, enveloping Robin in a bone-crushing hug.

Henri drew up short, gaze flitting between the two as Robin just stood there, stunned, in the young man's arms. They were close in height, the younger man just an inch or two shorter. Their fluffy blond hair was almost mirrored, and when the young man pulled back, Henri saw that their facial features, right down to those gentle hazel eyes, were nearly identical as well.

Robin blinked slowly, seeming to come out of his initial shock. His arms came up to encircle the younger man in a fierce hug. Tears overflowed down his rounded cheeks. After a moment, the younger man pulled away and looked up into Robin's face.

"What are you doing here?" the young man asked incredulously. "Are you a prisoner too?" Those familiar yet unfamiliar hazel eyes flicked to Henri and Fox, glaring.

"I...um..." Robin clearly didn't know what to say. Henri couldn't see much of his face from this angle, but it was as if Robin didn't know whether to be elated or terrified by the young man's presence.

The young man glared at Henri again, as if he was the reason for Robin's distress.

Robin dashed the tears from his eyes with the back of his hand and gently disengaged from the younger man's embrace.

"I'll explain later. Let's take a look at those cuts first." There was something different about his voice, a stilted upper-class edge seeping in. "You can handle the bandaging, right?" he asked Henri.

"Right."

Robin set to work assessing the new patients as Henri sat back down to bandage Fox's leg.

"Brother, you think? Cousin?" Fox whispered. Henri glanced up to where Robin chatted quietly to the reluctant recruits. The young man hovered near him like a worried mother hen. That, too, was so like Robin it was uncanny.

"Dunno. He has two brothers, so maybe." Robin didn't like to talk about his past, and his family was included in that. Henri knew he was from an upper-class Avardellan family, and was the middle of three sons, but that was about it. Robin got sad if Henri ever asked about it. After all, the judgment and expectations of his family were the reason he'd run away in the first place. They couldn't accept him as he was, and that had directly led him to being captured by the Deep Water Demon, and later meeting Henri.

Henri couldn't say he wished things were different. But he loved Robin, and he wished the thought of his family didn't pain him so.

Henri finished his task and patted Fox's leg. "Good as new."

"Damn, I was hoping you'd kiss it better," Fox quipped.

"You wish."

Fox's gaze traveled across the room to where the young man was glaring at them again over Robin's shoulder.

"Want me to stay just in case?" Fox asked.

"Nah, we've got it. Besides, I know you're itching to tease Rowan about what happened today."

Fox grinned and sprang up from the cot as if his injuries were non-existent.

"Damn right."

When Fox left, Henri approached the group of recruits.

"What can I do?"

Robin looked up from where he was stitching a laceration on a man's arm, and glanced around at the other recruits.

"Most of it is superficial, but could you clean up David's head?"

"David?" By the name, and the way the young man scowled, Henri suspected he knew who it was.

"Oh, right." A pretty blush spread to Robin's ears. "This is David, my younger brother. David, this is my..." He cleared his throat. "This is Henri."

Not his partner. Not his boyfriend. Just Henri.

Henri knew well enough how Robin's family was, but still, his heart sank down to his stomach. He loved Robin, and Robin loved him. But Robin came from another world, and deep down, Henri had always been afraid he'd realize this life wasn't for him, and they would have to part ways.

He swallowed down his melancholy and smiled at David, sticking out his hand to shake.

"Welcome aboard, David. It's nice to meet you."

David's gaze flicked down to Henri's hand, then back up to his face. He crossed his arms. Henri swallowed the lump in his throat, reminding himself that it was not Robin's eyes that were looking at him so distrustfully, but a stranger's.

"I'll wait for you," David said to Robin, inching closer to his brother's side. "You're a doctor."

Robin huffed, but he was back to stitching, and hadn't seen David snub Henri's offered hand.

"I trained him myself, Davy. He's perfectly capable of cleaning you up."

"I'll wait," David insisted, taking a step back like Henri would hurt him. The round-voweled Avardellan accent that Henri found so soothing and endearing from Robin's mouth was quickly becoming grating from David.

"I'm finished here anyway." Robin placed the final stitch and quickly wrapped a bandage around the man's arm. He looked up, and Henri couldn't help but melt a little under his gaze.

"Could you take the others back up to Logan?"

Henri nodded and gathered the other three men. Maybe once Robin got a chance to speak to his brother alone, he would smooth things over.

He found Logan on deck directing the movement of supplies between the ships. Henri left the recruits with him, then returned below before Logan could put him to work hauling shit back and forth.

Once he made it below deck, Henri's steps slowed. What were the two brothers talking about without him there? Was Robin explaining the situation? Would he tell David about his relationship with Henri?

Or was David convincing Robin to return to the family fold?

Anxiety clenched Henri's guts, and he rushed to the infirmary.

"...leaving?"

Henri stopped short just outside the open infirmary door, out of sight of the two brothers within. It was David that had spoken, his voice more haughty than Robin's. Henri knew he shouldn't listen in on their conversation. He should either leave or make his presence known, but he was frozen to the spot.

"Hold still," Robin sighed, not answering whatever question his brother had asked. There was silence for a moment before David spoke again.

"Why are you on this ship, Robin?"

"Why are you?" There was a familiar wryness in Robin's tone that Henri recognized as him being stubborn.

"I was commissioned to paint a portrait of the new governor of Kefrye, if you must know," David grumbled, obviously put out by his brother's avoidance.

"You've graduated from the academy, then?" Henri could almost see a smile of pride spreading across Robin's face.

"You'd know as much if you were home."

Silence again.

Robin broke it first this time.

"I'm proud of you, you know." His voice was gentle as always. "The Art Academy is no joke. And you even traveled all that way to paint the governor? My baby brother Davy is all grown up."

"Yeah well, I'm no doctor or heir," David mumbled. "And people don't call me that anymore, not since you left."

"Father and Mother must be proud," Robin countered.

"Not as proud as they are of you and Philip." There was a long pause in which David seemed to be collecting himself. When he spoke again, he sounded hesitant. "W-where have you been all this time?"

"I don't know what to say."

"Well say *something*," David hissed. "You've been missing for three years! We all thought you were dead!"

"I've been...Well I left, and my ship was captured and..."

"And they're forcing you to work for them," David finished for him. "Who was that guy? Your jailor or something?"

"N-no, that's not..."

Robin was floundering. Why was he unable to tell his brother the truth of the situation? Regardless of how they'd come into each other's lives, Robin had chosen to stay even after the Demon released him from his contract. He'd chosen Henri. So why couldn't he bring himself to tell David the truth?

Old anxieties simmered in Henri's gut. He clenched his hand into a fist, and fought down the urge to step in and set the record straight. If he did that it would just make it look like David was right.

"We can escape," David said fervently. "These deviants have to make land sometime, then we can go home."

"Davy stop! I-I can't. I'll talk to the captain and see if he'll release you, but I'm not leaving. I'm sorry."

Bittersweet relief flooded him. Robin was staying, but he hadn't told David about Henri. And Henri couldn't stand to listen anymore. He stepped through the doorway and their conversation fell silent.

THE UNFAMILIAR PRESS of the plug up Rowan's ass made him acutely aware of his body. It was not painful, nor necessarily unpleasant, yet with every step he took, his hole clenched and moved around the little silver bulb. With every sidelong glance the crew cast him, he became more and more convinced that each and every one of them knew.

Damn Yves for convincing him to agree to this when he was still cock-dumb in the afterglow of ill-advised sex. It was difficult enough going about his day knowing what awaited him when he and Yves were finally alone again, but on top of that, every time the plug so much as brushed more sensitive areas, he had to start deep breathing to stop himself from getting hard in front of the whole crew. The fact that he was wearing a skirt instead of pants, and had been too fucked-out to remember to put his underwear back on, didn't help either.

Blessedly, Yves came to find him after what seemed like forever but was probably only an hour. Rowan allowed himself a moment to feel relieved before he got the urge to wipe that self-satisfied smirk right off Yves's beautiful lips.

"What do you want?"

Yves quirked an amused eyebrow at him. "Is that any way to greet your beloved husband?"

"It is when he's a fucking menace to my sanity."

Yves leaned close, one hand on Rowan's waist. "How are you

enjoying my gift, darling? Is staying open and wet for me turning you on?"

"No," Rowan gritted out. Fighting down yet another boner as the simple sensation of Yves's hand on his waist sent his nerves into overdrive.

"Pity. Perhaps I'll have to hold off ravishing you till you *really* want it."

What a devious bastard he was, and Rowan loved him for it.

Rowan inhaled deeply through his nose and exhaled through his mouth, trying to steady himself as his overeager cock tried to twitch to life again.

"Did you just come to tease me? I have work to do."

"I would love nothing more than to tease you until you beg for mercy, but no, we must discuss the future of our little fleet. John and Logan are waiting in the *Sweet Lettie*'s captain's quarters."

The very room where Rowan had so recently been fucked into near oblivion. Yves really wasn't making this easy on him. Rowan hoped John wouldn't notice the mess they'd made of his new desk, and that Rowan's underwear had somehow gotten kicked somewhere John wouldn't find it. Though knowing John, he was already planning some subtle way to exact revenge on them.

Rowan remembered suddenly that he was meant to be annoyed at Yves for not only taking the risk of revealing their true relationship to outsiders—thereby necessitating that they keep the sailors as captive crew members—but also that he'd sprung this whole plan on Rowan and John without even discussing it with them first.

"Yes we *do* need to talk about 'our little fleet,'" Rowan agreed. If Yves heard the annoyance in Rowan's voice he didn't show it. He simply walked away, and Rowan followed.

Rowan hadn't gotten a good look at the room earlier, distracted as he was by being slammed against the door, then bent over the desk. Now his eye swept the room quickly, taking in the cabinets, the desk, the small table where John and Logan conversed quietly, and beyond a bank of cabinets and columns hung with sheer curtains, the bedchamber. His face heated as he saw the desk was now tidy. How much evidence of their lovemaking had they left behind? Or had John simply chalked up the scattered papers to the battle?

All hopes were dashed when he approached the table and John stared at him sternly.

"You owe me a new map of the Sunrise Sea," John said. "There are two distinctly ass-cheek shaped smears on mine. I can't imagine where they came from."

Rowan's face heated further, and Logan hid a chuckle behind his wooden hand.

"Ah...Sorry."

"Consider it done." Yves interrupted Rowan's embarrassed stutter. "Now, to the matter at hand." He took a seat on one of the four wooden chairs, adjusting his coat hem so it fell in pretty folds behind him. Rowan lowered himself gingerly into the other free chair, trying not to jostle the plug and failing. He clenched his teeth as lightning shot up his spine. Logan raised his eyebrows but said nothing. He, of all people, would never suspect what Rowan was currently experiencing. He'd probably ask Rowan later if he'd pulled a muscle or something.

Yves sat in a relaxed posture, but Rowan suspected he was keenly aware of every little flinch or hitched breath.

"Congratulations are in order, Captain," Logan said to John.

The corner of John's lip twitched. "Thank you. Though I can't say I expected it." His intense gaze moved to Yves. "Care to explain yourself?" John had never been overly respectful of Yves when he was the first mate, but now that they were on equal footing as captains, he seemed to be enjoying himself.

"I thought it was about time you were rewarded for your loyal service," Yves said calmly. "And we're in a good financial position to expand the fleet."

John raised his eyebrows. "Oh? Am I still under your command?"

"No, equal partners in the endeavor of pirating. Run your ship and your season how you like, but if you want to keep Illusion as a safe haven, you share profit equitably. The three of us make decisions together in regard to Illusion."

Rowan's annoyance spiked. Yves should've discussed this with him first. He wasn't opposed to John captaining his own ship by any means. John was as fair and competent as he was brutal. He'd be a fine pirate captain. Rowan just resented Yves making such a big decision without him. How long had he been planning this? Certainly since the last time they'd seen each other, when he'd asked Rowan to bring him the *Sweet Lettie*. He could've told Rowan then, could've even told him when they were alone in this room, but he'd waited to announce it in front of the entire crew instead.

"Fair enough," John said. He glanced at Rowan. "Are you amenable to this? You seem like a bee flew up your ass."

Yves snorted, and Rowan blushed. "I have no objections," Rowan answered simply. It wasn't the decision itself Rowan didn't like, it was the secrecy.

"I accept your terms, then. I'll return to Illusion at the end of the season, and share my newfound riches with you sorry sods."

"Excellent." Yves clapped once. "Now onto the next matter, choosing a new name for your ship and appointing a first mate."

John's eyes flicked to Logan and held his gaze. Logan shook his head subtly. "I'll choose Gaël as my first mate, if he agrees," John said when their gaze broke.

"He wouldn't leave Fox behind," Rowan said.

"I'll take that troublemaker too, if they're a package deal." John's voice was stern as always, but Rowan didn't miss the slight edge of amusement in it. Not even stoic John Hakon was immune to Fox's charms.

"Rowan? They're your crew. What do you think?" Yves asked.

A slight thread of anxiety crept through Rowan's chest. Gaël was his friend and a valuable crew member. And Fox was...so much more than that. He was practically family. Rowan's heart ached at the thought of losing them.

"If they agree to it, they're free to go." As much as he would miss Fox's lighthearted antics and Gaël's strong, quiet presence, he wouldn't hinder them if this was what they chose. Rowan hadn't missed the fact that Logan was clearly John's first choice and had turned him down without a second thought. At least his oldest friend would stay by his side.

"I'll fetch him." Logan got up and padded to the door, where he caught a passing crew member and sent them after Gaël.

"What of the *Sweet Lettie*'s new name?" Yves asked when Logan returned. It was traditional throughout the Islands to rename a ship when she passed into new hands, especially if those new hands belonged to a pirate. It left the old identity of the vessel behind and started anew. Not that the *Sweet Lettie* needed a fresh start, she was so newly built her wood was practically still green.

John thought for a moment.

"*Sweet Mercy.*"

Yves sat forward, dark eyes flashing. "Oh? Do you intend to be merciful? Perhaps I've misjudged you."

John smiled wickedly. "What could be less merciful than false hope?"

Yves grinned back, just as wicked. "I like it."

Gods, maybe it was a mistake to give a ship to John. He was almost as sadistic as Yves, and had a thing for fire. Yves sat back, satisfied with this answer, just as a knock sounded on the door.

"Enter," John called.

Gaël came in, honey brown skin streaked with sweat from moving crates in the sun, and closed the door behind him. "You called, Captains?" John's back straightened a little at being called captain again.

Not one to mince words, John said, "I need a first mate I can trust, if half my crew is going to be these press-ganged newbies. What do you say?"

Gaël blinked at him. "You want my recommendation?"

Logan chuckled, and Rowan smiled to himself.

"No, Gaël. I want you for the job."

"Oh, I..." It was clear this possibility had not occurred to Gaël. A small smile crept across his lips, quickly stifled. "I won't leave Fox behind."

"He's welcome as well," John said.

Gaël nodded, then looked at Rowan. "I'd need my captain's permission."

"You have it," Rowan answered. "Sad as I'd be to lose you."

"I'd like a day to think and discuss with Fox, if I could," Gaël said.

"Of course," John said.

"Best get back to your duties now," Rowan said. Selfish as it may be, he hoped Fox would refuse to leave the *Siren Song*. This was all moving too fast for Rowan's liking, his control over his own crew spiraling under Yves's whims. Gaël nodded and left, a slight spring in his step.

"Well if that concludes our business." Yves made to stand, but Rowan stopped him with a hand on his arm. He bit his lip as the movement jostled the plug.

"Not so fast."

Yves resettled into his seat. "What is it?"

"Only the small matter of appointing a new first mate for you."

Yves's gaze sharpened playfully. "Oh? You think I can't run the *Kraken* on my own?"

Now he was just being obstinate. Of course he couldn't run an entire warship full of pirates on his own. No one could run a ship effectively without a second-in-command for long. Yves needed a human buffer between him and the crew, but Rowan couldn't exactly say that in front of Logan and John.

"You need someone practical to temper your baser instincts. You don't always see what's in front of you."

"I see everything," Yves scoffed.

"Really? How long did it take you to realize you were in love with me?" If Yves could air their business in front of others, so could Rowan.

Yves quirked an eyebrow. "Quicker than you, darling."

True enough. He'd used a bad example.

"Enough of this weird flirting," John cut in. "I recommend Doe Adair for the role."

Rowan had heard the name before but it took him a moment to place it. A Laslandish woman who was married to Illusion's blacksmith. She and her wife had twins who often chased the cats around the village and snuck treats to Nephele. They'd been Gaël and Fox's little shadows for weeks over the winter when one of the cats in the main house birthed kittens in their room.

Laslandish people had an affinity for naming certain children after animals. Doe and Fox were two prime examples. It was an old traditional way that many still clung to. The Laslandish druids still roamed the island, presiding over births and deaths with their gnarled wooden staves. And every so often they would declare a newborn had the 'spirit of mischief.' Rowan had forgotten the proper name for it, but it was an old trickster god boiled down to myth and this last superstition. This ungendered god had three forms. Land, sky, and sea. When a child was declared to embody one, their parents named them after a creature from another in an attempt to trick the trickster, and hide the child from its influence.

When Rowan had first asked Fox about his name, Fox had told a story of himself as a wee babe of just a few weeks old. He'd looked up with his startling green eyes into the face of the visiting druid, smiled, and farted a fart so ghastly they all had to vacate the cottage. The druid had declared him for the sky. He'd ended up with the name Fox.

Now, Yves tilted his head questioningly. "Why Doe?"

"She's practical, smart, and loyal. She's been with you since the beginning, and knows your eccentricities," John said.

Rowan hadn't known that. He'd thought John the longest serving crew member of the *Kraken*. Yves looked at Rowan, who raised his eyebrows in silent challenge.

"Fine," Yves sighed. "Doe will be my new first mate."

CHAPTER 6

MAY 2ND, 1668

Rowan was practically sweating by the time he closed the door behind him, only a few hours after Yves had first placed the silver plug. Yves swept into the first of his chambers, a parlor elegantly appointed with a shiny oak dining table and a pair of ruby velvet armchairs arranged in front of the cold fireplace. Rowan had been in these rooms many times. Hell, they'd had sex on practically every available sturdy surface in Yves's quarters, and several unsturdy ones besides. But the ostentatiousness always struck him, reminding him how different he and his husband really were. They were both ambitious, sure, but Yves had a hunger in him that far surpassed Rowan's. He could never be satisfied. Always consuming. Always feeding more to the void within him. It was never enough, and sometimes Rowan worried that one day he would no longer be enough either.

Yves cast his coat over the back of one of the armchairs and continued further into his quarters toward his bedroom, expecting Rowan to follow. But Rowan remained by the door. Every time he walked, he was reminded of the silver plug buried in his ass, keeping Yves's cum inside him. Keeping him ready for Yves's cock. Even the roll of the ship caused his stance to shift, pressing the silver bulb against his sensitive walls.

As much as he wanted to follow Yves to bed and present himself to be ravished again, he couldn't quite make his feet move. There were things he and Yves needed to discuss, and if he let himself be fucked silly, he'd forget all about them.

Sometimes Rowan wondered if his inability to resist Yves's seduction was simply because he was weak, or if it was due in part to some otherworldly demonic draw.

Finally noticing that Rowan was not eagerly following behind him, Yves came back to his side.

"Do you think John will be able to make it on his own?" Rowan blurted before Yves could touch him. This was truly the least of his concerns, but he had to start somewhere.

Yves smiled at him indulgently.

"I paid him in advance for the season, and he's got the *Mercy*'s cargo to pawn. I'm sure he'll be fine," Yves assured him. "I'm more interested in how you're faring." He closed the distance between them, eyes growing hungry and dark. Rowan could have sworn he saw the man's mouth watering.

"Yves..." Rowan dodged around him, holding up his hands to fend him off. Yves's smile sharpened, thinking this was another game.

"Yes? Tell me, has it been a struggle to go about your day with my little gift inside you? As you captain these poor sods who are none the wiser that you're ready to be fucked at any moment?"

Rowan backed away more, his ass bumped against the edge of the table, jostling the plug and sending a shockwave of pleasure, pain, and humiliation through his body. His knees weakened for a moment before he caught himself on the edge of the table. Yves reached him, his long-fingered hands grabbing Rowan's hips and—

"Stop, please," Rowan gasped. Yves's body stilled, hungry mouth mere centimeters away, ready to devour him.

"Are we playing coy or is something wrong, darling?"

"I—" Yves's warm breath wafting across his skin was driving him to distraction. He pushed Yves away gently to give himself some breathing room. Yves's brow furrowed.

"Are you in pain? Should I take it out?"

"I-it's fine just...Why did you do that?"

"Do what?" Yves almost looked lost, standing there without his hands on Rowan's body. No outlet for his carnivorous lust.

"Those sailors know about us now," Rowan hissed. Yves had kissed him in front of outsiders, and Rowan was sure everyone on the ship knew exactly what they'd gotten up to in the captain's quarters of the *Sweet Lettie* as their crews guarded the prisoners. He was as much to blame for it as Yves for going along with it, but that was beside the point.

After the battle outside Wave Harbor and their subsequent reunion and marriage, Yves and Rowan had braced for news of their relationship to spread. They were not so naive as to think that killing Cyrus and Admiral Batteux would kill the information too, but no such rumors had spread. It seemed as if the two conspirators had kept it largely to themselves, not wanting to share the glory.

Yves graced him with a charming smile. "Must we talk about this now darling, when we both know your pretty little ass is wet and primed for me?"

Rowan glowered at him. They'd agreed to keep their relationship a secret from the outside world, and now that would be impossible, since they'd revealed it all in front of an entire crew they didn't know and couldn't trust. And what would they do if their unwilling new crew members found out about Illusion? The whole thing was a mess.

It wasn't that they were both men—though Rowan was sure certain factions of polite society would condemn them for that too—but that they were both wanted criminals. Murderers and pirates with such hefty prices on their heads that whoever might capture them would have a hard time deciding which country to hand them over to. If their relationship was known, it could be used against them. They could be used to hurt each other. Just as Cyrus and Batteux had used Rowan to lure Yves out and kill him at Wave Harbor. Rowan did not want to be responsible for another of Yves's deaths. Nor could he stand the thought of Yves being alone again if Rowan were to suffer a much more permanent fate.

"We agreed to keep it a secret, Yves," Rowan said, frustrated with his husband as much as himself for giving in so easily, as always.

The easy confidence seemed to melt away from Yves's shoulders.

"I couldn't wait."

"Why not?"

Yves shifted as if he wanted to get closer, a sudden vulnerability in his expression.

"Because I...I died again. And when I came back all I could do was miss you. It was hard enough to wait at the Teeth instead of hunting you down immediately."

Rowan's heart dropped to his stomach. He reached out to catch Yves's hand and drew him closer.

"How did it happen?" he whispered.

Yves hesitated for a moment before brushing a light kiss across Rowan's cheekbone just beneath his eyepatch.

"Do you really want to know?" His voice was low, as intimate as their embrace. As intimate as death.

Rowan didn't, truly. He was surrounded by death constantly, whether dealt by his hand or not. Yet the thought of Yves dying filled him with so much dread he could barely stand it, nor could he stand to let Yves go through yet another death alone.

"Tell me, if you want."

He felt more than saw Yves's sad smile as their cheeks brushed. "I would spare you the gruesome details, my love."

"Were you in pain? Did...Were you at peace after?" Rowan's eyes widened. "Does the crew know?" Thus far in Yves's illustrious career, he'd been able to hide his immortality even from those closest to him. As far as the crew was concerned, their captain was simply very lucky when it came to escaping the ultimate fate of all pirates. And if there were rumors that cut close to his true nature, well, sailors were known to tell tall tales, and it only served to fuel the fire of his legend.

"It is like a dream of floating in the sea. Calm, no matter how violent the death." Yves drew back to look at him, searching his face for a reaction to what he was about to say. "John knows. He got me below deck before anyone could see the extent of it."

Rowan shuddered, trying not to let his imagination run away with what damage could have befallen Yves's beautiful body, yet left no evidence behind.

"What will you do without him now that he is a captain in his own right? Is this *why* you made him a captain?"

"Not entirely." Yves's tongue poked the inside of his own cheek, a habit Rowan found endearing, even if it usually meant Yves was annoyed, or thinking thoughts that shouldn't escape into the world. "If we are going to have this conversation in full, perhaps we should take care of your delicate situation first?" Yves asked, his hand wandering down Rowan's waist.

Rowan had almost completely forgotten about the plug in the face of Yves's news. His muscles tensed at the reminder, sending another wave of not quite pleasure through his core. He bit his lip to hold back a whimper.

"I can't trust that you won't turn its removal to your advantage. You're not going to distract me that easily," Rowan said seriously.

Yves stepped back, his hand going to his chest in mock offense. "How could you say such a thing, darling? When have I ever used sex to distract you?"

Practically the whole beginning of their relationship, and just a few minutes ago, before Rowan had managed to steer the situation toward his questions. But Rowan didn't point that out; they both knew Yves's favorite little tactic well. And they both knew Rowan could rarely resist going along with it.

Rowan sighed, and the faux offense melted from Yves's expression, replaced by his usual charm. He stepped toward Rowan again, crowding him against the table. "At least let me take you to bed, so we can be ready if the mood strikes," he said playfully. Rowan didn't even have a chance to protest before Yves swept him up into his arms and began carrying him toward the bedroom.

"Yves, I'm serious!" Rowan growled. He tried to struggle, but the plug pressed on his prostate again and the struggle fizzled to a whimper. Yves sighed, diverting course to plant himself on one of the velvet armchairs and settle Rowan into his lap like a child. Rowan accepted this grudgingly. It was better than standing at least. He leaned his shoulder into Yves's broad chest, his legs thrown over the arm of the chair.

There was silence between them, broken only by the susurration of waves and the creak of the *Kraken*'s timbers.

"You die an awful lot for someone who's immortal," Rowan finally said.

"I do not," Yves protested, but there was not much argument in it. He'd died more than the average person, at least.

"At least three times since I've known you."

"To be fair, one of them was your fault."

Right, the bullet that was still lodged in Yves's heart. Rowan's was the only scar that still marred Yves's perfect body.

"One tends to get a bit reckless when returning is inevitable." Yves's tone was light, trying not to let his darkness show. His arm tightened around Rowan's waist. Rowan's heart squeezed painfully again, an old anxiety resurfacing like a bloated body.

"What if someday you don't come back?"

Yves pinched Rowan's chin between his thumb and forefinger, tilting his head so they were eye to eye.

"Not even your bullet could kill me for good, my love. Trust that I'll always return to you."

A shiver ran up Rowan's spine. He did trust that Yves would always come for him. And that was why Rowan worried. He couldn't let Yves sacrifice for him again and again, always returning, only to die again. What if there was a limit to his resurrections? What if one day he ran out of time?

A tide of possessiveness washed over Rowan then, an overwhelming need to keep Yves by his side and protect him from the world's ills. It was ridiculous. Yves was essentially immortal, and Rowan himself was mortally breakable. Was this how Yves felt about him all the time? Was this the reason for all those hungry looks, and his borderline obsessive need to fuck Rowan into submission every minute they were together?

Rowan leaned further into his husband's embrace, his lips brushing up the side of Yves's neck.

"You can't go on dying. What if you run out of lives?"

"I am a demon, not a cat," Yves said gruffly, then seemed to soften again. "I have thought of it."

"You don't know when you'll die for good?" Few people got such a luxury, yet for Yves not to know the true terms of his existence seemed horrifying all the same.

Yves returned Rowan's kiss, nuzzling into the side of his head as if he really was a cat. Rowan was unfortunately sitting with his blind side to Yves, and could not adequately see him. He shifted on Yves's lap but Yves held him fast. All the same, he could feel a shift in the air, hear the deepening of Yves's voice that heralded the demon becoming more present at the forefront of his consciousness.

Ever since learning Yves's true nature on their wedding night, Rowan had watched him closely. The two souls within him, the human and the unfathomable demon, were woven together so tightly that it was hard to separate one from the other. But sometimes one took the lead. The man, who loved Rowan and wanted to do right by his crew. And the demon, whose only humanity lay in loving Rowan in its own cruel and possessive way. They were one, but there were many parts of this whole. The murderous creature who hadn't recognized Rowan on the *Valliant*'s deck and almost killed him? That was the demon, always lurking just beneath the surface. The one who always kissed Rowan so tenderly after wrecking him? That was Yves.

"Believe it or not, this is the first time I—the demon," Yves corrected himself, "has possessed a mortal body. I..." He grit his teeth, clearly struggling with the nomenclature now that the demon was making its presence more known. Usually it came to the forefront when there was no time for talk. "*It* was not expecting our consciousnesses to meld so thoroughly. Perhaps we will be immortal forever. Perhaps one day my final death will come and it will perish alongside me, or return to its own form. We do not know what will happen. Just as the demon's presence has enhanced this mortal form, my fragile mortality has dampened some of its more godly abilities."

Rowan had the sudden urge to remove his eyepatch, to see both sides of the man he loved. He shifted in Yves's lap again to face him more fully and removed the little piece of leather that blocked Yves's demonic form from his view. Yves did not stop him, even as his eyes took on the black depths of the sea, and the shadowy blue tentacles unfurled against the back of the armchair. Rowan ran his fingers through Yves's luxurious black hair as one of the smaller tentacles revealed itself to be already coiling up his leg from ankle to thigh.

Rowan huffed. The tentacles sometimes groped him when they were in their imperceptible form, and Rowan had given Yves a stern talking-to about it several times. Yet this felt more like the demon side clinging on to him for comfort, so he didn't complain as the tentacle snaked further between his legs. Another had decided to invade his boot.

"You better not go dying again then," Rowan murmured, curling into Yves's embrace so their lips nearly touched. "Either of you."

His thumb traced over Yves's sculpted cheekbone. Yves's breath caught. His arms flexed around Rowan's waist, and the tentacle wound tighter. But he waited for Rowan's lips to capture his. It was just the lightest brush at first, deepening as Rowan's tongue slipped past his lips. A breathy moan escaped Yves's throat, and a bead of moisture slid against Rowan's thumb where it rested against Yves's cheek. He pulled back, astonished to see that Yves was crying.

"I-I'm afraid to die. I don't want to leave you alone," Yves blurted, clutching Rowan close as if he would disappear at any moment. Rowan sucked in a startled breath, and Yves blinked at him with wide eyes, as if he'd just heard something utterly ridiculous escape his mouth without his permission. As if neither soul that resided within him had quite expected the other to feel—let alone say—such a thing.

Which side had it come from? The man, who'd been drowned, hanged, shot, burned, and all manner of things, and was probably still so like that scared teenager who'd made a deal with a demon? Or the demon itself, who'd never expected to experience death at all?

Rowan cupped Yves's beloved face between his hands, wiping the errant tears away with his thumbs.

"Many people fear death," Rowan murmured. "You are not alone in that." It was unnerving, these flashes of vulnerability, of raw humanity, that sometimes gripped Yves. He always appeared in control, poised and perfect. Yet with Rowan he did not have to pretend. Rowan knew all sides of him. The ugly and the beautiful. To see those fathomless black eyes brimming with tears pulled at Rowan's heartstrings in a painful way.

As fast as the tears had begun, they dried up, blinked away as if they'd never been. Yves cleared his throat, watching Rowan from under his thick black lashes, still subtly beaded with tears.

"I don't know what came over me." Yves's voice came out low and rough.

As disquieting as it had been, Rowan found himself instantly missing Yves's openness.

"Don't apologize." He smoothed Yves's hair back from his forehead reassuringly.

"I'm sorry for revealing our relationship too. I should have controlled myself despite the circumstances."

Oh, right. That was how this conversation had started in the first place. Rowan had been angry with him. But he couldn't hold onto that anger. Not after Yves's confession.

"I've put you in danger," Yves said.

That had been Rowan's worry as well, but now the cat was out of the bag, and it could not be put back in.

"We'll just have to deal with it."

"I'll gladly kill them all, if you wish it. Dead men tell no—"

Rowan pressed a hand to Yves's mouth, silencing him. "We said they'd live if they joined up. I'll not go back on my word so carelessly."

Yves huffed in annoyance, but nodded, and Rowan released him.

"Your life is worth more than all of them," Yves said, his dark eyes trained on Rowan's face. Rowan tried to force his worries down, away from Yves's perceptive gaze. It was no use torturing himself over it when nothing would change. He'd do his best to convince Yves to be more careful, but there would be no answers to his questions about the bounds of Yves's immortality. The only creature who could possibly answer was already in Yves's head, and it was just as out of its depth as they were.

Rowan ducked his head against Yves's shoulder. His lips brushed Yves's exposed throat.

"Never mind that now. You won't have to kill anyone for me. I can do my own dirty work."

"I know you can." His deep demon voice vibrated through Rowan's body, deliciously suffocating. Rowan traced Yves's pulse with his tongue.

"What was that you said earlier about being wet and primed for you?"

Yves's body went still beneath him.

"Are you in the mood, darling? After all that talk of death?"

Rowan ran his hand up Yves's chest, savoring the hard planes beneath the soft, expensive fabric. He wanted to tear it away and get at the porcelain skin beneath. He could no longer stand to think of Yves's many deaths or his own fragile mortality. He wanted only to wrap himself up in Yves and forget everything else. He wanted to feel how alive his many-times-dead lover was.

Yves caressed Rowan's thigh with one elegant hand, long fingers tripping over the coils of tentacle.

"Did all that talk of my death turn you on?" Yves asked again.

Rowan sat up a little straighter, his lips finding Yves's sharp jaw.

"It just reminded me how alive you are. And that I should take advantage of all this beautiful blood pumping through your veins while I have the chance." He wiggled, grinding his ass down on Yves's lap. Yves's cock hardened at the pressure, and the silver plug, still buried deep inside Rowan, shifted. He let out a small, breathy moan.

Yves's hand whipped up from Rowan's thigh to crook one elegant finger beneath his chin, forcing his head up to look him in the eye.

"What would you like me to do to you?" His black gaze dipped to Rowan's lips.

"Anything," Rowan whispered.

Yves's lips captured his, their shared breath hot between them as Rowan opened his mouth to accept Yves's questing tongue. He kissed Rowan breathless, forcing the dark thoughts of their shared future into the background. They let themselves sink into the distraction, preferring instead to enjoy the pleasures of each other while they still could.

Before he knew it, his coat lay discarded beside the chair, and Yves's hands pushed up under the hem of his shirt. Yves's cock hardened further beneath Rowan's ass, and Rowan's body responded in kind, tenting the skirt in an obvious way. Before Yves, Rowan had never used to be like this. Desperate and needy and craving sex all the time. He wondered if this, too, was the result of some dark, demonic power that had him deliriously in its clutches. But truly, he didn't care one bit. He might love his freedom in all ways, but being subject to Yves's sexual prowess was a kind of freedom in itself. The act of giving himself wholly to the person he loved, knowing that he could show Yves any side of him, no matter how pathetic, desperate, or lost to desire. He could surrender himself fully and come out on the other side.

Rowan pushed himself up onto his knees to straddle Yves's lap, ignoring how the tentacle that was wrapped around his leg slithered over his bare skin. Yves's hands wandered from his waist to the hem of his skirt, which pooled around his thighs, still stained with the blood of battle. Had that been only hours ago? It felt like a lifetime. Rowan released the ivory buttons at Yves's collar, exposing a sliver of creamy chest and collarbone.

"So beautiful," Rowan murmured against his lips, fingers caressing the warm skin. He determinedly avoided touching the pink scar tissue over his heart. Sometimes Rowan was fascinated by it. The only mark to have marred Yves's perfect skin, left by him and him only. But tonight it only served to remind him of the uncertainty of Yves's existence.

Yves cupped the curve of Rowan's bare buttocks beneath the skirt, fingertips pressing to the flared base of the plug. It pushed deeper, brushing Rowan's prostate just enough to spark the stirrings of pleasure, but not enough to satisfy. As he'd gone about his day the plug had ceaselessly reminded him that he belonged to Yves. Not that he could ever truly forget. It was as much a brand of ownership as the ring on his finger. And it had been teasing for hours. Building his anticipation. His *wanting*.

Yves pressed a bit harder, smirking as Rowan whimpered.

"You never answered my question earlier, you know," Yves said.

"And what is that?" The tentacle snaked up his thigh, delicate suckers dimpling the supple flesh.

"Did you like our little game today?" His fingers pressed again, and Rowan's hips bucked in surprise as a lightning bolt of pleasure shot up his spine. "I can see you're quite enjoying it now."

"I like everything you do," Rowan replied breathlessly. He fumbled with the laces at the front of Yves's trousers, impatient now that he'd gotten a taste. He freed Yves's cock and stroked it once. "Your gift is wonderful, but I prefer the real thing."

"I must give you what you want then." Yves twirled the plug, eliciting another moan. "Or shall I play a bit longer?" He twisted the plug back the other way. Another tentacle coiled around Rowan's other leg.

"Please..." Rowan gasped. The two tentacles constricted and pulled Rowan's thighs apart quickly, so his knees pressed inside the arms of the chair and his hole clenched around the round sides of the plug. He imagined Yves's cum from earlier slicking his insides, keeping him wet for whatever Yves had in store.

Slowly, Yves pulled the plug out, its smooth sides sliding with ease. Rowan shuddered, gripping the front of Yves's shirt until finally it popped free.

All at once, the emptiness overwhelmed him. The only sound that of the solid silver plug thumping to the floor where Yves dropped it. A thin thread of liquid dribbled out of Rowan's hole as Yves fingered the rim. His eyes glittered with satisfaction.

"Seems like I was right, my darling. You're still wet for me. Your body is begging for it." The tentacles tugged at Rowan's legs again, and the tip of Yves's cock replaced his fingers at Rowan's entrance. Rowan's thighs tensed, aching to sink down and take all of him at once. To be filled with him and feel Yves's pulse thrum through his own body. But the tentacles restricted him, holding him fast.

"Please," Rowan begged again, his voice strained. Depressing thoughts of death had started to creep in again, and all he wanted was to give himself over to pleasure.

Yves must have heard the desperation in his voice. Wordlessly, he loosened the tentacles, and Rowan sank down quickly, gasping as Yves's huge cock penetrated and filled him. He took the entire length of it in one movement, the only lube the remnants of Yves's cum. The only preparation the hours-long stretch of the silver plug.

A twinge of pain raced pleasure through Rowan's flesh, and his hands fisted tighter in the front of Yves's shirt. Yves's hands settled onto Rowan's thighs again, and his black eyes slid closed, head tilting back to rest on the bloodred velvet.

They stayed like that for a moment, a kind of relief washing over them as if right here, locked together and intertwined, was the only way they could truly be at peace. Silence and stillness permeated the room, but for their softly labored breaths and the gentle undulations of the shadow tentacles, suspended as if floating beneath the water.

"Back where you belong," Yves murmured, as if to himself. His eyes remained closed. He seemed so at peace, like being buried deep within Rowan's insides was the only balm in his troubled life, the only sweet solace.

"Yes," Rowan agreed. He raised up on his knees again, legs already trembling as Yves's length slid against his walls. Both of them gasped. Rowan stopped when just the tip was inside. Waiting, he supposed, for Yves to open his eyes and look at him.

They remained closed, Yves's long lashes, like delicate raven feathers, resting against his high white cheeks. His full lips parted slightly, waited with bated breath for Rowan to take him in again.

When Rowan didn't move, Yves finally opened his eyes, those obsidian orbs so dark that Rowan could fall into them forever. Yves's gaze fixed on him with such pure adoration that for a moment Rowan forgot himself. His muscles slackened, Yves impaling him quickly again, their hips meeting with a satisfying *thwack* of flesh.

Hot pleasure tingled through Rowan's nerves. Yves caught Rowan's face between his hands as Rowan slumped forward with a moan. His eyes searched Rowan's features, the pad of one thumb brushing over the crisscrossed scars on Rowan's cheek and the outer corner of his eye that had barely faded with time. How could such soulless eyes hold such love? He was looking at Rowan as if *he* was the beautiful, godlike figure in this relationship, not Yves.

But he was not. He was just a man like any other. Stubborn and scrappy and maybe a little clever on a good day. A barnacle clinging to the marble skin of a sunken god.

Rowan would just keep getting hurt. Keep adding to his catalog of scars till he was more broken than whole. But Yves would remain the same. Unaged. Untouched by the violence they surrounded themselves with. Pristine and beautiful and perfect.

As if sensing his melancholy thoughts, Yves's fingers tightened against Rowan's scarred flesh.

"I love you, Rowan." His voice was deep and serious, only slightly tinged with an underlying current of lust. "I would protect you from all that seeks to harm you. Even from myself."

"*Do* you seek to harm me?" Rowan asked breathlessly.

Yves's thumb brushed lightly along the white-blond lashes that framed Rowan's jade eye.

"My love harms you. Your association with me puts you in danger."

Rowan rolled his hips involuntarily, his body seeking pleasure even as his mind drowned in sickly sweet melancholy.

"No more than I put myself in." His hips rolled again, Yves's cock rubbing at his prostate and dropping a heady veil of pleasure over his thoughts. He bent to kiss Yves hungrily, and when the kiss broke, he said, "If your lives are infinite, it is me who will hurt you. Eventually I will die and leave you."

The ghost of future pain flickered across Yves's face, and Rowan regretted his words immediately. Rowan kissed him again, his hips finding a steady rhythm now as he rode Yves. Was it strange to speak of death while their bodies were so viscerally, vitally alive?

"Despite all that, we won't let each other go," Rowan whispered, one palm pressing to the old bullet wound beneath Yves's shirt. "So show me that I belong to you, even beyond death."

The words seemed to snap Yves from his mood, all at once transforming sorrow to lust. He dragged Rowan back into a crushing kiss, his hips bucking up to shatter the fate looming between them. Bliss coiled through Rowan's body as he matched Yves's movements. Their bodies knew each other. Fit together, and danced to the melody of moans that spilled from their lips. Though often rough in the heat of passion, tonight they moved in sensual harmony as they drank in the fleeting rapture of each other.

Rowan could barely catch his breath, his lips bruised with kissing. Yves's hands stayed on either side of his face, catching his own snatches of breath as he drowned himself against Rowan's mouth.

One of the tentacles, moist with its own juices, wrapped around Rowan's manhood beneath the skirt and began pumping him, suckers puckering the taut skin like a dozen tiny mouths. It was strange how amazing it felt, a unique sensation that only Yves could provide. Warm tingles spread out from the center of Rowan's chest, mixing with hot euphoria.

"Yves," he moaned, reaching up to grasp Yves's hand where it still rested against his cheek. Yves's head was pressed hard against the velvet back of the chair, tendrils of black hair stuck to his sweat-slick neck. As beautiful and perfect and put together as Yves usually was, Rowan loved these rare times he could see Yves come undone. He sometimes wished he could wreck Yves the way Yves wrecked him, but this was more than enough. Seeing his depthless eyes hazed with love and lust in equal measure. Rowan would never let him go.

Yves's hips stuttered, his powerful legs driving his length up into Rowan with reckless abandon. A man lost to pleasure. Had his death affected him this much? Where was his usual control? His dominance?

"Fuck, Rowan. I'm..." Yves dragged Rowan into a hard, sloppy kiss, his breath ragged. He managed a few more hard thrusts before overwhelming euphoria pulled them under. Yves's cock throbbed deep in Rowan's core, and the tentacles constricted all at once, spasming with his climax, squeezing the supple flesh of Rowan's thighs and around his cock as the suckers slurped up Rowan's own streams of cum.

Rowan collapsed against Yves's chest, harsh breaths heaving from their lungs. Yves's hand moved to cup the back of Rowan's head, his other arm encircling his back. The tentacles loosened, and Rowan knew his thighs would be banded with puckered bruises by morning. The knowledge that the marks of this moment would be imprinted on his flesh for days to come sent a shivering aftershock through his exhausted body. His tongue flicked out, lips pressed to Yves's throat, tasting the salt from his skin.

"I love you," Rowan whispered. Yves's pulse fluttered against his lips at the words, and Rowan couldn't help but smile. Yves stroked Rowan's hair.

"I love you too," he murmured. "I promise to be more careful, if you do."

Rowan chuckled. "I don't think either of us can keep that promise."

Yves's arms tightened protectively around him. "I won't hold you to it. As long as you always come back to me."

"Deal."

CHAPTER 7

MAY 2ND, 1668

Fox dragged Gaël into their small room by the front of his shirt, planting a needy kiss on his lips as the door slammed closed on the day. He was tired, exhausted even, from days of chasing the *Sweet Lettie*. Then the battle. Then on top of it all, getting his damn leg wound stitched. It didn't help that Gaël had disappeared to speak with the captains and come back quiet and contemplative. It wasn't as fun to ogle Gaël's muscles glistening with sweat if Gaël was too distracted to get all blushy when he caught Fox looking.

But fighting always got Fox fired up, and he had one last bit of energy to burn off before he and Gaël could fall gratefully into bed. Maybe they should do it standing up tonight, because Fox suspected that as soon as his head hit the pillow he'd be out like a snuffed candle.

Gaël's strong arms wrapped around Fox's waist, and he returned the kiss almost desperately. Fox let out a low groan, sweet desire kindling in the pit of his stomach. He'd never get tired of all the ways Gaël could wreck him and put him back together again—and they'd tried many—but it was days like this, when they were both exhausted and satisfied and could come back to their little room on board the *Siren Song* and make love till they were both spent, or just cuddle and talk till they fell asleep, that made him understand the true depths between them.

Fox let his hand wander lazily down to cup the curve of Gaël's ass, wondering who would get to have who tonight.

Gaël broke the kiss.

"Fox." It wasn't the breathless call of a lover; his tone was serious. Fox pulled back, eyes searching his angular face.

"What is it? Is something wrong?" Gaël hadn't been hurt, had he? Surely he would have said something.

"John asked me to be his first mate," Gaël blurted. Fox's hands dropped to his sides. "I didn't say yes," Gaël added hastily. His arms tightened around Fox's waist, as if afraid Fox would pull away.

"So why're you telling me then?" Fox asked. His voice came out small, and he resisted the urge to clear his throat.

"Because I want to say yes. But I wanted to talk to you first."

Confusion warred in Fox's mind. He pushed gently out of Gaël's arms and went to sit on the edge of the bed. Gaël followed and sat beside him. He waited in silence for Fox to say something.

"Are you not happy here?" Fox picked at a hangnail.

Gaël took his hands gently, stopping the small act of self-destruction.

"Of course I am, Foxy. I'm happy to be wherever you are. Just... John is going to need someone trustworthy by his side, and I want to prove that I'm good for more than just fighting." He leaned a little closer, and Fox looked up. Gaël's expression was so tender, so earnest and open. "I know this is your home. I promised I wouldn't leave you, so I'm asking you to come with me. But I won't go if you ask me not to. I'll tell John no."

Leave the *Siren Song*? The only home he'd known since he was a twenty-year-old kid. The only home he'd ever had in his life that was stable and full of people who cared about him.

"I...I can't leave Rowan." Curious. He'd meant to say the *Siren*, but this was true as well. Rowan had saved his life. Rowan had brought him here. Rowan had stayed by his side and guided him out of the lowest point in his life. Without him, Fox would have ended up dead in some back alley long ago.

A flicker of sadness crossed Gaël's features.

"I understand. I'll tell John no."

"I didn't say you couldn't go."

It was as if he'd stuck his hand right between Gaël's ribs and squeezed his heart. Gaël looked lost for a moment.

"W-what are you saying?" Gaël managed to choke out. He sounded on the verge of tears, and Fox suddenly realized what his words had sounded like.

"That's not what I meant!" he blurted. He snatched his hands from Gaël's grip to cup Gaël's face instead. "I only meant you should go, and I should stay. No. That sounds bad too. Shit." He closed his eyes for a moment, trying to piece the words together. Gaël's hand came up to rest over Fox's.

"I only meant," Fox said slowly when he reopened his eyes, "that if this is something you need to do, I won't stop you. I still want you. I still love you. As long as you come back to me, as long as it's not forever, you should go."

The breathless heartbreak eased, replaced by grateful affection.

"Are you sure?" Gaël asked.

Fox put on a smile, despite his heart performing death-defying acrobatics in his chest. The thought of being without Gaël for even a day filled him with dread. But... "I have to learn to be without you sometimes."

They'd reunited nearly two years ago, and in the beginning, Fox had panicked whenever he'd woken and Gaël wasn't there. He'd relived the worst day of his life. But slowly, waking up next to the love of his life morning after morning, every day a reassurance that he was loved and would never be abandoned again, had caused that panic to recede into the background. Gaël was now able to come and go as he pleased in the mornings with little fear that Fox would become a blubbering mess because of it. Sometimes the panic returned; Fox never really knew what might trigger it. Maybe the angle of the light as his hand searched the other side of the bed in vain. Maybe cold sheets on his fingertips. Maybe nothing at all.

The point was, he was getting better, and he couldn't continue living in fear. He couldn't keep Gaël locked up in a cage of the past. He had to let Gaël go, for a little while at least.

Gaël kissed Fox's palm.

"You don't have to learn if you don't want to."

"I do want to." Fox smiled. "But maybe just for a season at first? See how it goes?"

"Deal."

Exhaustion dragged at Fox's consciousness now that the adrenaline of Gaël's kisses, then confession, had worn off. He blinked slowly and leaned forward to plant a kiss on Gaël's cheek. Gaël smiled, cheek dimpling beneath Fox's lips.

"You look sleepy." Gaël gathered Fox into his lap, then flopped back onto the bed, dragging Fox down with him. Fox nuzzled into his chest, fingers tracing the scar beneath Gaël's shirt. It still pained him sometimes, the muscles beneath never healing quite right.

"Don't let John work you too hard," Fox murmured.

"Of course. I have to come back in good shape for you. Who else can keep up with you?"

Fox's giggle turned into a sigh of contentment, tiredness making his body heavy, dragging his eyelids closed. Gaël's warmth wrapped around him, a safe cocoon in the uncertain world.

Henri didn't look up from his book as Robin entered their room. He could tell by the way Robin's feet dragged that he was exhausted, from both the day's work and from seeing his brother again after all this time. How long had it been? Three years that Robin had been away from the harsh judgment of his family. Three years in which he had slowly learned that he was not broken, not unnatural, not wrong.

Yet when faced with his brother again, Robin couldn't admit that he and Henri were together.

"Hey, love," Robin greeted him quietly, toeing off his boots. Henri grunted in response, turning the page even though his eyes couldn't focus on the words. Robin moved further into the room, doing all the usual things he did when he got home. Henri didn't move.

"Henri?"

Henri shifted where he sat on a thin cushion atop his sea chest. He could imagine the way Robin's brow furrowed beneath his fluffy fringe. Henri usually read stretched out on their bed, either with Robin tucked safely in his arm or waiting for him to be.

Today he didn't feel like it. If Robin couldn't acknowledge their relationship, he could do without the warmth that came with it.

"You okay?" Robin stepped closer in Henri's peripheral vision, and Henri nodded without looking up. The words on the page blurred but his eyes were dry. He was simply unfocused, adrift in his thoughts.

Robin pushed a small stack of penny novels to the side and plopped down next to him. Henri's gaze focused on the books. His collection grew with every port they stopped in and every ship they robbed. He liked the romances the best, though most of them only depicted relationships between men and women.

Robin stared at him, waiting to be acknowledged, but Henri ignored him. Instead he tried to return to the book. People were always surprised when they learned he could read. Most pirates—hell, most commoners—in the Islands couldn't. His maman had taught him as a child, and he'd always loved stories of all kinds. But he'd stopped reading when he left home after her death, and hadn't picked up a book again until he'd found a penny novel about pirates and princesses in the library at Illusion.

"Henri," Robin said again, and there was such worry in his voice that Henri instinctively looked up. Robin swallowed nervously. He gripped Henri's book with a gentle hand and slowly lowered it to his lap. "Talk to me?"

Robin might be an educated man, but right now he was being painfully obtuse. Wasn't it obvious why Henri was upset? Why should he have to tell him?

Obstinance itched in Henri's chest.

"Nothing, just tired."

"Let's go to bed then." Robin's fingers moved from the book to caress Henri's wrist, but Henri twitched away. If Robin would deny their relationship, it felt wrong to let him touch him.

"There's something wrong," Robin insisted. "Please tell me." His handsome face was so open, so worried.

Henri looked away, carefully marking his page with a scrap of paper and returning his book to the stack. He took a moment to gather his thoughts, letting the urge to be argumentative ebb away before he spoke.

"Are we not together?" His voice came out small, but no less accusatory.

"What?" Robin grabbed his hand. "Of course we are. What are you talking about?"

Henri didn't snatch his hand back this time. Despite being the source of this hurt, Robin's touch was still comforting. He raised his gaze to look Robin in the eye.

"I'm talking about David. You hid our relationship from him."

Understanding crept into Robin's soft hazel eyes. His lips parted as if he didn't know what to say, or how he could defend himself. They both stayed silent for a moment, staring at each other.

"I-I'm sorry," Robin said quietly after a moment. "I didn't notice."

That lit a spark of anger in the kindling of Henri's hurt. Robin hadn't noticed? He'd been about to say it when they were first introduced, yet course corrected and called Henri by name instead.

"Bullshit," Henri said, and Robin had the nerve to look startled. "You let him call us deviants. He thinks you're a prisoner. You could have corrected him at any time." He'd had so many opportunities to tell his brother about them, yet he hadn't.

Robin's expression hardened slightly. "*He is* a prisoner. It makes sense that he would think I'm the same. And you know what? He's not wrong. I was essentially a prisoner on the *Kraken* till the captain forgave my debt."

"*You* made a deal with him so you wouldn't have to go back to your terrible family!" Henri shouted. He snatched his hand back from Robin's hold, and Robin didn't stop him. He only bit his lip, and slouched back against the stack of books.

"They're not terrible," he said quietly.

Henri couldn't believe what he was hearing. He didn't know the exact details of Robin's past, but he knew this much, that his family had treated him horribly under the guise of love. They'd tried to force him into a marriage he didn't want.

"They drove you out of your own home," Henri argued. He knew the futility of it even as he said it. Robin was a gentle soul, and no matter how badly his family had treated him, he still loved them. And maybe somewhere deep down, he still believed them. Dread churned in Henri's belly, and he stood up, desperate not to stay still.

Silent tears tracked down Robin's cheeks, and he didn't seem able to look Henri in the eye.

"Sorry," was all he could say.

"Are you going to tell him?" Henri asked. He didn't know why it hurt so bad that Robin's brother didn't know about them. Maybe he wanted revenge on Robin's behalf. Wanted them to know that Robin was unapologetically happy with a man, despite how they had tried to stifle him.

"I don't see the point," Robin said quietly. Despite Henri's hurt, seeing Robin upset pulled at his heartstrings, and he wanted to wrap the taller man up in his arms and comfort him. But he stayed standing, his fists clenched at his sides. "If Davy knows about us he'll just be mad. And he'll try even harder to make me leave and..." He dropped his face into his hands, as if it was all too much to say out loud.

"So are you going home, then?" Robin had never wanted this life. Henri knew that well enough.

Robin's head snapped up, teary hazel eyes wide. "No! Of course not!"

"Then why are you so afraid of him knowing? If you have no plans to go back, who cares if they know?" Henri cared. He *wanted* them to know.

"I care!" Robin exclaimed, then his mouth snapped shut, as if he hadn't meant to say it.

So that was the truth of it. Robin still believed what they'd always taught him. Maybe he still believed he could go home like nothing had ever happened.

"You care because you're ashamed," Henri spat, feeling hypocritical even as he said it. Robin recoiled as if he'd been slapped. Henri bit his lip to keep the reflexive apologies at bay. He shouldn't have let it get this far. He never wanted to raise his voice to Robin. But the fear that Robin would turn his back on him stoked the flames of his anger higher.

Silence stretched between them, punctuated only by Robin's sniffles. Henri dug his nails into his palms to keep from reaching for him, soothing his hurt and saying it was all okay just to make him feel better. Because the truth was, it wasn't okay.

Henri took another step back. He hadn't realized before, but he harbored a deep hatred for Robin's family. They didn't deserve this sweet, doting man who only wanted to help people and give love. They didn't deserve the love he still held for them.

"They don't love you," he whispered. "Not like I do."

Robin sniffled again and Henri stepped toward the door, slipping his feet into his boots as he went.

"I'm gonna sleep somewhere else."

"Henri, wait—"

Henri was already out the door.

CHAPTER 8

MAY 2ND, 1668

The sea pressed in all around Nia, cool and soothing. She spun, relishing the salt in her nostrils and the push and pull of the currents on her body. She wanted to give in and let them take her where they would, far away from this place. Far away from imprisonment and pain. But that was not possible. So she dove deeper, searching for what Captain Stroud had ordered her to find.

A flash of light caught the corner of her eye, and she swam over. A small chest sat wedged between two spars of coral. She nudged it, but it was stuck fast and her lungs were beginning to burn, so she spun away and resurfaced.

The *Silverfin* bobbed in the water not far off. The weight of Silver Stroud's gaze settled on her as soon as her head broke the water's surface. His hand closed around the cord at his neck, and the urge to return to the ship pulled at her like a parent's guiding hand.

NIA GASPED AS SHE WOKE, and for a moment in the dark, she could still feel Stroud watching her. Still feel that tug at the very essence of her. The scar low on her back burned with the memory of when he'd cut that piece from her.

She gripped the sides of the hammock as it swayed, breathing hard. This was the *Monsoon*, not the *Silverfin*. Stroud was long dead, and the woman who'd killed him was captain of this ship. Somehow that thought comforted her. Like the Zanta of the past had reached out to protect her even before they met.

Nia tried to steady her breathing, reminding herself again and again that he was gone and she would never be his captive again. Except that wasn't true. She was still his captive even after death, because she couldn't return to the sea without the precious thing he'd stolen from her. She was so close to freedom, she could taste it like the lingering sourness of sleep on her tongue. All she had to do was find her treasure, and take it.

Slowly, noises from other parts of the ship filtered into her small, windowless storeroom. She must have slept for hours, dreaming of the past with no sun outside a porthole to wake her. She stared up into the dark and listened to the sounds above her head, reminding herself this was not the little closet in Stroud's quarters that she'd slept in from the age of ten. There was no lock on this door, and she could leave at any time.

She still remembered the rush of bitter elation when she'd finally broken free of that ship. He'd left the key on his nightstand when he went ashore, and though Nia couldn't reach her treasure, that tiny silver key gave her the courage she needed. When a crewman brought her meal, she bolted, running up into the wind. The pounding of her heart drowned out the pirates' shouts as she dove into the harbor. Her treasure was close enough that it didn't hurt right away, and she was a strong swimmer. But soon the salty water had seeped into every pore like knives, and when she'd limped onto the shore, she almost wished the sea had taken her after all. In a few years, she knew she would waste away just like her mother. But in the meantime she was free, damnit. She was free.

Nia touched the silver key at her waist to remind herself once more, then tipped out of the hammock.

Zanta had ordered her to report to the first mate, but Nia saw no reason to delay her grand plans. The more she'd thought of it as she drifted to sleep, the more she realized that perhaps she'd been too hasty with her plan of jumping straight to seducing Splinter Zanta. Too excited by John and Logan's gift, and mesmerized by the captain's beauty. She knew the chest was on the ship—she wouldn't still be alive otherwise—but she couldn't feel *where* it was. She should search the ship first before trying to seduce her way into the captain's quarters.

Nia sighed and stepped back into the skirt she'd worn since the day before, smoothing the wrinkles out of the fabric as best as she could. She'd really been looking forward to potentially using those beautifully carved gifts on Zanta, but she would have to content herself with only enjoying them herself for the foreseeable future.

Nia had never been good at sneaking, but she tried her best to move silently through the narrow passages belowdecks. The chest could be anywhere. It wasn't large, though it was made of iron, and could be easily concealed in the bottom of a crate or behind a stack of barrels, and she'd be none the wiser. Who knew what little nooks and crannies a pirate ship could hold.

She'd made it through several storerooms before someone came looking for her. She glanced up from rifling through a crate of fabric to find a man watching her from the doorway of the hold. Nia startled like a surprised rabbit, and hastily shut the lid of the crate with a thump.

"The captain sent me to find you," the man said, his voice deceptively light and accented with something that sounded halfway between Yarenen and Sounese. He was taller than her—but that wasn't saying much—with medium-brown skin and an attractively aquiline nose, pierced with two gold rings in the same nostril. He leaned his head of loose black curls against the doorjamb, warm eyes sweeping her in turn. His expression was serious, which didn't sit right on his naturally mirthful face. Small indents around his mouth spoke of frequent smiles.

Nia hastily got to her feet and dusted off her skirts. "Oh? What does she need me for?" Nia tried to keep her tone relaxed as if he hadn't caught her snooping.

He raised one thick eyebrow. "Just come with me."

Well, it wasn't like she could refuse. Nia followed the pirate up the stairs and down the hallway toward the back of the ship.

"What's your name?" Nia asked, hurrying to keep up with his bouncy strides. With every step his seriousness seemed to melt away, as if he was unaccustomed to being used to intimidate people on this ship.

"Laurent. I'm the cook here."

"She sent the cook to fetch an errant new crew member?"

His kohl-lined eyes flicked to her. "I wouldn't say crew member just yet. Though I think we'll be seeing a lot of each other."

They passed an alcove framed by moth-eaten curtains that contained a small statue of two intertwined sea serpents, the shelf beneath it scattered with offerings of small trinkets, coins, and dried flowers. No food. Never food that might rot and attract rats to the ship. They arrived before a door. Laurent knocked, then ushered her inside.

Shelves loaded with the spoils of piracy lined the walls to the left and right of the one-room captain's quarters like a library of thievery. Weapons both ornamental and practical, leather-bound books from the Islands and scrolls from the southern continent, shiny trinkets, and brass navigational instruments. Nia's gaze swept over them quickly, cataloging and dismissing it all when she did not see the iron chest. At the far end, a wide wooden bed was built into the cabinetry under a bank of arched and latticed windows, supporting a luxuriously plush mattress strewn with blankets and richly embroidered cushions. Envy sparked in Nia's chest at the sheer comfort it exuded. After spending the last five years of her life sleeping on a utilitarian bed in the attic of the Swan Inn, and far less comfort before that, Nia thought maybe she should try to seduce Zanta after all just to have a chance at sleeping in such luxury.

In the center of the room, Splinter Zanta sat on a low wooden chair piled with plush silk cushions, her bare feet resting on a rug patterned in geometric red and blue. She sat with her back straight and her head high like a queen, hands folded in her lap. She wore only a knee length shift, her long legs exposed. Nia almost caught her breath at that, willing herself not to react to the beauty displayed before her. There was no question in her mind why any man or woman would choose to follow this woman into battle.

Another Yarenen woman who Nia recognized from their flight from Roseforte Harbor stood behind the chair with Zanta's hair in her hands. The waterfall of dainty braids on Zanta's head was now being unraveled into a beautiful storm cloud, and Nia got the distinct feeling she'd been invited into a private moment.

"There you are." Zanta kept her head perfectly still as the other woman finished unraveling a braid and moved on to the next.

"Here I am." Nia resisted the urge to drop into a curtsy, knowing the strange way she was feeling about seeing Zanta in a state of undress was silly beyond measure. She had a job to do, and couldn't get distracted by feelings of *actual* attraction toward the woman who'd essentially kidnapped her.

"I caught her going through crates in one of the holds," Laurent ratted on her.

Zanta's eyebrows rose. "Thank you, Laurent. You may go back to your duties."

"You know, when you said I had something you wanted, I thought you were being flirtatious," Zanta said, once the door closed behind him. The other woman's fingers paused in their unbraiding for a moment.

"I was," Nia answered with no further explanation. The key to lying, she'd found, was to give no more information than you were directly asked for. And having a pretty face didn't hurt either.

Zanta's brows climbed higher. "So then what were you looking for?"

"Just getting acquainted with my new home." Nia shrugged. The woman behind Zanta huffed a laugh, and Nia smiled at her.

"I'll remind you that I can drop you off on shore at any time I please," Zanta said.

Nia glanced furtively around the room again. She'd made it to the captain's quarters sooner than expected, without having to try her hand at seduction. Now she was finding herself disappointed that not only was the chest definitely not among the other treasures sitting out in the open, but Zanta was now annoyed and distrustful of her, and it would take more effort to earn back her good favor.

"But you won't, will you?"

Zanta's full lips twitched to the side in amusement. "You're quite confident, aren't you?"

"It comes with the job."

"Is lying and sneaking around within the purview of a tavern maid as well?"

"Could be." Nia knew she was digging herself a deeper hole that she'd have to climb out of later. If she annoyed Zanta enough, she had no doubt she'd get dropped off at some backwater port with a few coppers and a wish of good luck. She couldn't let that happen till she had her treasure in hand.

"Speaking of jobs," Nia said, trying to steer the conversation away from her potential deception. "I'm sorry I didn't report to the first mate. I took a nap, then I couldn't find her." She tried to look bashful, which did not come naturally to her.

"Well, she's certainly not at the bottom of a crate." Zanta turned to the other woman. "Sabri?"

The woman left off with Zanta's hair and smiled. "We've agreed you will help in the galley and mess, and whatever else Laurent needs," First Mate Sabriye said. "It's almost dinner, so report to the galley right after you leave here."

"Yes, ma'am." Nia dropped into a quick curtsy and turned to go.

"And Nia." Zanta's voice curled through the air, smooth as honey. "Don't let me catch you snooping again. Or I'll keep my promise and drop you off in a fishing village instead of a port."

CHAPTER 9

MAY 3RD, 1668

The sun set in pink and orange on the horizon, casting the blunt shadows of the Teeth over the three tethered ships. All was quiet, the sailors of the former *Sweet Lettie* settling reluctantly into their new roles as pirates. Logan was exhausted from coordinating the exchange of goods across the ships and dividing up the sailors in a way that would cause the least amount of disruption. Yet despite the heavy weight of future muscle aches dragging at his limbs, he retrieved a bottle of wine from the storeroom and made his way past the crew members sitting around barrels betting on dice and carousing. From somewhere else on the deck, laughter burst into the growing darkness, and Logan smiled to himself as he made his way across the gangplank over the dark lapping water between the *Siren* and the *Sweet Mercy*.

A former crew member who'd volunteered to join John nodded to Logan as he stepped down onto the *Mercy*'s deck. Logan patted him on the shoulder as he passed. They'd doubled up the guard shifts on all three ships in case any of the new sailors got the idea to cause trouble. But Logan doubted they would. The combined threat of the Deep Water Demon and the Ghost Hawk would be sufficient enough intimidation to keep them in line.

Compared to the *Siren*, the *Mercy* was quiet and dark, a cloud of somber uncertainty hanging over it. Logan knocked lightly on the door to the captain's quarters with his wooden hand. John answered almost immediately. A small smile curved his lips as he stepped aside to let Logan in.

The captain's quarters were well appointed despite the relatively small size of the ship. The main area was half-stateroom, half-office. To the right sat a light maple desk, still scattered with papers and charts from the previous captain. To the left, a small dining table and chairs of the same wood sat on a pastel rug. Past them, the warm light of the mirrored brass sconces didn't quite reach the sleeping area on the other side of two banks of waist-high cabinets with curtains behind them.

"I brought wine," Logan said, lifting the bottle of dark red liquid.

John retrieved a pair of cups from a cabinet as well as a bottle. "I appreciate it, but I've already raided the late captain's stash." He tilted the bottle so the amber liquid caught the light. "Care to try some?"

Logan nodded and left the wine on the table as John poured them each a glass. They settled comfortably into their chairs, and John shuffled a deck of cards with ornately illustrated backs. They remained in comfortable silence as John distributed five cards to each of them. Logan retrieved a small tin from his pocket and ran his wooden fingertips over the yellow beeswax within so they would grip better. He carefully positioned the brass joints to hold the cards so his other hand would be free to switch them out as well as pick up his drink.

This had become a habit of theirs over the past year. Whether they were wintering in Illusion, or the two ships were meeting up for Rowan and Yves's marital reunions, the first mates convened in one or another cabin to drink and play cards and lament the antics of their captains and crews.

At least, that's how it always started.

They weren't together, and no one knew that these nights were sometimes more than just two friends chatting and playing cards.

They both sipped their drinks as they examined their cards for a game of Fluke. The strong brandy hit the back of Logan's throat and burned his sinuses. John preferred strong liquor while Logan was partial to sweets like cider, but he wouldn't pass up an expensive drink if his friend offered it. Their friendship had definitely hardened his alcohol tolerance, if nothing else.

"So," Logan said after they'd played one hand, which Logan lost, "did you know the Demon was going to gift you a whole fucking ship?"

"Ha!" John's bark of laughter accentuated the slap of him laying down the queen of diamonds on the pile of cards, winning the second hand. "I never know what that bastard is going to do. I guess this time it worked in my favor."

"Definitely an upgrade, Captain."

John's brown eyes flashed, and Logan smirked back over the rim of his cup.

"I like the sound of that."

Logan had noticed during their meeting with the other captains. "Of course you do. You have much more of an ego than you let on."

"I believe it's called confidence."

"Sure, sure. Whatever you say. Captain."

John tilted his head, spearing Logan with his intense gaze. Logan felt heat rising up his neck. No matter how many times John looked at him like that, he could never get used to it. He held John's gaze for a moment before averting his eyes to his cards.

"So where are you planning to head first?" Logan asked, trying to get the conversation back on track.

John examined his cards as well, switching two of them around. Logan didn't really know why they still played this game. He rarely won, and more often than not their games were left abandoned anyway.

"Maybe I'll visit Roseforte. See if our gift was delivered," John said nonchalantly.

Lightning crackled through Logan's nerves at the mention of the Talvan town where they'd had a threesome with a beautiful barmaid named Nia.

"Oh? You're going to visit her without me?" Logan said, trying to match John's tone. Last autumn they'd visited her again while hunting down information on a warship called *Trinity* that the captains had wanted to plunder, and she'd delightedly welcomed them back into her bed. Logan thought he might be half in love with both of them. But if he was honest with himself, he'd never actually understood love, so it was probably because they were the only two people he'd ever slept with.

Despite their yearlong casual affair, there was one thing he and John hadn't done.

Logan bit his lip, trying not to think of it. Maybe they'd just play Fluke tonight, and Logan would go back to his own small cabin on the *Siren* unfucked once again.

"It wouldn't be without you if you agreed to be my first mate," John said, bringing Logan out of his thoughts.

"I thought you already asked Gaël?" Logan laid down a jack of hearts, winning the hand. He dumped the cards out of his wooden hand for John to collect and shuffle. "Won't he be sad if you take it back?"

"I'm sure Fox could help him get over it." John smirked and redistributed the cards.

"No doubt. But it doesn't change the fact that Rowan needs me."

"What if I need you?" John asked with a mock pout. That was something about him Logan could never quite understand. He mocked love and vulnerability as if he was above it all, yet he said things like that. Even if he wasn't being serious, it made Logan's heart flutter. Was he merely being flirtatious? Or was the flirting obscuring something more?

"Sorry," Logan replied, keeping his tone light. "He's got seniority."

"Fair enough." John leaned forward, laying a card on the table between them, his hand lingering on the faded surface. His eyes met Logan's. "But does he suck your dick? I doubt it, considering he's married to Yves."

Logan almost choked on a sip of brandy.

John continued, "You know if we sail together, we wouldn't have to wait so long to...play cards." One eyebrow quirked up, and his hand inched closer over the table.

"As if you don't play cards with whoever you want when I'm not around," Logan scoffed. Their arrangement was unspoken, but clear as day. There was nothing more than friendship and sexual compatibility between them. Not that Logan necessarily wanted more from him, nor was he jealous that John inevitably slept with other people while Logan didn't. It wasn't that Logan couldn't sleep around if he wanted to. He just preferred the security of knowing John and Nia wanted him. He didn't like uncertainty.

John said nothing, and Logan glanced up to find John gazing at him over his cards.

"Does that bother you?" John asked, his eyebrows raised.

"N-no, not particularly," Logan answered honestly. Just because the rest of their friends were falling in love left and right didn't mean he wanted to.

When John spoke again, his voice was softer. "Are you sure?"

There he went again being unexpectedly considerate. If Logan didn't know any better, he'd think John actually cared about him beyond friendship.

Logan tilted his head to the side, trying to suss out a deeper meaning behind John's words.

"Would you actually stop sleeping with other people if I said yes?" Not that Logan would ask him to do that, but he wanted to hear John's answer.

John blinked at him. "Ah...I don't think so."

"Well then what's the problem, Captain?"

John sat back with a huff. "You keep calling me that."

Logan leaned forward, laying his cards face up on the tabletop and unbending his wooden fingers with his other hand.

"Well, you are a captain now. Aren't you?"

"But I am not *your* captain."

Logan quirked an eyebrow, enjoying having the upper hand in their flirtations for once.

"You could be, for tonight."

John stood suddenly, the chair scraping across the rug. He snatched up his half-full cup and downed the rest of the brandy. Logan remained seated, his gaze roving down John's body to where his cock already filled out his pants.

Gods, he was handsome, with his collar open and his chestnut hair gleaming in the warm light. Logan loved seeing him like this. When the mask of stoicism fell away and left only raw lust in its wake.

Logan reached out and hooked two fingers into John's waistband. He tugged him forward, and John let himself be led until he was standing between Logan's legs.

"You know..." Logan tried to keep the breathless anticipation from his voice. He'd tried his hand at seduction with John countless times, but somehow it was always John who gained the upper hand. "You are a powerful man now, John Hakon." He unhooked his fingers, running them lightly up John's stomach and chest. "You can go wherever you want. Do whatever you want. *Take* whatever you want." His hand closed around John's shirt collar and yanked him down. John's hand slammed onto the table to keep from falling. The cups rattled. Logan's mouth remained only a breath away from John's. John nipped for Logan's bottom lip, but Logan pulled back, just out of reach. His eyes raised to meet John's hungry gaze.

"What will be your first act, Captain?"

John yanked him to his feet and kissed him, mouth devouring, hands buried in Logan's blond curls. They stumbled a few steps, and Logan's bootheel caught on the wrinkled rug, bearing him to the floor with John atop him.

John's tongue aggressively parted Logan's lips and invaded his mouth. Logan couldn't restrain the moan that passed between them. They'd always met each other with eagerness. Sometimes passion, sometimes simple appetite, but this was different. It felt as if John would consume him. Ravish him.

Desire surged down Logan's spine, straight to his dick. He'd never used to be like this. Never even flirted or realized he was being flirted with till John came into his life. But something had fundamentally shifted in his world that day in the garden with John's mouth on him, and every time John had touched him since.

Logan's hand twisted in John's shirt collar, dragging him closer. He tried to flip John onto his back, but only managed to trap one of his legs between John's powerful thighs. John used his leverage to grind down once, then allowed Logan to roll him. Logan landed against his chest, leg still trapped.

Logan whimpered around John's plundering tongue, clinging to him, his real hand still balled up in John's shirt, the wooden one pressed hard to his chest. Logan imagined he could feel the pounding heartbeat through the wooden palm and brass joints.

John's own hand tightened in Logan's hair, deepening their kiss as his other hand tore Logan's shirt away from his shoulder. He wrenched Logan's head to the side and nipped the newly exposed flesh.

"Captain," Logan moaned. The title simply slipped out, and John's cock practically doubled in size between them. He growled, ripping Logan's shirt down the back then flipping Logan onto his back again, the delicate pastel wool chafing his skin.

John braced above him, hands pressed to the rug on either side of Logan's head.

"Are you going to keep calling me that?" John asked, slightly breathless.

Logan palmed John's cock through his pants, lips parted and inviting.

"You like it."

John's eyes slid closed, collecting himself, or maybe savoring the touch of the hand he'd created. He bent down, their noses brushing, lips tantalizingly close.

"What must I do to earn that title from you for real?" he rasped.

Logan never asked for what he wanted. Not directly. And especially not now, when all he wanted was to finally have John in his entirety.

Seeming to read this in his face, John's brown eyes darkened further.

"Logan." His hips rolled down to chafe his dick against Logan's wooden palm. "Do you remember the first time I took your cock into my mouth? How the flowers crushed beneath you and filled our noses with their scent?" He punctuated this question with a kiss, lingering only long enough to stifle Logan's answer and leave him wanting. "And do you remember when I first fucked your mouth? Stretched out your gorgeous lips that still tasted of Nia's cunt as she rode you?" He yanked Logan's pants harshly down his hips, his cock bouncing free. This time he left Logan's lips untended, free to answer, though his head swam with dizzying memories.

"Y-yes...I remember," he stuttered. He could practically smell the sun-warmed flowers, taste Nia's sweetness on his tongue like nectar.

"You were so sweet." John's hand closed around Logan's exposed cock, and Logan gasped, muscles going taut. "So innocent. And under my hands your little virginal petals have fallen away one by one." His brandy-laced breath invaded Logan's senses, his hand stroking Logan's cock almost lazily. "But there's one last petal of your flower for me to pluck, isn't there?"

"Y-yes, Captain," Logan moaned.

John captured his lips in another hard kiss, his hand pumping Logan faster, spreading precum down the shaft. Logan arched into his touch, nervousness twining with pleasure. It was happening; John was finally going to fuck him.

John's massive cock strained inside his pants. Logan's throat tightened, imagining that girth stretching and filling him up and...

Logan whimpered rather pathetically. If he hadn't let go of any sense of shame around such acts under John and Nia's careful tutelage, he'd have been embarrassed at such a sound coming out of his mouth. But it only spurred John on. His lips scorched a burning trail down Logan's throat and collarbone. His hand left Logan's dick for only a moment to rip away the remains of his shirt and lave his tongue over Logan's hard nipple. When his lips reached Logan's navel, he caught Logan's gaze.

"Are you sure about this?" John asked quietly, his voice laden with heat.

"P-please, yes," Logan answered, unable to disguise how far gone he was already, from a few simple touches. He was met by a self-assured smile as John seized him around the waist and lifted him almost effortlessly into his arms. Logan yelped in surprise and wrapped his legs around John's thick waist. They left the warm light of the stateroom behind as John carried him past the curtains into the shadows of the bedroom.

The wide bed was built into the ornate woodwork of the walls and cabinetry. It took up almost the entire bedroom space, framed by green brocade and sheer curtains and backed by a bank of leaded glass windows. Beyond the square panes, the sky had descended into velvety darkness.

John dumped Logan onto the bed, the mattress bouncing beneath him. John dragged his shirt off over his head. The half-moon outside provided no light from behind the clouds, and the sconces in the parlor backlit John where he stood at the edge of the bed. Warm light wrapped around the edges of his body, accentuating his thick muscles, revealing the anchor and laurel symbol of the Marran navy tattooed on his left pectoral. His face remained shadowed, obscuring his expression.

Before they'd begun this affair, Logan had always found John intimidating. And even now, some primal part in the back of Logan's mind shivered as John stood over him, half naked and breathing hard, like the beast he was nicknamed after.

Logan sat up, trailing his hand down John's broad chest, finding the line of hair beneath his navel and following it down to the waistband of his trousers. He tugged at it, looking up to John's shadowed face for help. He could manage his own clothes one-handed now, but others didn't have the same consideration in how they dressed.

John complied with Logan's silent request, unfastening the front of his pants and shucking them off without breaking eye contact. Logan's gaze inadvertently flicked down to John's cock, heavy and hard between his thighs. His own cock twitched in response as he ran his fingers lightly down the length of John's shaft, blood pulsing beneath his touch. John's eyes scorched him, and Logan licked his lips, anticipating the veins bulging against his tongue.

John caught Logan's chin as his lips met the flushed cockhead. He tilted Logan's head up, forcing Logan to look at him.

"I'm too impatient for all that," he said gruffly. "I want to hurry up and split you open."

Heat surged through Logan's veins, as if the words had poured molten honey into them. He barely bit back an unwarranted moan, and John's grip tightened on his jaw.

John moved first. He pushed Logan onto his back, grip moving from his jaw, down his throat to his collarbone, pinning him to the plush bed. John leaned over him, his other hand retrieving a small vial of lube from a drawer inset into the base of the bed. Logan's breath caught as John uncorked it with his teeth, and instead of spreading it over his fingers, poured a generous amount onto the base of Logan's cock, letting it dribble down his balls and over his hole.

John braced one knee on the edge of the bed, spreading Logan's legs wider. His finger teased Logan's rim for just a moment before breaching him up to the knuckle, forcing a moan from his throat. Normally they tried to keep their hookups quiet and discreet so their captains and crewmates wouldn't suspect them. But now John was his own captain, with his own ship, and it didn't seem to matter anymore, not with John's fingers inside him.

John pumped his finger gently a few times. The intrusion felt strange and new, yet with every stroke, Logan's tense muscles began to relax into the sensation pooling low in his gut.

John curled his finger up, seeking the sweet spot that would heighten Logan's pleasure. Sparks burst behind Logan's eyes as the pad of John's finger circled it. His back arched off the bed, and his legs widened ever so slightly, eager to take in more. John's shadowed lips turned up at the corners in a self-satisfied smirk. He teased Logan's prostate mercilessly, until Logan's head swam with drunken euphoria and his breath came in short gasps. The urge to beg tingled across Logan's lips. He wanted—no—*needed* more.

John's finger suddenly withdrew, and Logan whimpered, reaching for John's arm to urge him back. John leaned down to press a kiss to Logan's chest, teeth skimming across his peaked nipple. He added a second finger and after a while, a third. Despite the breathless pleasure coursing through Logan's body, he began to grow impatient.

"John...please..." Never in his life before they'd run into the *Kraken* had he thought he'd be begging the Beast of Whitestone Reef to fuck him, but John's effect on him was undeniable.

"Please what?" John asked, his voice silky smooth.

"Please, I need—fuck!" He interrupted himself as John rubbed circles into his prostate. "I need you inside me."

He felt, more than saw, John smirk in the half-light. "As much as I want to fuck you right now, you're not ready yet. Trust me."

Fear that John had changed his mind seized Logan's heart.

"But...you said..." he panted.

John leaned down, his lips brushing the curve of Logan's cheek in the dark. "Oh, don't worry. I'm glad you saved it for me. You just aren't stretched enough." His fingers continued their torturous movements. Circling. Thrusting. Stretching. "Taking a dick like mine requires a little extra preparation. And after I fuck you, you won't be satisfied with anyone lesser. I hope you're ready to crave my dick for the rest of your life."

John let his words sink in as he continued fucking Logan with his fingers. "You should know as much by now. You've had it down your throat often enough."

Logan groaned as the memories of every time he'd sucked John off flooded through his mind. The soft skin against his lips, John's hips pushing deeper, fingers in his hair to hold his head in place. The stretch and ache in his jaw and throat. He couldn't help but imagine that monstrous girth inside his ass, giving him as much pleasure as he'd provided.

But John said he had to wait. To prepare more to take it without damage. He thought he would go insane if he was denied even a moment longer, and he knew John must be brimming with impatience by now as well.

Fortunately, Logan had had years of experience observing Fox. He knew—in theory at least—how to seduce a man. He knew John wanted him. And he had a brand new trick up his sleeve.

"P-please, Captain," he whined, squeezing around John's working fingers. "I-I can't wait any more. I can take it. I promise!"

John's fingers stilled, a low growl emanating from his throat.

"You might come to regret those words."

"Don't care," Logan gasped. His hips twitched, seeking the friction of John's callused fingers.

John laughed and withdrew them torturously slowly, making sure to brush Logan's prostate on the way out.

"You might care when you can't walk for a few days."

Logan shivered both at the prospect of being at this man's mercy and getting fucked so hard he'd be incapacitated. Before John, he would never have thought such a thing. He would never have been excited by powerlessness or potential pain. Yet here he was, on his back with his legs spread, dick throbbing and ass dripping lube, hungry for John's cock.

John nudged his leg, and Logan suddenly realized he was waiting on an answer, an affirmation that this was still what Logan wanted.

Logan didn't have the words for all the contradictory feelings warring inside him, so he dragged John into a hard kiss. John groaned against his lips, letting Logan's tongue slip into the warm interior of his mouth. He tasted of brandy and a hint of tobacco. Logan's hand wandered down John's bare chest and stomach to wrap around his throbbing cock. He stroked it slowly, then guided it down to press against his loosened hole.

He broke the kiss, and gazed half lidded up into John's eyes.

"Fuck me, Captain."

John seized him, pulling him to his feet and turning him around to face the bed. John's arm snaked around Logan's waist, pulling their bodies flush together so Logan's back pressed tight to John's chest and John's cock throbbed against the curve of Logan's ass. John nipped at the tender skin of Logan's neck.

"Don't say I didn't warn you." John's other hand engulfed the back of Logan's neck and squeezed, bending him over the bed. Logan whimpered in anticipation as John's cock pressed against his entrance. Wet lube dripped down Logan's crack as John poured more into the place where they were almost connected. Logan bit his lip, bracing both hands on the soft mattress.

Everything remained still for just a moment before John pushed slowly in. Only the tip entered, and yet Logan already felt so full he could burst. He shuddered, and John's hands tightened on his body, reassuring yet demanding. Logan whined when the intrusion of John's girth withdrew slightly.

"I told you I have to open you up more," John said gruffly. Was this affecting him as much as it was Logan? Was this shallow pulsing torturous to him too? He rolled his hips forward again, penetrating a bit deeper. His girth throbbing against the stretch of Logan's hole. *Fuck.* Logan breathed out slowly, willing his muscles to relax and allow John further inside. He could do this. He *wanted* to do this.

With every shallow thrust, the stretch deepened. Each time, Logan thought that must have been it, it was all in, until the next moment when John's girth strained the limits of Logan's virginal hole even more. Wouldn't it be better to go all in? To get the initial pain and stretch over with? What was the use of prolonging it? John was breathing hard, his fingers digging into Logan's flesh like he was barely holding himself back.

The outward slide of John's cock made Logan want to cry in frustration. He liked this, he did, but it just wasn't...

Logan's muscles squeezed involuntarily to keep him inside, to draw him deeper. Logan glanced over his shoulder. He couldn't see John's expression in the dark, but the tips of his hair curled and glistened with sweat against the side of his neck.

"Captain, please..."

John made a sound like his will was breaking, and the tension in the air shattered almost audibly.

John's hips snapped forward, burying himself balls-deep with one stroke. Logan's body rocked forward with the force of it, his thighs hitting the edge of the bed frame. An agonized moan ripped from Logan's throat as John's massive cock stuffed him to the brim. His hole burned with the stretch, but what little pain came with it was overshadowed by the overwhelming pleasure of fullness. John didn't wait for him to adjust—he drew back halfway and slammed back in.

Fuck. For all John's warnings and questioning about whether this was what Logan wanted, it seemed he no longer had intentions of being merciful. He set a brutal pace, hips snapping sharply, penetrating as deeply as possible and abusing Logan's prostate with every thrust. His hand still gripped the back of Logan's neck to keep him in place, fingertips brushing the bouncing blond curls.

Pleasure crackled across Logan's nerves, and he let out a long, low moan which only served to spur John on. Logan was desperate to touch himself, but he needed both hands to brace against the bed and take what John gave him. The next stroke was the hardest yet, and Logan felt as if he was splitting in two, the sheer girth of the cock inside him opening the way to unimaginable euphoria. Pleasure built uncontrollably with every thrust, the impending orgasm rushing to consume him like an avalanche.

"John," he gasped. A dribble of drool dropped to the coverlet. John's thrusts slowed for just a moment, hand tightening on the back of Logan's neck. Logan's hips rutted back in protest at the sudden loss of pace. Even though he knew John was only giving him room to breathe.

"Please. More," Logan moaned when John did not reply to his unspoken demand. John's tight grip turned to a caress, trailing down between Logan's shoulder blades and over his sweat-slicked back. He grabbed Logan's waist, rubbing circles into the dimples on Logan's lower back, as if that would soothe the intrusion of his dick. Logan whimpered and rutted back once more, taking as much of John as possible.

"Fuck, you feel good," John groaned, his own hips twitching forward to bury himself deeper still. His voice held an edge, as if he was barely keeping himself together. John was usually so stoic, so in control in the face of danger and pleasure alike. Yet here and now, deep inside Logan, control had abandoned him.

Suddenly, John withdrew, and Logan gasped at the emptiness as his hole constricted. John pulled him upright with one arm tight around his waist. Bleary, already half delirious, Logan leaned his head back against John's shoulder, reaching up to thread his fingers through John's glossy chestnut hair. John's beard scratched against Logan's skin. They stayed like that, back to chest, both breathing hard. It would have been romantic, if they had those feelings for each other.

They spoke no words in this quiet moment. There was a reason Logan had waited to do this with John. A reason he didn't have the desire to sleep with anyone else. They knew each other well by now, and there was no awkwardness between them.

After a few more kisses, John eased Logan onto his back on the mattress. He dribbled more lube onto his own cock, his hand working over the veiny shaft to slick it up. Hunger pooled in Logan's belly. John Hakon was undoubtedly handsome, his body thick with underlying muscle, sweat gleaming across sun-tanned skin in the lamplight. John bent to pepper Logan's still heaving chest with more kisses and took his nipple between red lips. Logan gasped, clutching the coverlet beneath him as John spread his legs and lined himself up with Logan's entrance again. John's intense gaze met Logan's bleary, fucked-out one.

John thrust in, and Logan canted his hips up to meet it. The intensity of the stretch from this angle practically forced the air from his lungs. John's lips trailed over Logan's collarbone, up his neck and chin till he found his lips. Logan moaned into the kiss, and John thrust deeper this time, the veins of his cock dragging deliciously through Logan's insides. Logan clenched, unable to help the natural reactions of his body.

"You're gonna strangle my cock if you do that," John said in a low voice. But it didn't stop his cock from swelling in response.

Logan's responding moan sounded absolutely filthy in his own ears. He grabbed at John's arm for support. Then realized he'd done so with his wooden hand and settled for simply resting it against John's bicep.

John set a slow and deep pace, hungrily watching Logan's changing expressions. He placed his own hand over Logan's wooden one, curling the jointed wooden fingers around his arm so Logan could hold him.

Logan tried matching his pace, dick bouncing and aching against his soft stomach. "Ah...Captain, please, faster."

John pushed them further up the mattress, and Logan's heels dug into the soft surface, seeking leverage as the pace quickened. Pleasure threaded every nerve, weaving into an intoxicating tapestry. Logan grabbed his own cock with his real hand, stroking it a few times, hips arching off the bed.

"Fuck, you're hot," John moaned, thrusting faster, breath ragged. "Make yourself come for me. Show me how you jerk off when you're alone in your cabin, hm?"

A small wave of embarrassment washed through Logan's ecstasy, somehow heightening it. His hand moved faster, eliciting another string of moans as the pleasure sharpened. John watched him with hooded eyes and that, too, sent sparks sizzling through his body. It was one thing to have sex, to get one another off simply for the fun of it; it was quite another to show John what he did in private when he was completely alone. Pleasuring himself while John was inside him was somehow more intimate than anything they'd done before.

Logan squeezed his eyes shut, basking in the heat of John's regard. He imagined he could feel John's muscles flex beneath his wooden palm as he thumbed his own slit with the other hand and spread precum down his shaft. The whorls of his fingertips glided over the taut skin, sliding back up the shaft in a loose fist. His breath grew ragged, and he knew he was mere moments away from toppling over the edge. The pleasure from front and back overwhelmed his senses. He rolled his hand over the head of his cock, teasing the slit before stroking down again. Moans and gasps fell from his lips, unburdened by self-consciousness.

A particularly deep stroke that hit Logan's prostate just right had him coming into his hand, semen spurting warm and sticky across his belly and coating his fingers.

"Fuck, you're so..." John's voice cut off in a groan as Logan's hole clenched around him. "I'm close—keep going."

"Yes, Captain." Logan obeyed, eyes opening blearily as he continued to pump his fist over his dick. Cum squelched between his fingers, and John moaned, thrusting faster and deeper, quickly raising Logan up into the clouds of overstimulation. Small whimpers escaped Logan's lips, but he didn't stop fucking his own fist till he finally met John's intense brown eyes.

John grunted, and with one last thrust, spilled hard into Logan's achingly stretched insides. His body shuddered, and Logan reached up to clutch John's other arm, not caring that he was getting cum all over them both. John's muscles shifted beneath his touch as he bent to kiss him. Logan's eyes drifted closed again, drunk on the taste of brandy on John's tongue and the girth of John inside him.

The kiss broke, and John withdrew, dick squelching through the cum on its way out. Logan gasped at the gape he left behind, resisting the urge to cover it up with his hands. When he finally opened his eyes, John peeled Logan's wooden fingers from their grip on his arm and collapsed to the bed beside him.

John's fingertips trailed through the cum on Logan's stomach down to the place where his cum leaked out of Logan's hole. He fingered the rim, smirking when it elicited another gasp.

"So stretched out for me," he murmured possessively, almost reverently. Logan didn't move, and John withdrew to rest his hand on Logan's thigh. He didn't try to cuddle him, and Logan didn't expect it. Logan found himself staring up at the ceiling of John's new captain's quarters, directly into the eyes of a blond, rosy-cheeked cherub. He squeaked in surprise.

"You okay?" John murmured.

"I think we're being watched." He pointed one cum-soaked finger to the mural. It encompassed the entire ceiling over the bed, a blue and gold sky framed with rosy clouds and a cadre of cherubs with tiny wings and bare asses frolicking throughout.

John looked up and laughed, eyes crinkling.

"Great start to my captaincy, a bunch of winged babies watching me fuck."

"You should probably paint over it." Logan grimaced, both at the painting and the way his lower back twinged as he shifted.

John tilted his head thoughtfully, examining the mural. "I don't know. That one kinda looks like you. Maybe I'll keep it."

Logan swatted at him, wincing again.

"Was I too rough on you?" John asked.

"I think I'll be fine." Logan made to sit up. Sometimes they went back to playing cards after getting off, but the post-nut bliss was fading, and he suddenly felt like he should go.

His body had other plans. A jolt of pain shot straight from his stretched out asshole up his spine, and he fell back to the bed, wincing.

"Take it easy." John patted his shoulder. "You just got fucked by the biggest dick on the Broken Sea. Just lay down till you recover."

"Haha, very funny."

"I dare you to find a bigger one," John said with mock seriousness. "Just lay back down and count the number of disturbingly accurate cherub dicks on my new ceiling."

Logan covered his eyes with his forearm. "I refuse. You'll really have to paint over it or I'll never come back."

"Fine, fine," John chuckled. "I'll get a scene done of what happened here tonight. To commemorate your final deflowering."

Logan shot him a scandalized look. "Don't you dare."

John wrapped one arm around his waist, pulling him close against his warm chest. "Seriously though, rest for a bit."

The warmth of John's skin, his breath ghosting across Logan's cheek, and the soft press of his—admittedly huge—cock against Logan's thigh was already lulling Logan into a peaceful stupor. It couldn't hurt to stay a few more minutes. He would go back to his own cozy little cabin onboard the *Siren* after a short rest.

He closed his eyes, blocking out the artfully rendered cherubs above him, and didn't even notice when he dropped immediately to sleep.

CHAPTER 10

MAY 5TH, 1668

A yawning whirlpool of trepidation had slowly begun to swirl in Fox's gut since he'd given Gaël permission to become the first mate of the *Sweet Mercy*. With every night that brought them closer to Gaël's departure, the churning waters spun faster and faster. At any moment Fox would drop over the edge into that bottomless void and never resurface again. And every time Gaël left his side, even for a moment, Fox felt like he was being left behind.

His home shouldn't feel like that.

But tonight was their last night together, and Fox was determined to make the most of it. To stamp his presence on Gaël's very being so he would have no choice but to return unscathed. Fox pushed all the trepidation and anticipated loneliness into the bottom of the whirlpool as he shoved Gaël up against the closed door of their quarters, hands fisted in the front of his shirt, and kissed him breathless.

There were no words between them. All that was left unsaid could now only be spoken by their entwined bodies. Gaël's lips parted, accepting Fox's tongue greedily as his fingers threaded through Fox's wind-mussed hair. He moaned against Fox's mouth, unable to speak his name around the invading tongue. Fox's fists tightened further in his shirt, as if Gaël would disappear at any moment.

He could have changed his mind and asked Gaël to stay. Yet Fox couldn't let his own anxieties stifle Gaël's freedom. Gaël had been more than accommodating of Fox's insecurities since their reunion, and though Fox found himself incapable of leaving the *Siren*, that didn't mean Gaël must remain as well. Both of them understood this now, but that didn't mean Fox would let him go without showing him what he would be missing.

Fox rocked his hips against Gaël's body, anticipation heightening as he felt Gaël's cock harden beneath his pants. Fox's tongue stroked into Gaël's mouth, eliciting another moan. He stowed away that sound in his memory for the season of inevitable lonely nights that stretched ahead of him.

But tonight he wasn't lonely. He yanked Gaël's shirt up over his head, their lips parting momentarily as the fabric passed between them. The whirlpool spun faster and faster, turning Fox's movements frantic. Gaël hauled him close to his chest, his hands wandering down Fox's back to cup his ass.

Fox's lips scorched a trail down Gaël's throat and over his collarbone, his mouth open and wanting. Gaël leaned his head back against the door, still gripping Fox's body tight to his. His breath came in quick pants as Fox lavished his chest with attention. Fox flattened his tongue against Gaël's hard nipples, then nipped at them with his teeth, eliciting a gasp.

"I'm gonna wreck you tonight, baby," Fox murmured. "Would you like that?"

Fox found Gaël watching him, eyes clouded with naked lust. He licked his plush, parted lips.

"Do whatever you want with me, sweetheart. I'm all yours."

Arousal surged through Fox's body. He unfastened Gaël's pants and dragged them down his hips, practically salivating as Gaël's thick cock sprang free. Fox fell to his knees, too impatient for slow teasing. His own cock pressed hard against the inside of his pants. He framed Gaël's hips between his hands and sucked Gaël's cock into his hungry mouth. Gaël's moan redoubled as his cockhead breached Fox's kiss-swollen lips and slid against the inside of his cheeks.

Fox closed his eyes for a moment, relishing the slide of soft skin against his lips, savoring the salty precum on his tastebuds. Gaël's hips twitched as Fox's tongue swirled around him on the next downstroke. The head hit the back of his throat, and he swallowed around the intrusion. He inhaled the familiar scent of Gaël's musk, his nose buried in the dark pubic hair.

"Foxy," Gaël moaned, already breathless. Fox's eyelids fluttered open, holding his stormy gaze as he slowly began to pull back, his tongue swirling and pressing against all the sensitive spots he knew would drive Gaël mad. When only the tip remained inside he sucked on it, saliva pooling beneath his tongue, before he pushed forward up to the base.

Gaël gripped Fox's hair as Fox set a relentless pace. His hips twitched against Fox's restraining hold with every stroke, desperate to fuck Fox's mouth. The veins beneath his tight skin throbbed, mirroring his pounding heart.

Fox moaned around Gaël's cock, his own dick desperate to be touched. He let his teeth scrape lightly down Gaël's shaft, and Gaël shuddered.

"Fox, please. I..." Gaël's hips stuttered again, his grip tightening in Fox's hair. The desperate cast of Gaël's voice told Fox he was close. After a few more strokes, he released Gaël's cock with a lewd slurp.

Fox blinked up at him, knowing his wide green eyes and swollen lips would push Gaël even closer to the edge.

Gaël growled and tugged Fox's hair, urging him to his feet. Fox let the tug send tingles across his scalp and down his spine before he complied, rising slowly so they were face-to-face.

"Don't make me come too quick. We still have the whole night ahead of us."

Fox smirked and palmed Gaël's wet cock. "As if I can't make you come as many times as I want."

Gaël shivered at his words and followed Fox's tugging hand, allowing himself to be led to the bed.

There was always a moment between them, when they were skin-to-skin like this, where the fluid nature of their sexual relationship pulled taut with possibility. The sometimes unspoken question of who would give and who would receive. Gaël captured Fox's swollen lips in a deep kiss, their tongues ebbing and flowing together, sparring for resolution until something finally clicked into place in Fox's head.

Without breaking the kiss, Fox pushed Gaël onto the bed, hitching Gaël's thick thighs around his hips in a clear show of dominance. Gaël arched into his touch, accepting his role as easy as breathing. He dragged Fox's shirt off over his head and tossed it to the side before frantically unfastening the front of Fox's pants. Fox moaned when Gaël's hand slipped beneath his underwear to wrap around his cock. He thumbed the wet slit, spreading precum over the flushed head. Fox's hips involuntarily bucked into his hold. His impatience grew, thrusting into Gaël's loose grip as his mouth devoured Gaël's lips. He'd gone into this with a plan to drive Gaël mad so he would miss Fox terribly while he was gone. Unfortunately, Gaël had the same power over him. That was what happened when you were hopelessly in love.

Fox's grip tightened on Gaël's thigh, fingertips digging into the firm flesh. His dick throbbed in Gaël's grip, and he held back a whimper. He had to take back control and not let himself succumb to the natural seduction of Gaël's body.

Fox sat back to shuck off the rest of his clothes. Gaël reached for him, desperate for more contact, and Fox caught his hand to press a kiss to his palm. He trailed kisses up Gaël's arm to the inside of his elbow, as his other hand caressed up Gaël's thigh to brush his cock. Gaël bit his lip, watching Fox's face as Fox lavished his skin with kisses.

"Fox..." Gaël whined, and Fox smirked in return. Usually Fox was the impatient and needy one, but it seemed that Gaël was missing him already. He stroked Gaël's cock lightly, lips traveling down Gaël's muscular body. Gaël gasped as Fox's cheek skimmed down the shaft, then grunted when Fox pulled him to the edge of the bed. Fox lowered to his knees on the floor and propped Gaël's sturdy legs on his shoulders. His lips trailed along Gaël's inner thigh to the bottom curve of his buttcheek. Gaël's muscles tensed as he realized what Fox intended to do, and a small, whiny moan escaped his parted lips as Fox spread his cheeks and flattened his tongue against Gaël's puckered hole.

Fox continued stroking Gaël's cock, relishing the way Gaël's hole constricted against his tongue. Fox teased around the rim for a few moments, waiting for Gaël to relax again. His muscles loosened bit by bit as Fox lavished him with attention. When he was sufficiently relaxed, Fox pushed his tongue past the tight ring of muscle and lapped at Gaël's pliant interior. Gaël groaned, his hips twitching to impale himself further on Fox's tongue. Fox withdrew and thrust his tongue in again, eliciting another groan. Fox spread him wider, thrusting and lapping at his insides, unconcerned with the saliva coating his cheeks and chin. He only wanted to listen to the pleasured sounds falling from Gaël's lips.

Gaël's soft insides tightened around Fox's tongue with every thrust, and a sort of dizzy euphoria began to cloud Fox's mind, his own arousal heightened by his lover's pleasure. He shifted on his knees and redoubled his efforts, satisfied as Gaël's hole slowly loosened under his ministrations. He resisted touching his own cock to relieve the pressure that built with every twitch of Gaël's hips seeking deeper penetration.

Fox's thumb dipped in beside his thrusting tongue, circling and stretching more until Gaël's hips rutted back sharply. Fox replaced his thumb with one finger, then added a second, taking care not to let his own impatience hurry him. He couldn't let Gaël's first day on the job tomorrow be marred by a sore back.

Gaël's fingertips brushed the top of Fox's head, and when Fox looked up, Gaël passed the vial of lube they always kept under their pillows into his other hand. Fox held his gaze for a moment and slowly licked the saliva from his lips, giggling when Gaël shuddered.

One corner of Gaël's lips quirked up in response, revealing one of his absolutely devastating dimples. Fox's heart performed an acrobatic flip between his ribs, and he averted his gaze. How this gorgeous man could make Fox blush and fall in love all over again just by smiling when Fox was knuckles deep inside him was an absolute mystery. Yet of course he didn't mind. He'd do anything to make Gaël smile.

And even more to make Gaël moan his name.

Fox withdrew his fingers and coated them generously with lube before thrusting back in. Gaël moaned quietly as Fox began opening him up, occasionally pushing his tongue in beside his fingers. The coconut flavor of the oil and the taste of Gaël's insides coated his taste buds. He massaged the little bundle of nerves, watching Gaël's dick twitch at the stimulation, and beyond that, Gaël's beautiful pink lips open in a moan. Even just that was enough to push Fox close to the edge. He bit his lower lip, squeezing his eyes closed to block out the beautiful sight of Gaël all splayed out and needy for him. He had to focus on the task at hand. He scissored his fingers open, and when they came back together, rubbed them on either side of Gaël's prostate.

He rested his cheek against Gaël's inner thigh and listened to

Gaël cry out for him, committing every bit of his voice to memory. His deep tone. His breathless begging. What if something happened and Fox never saw him again? What if this was the last night they would ever spend together?

"Fox, please...I'm ready," Gaël begged, and Fox shook himself from the dark thoughts, refocusing on his lover's pleasure. He opened his eyes to see Gaël's head tilted back, hands clutching the sheets, back arched, and hips rutting against Fox's fingers as his flushed, hard cock bobbed against his stomach. The sight overwhelmed Fox instantly, and he leaned over Gaël's body to get a better look, never stopping his stroking fingers. Gaël's eyelids fluttered, and he reached up to cup the back of Fox's neck and draw him down into a kiss. Fox groaned as their lips met and his cock brushed against Gaël's inner thigh. He shifted to brace one knee on the bed and pressed at Gaël's prostate with his middle finger. Gaël gasped and released him, hand falling back to the bed beside his splayed onyx hair.

Fox kissed him harder, his tongue swirling around Gaël's and his fingers thrusting a bit faster. Suddenly, Gaël pushed him away, and he didn't even have a second to react before his back hit the mattress and Gaël was straddling his hips.

"Hey!" Fox's protest was silenced with a deep and hungry kiss. Gaël's hips shifted, and he reached back to quickly slick lube over Fox's cock. Gaël lined the tip up with his entrance and sank down with one swift movement, impaling himself as deep as Fox could go. Pleasure sliced through Fox's body as Gaël's soft interior closed around him, and he squeezed Gaël's thick thighs to keep from coming right then. Gaël stayed still for just a few seconds, presumably giving himself time to adjust to the intrusion, before he began to move.

Bracing his fingertips against Fox's stomach, Gaël lifted himself and slammed back down. His body shuddered as a deep moan punched out of him. He repeated the action, getting faster and faster with every stroke. The strong muscles of his thighs shifted beneath Fox's palms as Fox watched him ride his cock with fascination. He was gorgeous, honey-brown skin already gleaming with sweat, black hair falling away from his upturned face. Fox's gaze traveled down the corded column of his throat, over his scarred chest, his flat stomach, and his dripping cock bobbing in a thicket of black curls.

Fox could tell Gaël was putting on a bit of a show, making sure their last night together was one to remember. So he lay back and enjoyed the sight of Gaël fucking himself down onto Fox's cock.

"You ride me so well, baby," Fox groaned as Gaël's body undulated over him. Gaël's eyes cracked open to gaze down at him over high cheekbones, kiss-bitten lips parted around the string of moans that continuously spilled from them. One of Fox's hands wandered from Gaël's thigh to his cock. He thumbed the slit, smearing precum over the swollen head, and Gaël's hips stuttered to a stop for just a moment, lost in the bliss of having Fox inside him and around him.

Fox often mourned the fact that it was physically impossible to fuck and be fucked by Gaël simultaneously. Good thing both of them usually had the stamina to go two rounds. Fox hated ending a night unfilled.

Fox pumped Gaël's cock with a few quick strokes. Gaël leaned back, the line of his beautiful body rippling with muscle. He braced against Fox's thighs, fingers digging into the tattoo there. His hips rolled feebly, grinding down onto Fox's cock as Fox pleasured him. Fox bit back a groan as Gaël's insides clenched, sending tingles of pleasure racing across his skin. The next time Gaël raised his hips on shaking legs, Fox braced his feet on the bed and thrust up into him as deeply as he could, making sure to angle it just right.

Gaël jolted with the force of it, and a long, agonized moan clawed its way up from his stomach to his throat. Fox ground his hips against Gaël's firm ass before beginning to thrust in time with the strokes of his hand. The whirlpool of impending loneliness in Fox's guts had spun itself into a frenzy of pleasure. He was dizzy with it, but he couldn't let himself go until Gaël did.

With a few more thrusts, he got his wish, and Gaël came, his head thrown back, Fox's name ripping gutturally from his throat. Thick white cum spurted over Fox's chest, neck, and face. His hand tightened on Gaël's thigh to keep him seated on Fox's cock as a glob of cum splattered on Fox's eyelid and another on his lip. His tongue darted out to lick it away. Gaël's body quivered as the last of the orgasm left him, and he slumped forward, exhausted.

But Fox wasn't done. Far from it.

Fox unseated himself and flipped Gaël onto his stomach. He knelt behind him, pulling Gaël up onto his hands and knees.

"Foxy..." Gaël whined, but he pushed his ass back against Fox's cock, seeking more. Fox flicked the cum away from his eyelid, and dragged Gaël back to line his entrance up.

"Do you want more, baby?" Fox asked mischievously, walking his cum-slick fingers up Gaël's spine. He teased his pink and swollen rim with his tip.

"Please, more..." Gaël answered breathlessly. "Fill me up." He wiggled his ass alluringly, taking a page straight out of Fox's book of seduction.

Fuck, well, Fox couldn't say no to that.

He bottomed out with one stroke, a raw and unbridled cry ripping from Gaël's lips as he was filled up again. Fox didn't wait even a moment for him to adjust before he was hammering into Gaël's tight, wet heat, chasing down his own orgasm like a rabid dog.

Fire licked across his nerves, but this position wasn't quite enough. He braced one foot on the bed so he knelt on only one knee, then hitched Gaël's leg back and to the side to rest on Fox's thigh. The angle tightened Gaël's passage, and had the head of Fox's cock raking past his prostate.

"Fuck," Fox rasped, his fingers digging harder into Gaël's flesh as he fucked into him with reckless abandon. Dizzy pleasure clouded Fox's self-restraint—as if he'd ever had any when it came to Gaël.

Only small whimpers tumbled from Gaël's lips, his head hanging down between bunched-up shoulders. Exhausted. Yet from this angle, Fox could see he was starting to get hard again. He was simply holding on for dear life, letting the pleasure wash over him and pull him under.

The pathetic little sounds were driving Fox insane, but now he wanted to make Gaël come again. He redoubled his efforts, angling just so, and savoring the drag and squelch of his cock against Gaël's delicious insides. Fuck. He was definitely going to need a round two tonight if he was going to survive the rest of the season without Gaël.

Gaël cried out as Fox subjected him to a particularly deep thrust and pearly cum splattered onto the sheets. His walls clenched tight around Fox's cock, and Fox's orgasm hit him all at once. Euphoria enveloped every sense as he spilled hot and hard, his cock throbbing against Gaël's clenching walls. He managed a few more stuttering thrusts before they both collapsed to the bed, breathless and satiated.

Gaël reached back to card his fingers through Fox's sweat-damp hair, grinding his hips back to chase the aftershocks of pleasure. Fox kissed the back of his neck, slow and languid, memorizing the post-fuck taste of his skin. Fox locked his arms around Gaël's waist to keep them connected.

"Mmm," Gaël moaned contentedly, settling into Fox's arms so perfectly. Fox buried his face into Gaël's shoulder. This was where they belonged, tangled up in each other. But after six years apart, they were parting again. At least this time they had love in their hearts and a promise on their lips.

Their breathing evened out, and their sweat cooled. Fox's cock softened and he slipped out, causing Gaël to groan and turn over, threading his arms around Fox's waist. He pecked the tip of Fox's nose, and Fox giggled.

"Love you, sweetheart," Gaël murmured, gray eyes shining.

"Love you too." Fox was still a little out of it, basking in the afterglow. The words tasted bittersweet alongside the lingering saltiness of Gaël's cum on his tongue. In the morning Gaël would leave, and tomorrow night Fox would be in this bed all alone. He would no longer have the simple comfort of waking up next to the person he loved most in the world.

His arms tightened involuntarily, unwilling to let Gaël go. Unwilling to fall asleep just yet, because if he did, tomorrow would come much too soon.

Gaël's thumb rubbed over the whorls of Fox's thigh tattoo absently, following the path his life had taken. It had become a habit of his since their reunion, as if Gaël could learn every part of Fox's being by touch alone. The wavelike swirls wrapped Fox's thigh in bands of a story: little foxes traipsing through floating symbols of things that mattered. A pair of children curled up together, for their time on the streets. A hawk soaring overhead, for joining the *Siren* crew. A piece of honey candy, for the night Henri had saved his life in a tavern brawl. All floating down the inked current of his life. Occasionally Gaël's fingers would brush one illustration or another and he would say: *Tell me about this*, and Fox would recount the story as Gaël caressed his skin. Fox couldn't look him in the eye during those times. He didn't like the raw yearning he found there, the regret Gaël would always carry with him that he had not been there to share those adventures together.

Now, Gaël's fingertips found a section where the lines were broken, which he had never had the courage to ask about before.

"This is where I left you," he said, voice low.

It was a small gap, the threads of ink simply disappearing and reemerging on the other side of some invisible barrier. But it threw the entire tattoo into disharmony.

"Yes." Fox didn't have to look to know where Gaël's touch lingered. He knew it well. That blank space, severing his life into before and after. It sat pride of place right on the front of Fox's thigh, a constant reminder.

Sometimes, in the six years they'd been apart, he'd catch sight of it while being fucked by some other man, and his mind would disconnect from the pleasure his body wanted to give him. His emotions would go dull and distant. And in the back of his mind, he'd wish it was Gaël touching him instead. More than once he'd considered filling up the space, erasing what Gaël had done, but it was as much a part of him as the joyful memories. Without Gaël leaving him, Fox would have never joined the crew of the *Siren*—he would never have found the place he was meant to be.

It didn't matter now. They were together again, and even though Gaël was leaving as soon as they ventured from this bed in the morning, Fox knew he would always come back to him.

Now Gaël's gray eyes held that yearning again, that soft sorrow of time lost. A brief hope lifted Fox's heart that Gaël would choose not to leave tomorrow, that he would choose Fox. But that was selfish. He couldn't keep Gaël here any more than Gaël could make him leave.

"Can I ask you something?" Gaël said quietly.

"Hmm?" Maybe Gaël would finally ask about that time, but Fox wasn't ready to tell. He didn't want to ruin the night by airing out his suffering. The lowest of low points in his life.

"Will you be okay while I'm gone?"

Fox frowned slightly. "I told you I'll work on it. I'll miss you terribly and think of you every moment, but you don't have to worry about me."

"No I mean..." Gaël trailed off, as if unsure how to continue. His thumb pressed a little harder into the gap in Fox's tattoo. "I mean sexually."

"Sexually?" Fox roused from the last of his glowing stupor to look Gaël full in the face. "What do you mean?"

Gaël's other hand fidgeted with the edge of the pillowcase. "I mean, will you be satisfied with just yourself while I'm gone?"

Fox froze, Gaël's words like a stone in the pit of his stomach. Did Gaël think so little of him? That all he thought about was sex?

"I'm not planning to cheat on you, if that's what you're asking." Fox's tone was cold. He pushed slightly out of Gaël's embrace.

"No, no." Gaël hugged him back to his previous position. "That's not what I meant. I just...I mean..." He sighed and closed his eyes for a moment, collecting himself. Fox wiggled in the silence, previously blissful mood now soured.

"Fox, I love you so much," Gaël began, meeting Fox's green eyes with his gray ones. "I know me leaving is going to be a burden for you. I just want you to be happy. I want what you want so...If you need to sleep around while I'm gone, I'm okay with it."

Silence met his words as Fox struggled to comprehend what he was hearing. When had he ever given Gaël the impression that he couldn't go without sex? That he missed sleeping with a different person every night? Tears burned the back of his throat, and he swallowed them down. Gaël should know by now that Fox was more than the happy-go-lucky slut that most people viewed him as. Yet here he was assuming that Fox couldn't last a few measly months without his lover. The thought should have made him angry, but that small spark of anger was smothered by an all-consuming sadness instead. Maybe Gaël didn't know the true Fox beneath the outgoing facade. Maybe...

He extricated himself from Gaël's embrace, curling up so as little of his naked body was visible as possible. "Is that what you're going to do?" he asked quietly. Gaël was loyal to a fault. At least Fox had thought he was. Now, many previously true things seemed up in the air.

"N-no, of course not!"

"Then why would you think I would?" Fox snapped.

Gaël reached for him instinctually, then thought better of it. His gray eyes softened.

"I'm not enough for you, Fox."

"When have I *ever* made you think that?"

Gaël sighed, dragging his hands down his face in frustration. "This is not how I wanted this to go."

"Did you expect me to be happy that you're springing this on me *the night before you leave*? Did you think I would happily climb into someone else's bed as soon as you were gone? You must think so little of me."

This time when Gaël reached out, he grabbed Fox's hand and held on tight.

"That's not it. I swear it's not. It's..." He sucked in a deep breath. "It's actually the opposite. You're so full of life. And I love you so much the thought of you being alone and sad hurts. You're my whole world, but I'm just a small piece of yours and..." He tugged Fox's hand to his lips, murmuring the next words into the backs of his fingers. "I just didn't want my leaving to hurt you as much as it's already hurting me. I've never deserved you, Fox. I never deserved your forgiveness, and as much as the past year and a half has been the happiest of my life, I feel like I'm on borrowed time. I feel like one day you'll realize I'm not good enough for you."

Oh. Gaël was such an idiot. Such a beautiful, sweet idiot. It wasn't Fox he thought little of; it was himself.

Maybe Fox should have made Gaël work harder to come back into his life. Made him feel like he'd earned it. But Fox was, after all, a bit of a slut at heart, and he'd allowed Gaël back into his bed and his heart as soon as Gaël apologized. Now Gaël wanted to return Fox's gesture of good faith, letting Gaël go on this adventure as first mate of the *Sweet Mercy*, with a gift of his own—the freedom to satisfy his needs without repercussions. The freedom to take comfort in Gaël's absence.

Fox had a wealth of experience. He had many people—even on this ship—that would jump at the chance to be with him again. Yet Fox found the thought of sleeping with anyone else after Gaël held no sense of excitement for him. His heart had only ever belonged to one person, since that day when they were five and he'd found Gaël crying on a stoop, and brought him home. Gaël *was* enough for him. Gaël was the person whose absence in his life had left a space that could never be filled by anything else. How could meaningless sex with strangers or acquaintances compare to even the most tame night with the man he loved?

"Foxy?"

Gaël's voice was quiet, expectant.

Fox wanted to say all of that, but his mouth couldn't catch up with his mind. He squeezed Gaël's hand, and placed Gaël's fingertips back on the blank space in the tattoo. "There's no other blank space, because losing you was like losing part of myself. I gave my body to all of those people, because my heart wasn't free to be given. It was with you. Whether you believe it or not, you are enough for me, Gaël. No one else ever could be."

Some semblance of relief came over Gaël's features. He drew Fox a little closer, reverently kissing the inside of his wrist like he didn't deserve to kiss his lips. "I'll work hard to be the man you think I am."

Fox frowned at him. "You already are."

Gaël said nothing. He pulled Fox back into his arms, and Fox let him, still frowning a bit. Gaël hadn't taken back his offer. Fox wanted him to take it back, but he had a feeling Gaël wasn't going to.

Gaël smoothed Fox's sex-mussed hair back from his forehead. Their eyes met, gray and green like a forest in a storm. "I will return to you. I promise," Gaël whispered.

"I know."

CHAPTER 11

MAY 6TH, 1668

A bead of sweat trickled down the center of Nia's back as she ladled spiced stew made from chicken and root vegetables into a sailor's waiting bowl. He smiled a gap-toothed grin and thanked her politely in the Yarenen language, of which her miniscule vocabulary was quickly expanding. She said the appropriate "you're welcome" back—no doubt terribly pronounced and accented—but the sailor winked anyway before moving on to get a round of hard flatbread from Laurent.

Laurent smiled at her as well, proud of his new pupil. Over the past few days, when she wasn't slipping away to search the ship and coming up empty, Nia had learned he was from the islands between Yarene and Souna, and older than Nia had initially thought, his shoulder-length black curls shot through with gray. He and Nia had become fast friends. From the first time he'd teased her for under spicing the food, and when she'd caught him ogling one of the particularly well-muscled sailors, they'd joked and gossiped the days away as the *Monsoon* continued its course away from Roseforte and whatever trouble was brewing after the attack.

"I hope Laurent isn't working you too hard."

Nia looked up from her task to see Splinter Zanta holding out two painted porcelain bowls. Her hair was now unbraided, but for a few beaded strands, and was pulled back from her face by a green scarf.

"Nothing I'm not used to." Nia ladled the bowls full of heaping portions, steam laden with saffron, cumin, and some other spices she didn't remember the names of curling up between them.

"Come eat with me," Zanta said, gesturing with one of the bowls toward a small table in the corner of the mess.

"Are you asking me to abandon my post, Captain?" Nia teased.

"I'm sure Laurent won't mind. Will you?" They both looked to where the cook was not-so-subtly eavesdropping.

"By all means, give the captain what she wants." He smiled and took the ladle from Nia's hand, replacing it with two rounds of flatbread coated in olive oil and salt. Leaning close, he added conspiratorially, "She's quite the tyrant when she doesn't get her way."

"Is that so?" Nia smirked, as Zanta rolled her eyes. Nia stepped away from the steaming stewpot and reached back to untie her apron with one hand, holding the bread in the other. She didn't miss how closely Zanta watched her. Was it mistrust or interest? Nia pushed her ample chest out a little more as she teased out the knot at the small of her back.

She'd barely seen Zanta around the ship since being assigned to the galley. When they sat down at the table, Zanta pushed one of the bowls across to her.

"How are you settling in?" Zanta asked, scooping up a large bite of stew with a section of flatbread and chewing ponderously.

"Well enough. I've lived on a ship before."

"Have you?"

Shit. Nia shouldn't have said that. She was becoming too comfortable here after just a few days. More than a few times she'd found herself standing at the rail just watching the water, and feeling the salt spray on her face. This ship, being so close to the sea again, had lulled her into a dangerous sense of home she hadn't felt in years.

"As a child." Nia fished a piece of chicken out of the yellowy-orange stew with a spoon and chewed slowly to avoid saying more. She hadn't quite mastered the Yarenen tradition of eating with bread-based utensils. Zanta searched her face for a moment, then, seeming to sense Nia's reluctance to speak more on the matter, pivoted to other topics. She asked which crew members Nia had met thus far and if she'd been seasick, and before Nia knew it, her spoon scraped the bottom of her bowl.

"You must be hot working in that dress all the time," Zanta said.

Her eyes traveled down the curve of Nia's shoulder, and Nia thought they lingered on her bustline for just a moment too long before returning to her face.

Well, she was hot now with Zanta's lovely brown eyes on her. Did Zanta realize what she was doing, how Nia was reacting to just a simple lingering look? Why was she being so reactive anyway? Because Zanta was a beautiful woman seemingly showing interest after Nia had been with only men for so long? Or because Nia had already decided to try and seduce her if she couldn't find the chest elsewhere?

Nia looked down at the dress she'd been wearing since the day she'd first been dragged onto the *Monsoon*. It was definitely getting to the point of needing laundering, but she had nothing to change into. Especially nothing she could go prancing around a ship full of pirates in. Nia lifted the neckline of her dress, noting how the movement pulled Zanta's eyes down, and gave the fabric a delicate sniff. She wrinkled her nose purposely, though the clothes smelled more of cooking than sweat, no worse than any other sea dog on board.

"I could use a change of clothes, I suppose."

"Come on, then." Leaving their empty dishes on the table, Zanta led her to the hall. Nia threw an apologetic look toward Laurent as the door swung closed behind her. She followed Zanta to a storeroom close to the one that had been converted to her room. It was evening now, and the only light in the windowless room came from the deck prisms refracting the hazy almost-sunset over chests lining one wall and a wardrobe against the back.

Nia hadn't explored this room yet, and her eyes quickly scanned over the chests. None were the small iron box she was looking for, but a few were big enough to conceal it. Then again, if Zanta had somehow managed to open it—which Nia both dreaded and doubted—the treasure could be almost anywhere.

"See if you can find something that will fit." Zanta lifted the lid of the closest chest and began riffling through a stack of folded clothes and blankets within. Nia drifted further into the room, drawn by the tall wardrobe at the back.

"How about this?" The captain held up a pair of rough brown trousers that tied at the waist with a drawstring. Nia scrunched up her nose in distaste.

"What, you're jealous you're no longer the prettiest girl on your own ship, so you're going to make me wear rags?" Nia quipped. She opened the wardrobe, revealing several hanging gowns and practical dresses, most of which were definitely too small. "Ah, this is more my speed."

She heard Zanta scoff behind her. "These aren't *rags*. Trousers are much more practical for working on a ship."

"It's not like I'm going to be climbing the ratlines," Nia said without turning around. Her eyes roved over the dresses. Only three looked likely to fit her. An emerald silk gown that would set off her red hair fetchingly, but was definitely not suitable to wear on a ship. An austere ensemble consisting of a faded white blouse and an even more faded gray skirt that may once have been black. And a blue dress that was both practical and not completely drab.

"At least try the trousers," Zanta said.

"Find some that aren't brown or gray, and I'll consider it." Nia swept the skirts in the wardrobe aside. They did not reveal a concealed iron chest, nor did the corners or back of the wardrobe give away any clues to a false bottom or back. She heard Zanta rummaging through more chests behind her.

Well, it was one more place to check off her mental list of where the treasure was not. A small thread of unease thickened in the pit of her stomach. What if she couldn't find it? Would she get dumped back on land and have to start her life over once again?

"Why do you have all these dresses if you don't like them?" Nia asked to distract herself.

"Some belong to the crew. Others we couldn't manage to sell off for what they're worth. And some are for disguises," Zanta said. "How about these?"

Nia found Zanta kneeling beside a second chest, holding up a pair of puffy-legged burgundy trousers with vertical slashes of saffron yellow.

"You've got to be kidding."

"They're not brown!" Zanta said brightly, and Nia got the distinct impression she'd purposely found the ugliest pair possible just to spite her.

"They're hardly more practical than a skirt," Nia protested. "Who'd you steal those off of? A court jester?"

"You said you'd consider it." Zanta's lower lip stuck out slightly.

Well shit, with Zanta pouting on her knees, looking up at Nia with those big brown eyes, how could she say no?

"Fine, hand them over." Nia began to unlace the front of her dress to get at the skirt fastenings beneath.

"What are you doing?" Zanta had stood to hand her the trousers, but now averted her gaze, as if shy to see Nia undressing.

"Trying on the stupid trousers like you wanted," Nia replied innocently, secretly pleased she was having this effect on the other woman. She shucked off the outer layer of her dress and dropped it to the bottom of the wardrobe. Which disappointingly did not sound hollow when the heap of fabric landed on it. "I can't very well do that with all this nonsense on." She began undoing the ties of the inner skirt.

"Hurry up, then." Was that a slight blush rising to her cheeks? Nia dropped the inner skirt and stepped out of it toward the blushing captain, wearing only her chemise, stays, and underwear.

"Hand them over."

Zanta looked up, startled at Nia's sudden closeness. Her eyes caught first on the freckled tops of Nia's full breasts, half spilling over the top of her stays, then traveled down to her waist and ample hips. Nia took the ridiculous trousers from her and stepped into them, shimmying a bit to fit them over her rounded thighs and buttocks. Zanta hadn't taken her eyes off her, as if mesmerized.

Nia fastened the trousers. They were clearly made for a man, and stretched taut over her thighs and butt where they were supposed to be loose.

"Oh my." Nia's fingertips fluttered delicately to her chest in faux shock, as if she hadn't just stripped to her skivvies in front of Zanta to rile her up. She turned to give Zanta a full view of her round rear straining the fabric. "I fear it will cause a riot if your men catch sight of my ass in these."

This seemed to break Zanta from her spell. She snorted.

"Hardly."

Nia let her eyes go wide and innocent. "No? Is there something wrong with it?"

Zanta rolled her eyes. "Has your ass caused riots before?"

"I wouldn't know." Nia sniffed. "It's always behind me."

Zanta threw her head back and laughed. The kind of full-throated, uninhibited cackle that ripped out when shocked into laughter. The red and orange glass beads in her small braids clinked together, and the fading light refracting through the deck prisms played off the curves of her bare throat.

Fuck it. No use delaying her plans till she was done searching the ship. It always helped to have a backup plan. Nia closed the remaining distance between them, pulled Zanta flush to her half-undressed body and kissed her full on the mouth.

Zanta's laugh cut off abruptly as their lips met, and Nia found herself mourning the loss of it even as Zanta's plush lips parted in a faint gasp, allowing Nia's tongue to slip inside. Zanta melted into her embrace, eyelids fluttering closed. Her lips were soft, though slightly chapped from the wind and sea air, and the interior of her mouth still tasted of the warm and heady spices of dinner. Nia backed her against the wall opposite the open chests and tilted her head to deepen the kiss, her arm tightening around Zanta's waist. Arousal kindled deep in Nia's core, and her hand traced up the side of Zanta's waist to cup her face.

Zanta jolted and pushed her away forcefully, holding her at arm's length by the shoulders. Nia felt the loss of her warm lips like a sudden plunge into cold water after a fleeting moment in the sun. Zanta's eyes were wide, shocked.

"Sorry, I..." Zanta snatched her hands back and rushed from the room, slamming the door behind her.

All Nia could do was stand there. Bewildered. Had she misread Zanta's attraction to her? Or pushed too far too fast? Zanta had returned her kiss at first, so what went wrong? Nia touched her fingertips to her lips, the warm pressure of Zanta's mouth still lingering, arousal simmering in her gut.

Fuck. Nia dragged her palm across her mouth, as if to scrub the feel of Zanta's lips away. She had to be smart about this. If Zanta was willing to flirt but got cold feet in the face of something actually happening, Nia would just have to slow the pace. Draw her out.

That is, if Zanta was still inclined to keep her aboard. She might just decide to drop her at a remote village after all, for her indiscretions.

She grabbed the drab blouse from the wardrobe and pulled it on over her head, then gathered her own dress and the blue one and crept down the hall to her room. She really should go back and help Laurent clean up after dinner, but she suspected her cheeks were red, and she couldn't face any of Laurent's teasing right now.

Nia pulled the blouse off and struggled out of the tight trousers, intending to change back into her own dress. But her gaze slid to the wooden box carved with peach blossoms. Her belly clenched as she remembered the four objects contained within, and the heat in her cheeks deepened. She hadn't had the time or energy to try them yet.

Nia glanced back at the closed door. There was no use going back to the galley, and no one would come looking for her now that it was almost dark. She picked up the wedge of wood she'd been using as a lock and shoved it into the crack beneath the door. What better way to silence her worries than some sensual relief? She ran her fingertips over the wooden blossoms and undid the latch. The four gleaming wooden cocks sat nestled in their bed of peach velvet. Inviting and just begging to be used. Her mouth practically watered as she ran her fingers down the thick girth of the replica of John's cock. Then on to the others, finally ending with Logan's, slightly curved and the perfect size to take the edge off.

Anticipation building, Nia stripped down to her chemise. With only a swinging hammock instead of a bed, Nia took the box and knelt on the floor. She opened the compartment in the lid, finding the velvet straps and a small bottle of the coconut-scented lube that was favored throughout the Islands.

"How thoughtful," Nia murmured to herself, a flush of fondness for the two men warming her. Her offhand comment about missing them at the end of their weeklong romp last autumn had apparently inspired them.

After a brief struggle, Nia managed to fit the wooden cock into the appropriately sized ring and secured the straps around her ankles so that the cock pointed upward. All she would have to do was settle back on her heels for it to penetrate her.

Instead Nia leaned forward and braced one hand against the crates. Her other hand slipped down between her thighs. She was already wet from the kiss with Zanta and the anticipation of new pleasure awaiting her on that gleaming wooden shaft. She found her clit within the wet folds and circled it with soft fingertips. Slowly building up little waves of pleasure. Juices slicking her fingers. Nia closed her eyes, sifting through mental images of her conquests, particularly Logan, with his cherubic face and blond curls.

She wasn't usually one to pleasure herself—having a preference for penetration and no shortage of partners enthusiastic to fulfill her needs—but her fingers quickly found their own rhythm, stroking and teasing and waking up her nerve endings till she was wet and primed. Soft waves of pleasure lapped at her skin.

Without stopping, she uncorked the vial of lube with her other hand and leaned back to drizzle it over the head of the waiting shaft. Her fingers picked up their pace as memories of her one night alone with Logan flashed before her eyes. How he had suddenly become shy again without John there. How he had made her come three times on his tongue alone before she'd become desperate enough to pin him to the bed and impale herself on his leaking member without protection, his slight curve hitting all the right places, and riding him until he was a moaning and whimpering mess. She kissed him to stifle the moans, tasting her own juices slicking his lips. Only when he was about to come did he take charge and flip her onto her back, tongue bringing her to completion once again as his seed safely spurted across the sheets.

Now it was Nia who moaned desperately, rocking back against the wet head of the dildo, the movement of her fingers now sloppy and desperate. She wished they were Logan's shy tongue instead. She groaned in frustration, and abandoned her clit to reach back and position the dildo at her entrance.

Bracing one hand against the crate and guiding the dildo with the other, Nia slowly sank down to impale herself on the wooden member. She groaned as the rounded head penetrated and the shaft slid against her slick walls. It was less pliant than the real thing, so she went slow, missing the warmth of real cock, and the buck of hips between her thighs. But ultimately it didn't matter. With every hard inch that slid into her, her frustration floated further away. Her legs shuddered as her ass hit her heels and she was fully seated on the hard length, her slick insides clenching around the smooth surface. Nia's fingers moved to frame the place where it penetrated her then flicked over her clit again. Her hips stuttered as pleasure climbed up her spine, aided now by the girth filling her.

She gripped the edge of the crate harder to steady herself and rose slowly up on her knees, feeling every smooth ridge of carved vein as the polished wood slid against her insides.

Fuck, it was good. Not as good as a real, living and breathing partner, but delicious all the same.

Nia stopped when only the tip remained inside, her fingers still circling her clit faster and faster. She knew she should be gentle. She wasn't used to using toys on herself, but her nerves were already flushed with pleasure and excitement. She sank back down quickly, a breathy moan escaping as the curve hit her just right.

She set a quick pace, riding the wooden cock with images of riding Logan flashing behind her eyelids. The way he'd whimpered and bucked beneath her, his cheeks and chin still wet from her.

Nia brought her fingers to her mouth, sucking her own sweet and bitter juices from them as if she was tasting them from his lips. She rolled her hips down harder, taking the replica of his cock as deep as possible with every stroke. Her thighs burned with the movement. Euphoria shone through her body like sunlight, and it was not images of Logan or John or one of her many other conquests that came to her mind's eye now, but Splinter Zanta.

Zanta's warm lips on hers. Zanta spread out on a bed beneath her, perky breasts bouncing as Nia fucked her with her fingers...

A plaintive moan escaped Nia's mouth, pleasure rising like the morning sun and scouring away everything but the rapture of that hard length pumping in and out of her and the heady visions of Zanta coming on her fingers. Nia would make Zanta hers. Taste Zanta's sweet nectar and give her pleasures she wouldn't soon forget. At least until Nia found her treasure.

With one last thrust, Nia let out a cry, muffled by her fingers still in her mouth, and buried the dildo deep. Filling. Pleasure suffusing every inch of her. Her upper body collapsed against the crate, her core clenching around the delicious girth.

She wished she had someone to kiss. Someone to pull against her chest so they could listen to her pounding heart. But all she had was herself, and a box of polished wooden cocks to keep her company.

Zanta hurried straight to her quarters, not bothering to stop or answer when Sabriye tried to ask her a question. Her mind was awhirl. The curtains of the alcove the crew used as an altar to La and

Fa—the Yarenen sea serpents that were said to protect sailors—fluttered in Zanta's wake. She slammed the door of her quarters so hard the trinkets on her shelves rattled.

Zanta slumped onto the pile of floor cushions at the center of the room, staring at loose threads sticking out of the fabric that once held beads and shells. Her lips tingled, as if they were still imprinted with Nia's kiss.

Zanta thought she had healed from Emilie's death. She'd hoped that the fact she'd only been with men since then was just a shift in preference, not a symptom of the lingering trauma of holding the love of her life in her arms as she died. Of feeling Emilie's blood pour through her fingers so that they would never quite feel clean again. When Nia had finally acted on their flirtations and kissed her, Zanta's mind had gone pleasantly blank, until Nia cupped her face just like Emilie used to, and the guilt had crashed into her like a tidal wave. As if finally kissing another woman after all these years was a betrayal of the love she and Emilie had shared, and taking pleasure with another woman corrupted the memory of Emilie that she still held nestled like a fragile flame close to her heart.

A knock sounded on the door, and Zanta froze. Anticipation and trepidation both warred in her at the possibility it might be Nia. When she didn't answer right away, Sabriye's voice sounded from the other side of the door.

"Captain? You alright?"

Zanta opened her mouth to say, yes, she was fine, just tired, but nothing came out. She blinked, realizing a tear had slipped down her cheek to cling to her lip. She dashed it away, scrubbing off the imprint of Nia's kiss with it.

"Come in," she called, hoping the slight waver in her voice didn't carry through the door. It opened, revealing the concerned face of her first mate. Sabriye closed the door softly behind her.

"Did something happen?" Sabriye asked. She didn't approach, knowing from their many years of friendship that Zanta wasn't the type of person who craved closeness when she was upset.

"Nothing, just..." Zanta didn't want to tell Sabriye about the kiss. It felt like something she should keep close and secret. Not as close as she held Emilie's memory, but still something just for her. "Something just reminded me of Emilie."

Sabriye's expression softened, but her brow remained furrowed. "Did you hear what I said in the hall?"

"No, what is it?" Zanta patted her cheeks delicately. Making sure no more tears had fallen. It was late, but the job of a captain was never done, even for a pirate.

"We're being followed."

SURE ENOUGH, when Zanta made it to the deck and raised the spyglass to the encroaching night, there were a pair of ships clearly following in the *Monsoon*'s wake. Not close enough to make out their names, but closer than she liked any ship to be that wasn't friend or prey. These two looked suspiciously like they'd broken off from the small fleet that had attacked Roseforte, and that would mean the *Monsoon* herself was the prey.

She lowered the spyglass, and the uncomfortable feeling in her stomach quieted, pushed back in the face of an opportunity to do what she did best: captain her ship.

"How long?"

"Spotted them an hour ago, but they've been closing in, Captain," the lookout said. "Thought we saw them a few days ago too."

So while Zanta had been dallying and exchanging flirtations with Nia, some upstart captains had caught their scent and decided to pursue. Zanta scowled and looked to Sabriye. "Our bearings?"

"Smack-dab between Fontaine Island and Yellow Isle. Heading southwest," Sabriye rattled off.

Two islands in the string of Talvan-controlled lands between Souna and Lasland. Not the worst place to be chased, yet far from ideal. It would take several days to get out from between them and into the Center Sea. From there, they could run south to Yarenen waters where they were more comfortable and could lose their pursuers more easily.

"You said they were gaining on us?" Zanta asked the lookout.

The lookout pursed their lips. "Definitely closer than they were before. Whether they can actually catch us, I'm not sure." If these two ships really were chasing them, Zanta doubted they'd allow her the time to get back to her own familiar hunting grounds. But what else was she to do? It wasn't as if turning to fight was an option either. Two against one.

"Stay the course," she ordered Sabriye. "But put on some speed. Maybe we can put some distance between us and really see if they can catch up."

"Aye, Captain."

It was a solid plan. Not bold but not conservative either. Yet a sour weight settled in Zanta's stomach, a premonition that something had shifted and she was in for a world of trouble she could not yet see.

CHAPTER 12

MAY 6TH, 1668

When Henri was young, he'd thought pirates never cried. They never blubbered, sobbed, or even shed a single tear. Not in his maman's stories, told in front of the bakery oven. Not in the dozens of books he'd read since leaving home, even the romances. His father had never cried, not in front of Henri at least. And maybe other pirates didn't. Maybe they were all unfeeling cutthroats like in the stories.

The crew of the *Siren Song* was different. They were family.

The whole crew had gathered on the deck, gulls wheeling in the blue spring sky, screeching when Nephele swooped near to harry them. The *Sweet Mercy* was departing soon, the rigging in place, sails ready to be unfurled as her newly formed crew said their goodbyes. All around him, people who'd sailed together for years slapped each other on the back, embraced, reminisced, and made plans for the winter when they'd all be reunited on Illusion. No one mentioned that they might not all make it back. That there was always the possibility, even the likelihood, that disaster would strike.

None of the *Siren*'s crew really wanted to leave. But some saw opportunity for a bigger share among a smaller crew, a new adventure which few pirates could resist. And John, now Captain Hakon, needed people he could trust to temper the crew of the former *Sweet Lettie*. Across the water, the crew of the *Kraken* engaged in similar, if less tearful, farewells. Henri spotted the new captain up on the

Mercy's quarterdeck speaking with Doe Adair and the Demon. He still wore his old navy uniform with its mismatched sleeve, but it seemed brighter somehow, less like a vestige of an old life. John shook hands with the Demon, turning to survey his brand new ship, as the Demon crossed over to the *Siren*.

"Henri."

Henri found Gaël grinning tearfully up at him, Fox clinging to his side like a baby opossum.

"Congratulations, again." He clapped Gaël on the shoulder jovially. When Fox had told him Gaël was leaving again, all the protective instinct from Gaël's return in Fox's life had come flooding back. He'd almost made good on his promise to punch Gaël in the face for ever causing Fox pain in the first place. It was only Fox's reassurances that he really was okay that had stayed his hand.

But to be honest, he was still mulling it over.

Fox didn't really look okay at the moment. Henri could tell he was trying to put on a brave face and failing miserably, wearing his heart on the outside as always.

"Thanks." Gaël didn't seem to want to let go of Fox either. His arm was tight around Fox's waist. "I have to go soon, but can I ask you a favor? Will you look after Fox while I'm gone?"

"Does he need looking after?" Henri asked, one eyebrow raised.

"For a little while."

Henri could hear the strain in Gaël's voice, and wondered, not for the first time, why he'd agreed to leave if it was going to cause this much pain.

A sharp whistle split the air, sending the gulls into an annoyed frenzy overhead. The crew started to filter toward the *Sweet Mercy*.

Gaël let out a shaky breath, nodded to Henri, and steered Fox a short distance away. Henri tried not to pry, but he still heard the hitch in Fox's voice.

"Be safe."

Gaël drew Fox tight against his shoulder, murmuring assurances and love in his ear. They stayed like that as the *Mercy*'s crew started the last preparations without their new first mate. Gaël kept his face buried in Fox's wild hair.

When they separated, Gaël kissed him, and Henri looked away, his gaze landing on Robin as if drawn to him. He stood near the knot of conscripts, his dour-faced brother by his side.

"Last chance to tell me to stay," Gaël said to Fox, an attempt at good humor in his tone. Fox murmured something that sounded sarcastic.

Robin noticed Henri looking at him, visibly perking up like a puppy hoping for attention. Henri's heart twisted. He'd been giving Robin the cold shoulder since their fight, despite several attempts at reconciliation on Robin's part. The first night, Henri had slept in a spare hammock in the general crew quarters and woken with a sore back. After that he went to Logan's room, found it curiously empty, and crashed in his bunk. He'd slept there every night since, moving to the spare cot when Logan had come back from wherever he'd been, and only returned to his own room to grab a few things while Robin was out.

Each day when he saw Robin around the ship—even though he was avoiding him, they always seemed to run into each other—he looked more and more wrung out. Like he wasn't sleeping properly. It hurt to know it was because of him, but Henri couldn't bring himself to forgive yet. He knew Robin hadn't told David about them, and David was still acting like all of them were rabid dogs ready to snatch him up at any moment. No doubt he was in Robin's ear every day, poisoning him against the crew, trying to convince him to escape and go home.

Was there even anything to tell anymore? Henri had left in such a huff, and everything felt up in the air, like Nephele had kidnapped their relationship and held it hostage in the sky among the screaming gulls.

Henri shook those thoughts from his head. He might be mad at Robin, but he didn't want to leave him. And judging by the hopeful, sad puppy-dog way Robin looked at him every time, neither did Robin. Henri didn't even really know how they could fix all this. He didn't know anything, really.

Henri dragged his gaze away just as the Demon approached Robin and the small knot of sailors that had been conscripted to the *Siren* crew, most of whom shrank back like the captain was going to rip their faces off with his bare hands. Henri couldn't blame them, the Demon was one scary bastard. The only one of the group who didn't cower before him now was Robin.

Henri looked back over to Gaël and Fox in time for their final embrace, both clinging to the other like a lifeline. What must it be like to grow up with someone as your whole world like that, then be separated? Henri imagined it felt much worse than the chasm that currently stretched between him and Robin.

The two pulled apart.

"Don't get into too much trouble while I'm gone," Gaël said, thumbing Fox's chin affectionately.

"Only if you promise to come back."

"Promise."

Gaël stepped away and, casting one last lingering look at his lover, crossed the gangplank to his new ship. His arrival sparked renewed activity. Gangplanks were pulled, lines cast off, and the *Kraken* and *Siren* drifted away from the *Sweet Mercy*'s sides. Fox whirled, found Henri a few feet away, and tucked himself under Henri's arm.

"You okay?" The *Mercy*'s pristine sails unfurled under Gaël's orders.

A sniffle. "Never better."

"You can still go after him, you know. None of us would begrudge you leaving if it was to be with him." That wasn't entirely the truth. Rowan, Logan, and Henri at least would be heartbroken. Fox was the glue that held them all together.

"And deny you all the radiance of my presence? I'm not cruel," Fox joked, his voice still a bit teary. Henri handed over a piece of honey candy from his pocket without a word, just like the first time they'd met. Fox popped it into his mouth with a huff.

"Still mad at Robin?" he slurred, his tongue dampened by the weight of the sweet.

"Yeah." Henri didn't dare glance Robin's direction. He could feel David's glare creeping across his skin like a sunburn.

The *Mercy*'s crew pulled the planks and mooring lines as the sails filled with the spring breeze.

"Wanna make him jealous?"

Always the sly flirt, even if there was no longer intent behind it.

"I'm sure he's already suffering enough."

The *Sweet Mercy* pulled away, slowly tracking between the white islands. Fox peeked around Henri's body to glare back at David.

"You think so? Want me to dump the brother overboard?"

That was half tempting. "He's Robin's brother," Henri protested.

"I promise to fish him out before he drowns!"

"You're not dumping anyone overboard," Rowan interjected sternly, as he strode up to them. He ran an appraising eye over the pair of them. Fox disheveled and weepy, Henri no doubt looking as miserable and lost as he felt. "You two are a sorry pair. I should give you something to do to distract you."

"We're heartbroken, Captain. Leave us alone." Fox pouted.

"Should've gone with your lover then, shouldn't you?" Rowan said, ruffling Fox's hair. Fox leaned into the touch, and when Rowan tried to take his hand away, Fox snatched it and placed it on his head again. Was he going to be this clingy till Gaël got back? Maybe Henri really would have to keep an eye on him.

Fox pouted more when Rowan pulled his hand back after only one more pat. "Trying to get rid of me, Captain? I'm not that much trouble, am I?" He was putting on his bratty act, but both Henri and Rowan knew him well enough by now to see through it. Rowan's expression softened, and Henri squeezed Fox's shoulder.

"Of course not. What would we do without you? I'm just saying if you want to go with him, we understand." Rowan smiled, crossed scars tugging his cheek.

Fox sniffled. In any other circumstance, he would've offered up another joke, but he looked Rowan dead in the eye and said, "I'm not leaving my home. Not even for him," with all the certainty in his body.

Rowan's smile was as fond as Henri felt. He patted Fox's shoulder where Henri's hand still rested. "Run along and find something useful to do. And *don't* throw anybody overboard."

CHAPTER 13

MAY 6TH, 1668

"Enter," Rowan called, as a timid knock sounded at the door of the captain's quarters aboard the *Kraken's Fury*. Yves finished straightening Rowan's collar. The door opened, admitting David Beckett, his wooden box of paints and brushes tucked under one arm, and a canvas and folded easel under the other. His wide hazel eyes watched them from the threshold for a moment as Yves brushed imaginary dust from the shoulders of Rowan's jacket.

"Honestly, darling. I wish you would wear something more suitable," Yves sighed, but he wasn't really complaining. His gaze was sharp as it roved over his husband, no doubt planning in meticulous detail how he would divest Rowan of every stitch of roguish finery after the painter was gone.

Said painter made a small noise, as if to remind them he was there. Yet when Rowan looked his way, David's face was not flush with fear, as it was every other time one of the pirates talked to him. His expression was shuttered and disapproving, brows pinched together and lips thinned to a line. It was truly uncanny how much he resembled Robin. Though Rowan had never seen such a dour look on the good doctor's face, not even when Henri let Fox get him into mischief that was likely to land him back in the infirmary.

"Shall we begin?" Rowan said. David nodded curtly. He unfolded the easel and settled the canvas onto it. It contained the background of a half-finished portrait David had already been working on before capture. The subject, it seemed, had been hastily and recently scraped away. But Rowan could still see the faint lines of a woman in a burgundy dress on the canvas. Rowan found it fascinating how the amorphous layers of color slowly added up to the broad strokes of human form. The man was talented, despite his seemingly sour nature. Rowan was sure Yves forcing him to cover all his hard work to paint two pirate captains instead didn't add to David's already poor opinion of them. But Yves had been practically giddy at the prospect of having their portrait painted, so Rowan hadn't had the heart to ban him from bullying David into it.

Rowan dropped into the waiting chair, and Yves took up a position standing at Rowan's shoulder after planting a kiss against the short hair on the side of Rowan's head. David's expression soured further, and he mumbled something Rowan didn't catch.

Yves, however, tilted his head inquisitively.

"Care to share that out loud, painter?" he said coolly, annoyance and threat threading his voice.

David flinched, his brush halfway to the canvas with a small blob of black paint on its bristles. Rowan didn't know much about art, but he was fairly sure there should've been some sketching involved before paint went on the canvas. Painting directly over another work probably wasn't the best idea either. He hoped for Robin's sake that David would actually do a good job, or Rowan might not be able to save his brother from destruction at Yves's hands.

David seemed to collect himself after a moment, taking a deep breath as if to shore up his courage. "That's Master Beckett to you," he snapped, voice only wavering slightly. "I was trained at the Art Academy of Yrenmoor."

An amused smile curved Yves's perfect lips. "I call no man master, least of all a mewling pup like you."

David scowled.

"Let's just get this over with," Rowan said placatingly. "I have better things to do than sit here."

David remained where he was, brush poised in the air.

"Start painting, Beckett," Rowan reiterated.

"It's *Master* Beckett," David gritted out.

Yves's amused smile grew. "He also calls no man master...except for me."

That startled a laugh from Rowan, but David flinched again,

nearly dropping his brush. Red heat rose up his neck, and he quickly averted his eyes, mumbling something that sounded like *dirty sodomites*.

Ah, so that was his problem. Rowan suddenly remembered the reason Robin was on his ship in the first place. He'd run away from his bigoted family. It seemed that he was the only apple that had fallen far from the tree.

Yves's hand clenched where it rested on Rowan's shoulder. The amused smirk fell away. Rowan rested a placating hand atop his to soothe whatever murderous intent was boiling up in his chest.

"Just paint," he ordered David.

David's jaw worked as if he wanted to say more, but the paint finally touched the canvas. Tense silence unfolded as David's brush moved softly across it, his eyes flicking back and forth from the pirates to his work. Rowan and Yves remained still, their only movement that of Yves's thumb rubbing over the back of Rowan's shoulder.

Rowan began to grow restless, his legs tingling and neck aching from sitting in the same position too long. He rubbed at his eye, dislodging the eyepatch. A telltale shadow flickered in the corner of his vision.

"Yves..." Rowan said warningly. Yves said nothing. David glanced up at them, then back to his painting. The first cool touch of shadow caressed the back of Rowan's neck, his skin breaking out in goosebumps. The tentacle, still no more substantial than a ghost, spilled over his shoulder into his lap. The tip of it dipped between his legs, caressing his crotch over the laces of his trousers.

Rowan twitched and cleared his throat, hoping that Yves would take the hint and back off. It wasn't as if he could swat the tentacle away in front of David. No one but Rowan and Yves could see it.

David frowned. "Stay still, please."

Rowan nodded and folded his hands in his lap instead of lazily draped over the arm of the chair as they had been, trying to subtly fend off the tentacle's groping.

David let out a deep, put-upon sigh. "Put your arms back where they were, please."

"Maybe we should be done for the day," Rowan suggested.

"If you don't want the portrait, maybe you should let me go," David gritted out.

"Let you go?" Rowan raised an eyebrow. "I don't think you'd survive long on the Teeth." Maybe he should have felt bad for treating Robin's little brother like this, but the young man was absolutely infuriating. David's ears turned bright red, and he set his brush on top of the wooden box with a click.

"Look, I don't know what you have over my brother, but I want to bargain for his freedom." He looked as if he was about to pass out from fear, but he held strong. Rowan opened his mouth to tell David that his brother was, in fact, a free man and if anyone had condemned him to a criminal life, it had been David and his family. But Yves's fingers tightened again on his shoulder.

"Go on," Yves said lazily. "I hope you're not going to offer your painting skills or yourself in his place. Neither are worth our best physician."

David swallowed visibly and took half a step back, as if he thought Yves would leap over the easel and murder him if he said the wrong word.

"I-I know some information. The Ghost Hawk is being hunted."

"Oh? Do tell," Yves said. Only Rowan could hear the strain underlying his voice. The tentacle stopped its teasing.

David's eyes flicked between them.

"Well?" Rowan prompted, sitting forward. It was no secret that he and Yves had the biggest bounties on their heads of all the pirates in the Islands. But if someone in particular was coming after him, it was better to be prepared.

"Give me your word that you'll free Robin."

Their word? Who would trust the word of a pirate? David certainly didn't trust them, so what good would their word do? David seemed to realize this too, and followed up with, "Swear on your ships."

"It depends on the information," Yves said.

"It's worth Robin's freedom," David replied firmly.

"Fine. I swear on the *Siren Song* that he will be free to go," Rowan said. Robin was already free; it cost Rowan nothing to make this promise. And besides, he'd promised nothing about letting David go. It would be something to hold over him later, if the need arose.

David's gaze found Yves, expectant.

"He has no say in what happens with your brother," Rowan said. "I am Robin's captain."

David met his eye for a moment, judging his sincerity.

"I was hired to paint a portrait of the new Kefryean governor, and when you're the hired help, important people tend to think you can't hear them or that you can't understand what they're saying." David grimaced, as if he'd been lower class his whole life instead of the youngest son of a wealthy family.

"Is there a point to this story?" Yves drawled.

David sucked in a breath and snatched up his paintbrush again, clutching it to his chest as if it could protect him from Yves's ire.

"While I was painting, the governor took a meeting with a mercenary, some sort of exiled Kefryean noble and—"

A roaring in Rowan's ears drowned out whatever David said next. An exiled Kefryean noble, now mercenary? It couldn't be...

"What was his name?" Rowan interrupted. He didn't know when he'd gotten to his feet, but he found himself standing. Yves's hand had fallen away from his shoulder.

"I—What?" David blinked.

"What. Was. His. Name," Rowan gritted out.

"The new governor? He's—"

"Not the governor, the mercenary!" Rowan growled, taking a threatening step toward the cowering painter.

"It was..." David paused, wracking his brains to remember. "S-Shaw?"

Fuck.

Rowan's pounding heart dropped into his stomach, acid eating into its poor callused walls. Warrick Shaw, that motherfucking traitor.

It all came rushing back. Warrick's easy smile that had always seemed like he knew some amusing secret. The way he used to be so amenable to whatever Rowan wanted, never giving him any reason to doubt. He'd been Rowan's first mate before Logan, when Rowan was eighteen and a newly minted pirate captain and Warrick was just a year older.

That smile had indeed hidden a secret, but it was not an amusing one.

"Rowan?"

His own name brought him back to the present, and he realized he was breathing hard, staring at David who now cowered against the wall, still clutching his paintbrush. Yves's fingers brushed Rowan's arm.

"You know this Shaw fellow?"

"Yes," Rowan said, his voice curiously flat in his own ears.

Yves frowned and turned back to David. "Tell us what you know. Now."

"I-it's not much," David stuttered. "The Marrans are planning to invade the Sleeping Isles."

As if that wasn't shocking enough on its own. No one had ever tried to invade the Sleeping Isles, a mysterious archipelago north of Kefrye and Nanad. The last bit of unconquered land left before the Marran and Talvan empires would have to set their sights on valuable trade partners. Rowan often wondered what the empires would do once the last acre of land was consumed, whether they would finally turn their sights on each other as they'd wanted all along. He wondered if he would live to see it.

The Sleeping Isles certainly wouldn't be easy to conquer. Next to nothing was known about them due to the impenetrable wall of storms that surrounded them. Even only a few hundred years before, the isles had been more of a myth than a place real enough to put on a map. The only person rumored to have returned from the other side in living memory was the pirate captain, Silver Stroud. And the word of a pirate, of course, could not be trusted.

Rowan realized David had paused, as if waiting for permission to continue. "What do the Sleeping Isles have to do with me?" he asked.

"Shaw thinks you have something that can help them. S-something to do with that legend of Silver Stroud's treasure. His orders are to hunt you down and take whatever it is. You and another pirate... They said she's Yarenen, I think."

A Yarenen pirate who had something to do with Silver Stroud? It could only be Splinter Zanta. But Rowan had nothing to do with Stroud, least of all did he possess a piece of the treasure Stroud had supposedly brought back from the Sleeping Isles. Were there really rumors that Rowan possessed such a thing? Something that could make Marra's invasion of the Sleeping Isles easy? Or was Warrick Shaw taking an opportunity to finish what he'd started all those years ago, and finally take back his *rightful place* in Kefryean high society?

Silence unfurled. Words stuck in Rowan's mouth, weighing down his tongue while his mind raced through the possibilities and angles. He hadn't seen Warrick in nine years, but he knew his reputation as a mercenary.

For a few years, Rowan had heard nothing about the man and thought himself rid of the traitor for good. But Warrick had been in the Marran Empire's pocket ever since the war. He'd popped back up again with a small force of thugs behind him, putting down any fledgling rebellions and doing the dirty work the empire didn't want on the books. He had a reputation for not sparing those he deemed guilty, and didn't much care for evidence that contradicted his agenda. Rowan might be a pirate, but as far as he could tell, it was Warrick who had no morals. If Rowan and Zanta were now the ones in his sights, they were in grave danger.

Yves's hand tightened on Rowan's arm, grounding him.

"Is that all?" Yves asked David.

"Yes. I was dismissed for the day when Shaw took out some papers. I didn't hear any more."

"Then leave us."

David fled, leaving his supplies, and the barely started painting, behind.

"Rowan." Yves's deep voice quieted some of Rowan's frantic thoughts. "Are you alright?"

"We need to call a meeting."

Logan, Yves's new first mate, Doe Adair, and Fox—who'd been unreasonably clingy to whomever he could get his hands on since the *Mercy*'s departure that morning—gathered around the large table in Yves's stateroom. They were silent, sensing the oppressive mood between the two captains.

"We've had some news," Yves announced, when they were all seated. "There seems to be a new pirate hunter on the prowl, and he's coming for Rowan."

Rowan had told Yves nothing further about Warrick Shaw or their history together. He wasn't sure how Yves would react, but as they'd waited for the others to assemble, things had clicked into place in Rowan's mind.

"It's Warrick Shaw," Rowan said, his gaze locking onto Logan.

Both Logan and Fox sat up straight, as if a ramrod had been shoved down their spines. As the *Siren*'s longest serving crew members, both of them knew what had happened with Warrick. And Logan himself had been there to pick up the pieces of Rowan afterward.

"Warrick? You're sure?" Logan asked, his eyes trained on Rowan's face to gauge his mood.

"That's what we've heard," Rowan confirmed.

"From who?" Doe asked. She sat with her arms crossed over her chest, brown hair swept out of her face with a shell comb.

"The painter," Yves answered. "He overheard a conversation between the new Kefryean governor and Shaw. How do you know him, Rowan?"

"I—" Rowan's tongue still felt leaden. Maybe he should've explained it all while they'd waited for the others and saved himself the embarrassment of doing it in front of them.

"He used to be Rowan's first mate before me," Logan answered for him. All eyes swiveled in his direction.

Warrick had been more than Rowan's first mate. He'd been so many firsts. His first friend onboard the *Siren Song*, back when it was still a merchant vessel. He'd been instrumental in Rowan's hare-brained scheme to steal the ship out from under its bastard captain. Back then, Rowan had known nothing of Warrick's past, but they'd trusted each other. Or so Rowan had thought.

After months of sailing up and down the coast causing trouble and earning a tidy little bounty on his head, Rowan had sailed the newly renamed *Siren Song* to the eastern coast of Marra to collect Logan after he was finally discharged from the navy. Logan and Warrick didn't get along, but Rowan was just happy to have his two best friends by his side. As it turned out, Logan was a much better judge of character than Rowan.

Before that season was up, Warrick claimed another first for himself. He'd kissed Rowan one night out on the bowsprit. It wasn't Rowan's first kiss, but it was the first time he'd let it go further. Rowan thought he was falling in love, and in the months that followed, he only sank deeper.

Until Warrick, armed with Rowan's blind trust and adoration, led the *Siren* into an ambush. He was not a poor sailor turned pirate at all, but a Kefryean noble in exile. Cast out from his homeland for patricide. He wanted that status back, and he handed Rowan over to the Marran navy to get it.

Rowan, Logan, and the *Siren Song* had barely made it out alive, with only a handful of crew members. They'd limped into the middle of the Broken Sea. Rowan had spent days scrubbing the bloodstains from the deck, and longer nursing a broken heart.

Yves watched Rowan as Logan explained it all, leaving out Rowan's romantic entanglement. Yves must've known there was more to it. Suspicion sparked in his eyes, a slight downturn to his plush lips. Rowan needed to tell him.

"He's my ex-lover," Rowan said flatly, after Logan had finished his tale. He felt almost compelled to say it, as if he was confessing a sin. Yves's attention sharpened in the air around him. The others felt it too, shifting uncomfortably in their seats. Doe's nose, dotted with the typical Laslandish freckles, scrunched in distaste.

"He seduced you before turning you in?" Her voice was soft, almost motherly, in contrast to the wicked-looking knives strapped to her belt.

"More or less. He's the reason I don't sleep with my crew members."

"Besides Fox," Logan quipped, in an attempt to lighten the mood.

"What!" Yves, Rowan, and Fox all shouted simultaneously. Rowan and Yves in disbelief and horror. Fox with barely contained delight.

Logan blinked rapidly in confusion. "After Warrick left, we recruited Fox in Wave Harbor. I saw him sneak into your room half dressed, and he didn't come out till morning, so I thought he was... your...rebound." The words slowed at the end of the sentence as Logan realized he was just digging all of them into a deeper hole.

"Is that what you thought this whole time?" Rowan asked in disbelief. Yves was too quiet, and Rowan didn't want to look at his face for fear of what he would find. Of course both of them had had flings and lovers before they met, but all these revelations coming to light at once seemed like a recipe for disaster. Rowan knew if he ever met one of Yves's former lovers he would not be able to conceal his jealousy.

Fox's bright cackle split the tension like an overripe melon. He bent double in his seat, clutching his belly as uncontrollable laughter spilled from his lips.

"I mean I *did* sleep in Rowan's bed that night," Fox said, when he regained enough control to speak again. Yves's expression darkened, fists clenched, staring daggers at Fox as if he could barely keep from throttling him. Rowan grabbed his wrist.

"Unfortunately," Fox continued, either oblivious to or ignoring Yves's violent aura, "Rowan already had that pesky rule. He slept in a chair." Yves's tense muscles loosened, but his scowl remained fixed on Fox as he wiped a tear from his eye and dissolved once more into breathless giggles. "Gods...I think I'm dying."

Logan patted him on the back with his wooden hand, a small smile cracked across his lips. Doe looked on with a confused yet gentle expression, as if she wanted to pick Fox up and rock him like a baby. Rowan felt a fond smile spread across his own lips.

"You boys are a right mess. No wonder John hightailed it out of here at the first opportunity," Doe said lightly, as Fox's giggles finally faded. "I wonder if we can get back to the matter at hand?"

"Right." Rowan released Yves and stepped up to the table, placing his fingertips on its polished surface. "It's not just me that Warrick is coming after. He's hunting Splinter Zanta too. He seems to think that both of us have something from Silver Stroud's treasure that can help Marra conquer the Sleeping Isles."

"The Sleeping Isles?" Logan raised a skeptical brow.

"So you don't have what they're looking for?" Doe asked.

"Not that I know of. Though I can't say the same for Zanta. She's the one who killed Stroud after all."

"What's the play here, Captain? We definitely shouldn't hang around here much longer," Logan said.

Rowan was acutely aware that their current location in the Teeth was alarmingly close to the coast of Kefrye. Whatever their plan, sitting like a tasty morsel waiting to be gobbled up was not an option.

"Obviously you will return to Illusion and lie low." It was the first thing Yves had said since the revelations about Warrick. His presence remained heavy at Rowan's shoulder.

Rowan frowned. "We'd lose out on the whole season. Maybe longer. I won't turn tail and run based on a rumor."

Yves met his eye and held it. Their previous conversation about their futures and deaths came back to him alongside the memories of their fight a year and a half ago. *I won't be kept,* he'd said, before fleeing Illusion. He was a pirate, and a captain; cowering in the face of adversity was not an option. He didn't have it in him to hide.

Rowan broke Yves's gaze. "I think we should warn Zanta."

"And why would we do that?" Yves scoffed.

"Because she's our friend."

"It's a risk," Logan chimed in, voice soothing as always. "But she usually sails in the south, so at least it would get us away from Kefrye and the empire."

"And present one target for Shaw instead of two," Yves hissed. Rowan could feel Yves's anger building with every moment, like a storm on the horizon. The others watched them intently, curious to see how things would play out.

"Maybe you two should discuss this privately," Doe said. She stood without waiting for the captains to reply, and gave Logan and Fox a meaningful look. "Shall we?"

"I, for one, vote for Zanta. She's nice, and it sounds more fun," Fox said, as he followed Logan toward the door.

The three of them exited the room, Fox chatting excitedly at Doe about where in Lasland she was from.

Alone again, Yves stared at Rowan, seething. "You cannot go on a wild goose chase all over the Islands just to warn that woman," Yves said, clearly barely keeping his anger contained.

"*That woman* is my friend," Rowan retorted, his own irritation quickly descending to the same level as Yves's. Old feelings and old fights swirled between them like a whirlpool. "You would have me run and hide like a coward while people I care about are in trouble? Is that the sort of man I am?"

"You *promised* you would be careful," Yves growled.

"And I will be. But you're not going to ship me back to Illusion like a wayward child!"

Yves stepped close, aura threatening and oppressive. "You're a softhearted fool."

That was rich coming from him. He'd keep Rowan tucked safe and sound at home like a housewife if he could, even knowing that pirating was the only life Rowan had ever found joy in. Who was more of a fool? Yves for thinking Rowan would just accept subjugation? Or Rowan for still loving this controlling asshole?

"You're lucky I'm softhearted, and you're just as much a fool as me. If it were not so, we'd still be at each other's throats instead of in each other's beds. And this—" He pulled the gem-studded wedding ring from his finger and held it up before Yves's face. He knew it was a mistake by the way Yves's expression shifted, and the way his hand suddenly felt much too light. But he'd still done it. Anger spurred him on. "This would still be on the hand of whatever unfortunate sod you stole it off of."

The cool, suffocating embrace of the shadow tentacles enveloped him. Yves leaned close, glaring down his long nose. So close, but he did not touch. Fury edged his beautiful features. "And how I still long to set my teeth at your throat. To keep you chained to my bed, out of danger. But that is not what we're discussing."

"You've got some nerve falling in love with a fool, then scolding him for being one," Rowan said bitterly. He could not deny that Yves's words sent a shiver of fear down his spine.

He still caught Yves watching him hungrily sometimes. Not the hunger of lust—though that was ever present—but a hunger that filled Rowan's mind with images of being dragged to some deep underwater cave to be devoured whole.

Was Yves's possessiveness because he truly wished to protect Rowan? Or did he want to be the one who ultimately destroyed him?

"I will not stand by and let you put yourself in needless danger."

"Let me?" Rowan laughed mirthlessly. "You're not my keeper." It sounded petulant, and they both knew it. "I'm going south to warn her. You can come with me or go your own way, but you won't stop me."

Yves remained silent, simply gazing at Rowan with an unreadable expression. Was he hurt? Furious? Rowan truly couldn't tell, and the longer the silence stretched, the deeper the well of his own anger sank.

He grabbed Yves's hand and placed the ring in his palm, never breaking eye contact.

"I'm going. Follow or don't. I don't care." He brushed past, shoulder knocking into Yves. He slammed the door behind him and didn't look back.

He ran straight into Logan, Doe, and Fox milling about.

"We're leaving," he snarled, pushing past them. Logan fell into step beside him without missing a beat, and after saying goodbye to Doe, Fox followed.

"Going back to the *Siren* leaving, or...?" Logan asked.

"*Leaving*, leaving. We're going after Zanta, and I don't give a damn what Yves decides to do." Maybe that was too much information. He was too angry. He couldn't even remember if the tides were right at this time of day so they *could* leave.

"Maybe you should talk a bit more?" Fox chimed in. They'd made it to the *Siren*. Many of the crew members watched Rowan warily as he stomped across the deck, trailed by his closest confidants. Maybe he should heed Fox's advice, but he knew if he wavered Yves might charm him into compliance. Rowan didn't consider himself a weak man, but he was weak for his husband, and in this case, he needed to stay the course.

"We talked. This is what I decided. Ready the *Siren* to sail before nightfall."

PART 2

THE KEY

CHAPTER 14

MAY 6TH, 1668

The moon had long since reached its peak by the time Fox finally returned to his cabin. Most of the other crew members had gone to bed near dusk, exhausted by their hasty departure from the Teeth, but Fox had stayed up to play dice with the night watch. He wasn't tired—he didn't *want* to be tired. Restlessness skittered under his skin like beetles, and he knew without the distraction of company it would only get worse as the night wore on. Finally though, after Fox had won a dozen coppers off them, the watchmen had kicked him out of the game and he had nothing else to do but go back to his room and try to get some sleep.

His empty, cold room.

Fox slumped against the door. He'd shared a room with Logan for almost six years until he and Gaël had reunited. Now he was alone. His room, his home, looked empty without Gaël and his things.

A small well of emptiness settled into the pit of his stomach.

It was only the first night without Gaël here. How was he supposed to do this till winter? Maybe forever, if they ran into trouble—which was likely. Fox pressed the heels of his hands against his eyes, trying to smother the anxiety that threatened to crumble his edges. He couldn't think of the possibility of never seeing Gaël again. Of Gaël being taken away from him. In this line of work, there was always the chance they'd die before their time, but the thought that they might not be together when it happened, that Fox might never know what had happened if Gaël failed to return, would be too much to bear.

He had to stop. He had to figure out how to live normally without Gaël.

Fox pushed off the door, yanked his shirt off over his head, and toed his boots into the corner. He'd stayed up way too late trying to stave off the loneliness that was now settling in for the long haul. Fox collapsed onto the bed. He should just sleep. You couldn't be lonely or anxious if you were unconscious, right?

Fox curled up beneath the blankets, clutching the pillow close to his chest, and nestled his face into Gaël's scent. Gaël always teased that Fox slept like his namesake, a fox kit all curled up into a tiny ball to avoid being seen, an old habit from their childhood on the streets. The same habit that compelled Gaël to always sleep with Fox in his arms.

He should have said yes when Gaël asked him to go with him. Or, no, that wasn't right either. Fox couldn't stand the thought of being apart again, but he couldn't bear to leave the *Siren Song* either. There was no right answer. Either they were together and one of them was not where they wanted to be, or they were apart and miserable.

Fox hugged the pillow closer. His throat felt tight, but he was determined not to cry. He'd already wasted so many tears on Gaël. Besides, this time it wasn't forever. This time he'd given his blessing and knew Gaël loved him.

So why did he feel so alone?

Anxiety kindled in Fox's gut. He was pathetic. Not even able to spend one singular night alone. He'd assured Gaël that he wouldn't have to use the generous offer of *fulfilling his needs elsewhere* while Gaël was gone, but here he was craving physical affection like a parched man surrounded by salt water. And Gaël's warm scent on the sheets wasn't helping matters.

Last time he'd been alone, it was hell.

Fox rolled out of bed and knelt in front of his sea chest. He dug around in the dark till his fingers landed on what he was looking for: two lengths of old braided leather. The bracelet Gaël had made for him when they were kids, and the one Gaël had left behind when he ran away. Fox had kept them all this time, buried deep under his other possessions. Gaël didn't know Fox still had them.

After Gaël had abandoned him, Fox had kept wearing the bracelet. As painful as it was to carry around a reminder that Gaël had left him, it pained him even more to pretend Gaël had never been with him in the first place, that he'd always been alone. It was only after Rowan and Logan took Fox in, and he began to feel at home on the *Siren Song*, that he'd had the courage to take the bracelet off and stow it in his chest. He hadn't worn it in all the intervening years. He hadn't needed it.

But now he did.

Fox sat back on his heels, looking down at the two short lengths of leather side by side in his hands. The bracelets had been tight even back then on their skinny, half-starved wrists. All these years later, Fox was well-fed and muscled. There was no way the bracelet would fit. He contemplated them for a moment. Then began to pick apart the braided ends. The once soft leather creaked quietly as he unwound the strands, now stiff with salt and age. Once he was satisfied, he wound the two bracelets together end to end, interweaving the strands of Gaël's bracelet and his own to make one that would fit the man he was now. Fox slipped it around his wrist, and tied it tight.

Some of the anxiety quelled as the bracelets enclosed his wrist. But it wasn't enough, this symbol that they belonged together. The loneliness still remained.

Fox stumbled through the dark to the door. He didn't bother to put on his shirt or boots. He wouldn't need them.

His feet slapped against the floorboards as he made his way down the hall. Memory crept along at his heels like a friendly cat. His first night on board the *Siren Song* a year after Gaël had abandoned him, bruised and stabbed from a street fight, stitched up and taken in by Rowan and Logan and their scrappy little crew. Then being suddenly left alone, and succumbing to the swirling horror that was his own company without another person to distract him. He'd made this journey that night too. Same anxiety, same loneliness, same destination.

The door at the end of the hall wasn't locked. It rarely was.

"Captain?" Fox shut the door quietly behind him. Rowan probably wasn't his best option for a late night visit, but Fox's feet had carried him where they wanted. He scanned the room, dark but for the silver moonlight slanting through the windows above the bed.

"Rowan?" Fox said again, his voice quiet, almost shy. He ventured a few more steps into the room.

Rowan's slumbering figure shifted, one hand slipping beneath the pillow where he kept a knife, grumbling something Fox couldn't make out. Then he seemed to come awake a bit more.

"Fox? What is it?" Rowan's voice was rough and laden with sleep.

"I, um..." Now that he was here, he didn't know what to say. Anxiety constricted around his throat.

Rowan shifted again, eyes still closed. The moonlight fell across his messy blond hair, turning it white. He sleepily stuck an arm out of the nest of blankets and gestured Fox closer. Fox obeyed, stopping next to the side of the bed to look down at his captain.

"Um..." Fox scratched the back of his neck. His first night aboard the *Siren*, he'd tried to seduce Rowan, thinking sex was all he was good for. But Rowan had scolded him, told him he was worth more, that he didn't owe anyone access to his body. And when Fox had cried from shame and relief both, they'd played cards till Fox fell asleep. Rowan had carried him to this very bed and tucked him in. Rowan spent the night on an uncomfortable wooden chair, and it had been the first time Fox had felt safe since Gaël left him.

Now, Rowan flapped his hand at Fox again, still not opening his eyes.

"You miss him, right?" he mumbled, voice still heavy. "You don't wanna sleep by yourself?"

"Y-yeah..." Sometimes Rowan could be shockingly astute, and gentle. If Fox had had someone like him all along, maybe he wouldn't have turned out the way he did.

Rowan's eyes slitted open, one blue and one milky green, gleaming in the moonlight.

"Get in here then," Rowan sighed sleepily, moving the blankets aside.

Tears pricked at the back of Fox's eyes. He'd half expected to be scolded again, and planned to try Logan's room next. But now, in the silvered darkness of Rowan's cabin, some of the loneliness and anxiety dissipated.

Fox climbed into the bed and tucked himself under Rowan's arm. Nephele chirred sleepily from her perch in the corner as the two men settled under the covers. Rowan propped his chin on top of Fox's head and slowly petted his long hair. Fox sighed contentedly, nuzzling into the hollow of Rowan's neck.

"No funny business, okay?" Rowan joked.

Fox nodded in agreement. Rowan's fingers brushing along his scalp were already lulling him into sleep.

"Is the Demon going to kill me for sneaking into his husband's bed?" Fox murmured.

Rowan's chuckle reverberated through Fox's body.

"I won't let him."

CHAPTER 15

MAY 12TH, 1668

The sun was setting, long and slow, casting pink and orange light across the deck that fetched up against Nia's bare feet as she drummed them on the boards.

"Ha! Read 'em and weep!" She slapped her cards, a nine, ten, and fool of rubies, down on the top of the crate they were using as a table, then reached across to collect her winnings.

"Not so fast, missy." Laurent smacked her hand away from the little pile of coins and trinkets, and spread his own cards out like a fan, displaying them for all to see. A queen of hearts. A fool of hearts. And a king of hearts.

Shit. It didn't matter how good Nia's hand was, nothing could trump that. She groaned and rolled her eyes skyward as Laurent cackled and collected his prize.

"You celebrated too soon, chaton, nothing can beat a fool between a king and a queen," Laurent boasted. The other three pirates at the table, two men and a woman, chuckled at Nia's pout. But it was all good-natured fun. The money she was gambling with wasn't even hers. Laurent had given it to her so she wouldn't be left out of the game. It was only right he should win it back with the sheer force of his luck.

She'd become even closer with Laurent in her short time under his tutelage in the galley. He could be scatterbrained at times. Sometimes forgetting what he was about to say, or walking into the larder only to come out with a completely different ingredient than he'd gone in for. But he was a dab hand at cooking. Better even than Madame Durand, who was known throughout their neighborhood in Roseforte for her hearty, warming food. Laurent could've been a star if he worked on land instead of on a pirate ship. A darling of whatever culinary scene he set his sights on. Even if he did get caught up exchanging raunchy stories with Nia and sometimes burned the flatbread.

One of the men collected the cards and began to shuffle them. Nia pouted. She was completely out of money after only a few hands, most of which Laurent had gleefully won. She would've suspected him of cheating if his sleeves weren't rolled up to his elbows.

Noticing Nia's fake sulking, Laurent leaned forward and tweaked her nose.

"Don't be so heartbroken! You can still play. Right, friends?" He looked around at the others who nodded gamely. Laurent plucked a few coppers from the hefty pile in front of him and gave them to her.

Nia perked up. "Oh you're so good to me," she crooned, overly flirtatious. "We should run away and get married. You would make the best wife."

The corners of Laurent's eyes crinkled with amusement. "Alas, my fair lass, I'm saving my wifeliness for the right man. You don't have the equipment for the job."

Technically, she did. She had four of them sitting tidily in a bed of velvet in a box in her room. But she didn't tell Laurent that; it would only raise questions she wasn't prepared to answer.

"If I did, I'd marry you in a second, Laurent," Nia said, as the new hand of cards was doled out.

"Same," the other woman—a carpenter, by the sawdust dusting her hair—agreed. "Your fried sardines are to die for." She elbowed the card dealer. "You've got the right equipment, Colm. Quite impressive, from what I've seen. Think you could make an honest man of him?"

Colm, a big blond Laslandishman, blushed beneath his sunburn. The next card he dealt flipped face up, revealing the fool of hearts again. The whole group burst into uproarious laughter as he sputtered something Nia didn't catch. Laurent retrieved the card and handed it back to him with a wicked grin, the sunset casting blushing light on his face as well.

They settled into a merry mood as the game restarted. Nia had terrible cards and only bet a copper before bowing out to watch. She didn't miss the shy glances Colm now cast Laurent's way, nor that Laurent seemed to be returning them with his typical flirtatiousness.

Perhaps she'd have some juicy gossip to wheedle out of him come morning.

The sunset lingered, as if it wanted to bathe their little pocket of ribald joy in its light for a few moments longer. Nia hitched her skirts up to her knees and leaned back on her hands on the deck as the rest of the hand played out, enjoying the cool evening breeze.

No one jumped to attention when Splinter Zanta appeared on deck. The crew of the *Monsoon* was small and tight knit. They followed their captain's orders with practiced efficiency when they needed to, and most of them seemed utterly devoted to her, but they also knew when to relax. Nia's gaze tracked Zanta as she mounted the quarterdeck steps and had a quiet word with the helmsman.

They were being followed, everyone on board knew it, and for the first few days there had been a current of tension running beneath everything they'd done. The ships hadn't approached enough to get a good look at them or explain their intentions. Neither flew a flag, so they likely weren't military. But both were bigger than the *Monsoon*, and that meant trouble no matter which way you sliced it. Any number of people had reason to follow a pirate ship. Maybe they'd followed all the way from Roseforte, and were waiting for the perfect time to strike.

But now there was an air of hope about the crew, the tension dissipating like foam on the waves. Their pursuers had fallen back overnight, barely visible even with a spyglass, and it felt like Nia could breathe again.

Still, Zanta looked worried. Her thick brows knit tightly together as she surveyed the deck. When her gaze landed on Nia, warmth spread through Nia's body, and she pushed her chest out just a little more, showing off her assets to better effect, despite the drab dress covering them. Zanta had been avoiding her since the kiss in the clothing storeroom. Nia couldn't say she blamed her. Nia had come on a bit strong. She needed to ease into it more. Get some more flirting under her belt before making another move. It would be difficult. Nia wasn't used to rejection. Nor was she practiced in the art of subtlety. She was used to tumbling into bed with whomever happened to catch her fancy.

No matter. She enjoyed a challenge, and this really was her only option. Taking advantage of Zanta's cold shoulder, she'd used the time to search the rest of the ship, and found nothing relating to her treasure, not even in the several hidden compartments that were obscured by clever carpentry.

She would get into the captain's quarters. No matter what. And there was no time like the present to get started.

"Captain!" Nia affected a bright chirpy tone and waved Zanta over. "Come play with us! We need someone with enough skill to beat Laurent."

All the heads around the card game turned in Zanta's direction. Laurent snorted. "I don't think she's the one you want if you're looking to end my reign of tyranny," he said blandly, pushing a few more coins into the pile at the center.

"It's true. Our captain is shit at cards," confirmed the third man, a deckhand, eyeing his own cards skeptically.

"Nonsense!" Nia sprang up, and before any of them, least of all Zanta, could stop her, she bounded up the steps and threaded her arm through Zanta's. "Come, Captain, we can be a team."

Stunned, Zanta allowed herself to be tugged over to the group. Laurent scooted over to make room for them on the deck, and soon Zanta was sitting cross-legged between them, the puff of Nia's skirt touching her knee. Nia made a show of eyeing her own meager pile of coins. Then divided them up between her and Zanta, two coppers each.

Zanta raised her eyebrows. "Oh, I see now, you wanted to be a team because you're broker than a sailor in a brothel."

Laurent and the others laughed.

"Sailor in a brothel at least has something to show for it," Nia said sulkily. That earned a twitch of a smile from Zanta. Nia allowed herself to gaze at her lips a moment before looking away. The hand of cards finished up. This time with Colm taking the pot, though Nia suspected Laurent had gone easy on him. The carpenter shuffled this time.

"So are you two gonna be a team or not?" Laurent asked.

"Yes," Nia said, at the same time Zanta said, "No."

"What?" Nia was scandalized. "But I invited you into the game!"

"You're just using me for my potential money," Zanta laughed, easing into the banter.

"Well, are you gonna shell out or not?"

"Not," Zanta said firmly, her brown eyes glittering.

"I want my two coppers back," Nia sniffed. Zanta handed them over, then dug in her belt purse for coin of her own. The cards were dealt, and once again, Nia had a shit hand. She frowned.

"You don't have a very good card-playing face," Colm pointed out.

"I have a good face, overall," Nia protested. "I don't need to be good at cards."

"Weren't you a tavern maid?" Laurent chimed in. Nia stuck her tongue out at him and pushed two coppers into the pot.

"I was more of a 'kiss dice for good luck' type of tavern maid," she said primly. "One has no need for gambling when one is gainfully and *legally* employed." The others rolled their eyes.

Jovial banter accompanied the slide of cards and clink of coin, and in two more hands, Nia was flat broke again.

"Ah, I have no luck!" she lamented, rocking to the side and purposely letting her knee knock into Zanta's. The sun had dipped below the horizon by now, bathing the ship in dusky twilight and orange lamp glow.

"Guess you can't play anymore," Laurent said breezily, shuffling the cards in a bridge between his fingers. "No worries. The captain will take your place."

Nia pouted. Not playing would certainly give her more leeway to flirt with Zanta, but a better idea presented itself.

"I still want to, so why don't we make the game more interesting?"

Laurent's ears practically pricked up like a cat's at her mischievous tone. "Oh? Do tell, chaton."

"Alas, I have no money." Nia swooned toward Zanta, almost, but not quite, resting her head on her shoulder. Nia covered her eyes with the back of her hand, dramatic as a stage actor. When she uncovered them, she met Zanta's gaze directly. "But I do have clothes."

Zanta's eyebrows twitched ever so slightly. Laurent laughed again, loud and bawdy.

"Brilliant! Every round we can bet a piece of clothing, and whoever has the lowest hand, strips."

"Exactly!" Nia sat up, her fake swoon forgotten. She looked around the circle. Colm was blushing again, but the carpenter and deckhand seemed game. Zanta had an amused quirk to her kissable lips. "What say you, Captain?"

She didn't miss the way Zanta's gaze subtly traced her curves beneath the drab dress. "Aye, I'm game."

Nia clapped with glee.

"No fair, Nia's got on more layers than any of us," Colm protested, though he wasn't looking at her. His eyes had drifted back to Laurent.

"What I lack in coin I make up for in petticoats." Nia winked. "I'd be happy to take off a few layers to make it even, big boy." Colm's eyes snapped back to her, his blush deepening. Nia wondered if he was even sunburned at all, or if the pinkness on his nose and cheeks was a permanent aftereffect of all this blushing.

"No need for anyone to preemptively strip," the deckhand said, dealing out the cards. "Judging by the last few rounds, we'll all get an eyeful of Nia soon enough."

"Cur!" Nia exclaimed, leaning forward to whack him playfully on the arm, making sure Zanta got a full view of her backside in the process.

When she settled back in and picked up her cards, she made sure to let a brief flicker of disappointment cross her face, even though they weren't so bad.

"See?" The deckhand smirked.

"What's everyone betting this round?" Nia asked.

They went around the table, each declaring an item of clothing to bet. A hat, a belt, a neckerchief. Zanta bet her waist sash, and it finally got to Nia.

"My bodice," she declared. She might be wearing more layers than the rest of them, but the downside to a dress was that there was no need for a belt or anything of that nature. Hell, she wasn't even wearing shoes.

Laurent narrowed his eyes at her. "Now I can't tell if you have a good hand or a bad one."

Nia smirked. "I guess you'll have to see."

She did, of course, lose. Colm, in a stroke of modest luck, won. Nia undid the fastenings of her blouse, her breasts bouncing free of the musty fabric. She felt Zanta's eyes—as well as those of Colm and the deckhand—on her, and smirked.

In several more hands, Laurent was fully clothed but for one boot, Colm was shirtless, the other two were missing various belts and hats, Zanta had only lost her sash and one boot, and Nia—having decided she quite liked losing this game—was down to her chemise, underthings, and stays.

"You'll be naked before long," Zanta teased, nudging her arm.

"I'll get my revenge yet. The lot of you won't know what hit you when your dicks are swinging in the wind!" Nia declared. Another hand was dealt, and this time it was quite good.

Just then, a noise came from the crow's nest, and the lookout swung down from the ratlines. "Captain, we've got a problem." His expression was grim.

Zanta was already pulling on her boot. "Talk."

"There's a blockade ahead."

Fuck. They all scrambled to dress as the lookout explained. "I thought we might be headed for land at first, but it's bow lights. There's at least a dozen that I can see."

Zanta retrieved a spyglass from the helmsman, who'd previously been watching their game with amusement, and trained it in the direction the lookout indicated. She swore under her breath in Yarenen. Nia and the others crowded around. But they couldn't see much in the dark.

"Could you tell what nation they are?" Zanta asked.

The lookout grimaced. "My best guess? The Talvans are defending their waters after the attack at Roseforte."

"Seems likely." Zanta kept her eye trained on the dark horizon which bled into the sky. A faint breeze kicked up, ruffling her loose shirt. "And if that's the case, we aren't getting back to Yarene anytime soon."

"What should we do, Captain?" the helmsman asked.

Zanta swung the spyglass in the other direction. "We can try to run it, but seeing as our friends are still hanging back, I say we turn around and head north. No use getting caught between a rock and a hard place when we have all that open sea to our backs."

"Aye, Captain."

And just like that, the jovial mood shifted, each one of them reminded that they were outlaws, and they were being hunted.

CHAPTER 16

MAY 14TH, 1668

"Watch out!"

Henri shielded his face with his arm as Fox ran and leapt into the blue waters next to him. It did almost nothing to prevent the resulting tidal wave from slapping Henri in the face. It was a rare hot day, the days before still battling between late spring and early summer. And it was perfect. Henri splashed Fox as he resurfaced, sputtering and grinning.

"Did I get you? Sorry." Fox didn't seem sorry at all. He'd aimed his jump to land directly next to Henri. He was still sticking close to Henri, Rowan, and Logan ever since the *Sweet Mercy* had departed with Gaël on board, but had been especially clingy to Henri since Henri and Robin weren't exactly on speaking terms at the moment.

"Of course you got me, you rat bastard." Henri splashed him again, but he couldn't help but grin back. Around them in the water, several other crew members who'd rowed out to the rocky outcropping and its shallow sandbar were laughing and chatting while they rubbed sand into their skin before soaping up their bodies, washing away the grime of the past few days. None of them had gotten a proper bath since leaving the Teeth, only able to scrub themselves down with soapy rags and dump buckets of water over their heads. But today, the heat, the sun, and the sandbar made the perfect day for sea bathing. It would probably be their last chance till they reached proper land again.

Henri ducked low in the water, so only his neck and head were above the gently lapping waves. He quite enjoyed sea bathing, even if he wasn't looking forward to washing the salt out of his hair later. He scooped up a handful of fine sand and scrubbed it over his arms and shoulders, as Fox did the same.

"Where's Robin today?" Fox asked in that innocently searching way he had when he was sniffing for gossip.

Henri grimaced. "Probably with his brother."

"Sea bathing too homosexual for them?"

"Probably," Henri snorted. He cast a glance at the other crew members sitting around them, all of them stark naked regardless of gender, their clothes tucked safely into the beached rowboats. He didn't want to think about the kinds of things David was whispering in Robin's ears these days. David was rude to everyone, refused to do the work assigned to him—or did it so badly Rowan didn't dare assign him those tasks again—and it was isolating Robin by association. Every time Henri saw Robin around the ship, he had David at his elbow like a guard dog. Robin didn't even perk up when he saw Henri anymore. He looked lonely, and Henri wanted to go to him and make up. But he couldn't quite bring himself to do it just yet. Robin was still hiding him, and letting David terrorize them all with his bad attitude on top of that.

"Pity, David could use a good wash," Fox quipped, earning another snort from Henri. It was true. Every time David said or did something rude and Rowan got wind of it, he assigned David to duty on the bilge pump. Which essentially involved standing in a foot of fetid, brackish water and turning a crank to pump the water out of the bowels of the ship. It was smelly, back-breaking work, but instead of subduing him, it had only made David hate them even more.

"When are you gonna make up?" Fox asked, accepting a lump of soap from one of the other crew members and scrubbing it through his hair. "I hate seeing my favorite couple at odds."

"We're your favorite couple? I'm flattered." Henri didn't have the answer to the question/ He preferred instead to indulge Fox's banter.

"Of course you are. You're the most stable." Fox paused, his mouth twisting thoughtfully to the side. "Or you were."

"Wow, thanks for your vote of confidence."

Fox waved him away, soap suds flinging off his hand. "I'm sure it will work out. You haven't seen how he looks at you these days. The level of yearning is sickening, honestly."

That somehow made Henri feel all the worse. This was his first romantic relationship, and their first actual fight as a couple. He was out of his depth. Knowing Robin was suffering too put him on edge.

"I'm waiting for him to say sorry," Henri mumbled. Fox passed him the soap.

Fox took a deep breath and leaned back to dunk his soapy head. When he resurfaced, he leveled Henri with a stern look that did not sit well on his face. "Judging by how you've been acting, he probably feels like he can't talk to you."

"How I've been acting?"

"You look like you're gonna throw up every time you see him."

"I do not!" Henri flicked water at him half-heartedly.

"Yes you do. You get this weird, uncomfortable look on your face! He probably thinks you hate him."

Fox was a little shit, but he wasn't wrong. Ever since their fight, Henri *had* been avoiding Robin. Partly because he was still mad and hurt by his cowardice, partly because every time he was reminded of their fight, he got this raw, anxious feeling in his diaphragm, like it had been scraped over some rocks and no longer had the strength to drag air into his lungs.

Still, he didn't want Robin to think he hated him. He just couldn't stand that Robin was hiding him. He'd thought a few times of just marching up to David and telling the truth straight to his face. But that would probably hurt Robin even more, so he stayed away. They both knew David would never accept Henri. There were too many prejudices in the way. Strike one, Henri was a pirate. Two, he'd grown up in Talva, their country's enemy. Three, and probably most importantly, he was a man.

"I don't hate him. I just want him to acknowledge me."

Fox gave him a sympathetic look.

"Is Rowan gonna let David go, or are we stuck with him forever?"

Henri shrugged. "Last I knew, Robin was going to ask."

"And if David leaves but Robin doesn't tell him? Would that solve anything?"

They'd certainly be able to go back to openly being a couple, but Henri thought the hurt would still remain under the surface. He shook his head.

"Oi! Let's go!" The other crew members, having finished washing, were wading toward the rowboat.

Fox waved to them to show he'd heard, then stood and patted Henri on the shoulder. "Good luck."

THE *SIREN* WAS ALMOST ready to depart when the little contingent of freshly-washed crew returned. Henri made his way down to Logan's room to change clothes, not realizing until it was too late that his feet had carried him toward his and Robin's shared room out of habit. Sighing, he turned to go back, and came face-to-face with Robin.

Robin, without his gloomy brotherly shadow.

He seemed just as surprised to see Henri. A faint smile curled his lips before he remembered they were fighting, and it dropped away.

"You're back," Robin said, clearly trying for a neutral tone.

"Yup, I just needed clean clothes..." Henri trailed off, picking at a hangnail. Unsure what else to say. The antsy feeling had returned to his chest, threatening to overwhelm him. He moved to push past Robin just to get some air.

"Wait." Robin reached out, but didn't touch him. Because he was afraid David might see? Or was he respecting Henri's boundaries?

"What?" Henri asked, exhausted already.

"It's wash day right?" Robin said, fidgeting with the hem of his shirt. "Do you...want help?"

Henri blinked at him. Was this his way of apologizing, or was he just trying to go back to their usual routine like nothing had happened?

What had started out as Robin helping Henri bathe due to his injuries when they first met had morphed into a comfortable weekly ritual between them. Ever since he was a kid, Henri had found wash day to be a tedious chore. It annoyed him to spend time washing, drying, and oiling his locs when his friends could wash quickly and go out to play. He was already different from them, and back then, he resented the necessity of this care.

His feelings worsened after his mother's death. All those months bathing her by hand as she slowly got weaker and frailer, until that final wash to prepare her body for burial. And all of it he'd done taking special care with her hair because she'd have wanted that.

Caring for his locs properly left a sour taste in his mouth after that, but he'd never been able to bring himself to cut them off. Maman had always loved his hair this way, and several of the beads were gifts, so he kept it. Since Robin had begun helping him, most of Henri's anxiety around it had eased; he could simply lay back, talk and joke, and enjoy the ministrations of his lover's hands.

He contemplated Robin's question for a moment. Even though he had just returned from bathing, he hadn't washed his hair yet. He'd already been trying to muster up the motivation to do it since he'd stepped back on the *Siren*. He was still upset at Robin, but if he delayed too long, the salt would dry in his hair and get itchy.

"If you're offering," Henri agreed. Maybe being pampered by Robin would actually make him feel better.

Henri pulled his shirt off over his head in the privacy of their shared room as Robin fetched a bucket of rain from the cistern. He knelt next to his sea chest and dug out the bar of soap and a little bottle of hair oil.

Robin slipped back into the room, hauling the wooden bucket. Neither of them said anything as they set up with practiced movements. When everything was ready, they both settled onto thin cushions on the floor. Robin's long legs wrapped loosely around the base of the bucket. His gentle hand cupped the back of Henri's neck as Henri leaned back, guiding him to rest his shoulders against Robin's thigh so his neck could rest on a rolled up cloth on the lip of the bucket.

Their eyes met for a moment before Henri glanced away. He let his eyes slide closed as Robin scooped up some water with a wooden mug and let it trickle over Henri's hair. Robin did this a few more times until it was soaked through, then grabbed the lump of soap that smelled of rose, clove, and some other herbs Henri couldn't place. Robin had traded medicine for several bars of such soap with Splinter Zanta at the final rendezvous of the season the year before, and this was their last bar.

Henri relaxed into the familiar ritual as Robin lathered it through Henri's hair, and began massaging it into his scalp. The herbal scent and Robin's fingertips lulled him into drifting peacefulness. For a few moments, he was able to forget that they were fighting. That he was meant to be mad. But as far as he could tell, Robin had not told his brother about their relationship, and even though Henri missed him, he was determined to stand firm until Robin either confessed or gave a good reason why he shouldn't.

The cold water made Henri's skin tingle as Robin rinsed the soap from his hair, one hand against his forehead to block it from running into his eyes.

"Henri."

Henri's mind resurfaced at the sound of Robin's soft voice. Robin poured another mugful of water over his hair.

"Hm?" He wished he could remain in this blissful state for just a little while longer. But he knew he couldn't give his lover the silent treatment forever. He opened his eyes and tilted his head back to look up at Robin. Robin's lips parted, then closed again, as if he was rethinking what he wanted to say.

"You can sit up now."

Henri's brow furrowed. He'd definitely been expecting something else, but he sat up anyway, little rivulets of water running down the back of his neck. Robin pushed the bucket aside and moved to sit on the edge of the sea chest. Neither of them spoke as Henri settled on the floor between his legs, back to the chest, and Robin began squeezing out the excess water with a cloth.

The silence grew between them like mold, festering Henri's relaxed mood.

"I'm sorry," Robin finally said quietly. His hands didn't stop moving so Henri couldn't turn to see his expression. He sounded sad. Truly repentant. Henri leaned back against the side of the chest, drawing his knees up and wrapping his arms around them. He said nothing, not yet ready to forgive without a solution in hand.

Robin set down the towel and uncorked the bottle of hair oil, the scent of sweet almond permeating the air as Robin poured a small amount into his palm and began to work it through Henri's locs. The scent reminded Henri of sitting just like this at his maman's feet in front of the fireplace in their apartment above the bakery, waiting to see if his father would come into port before the first snows blanketed the harbor.

The memory made his heart ache. Maman was gone now, dead of a disease that had slowly wasted her body away over years. Henri had only been twenty-one when she passed, long after his father had visited one final time after years away. He later found out his father had died the same year, without Henri ever seeing him again. Henri had never even gotten a chance to ask him about all the strange things he said the last time they were together.

But those childhood winters when they were all together—his Kefryean pirate father, Yarenen former-pirate mother, and him, all settled on the northern peninsula of Talva—those had been the best times of his life.

Henri blinked, realizing he'd sunk too far into the memories of the past and missed the next thing Robin had said.

"Sorry, what?" He leaned his head back to look at Robin.

Robin's throat bobbed as he swallowed.

"I'm really sorry I hurt your feelings," Robin said quietly, his fingers still in Henri's hair despite being done with the oil. "I didn't mean to pretend we weren't together. My mind just kind of blanked out when I saw Davy and slipped into my old mindset of keeping everything secret."

He paused, looking down into Henri's upturned face, his eyes pleading for Henri to understand. His fingers slipped down the side of Henri's neck, soft from where the oil had soaked in.

"You used to keep everything secret?" Henri asked. He'd never really pried into the details of Robin's life before he ran away. But now he wanted to know. To understand his lover on a deeper level.

Robin bit the inside of his cheek.

"I don't really want to talk about it," Robin mumbled.

"I think you have to," Henri replied. "It's not healthy to keep it all inside, especially when it's affecting us." He reached up to brush the back of Robin's hand where it rested against his neck.

Robin sighed and leaned down to rest his forehead against Henri's. Falling back into this level of quiet intimacy felt so natural. Henri let out a long exhale as Robin's arms wrapped around his shoulders. He waited until Robin was ready to speak.

"I used to keep a lot of secrets," Robin said, not moving from their current position. "At first I didn't know what was wrong with me. Sometimes I said or did things and I'd get punished but I didn't know why. So eventually I just stopped talking and kept my true thoughts inside. And then I figured out that I liked other boys, so everything had to become a secret. I couldn't even get too close to my friends because I didn't want to seem suspicious." Robin's words came quickly now, gaining momentum as he clung to Henri like an anchor.

"Then I went away to university. For the first time, my parents and brothers weren't constantly looking over my shoulder, and I fell in love."

Henri's breath caught, and Robin chuckled self-deprecatingly.

"Don't worry, the feeling wasn't mutual," Robin whispered.

"I'm sorry." Henri didn't quite know what he was apologizing for, but he said it anyway.

"Thanks." Robin's arms tightened around Henri's shoulders ever so slightly. Henri's neck began to ache from being bent back at this angle, but he didn't dare move and disrupt this fragile equilibrium.

"Anyway," Robin continued, "you're right. I shouldn't have to keep secrets anymore." Henri's heart sped up at his words. After a slight hesitation, Robin moved so his lips pressed against Henri's forehead instead.

"I will tell him about us, Henri. I swear I'll tell him before he leaves. Just give me a little time, okay?"

That was all Henri wanted. Not just for himself or their relationship, but for Robin's sake. If he could tell his family about their relationship, that he was happy, maybe he could truly let go of the guilt he felt for leaving them and being happier without them.

"Rowan agreed to let him go?"

Robin nodded. "The next time we make land. Davy says he'll believe it when he sees it. And he keeps insisting I go with him."

"But you won't, will you?"

"Of course not."

"So how long do I have to pretend?"

"You won't have to, love. I swear I'll tell him as soon as possible. Please believe me when I say I never wanted to hide you."

Henri relished the feel of Robin's lips. He ran his fingers down Robin's forearms and laced their fingers together.

"I believe you," he murmured.

"Will you sleep here tonight?" Robin asked.

Henri contemplated this. He was still a little hurt, but all the nights apart had been so lonely that there wasn't really a choice.

"Yes."

Robin's lips smiled against his skin.

CHAPTER 17

MAY 16TH, 1668

The north coast of Lasland appeared on the horizon, craggy as a toad. The lookout whistled down from the crow's nest to alert them, and Nephele—who liked to sit up there and keep the crew company, especially if they had food—took to the air with a screech, flying ahead as if to scout the *Siren Song*'s way to safe harbor. Unfortunately for her, Rowan planned to turn east toward Souna, and from there, skim the coast down to the Sunrise Sea, Zanta's usual stomping grounds.

The small dot that was Nephele grew even smaller, and eventually disappeared into the distance. They would have to put into port at some point to gather information on the whereabouts of the *Monsoon* and possibly resupply. But at least they were sailing away from Kefrye and hopefully Shaw. Rowan was well aware that this plan was ultimately a foolish one, but Yves's immediate insistence that he should retreat back to Illusion like a gutless worm had rubbed him the wrong way and brought out a stubbornness to rival even Fox's obstinance.

Now Rowan was determined to see his decision through. Not only to warn Zanta of the trouble coming her way, but also to prove Yves wrong and force him to apologize for once. As much as Rowan loved Yves's domineering manner in the bedroom, he did not appreciate it in other aspects of their lives.

Rowan would never admit out loud that leaving things the way he had with Yves unsettled him, which in turn made him miss the bastard all the more. If Yves just apologized and agreed to help him, or at least not hinder him, Rowan would consider forgiveness. But Yves was probably well on his way in the opposite direction, ready to stalk the deep waters once again.

Being parted from Yves in anger reminded Rowan of how he had fled from Illusion, determined to never see him again. This fight was not quite so severe, and Rowan regretted leaving his wedding ring behind and what that might mean for Yves's volatile mood. Last time, Yves had marauded across the seas with a ferocity that terrified even other pirates. What would he do this time? Sink a dozen ships and pillage a dozen more? Raid the Marran coast?

Rowan contemplated the gray sky where Nephele had disappeared. Never mind that Yves's own actions would put an even bigger price on his already expensive head. How was being hunted by Warrick any different than what they usually got up to? It wasn't just Rowan who'd promised to be more careful—though he was definitely the more breakable of the two.

Rowan stilled, an unsettling thought forming. Yves was obsessed with protecting Rowan to the point that he had to actively stop himself from locking Rowan up for his own good. But seeing as Rowan's stubbornness was sailing him toward further danger by placing both him and Zanta in one place, what better way to protect him from afar than by eliminating the threat?

What if he was going after Warrick?

A sharp whistle from the crow's nest split the peaceful air. The signal that they'd sighted a ship. Rowan spun, fear and anticipation that Warrick had already found them pounding through his blood. He could see nothing of the other ship from this low vantage point. He drew his own whistle from its place on his belt and piped up to the lookout.

Friend, foe, or prey?

The whistle came back. *Unclear*.

Great. A mystery ship behind and Lasland ahead. They were fast approaching land, and he would soon have to make the decision to keep with the plan and veer east toward Souna and Talva, where there would be a higher presence of enemy ships, or abandon the plan altogether.

He scaled the lines of the main mast till he was halfway up and settled on the yard. The tall masts of the other ship appeared over the hazy line of the horizon. The *Siren Song* had slowed as it neared the coast, and if the other ship *was* following, they were gaining.

Wind ruffled Rowan's hair like a lover's touch. He set the spyglass to his eye and peered at the other ship as it closed the distance. It was three-masted. Large as a warship. It ran up its colors, a white skull and tentacles on a dark blue field. The *Kraken*'s flag.

Rowan snatched the spyglass away from his eye. His heart lifted even as his stomach plummeted. Yves was not going after Warrick. He was coming after Rowan.

To what end? Forgiveness? Or had he decided to chase Rowan down and drag him back to the safety of Illusion after all?

A hawk's screech drew Rowan's eye back to the crow's nest, where Nephele had returned to circle before diving down to perch beside Rowan, her sharp talons digging into the wooden yard.

"It's the *Kraken*," the lookout called, his voice carrying easily to Rowan's new perch. Rowan nodded but didn't answer, his mind ticking through Yves's possible motives while his heart and stomach battled it out over how to feel. The lookout raised his own spyglass again and called down, "They're hailing us."

So they were. The blue and yellow upright bars of a hailing flag had been run up the mast beneath Yves's colors. Rowan raised the glass again, gaze roaming over the tentacle carvings on the hull.

"Want me to reply, Captain?" The lookout unfurled both the *affirmative* and *negative* signal flags. Rowan's insides still warred with each other, the weight of indecision paralyzing him. Even if Yves was here to apologize—which was unlikely—Rowan was still mad. This casual contact and his traitorous body's eager response only heightened that. He wasn't some dog happy to heel to Yves's beck and call. He was the Ghost Hawk, and if Yves thought he could be forgiven so easily, Rowan would let him sweat it out.

The pad of Rowan's thumb found the callus at the base of his ring finger, left there by his absent wedding band.

"No reply," Rowan answered, "we're ignoring them."

~

May 19th, 1668

The straight razor glided across Rowan's throat, slicing away the soft fuzz of stubble he'd let accumulate over the past few days. Nephele's talons clicked against her brass perch in the corner as she tore into a bilge rat the crew had caught for her breakfast. It was the third day since the blue and yellow hailing flag had flown atop the *Kraken*'s mast, and Rowan was holding strong. He hoped his refusal to meet was making Yves dwell on his actions. He'd made Rowan feel small. Like someone to be pushed around and sent off to hide. Not like an equal. Rowan put up with a lot to love Yves, but he refused to be treated like a subordinate in his own marriage.

Now, the *Siren Song* skirted along the coast of Lasland, heading east and staying well enough away so as to not be seen as a threat to the coastal towns. The same could not be said for the *Kraken's Fury*. While the *Siren* was small and quick and could pass herself off as a civilian vessel, the *Kraken*, with her great bulk, could not be mistaken for anything other than what she was: a vessel of power and violence. And on top of that, Yves was doing nothing to hide. The *Kraken*'s deep blue sails hung proud and full on her masts beneath the snapping skull and tentacle flag.

After it had become clear that Rowan was ignoring his overture, Yves had dropped the niceties. There were no further attempts at communication. Instead the *Kraken* dogged the *Siren*. Sometimes close and sometimes from afar. But never close enough for Rowan to see Yves on deck, and never far enough to lose sight of them. The *Kraken* courted a violent reaction, trying to bait Rowan into acknowledging them in any way.

Rowan grimaced at his reflection in the mirror, then schooled his face to stoicism so the razor wouldn't catch on the raised scar tissue on his cheek. He'd grown increasingly exasperated over the last few days. Yes, he was being petty by refusing to acknowledge Yves, but was it not just as petty for Yves to match his energy and use his bigger ship to try and intimidate them into submission? He should have come to Rowan hat in hand, an apology on those beautiful lips. He should've decided to hail them again instead of matching Rowan's obstinance with intimidation.

So they played a new game of cat and mouse now. One that would likely not end up with them in bed together this time. Who would break first and give in to the other's silent demands?

A few times, Rowan had thought of running up the signal flag and getting it over with. But his pride wouldn't let him. Yves was just *so* infuriating. He couldn't help but give in to the anger Yves sparked in him. He'd always played second fiddle to the Deep Water Demon as a pirate. He refused to do the same as a man. Their relationship must stand on equal footing or not at all. So for once, he would let Yves come begging.

The tearing of rat flesh accompanied the *tink* of his blade on the edge of the soap bowl as he scraped suds and hair off.

These broody contemplations were interrupted by a protesting shriek from Nephele when Fox burst into the room without knocking. He'd become even more comfortable in Rowan's quarters the past few weeks, still creeping in most nights to climb into Rowan's bed just to have someone next to him.

"They've signaled!" Fox declared, almost giddy, as if the standoff between the two captains was a dramatic bit of theater that had finally come to fruition.

Rowan hastily set the razor down and wiped the soap from his face with a towel.

"What flag?"

Fox made a face, and crossed the room to make little soothing noises at the disgruntled hawk. "He wants to talk, dummy, what else?"

A part of Rowan thrilled at that. Yves had broken first. Rowan had won. But another part couldn't help but remain suspicious of his husband's intentions.

They hurried to the quarterdeck where Logan met them. "Orders, Captain?"

Rowan looked to the *Kraken* cutting through the waves behind them, the blue and yellow hailing flag flying like a tail tucked between a dog's legs. Had he reflected and managed to overcome his probable feelings of annoyance at Rowan's brattiness? Or were they going to argue again? Rowan considered ignoring his husband once again. The *Siren* could easily outpace the *Kraken*, and the temptation to show Yves just what he and his little ship could do nearly tipped his hand. But ultimately, curiosity got the better of him.

"Signal affirmative and let them catch up."

The morning was clear and bright, perfect weather to accept a groveling apology. Rowan allowed himself to indulge in a daydream of Yves on his knees, begging forgiveness and proclaiming Rowan right for both their crews to hear.

Such indignity would never suit him, but it was fun to imagine.

The *Kraken* caught up in no time, and was soon pulling up alongside. Rowan tried to seem nonchalant, standing on the main deck with a relaxed posture. But his gaze flicked back and forth across the *Kraken*'s deck, searching for Yves.

Finally, he appeared, bloodred coat and raven hair contrasting with pale porcelain skin. Rowan took in the sight of him like a drink of cool water. All the while pretending not to have noticed his presence. Yves was gorgeous beyond human comprehension or words, a fallen god among mortals. Rowan desperately tamped down the arousal that threatened to overwhelm his anger and pride. Why was he so pathetic? Immediately casting aside his convictions at the mere sight of his husband. No, he must stoke his anger higher so as not to be swayed by anything less than the apology he deserved.

He thought of the way Yves had told, not asked, him to hide on Illusion. The way he acted as if Rowan was his to command, and a dozen other little slights and annoyances that had built up over the past year of their marriage. Stone by spiteful stone Rowan built himself a wall of anger against Yves's beauty until it surrounded him like a tower.

But when Yves walked over to the rail and met Rowan's gaze for the first time in two weeks, that carefully constructed wall threatened to buckle. Despite Rowan's eyepatch obscuring his view of the otherworldly, he could tell the demon lurked close to the surface. If he removed his eyepatch, he was sure the shadow tentacles would be writhing angrily in the bright sun. Rowan practically choked on the seething anger rolling off his husband in waves like a dark miasma. Beautiful and terrible.

Rowan was definitely not getting an apology today.

The two ships were drawn together by ropes, and everything stilled. Both crews waited with baited breath to see who would speak first. Yves stared down at him from the greater height of the *Kraken*, silent and impassive.

Trepidation stoked in Rowan's belly. Yves had called this meeting, yet already they were at an impasse.

"You wanted to talk. So talk," Rowan said, loud enough for every ear.

The well of Yves's anger deepened, pulling Rowan down into its inescapable depths. He almost gasped for air.

Yves didn't say a word. He simply stepped onto the rail of the *Kraken* and dropped onto the *Siren*'s deck with a thud much softer than his size should have allowed. A dark god descending. Several of Rowan's crew members drew back as if they too could feel the demonic rage roiling around the other captain.

In two strides, Yves was before him. Between Yves's suffocating aura and overwhelming beauty, Rowan couldn't catch his breath. Words died in his throat. Yves was even more beautiful up close, the light catching his dark eyes like the first flush of sunrise on a stormy sea. Under the bloodred coat, a large onyx broach sat at the hollow of his throat, as black as Yves's demonic eyes and so shiny it reflected Rowan's own half-stunned, half-mulish expression back at him. A profusion of pristine white lace spilled from beneath like a waterfall, drawing Rowan's gaze down to high-waisted trousers cinched dangerously tight, and further, his thighs—

Rowan snapped his attention back to his husband's face. Wondering—not for the first time—if there was something demonic in the way Rowan became utterly captivated by Yves whenever he saw him.

Yves seemed to have no reaction to Rowan's wandering eye. His lips, so pink and tempting, parted around stilted, formal words. "Ghost Hawk, would you do me the courtesy of speaking in private?"

Rowan's breath caught. Not only at his pirate moniker, which Yves had rarely used since the first time they'd met, but at the overly polite request hiding whatever true intention Rowan could feel in this all-encompassing anger. What game was he playing? Had he taken Rowan's returned ring and departure as something more than Rowan intended?

Unable to form words around the walnut-sized bitterness in his throat, Rowan gestured for Yves to follow. The crew drew back hastily to make way as the two captains retreated toward Rowan's private quarters. Logan opened his mouth, no doubt to ask if Rowan wanted his attendance, but Rowan shook his head. Once they were away from prying eyes, he would demand an explanation.

But they did not make it to Rowan's quarters. As soon as the hall door swung shut behind them, Yves seized Rowan by the throat and shoved him against the wall so hard Rowan imagined it rocked the ship. The eyepatch dislodged, uncovering half of Rowan's jade eye and allowing him to see his husband's true form. Black eyes like a shark. Dark blue tentacles filling every corner of the hall behind him. Rowan's own hand moved on instinct, drawing his dagger lightning fast and pressing it to Yves's throat just above his high collar.

Something dangerous sparked in Yves's black eyes, and instead of shying away from the blade that could end his life once again, he leaned into it. A bright line of blood bloomed along the steel edge.

Rowan hissed, not wanting to hurt Yves yet unwilling to be defenseless. Yves's breath wafted across his face, lips a mere moment away from capturing Rowan's.

"Do not speak." Yves's voice resonated deep with the demon's echoes. The shadow tentacles filled the hallway like a dense fog, darkening the already dim light to near blackness. But still, Rowan could see the way Yves's eyes glittered with malice. He tried to speak, but it was as if Yves's command had siphoned away his voice. Nothing came out but a frightened exhalation. Yet his traitorous body reacted to Yves's closeness. He yearned to close the distance between their lips, to lean into Yves's violent embrace as if it was a loving one. For them, the lines between violence and love, aggression and lust, had been blurred since the day they met. The two were entwined as closely as their bodies. Dominance and submission, control and freedom, were mere toys for their passion.

A rivulet of blood, nearly black in the gloom, slipped down Yves's skin to soak into the snow-white lace of his collar. Saliva pooled beneath Rowan's tongue, eager to lick it up. To dip his tongue into the wound and draw out the words of contrition he ached for. But Yves's long fingers tightened on Rowan's throat, thumb pressing to his thundering pulse. Their eyes met, and Rowan knew in an instant Yves was thinking the same unholy thoughts as him.

Rowan surged forward, desperate to kiss those cruel lips. But Yves held him tight to the wall. His breath was ragged as he wrenched open Rowan's belt like the buckle and leather were no more than a knot of thread. He unfastened Rowan's pants as quickly as Rowan had drawn his blade. But his lips remained just out of reach. Torturous with their nearness. When Yves drew out Rowan's achingly hard cock, a choking gasp escaped his mouth, still soundless.

The pressure on Rowan's throat disappeared as Yves fell to his knees, not even flinching when the edge of Rowan's dagger scraped up his neck like a close shave. Rowan's arm dropped down to his side, already too delirious with lust to question what was happening.

The plush softness of Yves's lips meeting the head of Rowan's cock sent sparks dancing across his vision, and the dagger clattered to the floor from nerveless fingers. Yves did not draw out the teasing. He sucked Rowan's length into his mouth down to the base. Rowan's lips parted in a silent plea, still unable to make a sound despite nothing restricting him now. He buried his hands in Yves's onyx locks as Yves aggressively sucked him off, teeth and tongue working in torturous tandem to cause both pleasure and pain. Rowan's hips bucked forward into the wet heat of Yves's mouth, abandoning any thoughts that he could hurt him. He wanted to hurt Yves. To slake his anger on Yves's body with no concern for the consequences. Because this was not an apology. Yves was on his knees, but he was the one in control, still so furious that it filled every crack and corner of the hallway.

There was no love in this, only anger and passion. Ecstasy climbed up Rowan's spine like toxic rot, engulfing every sense as he fucked Yves's beautifully cruel mouth, which had so recently commanded him, and spoken formally to him as if they had never known each other like this. Yves's nails dug into Rowan's hips, little pinpricks of pain amidst the pleasure. His tongue swirled around Rowan's shaft, and with one last thrust, Rowan came—hot and intense—down Yves's throat. His vision whited out for a moment, body shuddering as Yves milked him dry.

Yves withdrew swiftly and stood. He caught Rowan in his arms, pinning him to the wall. He leaned close, and Rowan thought he would finally kiss him. But Yves spat a mouthful of cum into his own hand, and used it to slick up Rowan's inner thighs. Not bothering to wipe his hands, he released his hard cock from the front of his trousers and squeezed Rowan's thighs back together.

Still without a word, Yves thrust between Rowan's soft thighs. Rowan couldn't protest even if he wanted to, his mind still hazed with the aftershocks of orgasm, his body weak and pliable. He would've let Yves do anything to him in that shadow-darkened hallway. Would have let Yves fuck him raw with only his own cum as lube if he wanted.

Yves thrust between Rowan's thighs again, quick and hard. A small pearly bead of Rowan's cum flecked his delectable lips. So close. Rowan didn't care anymore that they were fighting, though his anger still seethed among the afterglow. He grabbed Yves's bloodied shirtfront, ignoring how wrecked and desperate he looked in the broach's reflection, and dragged him closer for a kiss. But Yves snatched his wrist and slammed it against the wall. Rowan gasped. His other hand clutched Yves's shirt so tightly the bloodied collar ripped, revealing the edge of a silver chain around his neck. Rowan could barely make it out in the shadows, smeared with Yves's dark ruby blood. Strange. Yves wore jewelry, but never like this, under his clothes where it couldn't be seen. Rowan reached for it, intending to draw it out into the dim light. But the oppressiveness in the air sharpened, causing his fingers to flinch away.

Rowan's gaze rose to meet Yves's eyes, as black as the shadows around him. His cock throbbed between Rowan's cum-slick thighs, pumping faster and faster. His fingernails dug into Rowan's wrist, keeping him pinned as his breath grew harsh.

Yves growled, the first real sound since he'd ordered Rowan to silence. The shadows seemed to coalesce and thicken around them. Suffocating. But not a single one touched him. Rowan whimpered, and hot liquid gushed between his thighs, splattering the wall behind him and squelching as Yves rode out his orgasm.

Finally, Yves's body stilled. He gazed back at Rowan, still full of anger. Rowan wanted to kiss him, to know that he was loved despite it all. His breath caught in anticipation, sure that Yves would finally give him a taste. His eyelids fluttered, his lips parted. Ready.

Yves withdrew and released Rowan from his grip, leaving behind small crescent indents on Rowan's skin. He tucked his length back into his trousers, drew a lacy handkerchief from his sleeve, and dabbed the bead of cum from his lower lip. Without a backward glance, he flipped the handkerchief in Rowan's direction and left. The shadows trailed behind him like a widow's veil. The handkerchief fluttered to the floor as the door slammed behind him.

It was as if all the air had been sucked from the room. Silence even more deafening than when the shadows and anger had filled it. Rowan's legs finally gave out, and he sank to the floor. He knew he should clean up. Knew that when Yves stormed across the deck with blood on his collar, Rowan's crew would come looking for him. And he couldn't face them like this, pants halfway down his thighs, covered in two loads of cum and delirious out of his mind.

He regained his feet shakily, moving in a trance. He hiked up his pants, but his belt buckle was broken, wrenched apart by Yves's impatient hands. The handkerchief lay in a heap on the floor, and

Rowan snatched it up, cleaned the cum from the wall, and retreated to his quarters.

Fuck, what was wrong with him? Rowan fisted his fingers in his hair with no regard for cleanliness. The anger had not lessened, but now it was laced with both confusion and shame. He'd let Yves come in here and do whatever he wanted. He'd *wanted* Yves to ruin him, hurt him, and use him. Yet now that it was done, he did feel used. Was Rowan not even worth a kiss? A word? Yves had only come here to slake his thirst, nothing more.

Rowan fell back onto his bed, head spinning. He pressed a dry corner of Yves's handkerchief to his nose and inhaled the scent of him. Sex and seawater and expensive cologne. Hating himself for falling so pathetically under Yves's spell.

CHAPTER 18

MAY 19TH, 1668

Zanta closed her eyes for only a moment, letting the sway of the waves far below lull her stress into silence. They'd managed to slip away from their pursuers for now, dodging around one of Souna's far-flung islands and heading north, away from their home waters, the opposite of what the enemy expected of them.

They were currently out of sight, so Zanta had sent most of the crew to bed. The smaller night crew still had the *Monsoon* under full sail, widening the gap between them. But Zanta couldn't sleep, so she'd climbed up to the crow's nest and was now laying on her back, her legs dangling over the edge.

She needed to think, and this was the only place her mind could run free.

The sky spread vast and black above her, ribbons of stars unspooling across the darkness like a spilled cache of diamonds, and Zanta's thoughts spilled with them. The mystery of their pursuers hung heavy in her chest. The two ships had to be connected to the attack on Roseforte. It was too much of a coincidence that they'd started following the *Monsoon* only days after it had fled the harbor. But who had attacked? And why were they following Zanta's ship? The attackers hadn't had any national or military markings as far as Zanta had seen, and their pursuers didn't either. But that didn't mean they weren't on someone's payroll. The animosity between the two empires was palpable, but the war between them had long gone cold. There hadn't been a direct attack against each other in a decade or more. They'd set that aside in favor of the empire race.

But everyone knew the lands yet unconquered were few. Only Avardel, Lasland, Yarene, and the Sleeping Isles remained. Avardel was allied strongly with Marra, treaties and royal marriages ironclad. Lasland was large and neutral, a valuable trade partner to both empires. Yarene was the gateway to the southern continent, and neither empire could invade it without incurring the wrath of the continental allies. That left only the Sleeping Isles, mysterious and naturally impenetrable. The last bit of free land between the two empires' expanded territories. Anyone would be mad to mess with those storms.

Had Marra finally snapped and decided to reignite war? If they had orchestrated the attack on Roseforte, it meant every country would be sucked into an all-out war that would likely last a decade or more. And where did the *Monsoon* fit into it all? She had no answers.

Zanta's endless musings were interrupted by the creak of weight on the ratlines. She sat up just as Nia's fiery head popped up over the edge of the crow's nest.

"Oh," Nia said, as if surprised to find her there. Though there was no way she could've missed Zanta's booted feet hanging over the edge of the platform. "Do you mind if I join you, Captain?"

Zanta couldn't very well say no after Nia had climbed all this way. "Be my guest."

Nia climbed up and Zanta lay back down, hair beads clacking on the wood. Nia copied her, lying flat on her back on the other side of the mast, so that it blocked her middle but she was visible from the chest up. They would be face-to-face if they turned their heads.

Nia twitched, then pulled out a hairpin that had presumably stabbed her scalp, and settled again. Both women remained in silence for a little while, just watching the stars high above while the sea undulated far below. They were caught halfway between. All alone, suspended together in the dark.

It was a disconcertingly intimate place to be for relative strangers. Especially ones who'd shared an ill-timed kiss not too long ago. But Zanta had found herself warming to the other woman, despite herself. Nia had befriended most of the crew members in a matter of days, and Zanta often found herself watching closely how she interacted with them. Noticing the way her smile produced deep lines in her cheeks, the way her laugh seemed to skip right to Zanta's ears.

But she'd also noticed the quiet moments when Nia thought no one was looking. How she seemed to relish when the sea sprayed up across the bow and pattered her with salty drops. How her green eyes took on a wistful sheen when she looked out over the waves.

At first Zanta had worried Nia would go back on her word, and jump after all. But as more and more days passed without an attempt, Zanta wondered what Nia was thinking in those moments. Why did she look so sad?

Just when Zanta thought the silence would stretch on forever, Nia spoke.

"Are you really going to make me leave?"

This again. Zanta couldn't make up her mind whether she wanted Nia to stay or go, especially now that they were being followed. There'd been no discussion of it at all since the kiss.

"Why is that so bad?"

"Well." Nia seemed to think hard about what to say. "I've become quite attached."

At first Zanta thought Nia meant attached to *her*, but Nia continued.

"Laurent especially will be heartbroken if I leave."

"You've become close quickly."

"I'm good at making friends."

"But you don't miss your friends in Roseforte? What about your family?"

Nia remained quiet for some time, the susurration of waves filling the silence, before saying, "The problem with living in a port is friends come and go often and easily. Family just goes."

"The innkeepers, they aren't family?" She'd claimed to be an orphan, but...

Nia chuckled. "No, you think they'd let their precious daughter or niece sleep with any sailor who caught her fancy?"

Ah right, that's what Nia had been busy with when Zanta went to deliver Logan's package. Zanta had nearly forgotten. She was grateful she hadn't been allowed to interrupt. Not only for propriety's sake, but also because it meant Nia was now here and safe.

With her.

Zanta shook the thought from her head, as Nia said, "I'm just an employee who rents a room in the attic. They do care about me, but not like family." She said this last part as if familial love was something she'd long been skeptical about.

"You really are an orphan, then?"

Nia looked at her, such a strange and unreadable expression on her freckled face that Zanta wanted to pull the truth out of her like she'd pulled the pin from her hair.

"Yes," Nia answered simply. "Are you?"

She wasn't. Her parents and siblings awaited her back home in Yarene. "No."

"Do they love you?"

This was getting too personal, even though Zanta had started this line of questioning in the first place. She changed the subject.

"Did you only come here to ask if I was going to kick you out?"

Nia turned back to the sky. "Not really. I like it up here. I used to do this all the time with—" A weighty pause. "I used to do this all the time."

Right, she'd lived on a ship as a child. Zanta wondered about that but didn't press further. Not wanting the personal questions turned back on her again.

After a while, Nia lifted her arm straight up, palm to the sky as if she could touch it. "The stars are so different in the summer."

Zanta did the same, closing one eye to focus. Her hand blotted out the Pearl Crab constellation, her middle finger and thumb balancing its two bright anchor stars on their tips. Wind whipped through her clothes, sailcloth snapping all around them.

If Zanta was truthful with herself, she wanted Nia to stay. Not only because they couldn't go back to Roseforte, or because she didn't want to drop Nia off in a random port with no resources, but because she'd seen how easily Nia had slipped into place amongst the crew. She was quick to kindness and radiated confidence in whatever she did. More than once, Zanta had caught herself smiling just because Nia was.

Zanta closed her fingers slowly, revealing the Pearl Crab like a shining version of the smatter of freckles on Nia's face. If she explored them, looked for more than the moment or two she allowed herself, would she find the constellations reflected on Nia's skin?

She looked at Nia once again. Nia had let her hand fall away from the sky too, and it now rested over her chest, as if she was feeling her own heartbeat. Even in the dark, with only the lantern light below and moon and stars above, she was one of the most beautiful women Zanta had ever seen. Her fiery hair, half tumbled from its pins, seemed even brighter in the low light. The bare skin of her neck a creamy river that flowed over her clavicles to the swell of her breasts beneath her hand.

Zanta's lips tightened into a thin line, trying to dislodge the memory of their kiss. She'd thought about it too often in the intervening days.

As if sensing Zanta's gaze, Nia finally roused from her thoughts, limpid green eyes on her, pupils wide and dark in the low light. One red curl fluttered across her brow on the wind, and Zanta resisted the urge to tuck it away.

Would it be so bad to keep her around a little longer?

"I guess I can—"

The boom of cannon fire shattered the peaceful night, followed by the splash of the shot hitting the water much too close for comfort. Zanta scrambled to her knees, searching the darkness for the source of the sound.

"Shit." The two ships blended in with the dark against the water, not a lantern to be seen. Of course they'd managed to get close. There was no way the crew on deck could've spotted them. The only indication they were there at all was the occasional glint of moonlight catching on brass fittings and glass portholes. Zanta should've been keeping watch.

Zanta started to scramble down from the crow's nest. Nia didn't follow. She seemed frozen, her gaze pinned to the enemy ships.

"Nia, come on."

She didn't move, but to sway slightly as the *Monsoon* banked to starboard.

"Nia." Zanta reached over to tug at her ankle, and Nia blinked, as if waking. "Let's go," Zanta said again. Nia followed her shakily down the ratlines.

When their feet hit the deck, Nia still seemed dazed, even as the night crew swarmed around them. The two ships were gaining fast, and even if the *Monsoon* could run again, it was looking like they'd have to fight for it. The aft bell started clanging the alarm.

Zanta grabbed Nia's hand. "Get below. You're not safe up here." She dragged her toward the doorway, where sleepy crew members already spilled out into the night.

"I can help," Nia said unconvincingly.

"Can you fight? Load a cannon?"

"No."

Zanta squeezed her hand. "Then you need to go below, where you're safe and out of the way."

Nia nodded, but for a moment, neither of them let go. Finally, Nia seemed to gather her wits again. "Be safe." She disappeared through the door.

ALARM BELLS HOUNDED Nia's footsteps. All around her, the *Monsoon* sprang to life. Pirates rousing from their slumber to answer the call to action. Nia wished she could help; it was true she didn't know the first thing about fighting, but Zanta sending her away left a sour taste in her mouth. She was only useful for one thing when it came to pirates, and without her treasure, even that was lost to her.

Nia stumbled on the last step as a crew member pushed past her. Even in trying to get out of the way, she was an obstacle. She tucked herself far into the corner next to the stairs until there was a lull in activity, then dashed toward her room.

Boom!

The second cannon shot sounded far closer. The first had been a test. Their pursuers breaking the element of surprise because they thought they were in range. This second shot was confirmation that the *Monsoon* was in their sights. It set Nia's nerves on edge, snaring her mind in memories she would rather not relive. Her breath shallowed, and she squeezed her eyes shut. This was not then. This was not the *Silverfin*. But the memories overtook her anyway. She dashed into the first room she could find, slamming the door behind her.

The interior was dark as pitch, but in the brief flash of lantern light from the hall, Nia had seen it was the storeroom with all the clothes. She could hide here. She could wait out the battle and the memories that came at her from the dark.

Nia stumbled toward the back of the room, barking her shin against the corner of a trunk. But she couldn't feel the pain. Her brain barely registered her surroundings. Her hands found the cool wood of the wardrobe at the end of the room and wrenched the doors open. She climbed in, tangling in the fancy dress as it fell from the hanger, and slammed the doors behind her.

Nia curled up into a ball, her side pressed to the back of the wardrobe. The heavy dress settled onto her, its weight an odd comfort. She clutched it to her chest, burying her face in the folds of silk.

Breathe, Nia, breathe.

But her breath only came in short, uneven bursts, and memory dragged her down into its depths.

She was a child and alone. Her father had locked her into her tiny, hidden room within his quarters as a battle raged outside. The *Silverfin* had stumbled upon a tax ship sailing from Souna to Talva, and her father was determined to obtain its riches. It was all coin, nothing that could be destroyed by water. So it didn't matter if the pirates sank it, Nia could always retrieve the goods from the wreck.

As always, she remained in pitch darkness. No lantern or window to light her nightmares. Because really, the room was a closet, and there was only room for Nia's hammock strung overhead, and a chamberpot and small trunk on the floor. Nia had huddled in the corner, her back pressed so tightly to the chest the iron filigree left imprints in her skin. She did not have the key to it, but it contained her life.

Her pelt, her true skin. Locked away from her and the sea.

Maybe if she had had it, she would not have been so afraid of the constant thunder of cannons around her, the shouts and screams of her father's crew. Though she was a child, she knew deep down that by locking her in this room without access to her pelt, her father had condemned her to death if the ship went down. If she had her pelt in its entirety, she'd be able to leave this place. Dive beneath the waves, beneath the battle, and go home.

Not that there was anything waiting for her there either.

For there was one more thing in the cramped room with her. She held it clutched to her chest, its weight like a hug. Her mother's pelt. The pelt her father had taken with him when he left her mother behind with Nia in her belly. The pelt whose absence had caused her mother to wither away and finally die when Nia was only nine or ten. The pelt her father had finally brought back when it was too late.

After all that, he'd stolen the valuables off the body, and kidnapped their daughter away from the only home she'd ever known.

Nia pressed her face into the gray leather of the pelt, inhaling the slight, salty smell, and pretended she was hugging her mother. If her mother had had to die, she wished her father had never found her. Had never taken their daughter away and exacted the same cruelty onto her by separating her from her pelt as well.

Now in another dark room, in another closet, another battle, Nia remembered all of this with such intensity it felt like it was happening all over again. The grief of her mother's death. Confusion over her new life, and whether she should love or loathe her new captor, her father. The square wound, fresh and raw on her back where he'd cut away a piece of her pelt to keep with him so she could never escape.

~

THE *MONSOON* MADE a good run of it for a short while, the lead ship firing a few intimidating shots off their aft. But before long the two ships moved to flank them, and all hell broke loose.

The one on the starboard side swooped close enough that Zanta could make out the name emblazoned in red and black paint on its side. The *Marigold*. Despite the color scheme, it didn't bear the M.W.S. prefix that would mark it out as a royal Marran ship. In fact, if Zanta squinted hard, she thought she could make out the remains of the now defunct Kefryean prefix Q.R.S. beneath the new lettering.

So they were mercenaries. Or what amounted to it. Zanta lowered her spyglass with a huff. After Marra had conquered Kefrye, with no small help from a faction of Kefrye's own nobles, they'd disbanded the armed forces. The Kefryean fleet no longer existed in an official capacity. Marra had renamed them all. They had absorbed some into the Marran fleet, but it was an open secret that several ships had been reconditioned in a more unofficial capacity as mercenaries and privateers. Now the evidence was in front of Zanta's eyes. Typical of Marra to use the ships of a conquered land to do their dirty work for them. If these were indeed two of the ships that had attacked Roseforte, nothing could officially be pinned on the Marran Empire. Even if Talva suspected they were behind it, they couldn't retaliate without reigniting the cold war.

The other ship dashed closer and Zanta trained her glass on it, fingertips going cold as soon as she spotted the mermaid figurehead. She'd been repainted: gone were the iridescent silver scales and flowing orange hair. Now the wood was dark-lacquered like the rest of the ship, but there was no mistaking the raised arms holding a conch shell or the hauntingly realistic eyes. Zanta's gaze darted to the ship's name. *Lonesome.*

But there was no mistaking it. The *Silverfin*, Silver Stroud's former ship. The ship Zanta had used a shard of to stab Stroud in the heart. The ship she'd sold to the Marran Empire for the reward money when she couldn't stand to sail it anymore, haunted by Emilie and Stroud's deaths.

Grief welled up in her, and she forced it down like bile. She couldn't afford to let it prevent her from getting out of this situation. Both ships closed quickly. Zanta was under no illusions they could get out of this if it came down to a contest of brute force. She knew the *Silverfin*—now *Lonesome*—and its capabilities. She'd have to outrun them, and Zanta knew of only one sure advantage her fan sails had over the mercenaries' square-rigged ones. Maneuverability.

The first volley of cannon fire from the *Marigold* shattered Zanta's thoughts. Most shots fell short, but one nicked the bow.

"Man cannons!" Zanta shouted, and her crew jumped to obey, despite most of them still being half asleep and half dressed. She spared a fleeting thought for Nia. She'd frozen when the mercenaries approached, and Zanta hoped she wouldn't freeze again if it came time for her to take action.

Zanta shook her head. Nia would be fine for now. She had to focus on getting them out of this situation first. She took up position next to Sabriye, who'd taken over from the helmsman and now stood with both hands on the wheel.

"Stay the course," Zanta said quietly.

Sabriye raised an eyebrow. "Is that an 'I'm still thinking' stay the course or an 'I have a brilliant plan' stay the course?"

"Little of both."

Sabriye nodded, and the *Monsoon* continued gliding forward, the two enemy ships on either side at the edge of cannon range. Zanta waited.

The *Lonesome*, emboldened by the lack of retaliation or evasive maneuvers, banked closer.

"Fire to port!" Zanta barked the order like a general. It was relayed to the gunners below, who touched smoldering linstocks to cannons. The sound ricocheted through Zanta's brain as all eight guns on that side fired.

"Reload!" She turned to Sabriye. "Tack starboard." Sabriye adjusted the wheel, and the *Monsoon* banked away from the *Lonesome* toward the *Marigold*, getting just out of range as the *Lonesome* fired and missed the *Monsoon*'s side by mere yards.

Now there was the *Marigold* to contend with.

"Fire starboard!" Zanta ordered, just as the *Marigold*'s cannons thundered, almost drowning out her voice. But some of the crew had caught onto her game already. The starboard cannons fired in unison, and two shots pummeled the *Marigold*'s side near the aft quarters.

This time, Sabriye didn't need Zanta to tell her what to do. She swung the wheel back the other way with the cooperation of the crew in the rigging, taking the *Monsoon* just out of the *Marigold*'s range and into the *Lonesome*'s. This wouldn't work for long. The Marran mercenaries were closing in, tightening the pincer around them, and soon the *Monsoon* would be trapped in the perfect position to be in range for both without the risk of them shooting each other.

She had to draw them in, make them each forget their ally waited on the other side.

The thunder of simultaneous cannon fire left Zanta's ears ringing. She didn't miss a beat, and neither did the crew, as several cannonballs ripped through the *Monsoon*'s rails. One barely missed Laurent, who yelped and dove behind a bundle of cargo.

"Load bar and chain shot!" Zanta ordered the port crew, even as the *Monsoon* swung back the other way. For her plan to work, they had to slow the other two ships enough that the *Monsoon* would be able to slip away without being followed. The best way to do that was by damaging the sails and rigging. If they ended up taking a good chunk out of the crew too, all the better.

They took another hit from the *Marigold*, one of Zanta's newer crew members speared by flying debris as a cannonball burst through wood. Laurent grabbed the man and hauled him below. They came into range of the *Lonesome* again, the bar and chain ripping the other ship's foresail.

"Fire when in range!" Zanta bellowed, trusting her crew to make the call of when to attack and when to rest. The *Monsoon* weaved her deadly path between the two ships as the vise closed further and further and it became more difficult to maintain the delicate balance. But the *Marigold*, at least, was slowing. Having taken a significant hit to her bow, and with several lesser sails shredded, she began to fall behind, but not enough to throw Zanta's plan into disarray.

Both ships suddenly banked inward toward the *Monsoon*, closing in for the kill. Soon the *Monsoon* would be trapped.

"Ready gull wings and be sneaky about it," Zanta ordered. The wings were a pair of modified studding sails that dropped down to either side of the ship's body. She and Sabriye had designed them together. Sure, they would make the *Monsoon* wider and harder to turn, but they would also increase their sail surface area, and therefore their speed, just enough to get them out of here.

But not before Zanta made sure the mercenaries couldn't readily follow.

Heart in her throat, Zanta watched the two ships closing in until she could practically see the old paint beneath the *Lonesome*'s new varnish. She swallowed her nerves and stepped in front of the wheel column, issuing a series of orders in a clear, steady voice that had the crew scurrying to do her bidding. On either side, the *Lonesome* and *Marigold* readied to strike a final, decisive blow, drawing ever nearer. Zanta could hear Sabriye's shallow breaths behind her as she stood clutching the wheel spokes with white knuckles, awaiting Zanta's order.

For just a few breaths, everything felt still. Distant cries of *Fire!* rang from the enemy ships.

"Furl sails!" Zanta shouted.

The *Monsoon*'s fanlike sails snapped shut, and their forward momentum slowed as the enemies' linstocks touched to fuses. The *Monsoon* dropped back out of danger as the two ships delivered a full complement of deadly iron and lead right into each other's sides.

"Turn about!"

Sabriye wrenched the wheel, slowing the *Monsoon* even further as it began to turn. They'd have to time this just right or they'd be dead in the water. Screams and shouts echoed from the mercenary ships, curls of cannon smoke lingering over the water so recently occupied by the *Monsoon*.

"Release starboard wing!" Zanta ordered, and it was done. Saffron canvas snapped as the sail filled and pushed them deeper into their turn, until they were almost facing into the wind.

"Release sails and port wing!" Zanta snapped, even as Sabriye frantically straightened the wheel. A cheer went up from the crew as the *Monsoon*'s sails filled and she surged through the waves once again, leaving the two mercenary ships behind.

CHAPTER 19

MAY 19TH, 1668

"Stay alert. I'll be back soon."

Zanta didn't stay to see Sabriye's nod. The *Monsoon* had left the two mercenary ships far behind, and still wove a circumspect course to throw off their trail. They weren't out of danger yet, but it was all that could be done for now.

Zanta stalked belowdecks. Now that the danger had passed, her thoughts turned back to the vacant, haunted look on Nia's face. Worry still thrummed in her chest, a persistent and unfamiliar beat that said, *Nia. Nia. I have to find Nia.* She did not know what she would do when she found her. Only needed to know that she was safe. They'd escaped the mercenaries for now, through sheer luck. But they'd need to put enough distance between them, or find a place to hide before morning. She didn't know why they were following the *Monsoon* so doggedly. Yes, Zanta and her crew were pirates, but it seemed like more than that. Why would mercenaries connected to Marra risk pursuing her through Talvan-controlled waters? Why follow her all the way from Roseforte, if indeed these ships had been involved in the attack? She was successful, but she rarely ventured further north than Lasland's south coast. She was of no consequence to them, surely.

Unless she had something on board they wanted.

Or someone.

The thought stopped Zanta short in the hallway. Who was Nia, really? Zanta had been able to tease little snippets out of her here and there. Nia had lived on a ship as a child. Nia was an orphan. Nia watched the sea like she longed for it. And Zanta knew other things about her too. She was kind, hardworking, flirtatious. She had a joyous, insatiable appetite for life. Yet that strange melancholy was a part of her too, and it tickled Zanta's curiosity.

Despite all this, Zanta knew next to nothing about who Nia was beyond the confines of the *Monsoon*. Could she be in trouble with the mercenaries somehow? But what would warrant sending several ships after her right to their greatest enemy's doorstep?

Zanta shook her head, trying to dislodge this line of suspicion. Right now, all she had to do was find Nia.

She hurried down the hall and stopped in front of the room Nia had been staying in. That thrum of worry still beat in her chest. She knocked.

No answer.

She knocked again. "Nia? It's over, you can come out now."

No answer. Zanta's chest tightened. Nia couldn't have fallen asleep. Not with that ruckus going on outside. Had she been hurt somehow? Zanta tried the handle, and the door swung open easily, revealing a dark room.

A dark, *empty* room.

The thrum loudened. Insistent. A flash of memory assaulted Zanta's mind. An image of Nia climbing the rail of the *Monsoon*. Desperate. Ready to jump into Roseforte Harbor. What if she'd actually done it this time? Or been hurt in the battle even after Zanta had sent her to hide?

Zanta turned from the empty doorway and ran.

"Nia!" Her voice sounded panicked, when just half an hour ago she'd been perfectly calm shouting orders in the middle of the attack. She opened the next door. Nothing. Then the next and the next, her panic mounting with every moment Nia didn't appear.

She had to be here somewhere. Zanta's foot hit something and sent it pinging against the wall. She skidded to a halt, picking up one of Nia's hairpins. It had been on the floor in front of the storeroom her crew had jokingly dubbed the atelier. Zanta tucked the pin into her pocket and wrenched the door open. Nothing. She made to move on to the next, then paused.

The room was as dark as the others, but a beam of orange light from the hall fell through the doorway and illuminated the large wardrobe on the opposite wall, Zanta's own shadow blotting its doors.

It would be a terrible place to hide. Obvious. No avenue for escape if you were found. There were loads of better hidey-holes on board the *Monsoon*. But Nia wouldn't know any of those. She'd only been on board for a few weeks and was not yet fully trusted. Not permanent.

No, that wasn't true. Zanta did trust her. They were well on their way to becoming friends.

Zanta stepped over the threshold, closing the door partway behind her so a small sliver of light illuminated her path.

"Nia?" she called softly. No answer. She crossed the room quickly. A swath of rich fabric was caught in the bottom of the door. She knelt, not wanting to loom over the frightened woman if she was indeed in the wardrobe.

"Nia?" She reached for the door handles.

The wardrobe's doors burst open, nearly whacking Zanta in the face. Nia half fell, half lunged out in their wake. For a split second, Zanta tensed for an attack. Maybe Nia thought she was an enemy—but the tavern maid's strong arms wrapped tight around her waist, Nia's face buried into her shoulder. They swayed back with the force of her exit, almost toppling to the floor.

"Zan—" A choked sob drowned the rest, Nia's voice muffled where her face pressed into Zanta's chest.

Zanta's arms came up to clutch Nia to her, relief edging out her panic. Nia was here, alive, and seemingly unharmed despite her fright.

They stayed like that for long moments, clinging to one another. Zanta on her knees and Nia sprawled half in, half out of the wardrobe. Nia must have been clutching the noble's dress as she hid, for it was now trapped between them, subject to Nia's tears and the crush of their bodies. The voluminous skirts piled around and under them like a drift of blown leaves.

"There, there." Zanta had never been much good at comfort. She patted Nia's soft orange curls, perpetually falling out of their pins, and experienced a stab of something foreign through her chest. Affection, maybe? Or was it merely relief that her stubborn charge had survived that harrowing brush with the mercenaries?

She tried to clamp it down. Now was not the time to puzzle over anything like that. It was clear the *Monsoon* was being hunted, and the frightened, shivering woman in her arms might have something to do with it.

Nia's shaking shoulders stilled, her arms loosening their hold. Zanta found herself reluctant to let go. But she let Nia sit back.

The sliver of light from the hall sliced across her face, illuminating one pale green eye, and a stretch of tear-reddened, freckled cheek, a loose lock of hair falling across it.

Oh. She was beautiful like this. Her bawdy confidence washed away with her tears, leaving only the raw, unmasked woman in its wake.

All questions about Nia's potential involvement with the mercenaries fled Zanta's mind. She held her breath.

"I'm...sorry," Nia hiccupped, scrubbing her sleeve across her nose in a very unladylike manner. "I don't know what came over me. It's just..." She stopped herself, collecting the words she'd been about to say and stowing them away inside herself. Her eyes rose to meet Zanta's shadowed face. "The battle is over then? We won?"

Zanta let go of her breath. "We escaped. They might come after us again."

Nia's eyes widened. "What do they want?"

The question seemed genuine, and Zanta dearly wanted to believe it was, that Nia had nothing to do with the attack.

"I don't know," she answered sincerely. She searched Nia's expression. But again, was caught by her loveliness in the half light. "Are you okay?" She couldn't stop herself from reaching up to tuck that copper curl behind Nia's ear.

Nia stilled. "I...I'm fine." She seemed to take stock of Zanta for the first time. "Are you injured? It sounded..." Her words trailed off as Zanta's hand moved to cup the side of her face.

"I'm fine," Zanta assured her. By the Serpents, what was Zanta doing? Nia had just been crying. Zanta had just fought for their lives. And yet, in the beat of quiet, Nia leaned toward her ever so slightly. Zanta mirrored her movement and kissed her.

Nia made a small, pleading noise against her lips, her hand coming up to rest on Zanta's shoulder. It was nothing like their first kiss, all full of lust and false passions. This was tender, almost reverent. Nia's lips tasted of tears.

They broke apart, and Nia's fingers snagged in the shoulder of Zanta's shirt, as if to stop her from running away again.

But Zanta didn't feel like running this time. Residual adrenaline from the battle coiled in her gut, mixing with the salty taste of Nia's lips, the sight of her green eyes, confused yet open.

"Zanta, I—" Zanta pulled Nia to her, and their lips met again, more insistent this time. Nia's body shuddered, and she leaned into the kiss, her lips parting. Warmth tingled across Zanta's skin as Nia's tongue slipped between her lips. The tension in her core coiled tighter, and she pushed Nia against the back of the wardrobe, her hand moving down the side of Nia's neck. Nia arched into her touch, sighing as their kiss deepened.

Zanta wanted her, all of her. She disentangled the voluminous dress from between them and cast it away, barely breaking the kiss. She slotted her knee between Nia's thighs, pushing one of them gently to the side. Nia's hands wandered to the hem of Zanta's sweat-soaked shirt, pushing it up her torso and framing her waist. Zanta kissed a trail down her neck to her breasts and buried her face between them. Gods, Nia was so soft and lovely. Zanta inhaled her scent as the pillowy mounds pushed at her cheeks with every breath.

Zanta's knee hitched higher, brushing the junction between Nia's thighs. Nia's hips twitched in response, grinding her still-clothed sex against the muscles of Zanta's thigh. She groaned, her hands moving to cup Zanta's ass and keep her there.

"Gods, I want you," Nia gasped. Zanta looked up, finding Nia's face flushed with arousal. Cheeks pink. Lips kiss-bitten.

"How do you want me?" Zanta's voice was low, almost a whisper. Nia rolled her hips again. Her pupils were wide in the dim light, almost entirely engulfing the beautiful green.

"I want"—another roll of the hips—"your fingers. Please." The words kindled in Zanta's core, spurring her to action. She slipped a hand down Nia's leg and found the rumpled hem of her skirts. She hitched them up Nia's thigh, realizing too late that her hands were still dirty from the battle when her fingers left a smudge of gunpowder on the silken fabric of Nia's stocking.

"Fuck." Zanta couldn't use her fingers on Nia when they were grimy like this, but she didn't want to leave and find some place to wash them. Well, there was no other option. Her gaze flicked up to

Nia's. "Bad news, princess, my hands are dirty. You'll have to make do with my mouth instead."

A shiver ran through Nia's body. She already looked debauched, and Zanta had barely even touched her yet. Zanta wanted to rip the pretty, pastel dress from her voluptuous curves and see the glory of her bareness. Her decadent sensuality that she wore so confidently for all to see. But here, leaning up against the inside of the wardrobe with her hair spilling out of its pins, her skirt up and her eyelashes still wet, her true wanton need shone like a beacon, and Zanta desperately wanted to taste it for herself.

"Please," Nia gasped, and Zanta didn't wait for further permission. With one last kiss to Nia's breast, Zanta lowered herself between Nia's legs. The sword at her belt thunked against the decking as she shifted.

Nia's aroused heat almost took her breath away. She mouthed at the stretch of bare thigh between Nia's stocking and underwear, her fingers tracing beneath the garter that held the stocking up. Nia spread the other leg wider, making room for Zanta's shoulders. Bumps raised on her skin as Zanta's breath wafted over it. Zanta's fingers found her undergarments and pulled them down.

She took her time resettling between Nia's legs, her lips trailing tantalizingly from Nia's ankle to knee, never breaking eye contact. Even this had Nia shivering in anticipation, and when Zanta reached her inner thigh, she whined. Zanta had wanted to go slow, to take her time savoring everything about this beautiful woman, but that whine pushed her over the edge.

It became a whimper when Zanta's tongue sank between her moist folds. Zanta groaned in turn, heat flooding between her own legs at Nia's sweet taste. She hadn't been with another woman since Emilie, and a small twinge of guilt slowed her for a moment before Nia's hand found her hair and brought her back to the present.

Her tongue traced the edge of Nia's labia before flicking lightly over her clit, eliciting a soft moan. Zanta couldn't see Nia's face past her bunched up skirt, but the sounds she made were enough. Zanta took to her meal with abandon, tasting every part of Nia until her sweet nectar ran down Zanta's chin.

She let her tongue lave over Nia's clit and down to her entrance, wishing she could slip her fingers in and feel Nia all around her. Nia moaned when Zanta's tongue penetrated her, fingers fisting in Zanta's hair and dragging her deeper.

"Please...Zanta..." The sound of her name so desperately spoken only spurred Zanta on. She squeezed her thighs together, trying to alleviate some of the ache of her own arousal as she slowly thrust her tongue in and out, letting her breath pool in the humid heat between Nia's legs. Nia clenched around her, and Zanta groaned again, wishing, not for the first time, that she could simply grow a dick at will so she could feel this with more than her tongue.

She curled her tongue up, tastebuds dragging along Nia's honeyed walls, nose buried in her petal-like folds, so that with every breath Zanta inhaled the essence of her arousal. Nia's cries cut off, coming out muffled, as if she'd clamped her other hand over her mouth to stifle them. Her shapely thighs closed around Zanta's head, and Zanta eased them back open, fingers digging into her soft flesh. Her nose nudged Nia's clit, and Nia's hips bucked, her muffled cries growing more frantic with every amorous lap of tongue. She was close. Zanta could feel it in the contraction of her pussy, and in the extra wetness that suddenly flooded Zanta's mouth with the taste of overripe peaches.

She groaned, burying her tongue as deep as it would go. Wondering what the true depths of Nia's insides felt like.

"Fuck," Nia gasped, her hips writhing against Zanta's face, her pussy clenching down hard on Zanta's tongue. But she responded with equal enthusiasm, fucking Nia with her tongue as Nia rode her face.

"Zanta," Nia moaned, her voice desperate and shaking. "Don't stop. I'm going to—" Her words cut off in a moan, and sweet liquid gushed around Zanta's tongue as Nia's desperation came to a shuddering halt. Zanta kept her mouth on her through her orgasm, until one by one Nia's tight muscles loosened and went slack.

For a moment, Zanta considered continuing. She wanted to feel Nia come on her tongue again, but Nia's hand moved from Zanta's hair to her cheek and guided her up.

Zanta didn't bother wiping Nia's juices from her mouth and chin as she leaned over Nia's exhausted body and planted a kiss firmly on her lips. Nia shivered, her arms wrapping around Zanta's neck. For only a moment they lingered there in the dark, Nia's afterglow practically lighting up her peachy skin.

Then Nia shifted, and Zanta found herself beneath the redheaded seductress, her back pressed into the lavish billow of discarded skirts.

"Your turn," Nia murmured, her eyes still glazed with lust. She captured Zanta's lips before she could answer, her hand slipping down to cup Zanta's breast.

Zanta held back a moan, even the simplest touch sharpening the ache in her core. She wanted Nia. Badly. The taste of her still sweetened Zanta's tongue.

"It's okay." Though eating Nia out had pushed guilt to the back of Zanta's mind, it still flickered there even as she leaned into Nia's next kiss. "I've been gone too long. I should get back."

Nia paused, her exploring hand already halfway down Zanta's waist.

"Oh." She pulled back, her enraptured expression falling. And suddenly Zanta's guilt was not over abandoning her post to touch Nia here in the dark, or even over betraying Emilie's memory, but because she had disappointed Nia.

She couldn't stand for that.

Zanta reached for her and drew Nia down into a kiss. Nia hesitated for a moment, then melted into it, her lust rekindled.

"I guess I could stay a little longer," Zanta said. "Only, don't frown at me like that. You're too pretty for it."

Nia chuckled, squeezing the curve of Zanta's waist, and settled over her, straddling Zanta's thigh, the sword trapped between Nia and Zanta's legs.

"I should..." Zanta's fingers moved to her sword belt, but Nia's legs only squeezed tighter.

"Leave it on," she whispered, eyes glittering.

She wasted no time in unfastening Zanta's britches and slipping her hand beneath.

"If you're in a hurry, I'll get right to the point," Nia murmured. Her thumb stroked over the downy curls concealing Zanta's sex. She nipped at Zanta's ear. "Just relax, beautiful. I'll take care of you, and we can take our time next time."

Next time. Zanta wasn't sure there would be a next time. She'd never planned to give in to Nia's flirting. But seeing her so raw and vulnerable, holding her in her arms after thinking she'd been hurt, had pushed Zanta over the edge.

All thoughts of their potential were replaced with *now*, as Nia's middle finger delved into the curls to circle her clit. Zanta gasped, tingles racing across her skin, the ache of desire turning into an all-out throb. She clutched Nia's waist, dragging their bodies flush with each other.

Nia trailed kisses behind Zanta's ear and down her neck. Her fingers stroked and circled expertly until she had Zanta gasping. Pleasure pulsed through her as strongly as worry had before. Nia leaned close, stealing another kiss from Zanta's breathless lips.

"How was it to be inside me?" Nia murmured. Her fingers played Zanta like a harp, setting Zanta's body quivering, the sweet music of euphoria singing from her lips. "I'm told it's divine." A smirk pulled the corner of Nia's lips into shadow.

Zanta barely had the strength to answer, but a particularly delicious flick of Nia's fingers brought out the truth.

"They were right...Y-you're sweeter than stolen wine."

"How flattering." Nia's confidence had returned now that Zanta was at her mercy. Her fingers circled, and Zanta's back arched, her still-booted feet bracing against the billow of skirts.

"F-fuck..." Zanta gasped. "Between your legs lies the gates to paradise itself." Nia drew the words out of her with each stroke. "Tasting you is..." Nia cut her off with a kiss, and when they broke apart again, she leaned her forehead against Zanta's so that her mouth rested close to Zanta's ear.

"Shall we see if I can't help you find your own paradise, my beautiful captain?" Her fingertips were at Zanta's entrance, all she needed to do was say...

"Yes, oh gods, yes." And Nia pushed in, fingers curling and stroking, sending waves of euphoria through Zanta's quivering body.

"Next time I will taste you as deeply as you tasted me," Nia whispered. Zanta clutched at Nia's shoulder to ground herself, but it was of no use. She soared on the wings of Nia's touch and words. Pleasure coursed through her like a raging current.

"Nia, I'm..."

"I know, beautiful. You're squeezing me so tightly. Come for me."

Finally, Zanta came with a cry, her orgasm hitting her like the crash of a wave on shore.

"Shh...shh." Nia peppered kisses over Zanta's gasping lips,

stifling her cries. And when Zanta's body finally went slack with relief, Nia withdrew, and brought her slick fingers to her own lips. Her tongue curled between them, a promise of what was to come. "You taste just as sweet, Captain."

CHAPTER 20

MAY 22ND, 1668

Rowan stepped unsteadily from the gangplank to the Kadling Kay docks, taking a moment to let his equilibrium adjust from the constant sway of the ship to the unfamiliar solidity of land. When he'd been younger, letting his mind wander as the rocking of his navy-issued hammock aboard the *M.W.S. Wolf* lulled him to sleep, he'd imagined that he was born for the sea. A magical creature of the deep who'd mistakenly been born on land. Though it was a decision born of selfishness, Rowan's father had ultimately done him a favor in selling him into indenture to the navy, for now Rowan couldn't imagine he would have ever found his true calling had he stayed on land.

But he was only a human. Despite such stories weaving through the very fabric of culture throughout the Islands, Rowan had quickly stopped believing in mythical sea creatures after a year or so at sea. Now he had seen one, taken him to his bed and in marriage. And that creature was as cruel and changeable as the sea itself. And if Rowan wanted to keep him, he would have to learn the depths of his own inhumanity.

A faint breeze lifted Rowan's hair off his neck. The members of his crew that had been granted shore leave flowed around him toward the taverns and trinket shops that lined the streets just beyond the dockside warehouses. The docks bustled with all manner of sailors, tradesmen, and the like. Most spared the *Siren* and her disembarking crew a long enough glance to clock them as pirates and give them a wide berth as they passed by.

Though Rowan had done his best to maintain secrecy on the voyage along the Laslandish coast, up close there was no point in hiding what the *Siren Song* was. She and her captain were famous after all. But even for the Ghost Hawk, there were legitimate ports on most coasts that were—if not friendly—at least not openly hostile toward pirates, even the infamous ones, as long as those pirates spent their ill-gotten gains and caused no more trouble than the average sailor. Kadling Kay had always been a good option for a short-term stay, even if the *Siren* crew had been run out of town because of a tavern brawl once or twice.

They'd lost sight of the *Kraken* in the last few days, and Rowan silently thanked the gods for it. It was one thing to have the Ghost Hawk and his crew stop over in a town. It was quite another for the Deep Water Demon to grace the mere mortals with his presence. While Rowan might be second in reputation only to Yves, he did not strike fear into the public's hearts quite the same. Rowan had witnessed more than one hardened sailor piss themselves in fright just from seeing Yves with a sword in his hand.

Funny how no matter which direction Rowan's thoughts blew, they always turned back to Yves, as if he was the north to which the compass of Rowan's heart pointed. Even when they were fighting.

Shaking the man from his head, Rowan started down the dock. He was here for a reason. To find any information he could about Warrick and Zanta. They'd seen warships on the horizon once or twice on their way down the coast, though Rowan couldn't tell what country they were from. It was only a matter of time before Warrick tracked one of them down.

A fearful gasp from a woman near him had Rowan lifting his head, reassurances already on his lips that he wasn't here to cause trouble. But it wasn't his scarred and one-eyed countenance that had caused it. The woman wasn't even looking at him, but out over the water.

By the utter fear in the woman's eyes, Rowan knew what she saw before he followed her gaze. Sure enough, the *Kraken's Fury* was out beyond the harbor mouth, appearing suddenly like something out of a nightmare. Yves had not even made an attempt to disguise it. The deep blue sails hung taut with wind, displaying their well-known skull and tentacle insignia proudly. Thankfully, Yves had the grace not to fly his flag, but neither had he chosen to fly the white flag of peace, as Rowan had done in an attempt to put the citizens at ease. Rowan groaned. Would it kill Yves to have some care for once? Some tact? Maybe it would. But it wasn't as if he'd stay dead anyway. He had to know the terror he was currently inflicting. Maybe he enjoyed it.

Others had seen the *Kraken* now too. Some had already fled, and some, like the woman beside him, seemed to be frozen. Rowan placed a gentle hand on her arm, and she nearly leapt out of her skin, wide eyes panicked.

"He won't hurt you, ma'am," Rowan tried to assure her, gentling his voice as much as possible. "I swear it."

The woman seemed not to comprehend his words, but she was thawed now, and scuttled away from the docks as quickly as possible, clutching her shopping basket to her chest.

Yves wouldn't attack. Though the legend of him ignored it, the Deep Water Demon never raided ports. Like Rowan, he stuck to hunting other ships. It just wasn't challenging to go after a town, which could neither run nor chase, though they could fight back. It was like slaughtering an animal already caught in a trap. It might give you meat, but there was no sport in it.

Besides, Yves could only be here to hunt one thing and one thing only. Rowan.

Rowan sensed the moment Yves stepped foot on land. It was as if the ground itself trembled beneath his feet. He stopped in his tracks, letting the flow of the market continue around him. No one else seemed to notice the trembling. Was it all in Rowan's head? Had Yves's power expanded and reached out to Rowan across the distance? Or was Rowan now so attuned to him that he could divine his nearness by the way the gravel crunched beneath his elegant, spurred boots?

Rowan resumed walking, even as anticipation mingled with fear raced up his spine. No matter where he was, he knew Yves would find him like a lodestone. Even without the ring on his finger, even fighting, they were irrevocably connected. It was sickening really, how much Rowan still longed for him, even as anger still simmered in his guts. Maybe after Yves rearranged them a few more times, the anger would dissipate.

He wove through the dockside market crowds toward more deserted streets as Nephele soared high overhead. He didn't know what Yves would do when he found him. Maybe he'd finally apologize, maybe he'd fuck him into oblivion. Whatever it was, Rowan had the feeling he'd rather not be around too many people when it happened.

A ripple coursed through the crowd behind him, gasps and shuffling footsteps, as if people were scrambling out of the way of something. Rowan told himself not to look back. If he saw Yves now, there was no guarantee he wouldn't run into his arms just to hasten their reunion. He had to keep at least *some* of his dignity intact.

He'd almost reached the edge of the market before the breathless pressure of being Yves's prey became too much. His gaze sliced to the shine of a mirror hanging in a trinket booth, catching a glimpse of his husband reflected within.

Yves prowled the crowded street, resplendent in a deep black coat with whorls of gold embroidery. He made no secret that he was following Rowan. His fathomless dark eyes were locked on him as he cut through the crowd like a shark through water, unconcerned with the wash of humanity all around him or the fear left in his wake. They knew him; of course they did. No one else could be so beautiful yet terrifying. He oozed danger.

Danger and sex.

Yves's focus remained solely on his prey. Solely on Rowan.

And he was still angry.

All the little hairs on Rowan's body stood on end, and he dragged his gaze away from the mirror with difficulty, realizing he'd frozen in place as soon as he saw his husband. He might be desperate to get his back blown out in another whirlwind of angry, brutal sex, but he couldn't let Yves know just how desperate. He resumed his walk, leaving the market and its inhabitants behind, and winding through the increasingly deserted maze of side streets and alleyways.

Rowan didn't look back again. He could feel Yves following, the oppressive darkness of his anger like a storm cloud. He couldn't help but add an extra swish to his hips, a slight arch to his back. Enticing.

He turned down a deserted alleyway. The stone and half-timbered walls on either side leaned precariously toward each other like two lovers across a chasm, until they almost touched overhead and blocked out most of the daylight. A short flight of crooked stone steps led toward the other end of the alley, the greater light of the sun tinged green, as if a garden lay just beyond. The scent of moss and other growing things met his nostrils, and he started forward, determined to discover what was down there.

A hand closed over his mouth, yanking him roughly off his feet and pressing his back to a firm chest. Rowan's muscles tensed for just a moment before he recognized it was Yves. He would know those beautiful long-fingered hands anywhere. They'd touched every part of him.

Rowan's cock twitched to life almost immediately. So much for appearing not desperate. Yves didn't say a word. But his breath was hot against the chilled side of Rowan's neck. He forced Rowan against the cold stone wall in the gloom. His wedding ring twisted around his finger, and the edge of the ruby cut shallowly across Rowan's cheek as Yves's hand dragged across his face.

Rowan gasped, back arching to press his ass to Yves's already hard length, too hungry already.

"You knew you were being pursued, you fool. But you didn't even look. What if I had been Shaw?" Yves growled.

"I knew it was you. I could feel you."

Yves's other hand pressed to Rowan's hip. His lips ghosted over the fevered skin of Rowan's neck. It was the closest thing to a kiss Rowan had had since their fight, and it sent a shiver down his spine. He braced a hand against the wall to steady himself as Yves's intoxicating touch clouded his thoughts, already overpowering all of his defiant intentions. Yves removed Rowan's eyepatch, allowing it to fall to the cobblestones before gripping his face again. The act of removing the barrier between Rowan's perception and the demon felt intimate, dangerous, like Yves wanted him to know his human side was not the one in control. His ruby ring dug harder into Rowan's skin, a sharp counterpoint of pain that only dropped him further into the haze instead of clearing it. His breath came out harsh and loud in the silence after their words. No one passed the mouth of the alley. No one watched them from the shadowed windows overhead. They were completely alone.

Yves's other hand slipped down Rowan's thigh, catching the hem of his skirt.

"Did you wear this for me?" Yves murmured. The light filtering in from either end of the alley darkened as the shadows coalesced into something closer to flesh.

Rowan pressed his lips together, not willing to admit that he had gone back to the *Siren* to change after seeing the *Kraken* in the harbor. Yves's hand on Rowan's face moved to grip his jaw as the other skimmed up his bare thigh beneath the skirt.

"Are you still angry with me, darling?" Yves asked coolly. Rowan barked an almost hysterical laugh in response. The notion was ridiculous. Of course he was. And so was Yves. Anger simmered between them as tangibly as the tentacles' cold touch on his bare leg.

Yves's breath huffed as his fingers found Rowan's undergarments. He swiftly dragged them down Rowan's hips. His thumb traced the edge of Rowan's plump ass until he found the surprise Rowan had in store. The base of the silver plug nestled between his cheeks. Yves exhaled long and slow, as if to steady himself, but Rowan felt the other man's clothed dick throb in response.

Without another word, Yves hitched Rowan's skirt up his hips, exposing his ass to the open air. In the same breath, he released his throbbing length from the front of his trousers and pressed it between Rowan's thighs. Rowan gasped, his hips twitching back.

"So fucking desperate for me." Yves's teeth caught the shell of Rowan's ear, clicking against his earrings. His thumb pressed on the plug, sending a jolt through Rowan's nerves. He tried to bite back a moan. One of the tentacles, just barely substantial enough to feel, coiled around his right leg, suckers puckering his bare skin and anchoring him in place.

Yves twisted the plug in a vicious motion, simultaneously pushing it deeper as the tip of a tentacle reached between Rowan's legs and squeezed his balls. Rowan whimpered, pressing his forehead to the rough stones.

Rowan was a man who had always worked to overcome his own powerlessness. Yet with Yves he was truly powerless, unable to resist giving in to him utterly. His legs already trembled, arousal coursing like a drug through his veins.

It was disgusting how much he wanted this. How much he desired to be dominated by his demonic husband.

The tentacle quested up his crack, slicking his skin with its juices. He gasped as the tip feathered his rim, then slipped in beside the smooth bulb of the plug. With one last twist, Yves popped the plug free and Rowan moaned, clenching around the insubstantial tentacle tip as its juices dribbled out of his hole to wet Yves's cock. The silver plug hitting the cobblestones at their feet rang through the alleyway.

Rowan's hips ground back again, desperate to be filled now that he found himself suddenly empty. The tip of the tentacle ran around his rim again, and he tried to take it in, but Yves kicked his legs wider and forced his hips against the wall. His aching and neglected cock pressed to the stones through his skirt, and he involuntarily rutted against it, desperate for any friction and already out of his mind with lust. Yves had barely even touched him yet.

So when he felt the press of Yves's cock at his clenching entrance, his whimper was the most pathetic sound he'd ever made.

"Please."

Yves's grip tightened on his jaw, the ruby cutting deeper. A drop of blood trickled down his chin to his throat. Last time, it had been Yves with blood on his skin. How many times would they make each other bleed until they could forgive each other? How many times would he let himself be fucked lovelessly against a wall before he clawed back some modicum of self-respect? He didn't want to go back to the way it was before. Simply rivals who fucked because they were intrigued by each other. No room around their obsessive lust for soft feelings.

Yet despite it all, he still believed Yves would not hurt him. Not in a way that was unwelcome, at least.

An agonized moan ripped from his throat as Yves penetrated him suddenly. The stretch of his massive cock burning from Rowan's rim to the deepest reaches of his body. Rowan's legs threatened to give out from under him, but Yves kept him pinned.

Pleasure climbed up his spine beside the pain, even as Yves pulled back and pounded into him again and again, not giving him even a moment of reprieve. Yves's hips snapped with reckless abandon, the slick juices of the tentacle squelching with every stroke and running down Rowan's thighs. His cock rutted against the wall, and in the back of his already fucked out mind, he was grateful the fabric of his skirt shielded him from being rubbed raw on the rough stones.

Rowan whimpered as the fabric chafed his sensitive skin, and Yves growled in response, the aggression in his thrusts redoubling.

Mercy and gentleness had no place in this alleyway. Pleasure and pain ripped through Rowan's veins like fire. His hole stretched and soaked with tentacle fluid, insides clenching around Yves's inhuman girth.

Something else coiled just beneath the euphoria. He trusted Yves completely, but there was no love in this act, no promise of tenderness after the brutality was done. Rowan supposed he only had himself to blame for falling in love with a man who was only half human, and had fucked him into a stupor the first time they met. But even back then Yves had kissed and held him. Now his anger was sour on Rowan's tongue.

Doubt seized Rowan by the throat just as Yves had back in the hallway aboard the *Siren*. What if they couldn't find their way back to normal? What if no matter how many times they took their anger out on each other like this, Yves's limited ability to love had run its course the moment Rowan placed that ring back in his hand?

Rowan reached up to grab Yves's wrist, to gain some semblance of tenderness between them, but Yves snatched it away, instead forcing Rowan's bleeding cheek against the cold stones with a hand on the side of his head. Rowan moaned, his hips bucking back to take Yves's pounding. Body moving of its own accord despite the way his heart dropped.

What did it say about Rowan that he so willingly gave in to Yves's carnal desires even when he knew this would happen? What did it say about him that he'd fallen in love with a man like this?

Voices from the street cut through the haze of pleasure clouding his mind. Hot shame flooded Rowan's body, and for the first time in his life, he didn't act in the face of danger—he froze. Yves must have heard it too, but he didn't stop. The voices came closer, and Rowan squeezed his lips together against the moans that tried to force their way up his throat, silently begging whomever it was to realize they'd forgotten something, or discover they were going the wrong way, and turn back before they passed the mouth of the alley.

"So I said to him..." The voices, accompanied by the susurration of boots dragging tiredly on the cobbles, grew closer. Rowan's cheek was pressed tight to the stones, face turned toward the three men who now crossed the mouth of the alley and stopped. Yves's body contracted against Rowan's back, teeth latching onto the space between his shoulder and neck hard enough that they could've drawn blood. Like a possessive wolf guarding its kill, still buried deep inside.

"What the fu—"

Before Rowan could stop him, Yves's pistol had cleared its holster, aimed, and fired without so much as a glance toward the intruders. The bullet cracked into the corner of the building over their heads, and they fled with a shout, boots pounding down the street.

Rowan had never known Yves to miss. It must've been on purpose, a warning shot. Or else he was too distracted by his length buried in Rowan's insides, slowly taking him apart.

The next brutal thrust had Rowan's cheek scraping against the stones, and his vision burst into stars at the edges. He cried out, half pain and half drowning bliss. Fire roared through his body, and all at once it broke over him, milky ropes of cum splattering the inside of his skirt and dribbling down the wall.

Yves's hand fisted in Rowan's hair, and he yanked Rowan's head back. For a moment Rowan thought Yves would finally kiss him. But Yves's upper lip curled, a rabid snarl forcing its way out of him with the last few savage strokes. His cock throbbed, seed spilling into Rowan's clenching hole and overflowing as Rowan trembled through the aftershocks.

All he wanted now was comfort. For Yves to wrap his arms around his abused body, soothe his scrapes, kiss his cheeks. Even if they were still angry with each other, surely Rowan deserved that much.

But that was not what happened. Yves pulled out quickly, letting Rowan's skirt fall over his exposed, leaking hole, and stepped away. Rowan turned on trembling legs, bracing against the wall. He reached for his husband, intending to pull Yves to him and end this coldness. But Yves either didn't see or didn't care. He tucked his cock back into his trousers and strode out of the now silent alley without a backward glance.

Right. Rowan hitched his underwear back into place and slid down until he was seated on the cold cobbles, skirt tucked beneath him, head resting against the wall. Their anger was greater than their love.

Despair overwhelmed him all at once. What was he doing? Why was he so willing to play into this? Their sex life had always been rough, but never like this, never with true anger behind it. He choked down tears and pressed his hand to his mouth to stifle the gasps and half-hitched breaths that accompanied them.

He couldn't go through this again. Next time Yves came to him, Rowan would refuse. Another drop of blood slipped down his chin like a tear, and Rowan wiped it on his sleeve. He must harden his heart like the stones that had scraped across his face, like the ruby that had cut his skin, like Yves's inhuman heart which still contained a bullet from Rowan's own gun. He could not be content as Yves's mere plaything. He couldn't allow himself to slip further than he already had.

He wouldn't allow Yves to touch him again until he showed Rowan that he was loved, and not just another body for Yves to fuck.

THREE TAVERNS already and nothing to show for it. Logan smoothed his blond curls back from his face and plopped his wide-brimmed hat back onto his head. The further south they'd traveled had seen the weather go from the fresh coolness of spring to the humid heat of summer.

Maybe at the next tavern he'd actually get a drink. Thus far he'd just been asking after the possible location of the *Monsoon* and its captain, Splinter Zanta, with no luck. All the sailors he'd asked had either been tight-lipped or didn't know anything. The robust flow of gossip between seafaring folk was not working in his favor today. It didn't help that most of them already knew about the two pirate ships sitting menacingly in their waters, and had their guard up around strangers. Maybe he just needed to go to a seedier area.

A gust of wind kicked up, almost blowing his hat off as he arrived in front of a tavern with an anchor painted on the bricks. A cannonball nestled in an indent in the road propped open the door to let in the fresh air. Logan recognized it as the tavern where they'd met Henri, and hoped he wasn't still banned. He swept his hat back off his head as he stepped inside, eyes quickly scanning the patrons for the most likely group to talk to. Most of the worn wooden chairs were full of sailors and dockworkers, and even a few Laslandish naval sailors with the hare and oak leaf stitched into their wide, vaguely oak leaf-shaped lapels. Logan debated whether he should approach them.

They might realize he was a pirate, but they might also have the most accurate information he was likely to get. He didn't want to seem too much like he was fishing for information, but at this point his patience was wearing thin, and he just wanted to go back to the *Siren Song* to sleep off the stress and heat.

One of the sailors glanced at him, a frown tugging down his ale-foamed mustache, and Logan decided not to bother them. He sidled over to the bar and ordered a mug of ale instead. He leaned against the bartop, found it sticky, and grimaced as he had to unstick his sleeve from its surface. The bartender set the mug in front of him and bustled away with his coins. Logan took a sip of the ale and grimaced again. It was about to turn. The sourness lingered in the back of his throat.

A sudden longing for the brandy in John's quarters aboard the *Sweet Mercy* struck him. John had been right at the time; Logan's back and rear had been sore for days after. He'd tried to hide it, of course, and he thought he'd done a good enough job of it. Yet every so often, he caught Fox giving him sly glances. But then again, Fox was Fox and could have been doing that for any number of reasons. He was always up to something.

It didn't really matter if the others found out about the true nature of Logan's relationship with John. He knew they wouldn't judge him. The most he'd get was some good-natured teasing, maybe an attempt to talk about it. But the thought of telling them still filled him with unease. He didn't really know what this thing was between him and John, and he didn't want to explain it to anyone else.

Logan shook his head and took another sip of the ale, willfully drowning out thoughts of John. He tried to listen in on the conversations around him, but the voices all blended together into a blur. He caught a barmaid as she passed by.

"Do you know if there are any sailors here who might know the whereabouts of the pirate ship *Monsoon*?"

The girl's eyes widened, and she cast a furtive glance around the busy room, as if murderous pirates would rise up from between the tables, summoned by Logan's words. She seemed not to have recognized him or noticed his wooden hand, concealed as it was by a glove and tucked into his lap.

Apparently seeing no danger in passing whatever information she had, she leaned closer.

"I heard the *Monsoon* was seen fleeing the attack at Roseforte a few weeks back," she said, half whispering.

Logan's skin went cold. "Roseforte? There was an attack on Roseforte? By who?" Never mind looking for Zanta. Nia lived in Roseforte. Was she okay? Had she survived?

The barmaid chewed her bottom lip before leaning closer. This was why Rowan always sent Logan on these fact-finding missions—people tended to trust an innocent face no matter whom it belonged to.

"They're saying it was a sneak attack. Privateers or mercenaries disguised as merchants. Whole harborfront burned to the ground." She shook her head, dark brown curls bouncing around her shoulders. "I can't imagine all those poor people dead. First that attack on Wave Harbor a year back, and now this?"

If she said anything more, Logan wasn't listening; his thoughts raced faster than he could catch them. But one single thing pushed its way to the surface, connecting dots. Months back, Logan and John had asked Zanta to take a gift to Nia in Roseforte as she passed through. Her ship could be disguised, and she had convincing enough merchant papers. Was that why the *Monsoon* had been there? Had Zanta and Nia met? And had they been caught in the crossfire of the attack?

"...the blockade."

Logan zoned back into what the barmaid was saying. "Blockade? What blockade?"

She gave him a look like she had *just* explained this. Which she probably had. "Everyone's talking about it. The Talvans are treating the attack as an act of war from Marra, even though there's no real proof it was them. They've mobilized their entire armada, and their waters are crawling with navy ships. If you were planning on heading south, best to turn around and not deal with it."

"Thank you." Logan left the still mostly full mug on the bartop, sure it would probably go right back into whatever barrel it had been served out of, and rushed back out into the sun and down to the harbor.

ROWAN HAD NOT RETURNED to the *Siren* by the time Logan arrived. He huffed in frustration and paced the deck twice. Then, realizing the crew members on duty were giving him nervous sidelong looks, went below to pace in Rowan's quarters instead.

"Logan!"

Logan had only made it halfway down the hall, nervously chewing his thumbnail, when he heard Robin's voice behind him. He found the tall doctor hurrying to catch up.

"Robin, is anything wrong?"

"Nothing urgent," Robin said, stopping next to him. "It's just that...The captain is still planning on letting the captives go, right?"

Oh, right, Robin's brother was among the sailors from the *Sweet Lettie* that Yves had forced to join them in some asinine display of power. Robin had asked Rowan to let David go shortly after, and Rowan had agreed. David Beckett was making them all miserable. He was a painter, not a sailor, and snooty to boot. He refused to do anything except follow Robin around like a scared puppy. He wouldn't speak to anyone but Robin or the other captive sailors unless it was to mutter insults, and he sneered at any display of affection between two pirates of the same sex.

Rowan hated disharmony among the crew, and after the third time he'd heard a report of David muttering slurs about both pirates and the lovers they took, Rowan had sent him to work the bilge pump as punishment. Of course, being given the grossest, dirtiest job on the ship had only made David hate them more. Ultimately, Rowan had decided to release all the captives as soon as possible and be done with the whole ordeal.

With questions about Zanta and Nia crackling through his brain, Logan had forgotten all about it.

"I'll mention it to him when he gets back," Logan said. "But I don't see why not. This port is as good as any to drop off unwanted guests."

Robin nodded. "I'm guessing I shouldn't tell David ahead of time."

Logan clapped him on the shoulder sympathetically "Best not get his hopes up. Rowan has a lot on his mind, especially with what I'm about to tell him."

Worry furrowed Robin's brow. "Anything I can help with?"

Logan tried to smile up at him, though his stomach still churned with unease. "Let me worry about it for now."

"If you say so." Robin left, and Logan hurried to Rowan's quarters. The room was empty, his captain nowhere to be seen. Logan wondered if he had heard the same information Logan had. Though if the *Kraken's Fury* being anchored out in the harbor was any indication, Rowan would be distracted by yet another marital drama with the Demon.

Logan resumed his pacing, boots thumping from wood to rug to wood again as he crossed the room, circled the table and chairs, then did it all over again. Beneath the windows, Rowan's bed was messy and unmade, as always without the Demon there to straighten Rowan's unorganized habits. It seemed especially messy today, and Logan decided not to wonder whether that was due to Fox spending nights here. He didn't want to make incorrect assumptions again.

Instead he worried about everything else. Rowan didn't know about Nia, nor about John and Logan asking Zanta to stop in Roseforte for them. Which meant Logan might have to tell him about the true nature of his relationship with John. There really was no way to avoid it if they wanted to find Zanta. He wanted to help Nia too, but wasn't sure how without taking a detour to Roseforte, which was sure to be crawling with enemies.

Rowan would have a plan. Rowan always had a plan.

It felt like he'd been pacing for ages when the door of the captain's quarters opened and Rowan sagged against the doorjamb, before spotting Logan and quickly straightening up.

"Did you find something?" Rowan asked, closing the door behind him. He looked exhausted, eyes red-rimmed and a few shallow cuts and scrapes on one side of his face.

"What the hell happened to you?" Had he gotten in trouble for asking questions in the wrong place? Or... "Did the Demon do this to you?"

Logan reached up to examine the already scabbed over cuts, but Rowan batted his hand away. "It's nothing."

"That's not a no." Logan followed him to the table, where Rowan slumped into one of the chairs. He leaned his head against the wooden back and looked at Logan sidelong as Logan fidgeted.

"It's fine. It was consensual. Got a little rough, that's all." He seemed not to have the energy to feel embarrassed over telling Logan this, though Logan felt his own face heat. "I'm not hurt, Logan. So don't worry about it."

This did not make Logan feel better. He trusted Rowan to take care of his own business, but Rowan had a blind spot when it came to his husband. He subjected himself to things he would never accept from anyone else.

"Rowan—"

"Drop it. Tell me what you heard about Zanta."

Right. Zanta. And Nia, and everything else. He dropped into the seat across from Rowan, bolstering his courage to potentially tell Rowan his secret and how it related to their search for Zanta.

"Roseforte was attacked by mercenaries or privateers. The Talvans suspect Marran involvement and have mobilized. They've set up a blockade, so we're not going south any time soon."

Rowan sat up, interest sparking in his blue eye. "Go on."

"The *Monsoon* was apparently seen fleeing during the attack." He should have just spilled all the information right there, but embarrassment held him back.

Rowan frowned. "She was in Roseforte? That place is crawling with military, why would she—"

"It's because of me!" Logan blurted. Rowan just raised an eyebrow, so Logan continued, a flood of words pouring out all in a rush. "When I went to Roseforte to hunt down Cyrus, I ran into John, and we slept together." Rowan leaned forward further, eyebrows climbing higher. Logan had never been able to keep anything from him, least of all when he gave Logan that demanding look. Even as kids, there had been no secrets between them, and suddenly Logan realized the pressure he'd been putting himself under by keeping this from his best friend. Logan soldiered on. "But, uh...it wasn't just us. We also slept with a woman named Nia."

Rowan made a sound that was half disbelief, half laugh, a slow grin breaking across his face.

"John and I have been occasionally fooling around since, but we visited her again last fall when we went to gather information on the *Trinity*. And, ah, John and I decided to give her a gift, but we didn't know when we'd be able to visit again, so we gave the gift to Zanta because she was going that way anyway, and I think that's why the *Monsoon* was in Roseforte so..."

Logan's words finally failed him. Oh gods, why had he let John talk him into letting him carve their dicks out of wood to give to their sometimes lover just because she'd said she would miss them? He prayed Rowan wouldn't ask what the gift was. His face already felt like it was bright red, and if he got any more embarrassed, he might keel over dead on the spot.

Rowan was grinning mischievously at him from across the table. "Logan, you dog you. How long has this been going on?"

Logan felt his ears turn even redder. "Since before I lost my hand," he mumbled.

Rowan's expression sobered at that, but amusement still lived at the corners of his mouth. "And is this affair serious?" he asked innocently.

"I care about them greatly as friends," Logan replied. The only way he was going to get through this was just answering Rowan's questions without thinking.

Rowan whistled. "Some friends."

Logan covered his red face with his hands. "Can we discuss the matter at hand please?"

"Sure. I won't ask any more questions about your relationships if you don't question mine."

Logan frowned. The two situations were very different. Logan's secret was just a juicy bit of gossip; Rowan seemed like he might actually be in danger. But if agreeing for now got Rowan off Logan's back, he couldn't refuse.

"Fine."

"Besides, Fox will do all the asking for me."

Logan's head snapped up. "Don't you dare tell him."

Rowan chuckled and waved him off. "Okay, okay. You know you won't be able to hide it from him forever though." He paused for a moment to let Logan calm down. "So you think Zanta was in Roseforte to deliver this gift? Knowing she had a reason to be there does lend credence to the sighting. Did they say which way the *Monsoon* sailed?"

"No, I didn't hear anything about that. I rushed back because I was worried about..."

Rowan's expression softened. "You're worried about your *friend.* What's her name again?"

"Nia."

"You know we can't dock in Roseforte directly, especially now that it will be swarming with soldiers even more than usual, not to mention wherever the attackers are now." His eye widened as a realization dawned on him. "Do you think the attack was Shaw?"

"He wouldn't attack a military port just because Zanta was there, would he? I know he's crazy, but that's an act of war."

Rowan sighed. "The empires might as well already be at war, but you're right. It's too bold even for him."

Logan's worry spiked, not only with anxiety over Nia's fate, but the fact that Warrick Shaw was after them again. This was the man who'd almost ended their pirating careers and lives before they really began. The man who'd tricked Rowan into falling for him so he could betray them to the Marrans to gain back the title he'd lost by murdering his own father.

"So what are we going to do?" Logan asked. He wanted to rush to Roseforte to find Nia and make sure she was okay. But he knew that wasn't the priority of the crew as a whole.

Rowan leaned his cheek on his hand. "If there are blockades to the south, Zanta must still be around here somewhere."

They sat in silence for a moment, both thinking it over. If they attempted to get close to Roseforte, they risked sailing straight into a nest of vipers and getting caught up between the two empires once again. Last time that had happened, both the *Siren* and *Kraken* had lost many crew members, and the *Kraken* had barely managed to limp back to Illusion. But barring that, even if they were right that Zanta had fled north, there were the entirety of the Broken and Center Seas to contend with. If she was desperate to get back home, she might circumvent Lasland to end up west of Yarene. She probably wouldn't risk sailing north through the Storm Gap, not with the danger of skirting so close between the Storm Ring and the Nanadie coast. The *Monsoon* could be anywhere.

"Maybe we should give up on this," Logan said quietly. "We don't know where she is, and it's getting serious."

Rowan scowled at him. "I'm not gonna back down. We'll be stronger together than apart."

But that wasn't the only reason, was it? Rowan wasn't going to admit defeat to the Demon, and he wasn't going to allow Shaw to defeat him either. How far would this go before the Demon and Rowan forgave each other and chose to put their crews before their marital squabbles? Logan supported Rowan's choice to warn Zanta, they were friends after all, but not if it meant getting stuck in the middle of a war.

Logan scowled back. "If we're going to keep pursuing this, we can't let ourselves get trapped again. We've got to have an escape plan." As much as he cared about Nia, their crew came first.

"We'll head northeast and get the lay of the land. I don't wanna give up on this yet. But if we get into trouble or can't find out anything about Zanta, I'll drop it. I promise."

Logan nodded. This was about as close as he was going to get to compromise. Still, he wished he could run off and find Nia and make sure she was safe.

"I don't suppose you know where John was headed with the *Sweet Mercy*?" Logan asked hopefully.

"Up the Avardellan coast, I think. Why?"

"Never mind." The *Sweet Mercy* wasn't a known pirate ship yet. John could've slipped in and gotten Nia no problem. But Avardel was about as far from Roseforte as one could get in the Islands, so that avenue was closed to them. He sat for a moment, hoping beyond hope that Nia had survived the attack. She was smart. Capable. It was entirely possible she was fine, right? And speaking of capable people, there was one more thing he had to discuss with Rowan. "Robin asked if we were going to let the captives go at this port."

That slow smile was back. "That would piss Yves off. Let's do it."

CHAPTER 21

MAY 22ND, 1668

They caught the trade winds west, intending to head around the north coast of Lasland. If they could circumvent the blockade, they had a chance to get back to familiar waters. The mercenaries were nowhere to be seen, and Zanta felt like they'd finally slipped the noose of these past weeks of strange happenings. For a few days at least, Zanta and her crew were free again.

Until the *Lonesome* caught up. Sabriye spotted it before they even had the Laslandish coast in sight. It wasn't as damaged as Zanta had hoped, but the *Marigold* wasn't beside it. It bore down on them quickly, and fired several shots off the *Monsoon*'s bow, harrying them until they were forced to turn north instead.

Truthfully, Zanta was almost glad for the distraction. It kept her from thinking about Nia.

The next morning Zanta stepped, yawning, into the crisp dawn air. The days had already given way to summer heat this far south, but the mornings still belonged to spring. Zanta stopped short on the top step, yawn aborted, leaving an unfinished feeling in the back of her throat. The orange disk of the sun crested the horizon, painting bright stripes on the sea and sky, and silhouetting a lone figure.

Nia sat with her skirts tucked around her legs, chin resting on her folded arms on the rail. Her hair shone rose gold in the light, at peace with the morning and the sea. She didn't turn at the sound of Zanta's footsteps, mesmerized watching the sun's blush on the waves. What Zanta could see of her profile held longing in every line.

Zanta drifted toward her a few steps before she stopped herself. What was Nia thinking about? Was she missing home? Wondering about the people she'd left behind?

Or was she wondering why Zanta had been avoiding her?

Zanta tore her eyes away from Nia's beauty, guilt tightening her belly. It had taken exactly one night for the weight of what she and Nia had done to fully settle onto her. She'd been taken in by Nia's vulnerable beauty in a moment when the adrenaline of battle still sang through her blood. She could almost say she'd been bewitched, if she believed in that sort of thing.

The rational side of Zanta's mind said that they'd done nothing wrong. She and Nia were grown women who'd let a storm of high emotion turn into physical passion. There was nothing wrong with that.

But the other side, the side that still loved and grieved Emilie, had already condemned the act. When Nia had seen her the next morning and smiled that bright, sunny smile, freckled nose wrinkling, and leaned in for a kiss, Zanta had run. And she'd been avoiding her ever since.

It had broken something in her to see Nia's smile fade away, but Zanta couldn't quite get past the overwhelming feeling that she'd cheated on Emilie.

"Captain?"

Zanta snapped from her reverie, realizing that she'd been gazing at Nia for much too long, tracing the slope of her nose, the curve of her neck limned in sunrise. Nia's head snapped around at the sound. The helmsperson made their way down the steps and clapped Zanta on the shoulder.

"Been here since before dawn." They nodded toward Nia, speaking quietly so she wouldn't overhear. "Thought she might be fixing to jump again, so I kept an eye out. But she just watched the water."

"Thank you."

They shrugged. "All's quiet with the mercs."

Zanta nodded. The *Lonesome* maintained its place off their port side, still preventing them from turning west toward Lasland.

The helmsperson nodded and retreated below for a much needed rest.

"Zanta."

Shit. Nia stalked toward her, soft face no longer wistful, but determined. Zanta retreated up the quarterdeck steps, but Nia only followed.

Shit, shit, shit. Zanta should've escaped below while she still had the chance. Now she was going to be trapped up here.

"Go check the lines," Zanta murmured to the relief helmsman, and took the wheel from him. He took one look at Nia's stormy expression and retreated down the opposite set of steps.

"Zanta!" Nia barked. Gods, she was so close. Zanta didn't look at her.

"I'm busy." She could practically hear Nia roll those bright green eyes.

"Busy avoiding me," Nia scoffed. "Is it your habit to kidnap women, seduce them, then ignore them? Or am I special?"

The ire in her voice finally forced Zanta to look at her. Color had risen high on her cheeks, her hands on her ample hips and a half scowl, half pout on her lips. Gods, even like this, Zanta found her adorable. She imagined how devastating Nia must look scolding wayward sailors at the inn. Zanta wasn't into degradation, but she could happily make an exception for this woman.

"You're not special."

Nia's mouth dropped open in shock, and Zanta almost fumbled the wheel spokes when she realized how it sounded.

"No! I mean..." Zanta wanted to bash her own head against the wheel. "I don't do this. I never do this."

"So I am special." Nia cocked an eyebrow.

Oh, she was being obstinate now. Why wasn't Zanta annoyed?

"I didn't kidnap *or* seduce you," Zanta argued, trying to get back on track.

The eyebrow arched higher. "Eating me out on the floor of a storage room isn't seducing?"

"Oh yes, you and your flirting and big teary eyes had *nothing* to do with that!" Zanta shot back.

"So it was pity that led your tongue to my cunt? How generous of you!" Both their voices climbed higher, and Zanta flinched. The morning shift would be making their way up soon, and she didn't want to hash this out in front of them.

"Lower your voice!" Zanta snapped.

"Oh forgive me, Captain, for speaking out of turn. I forgot I'm not worthy of even a passing word, let alone a morning after kiss!" Nia's voice dripped with venom, but her pale eyelashes darkened with tears. She whirled. "I'll take my leave."

"Wait!" Zanta caught her hand before she could think. Instead of wrenching away and storming off, Nia's fingers tightened in hers.

"I'm sorry," Zanta said.

"I don't appreciate being ignored," Nia sniffed. Some of the fight had gone out of her.

"I shouldn't have done that." Zanta tugged Nia a little closer. The guilt ate at her edges, but Zanta pushed it away. "I...It's complicated."

"Didn't seem complicated when you were moaning my name," Nia grumbled.

"Nia, I'm going to tell you something."

Nia met her gaze, peridot sparkling in the growing light.

Zanta continued, "I had a fiancée, years ago. She..." Gods, how could Zanta describe the horror of Emilie's death? The way it had reshaped her whole life? "She died five years ago. I haven't slept with another woman since, and what we did that night was overwhelming. I felt guilty for betraying her." Truth be told, she'd barely slept with men either. She'd attempted with Rowan and been rejected.

Nia remained silent for a few seconds, processing, lips parted ever so slightly. Zanta bit her lower lip to keep from kissing her.

"What was her name?"

Even this felt like giving away so much. "Emilie."

Nia looked away, toward the rising sun.

"It doesn't have to mean anything," she finally said quietly. She crossed the arm not held by Zanta over her belly. Defensive.

"What?"

Their eyes met again, fingers tightening. "You said you felt guilty," Nia said. "You don't have to. You obviously still love her, but what we did doesn't lessen that. It didn't mean anything."

Zanta tried to swallow her heart back down, but it stuck in her throat. "I..." Her words were arrested by Nia's smile as she stepped closer.

"Guilt doesn't look good on you, Captain." She reached up to smooth the crease from between Zanta's brows. "Go on loving her, but don't feel bad that you're attracted to me. You deserve pleasure, and I can give you that. No strings attached."

Oh. Why did it feel like a flock of deranged birds was trying to burst from Zanta's throat? Nia was offering her an out. A way to assuage her guilt and still have Nia, for as long as that might last.

The morning shift was starting to filter onto the deck below. Nia tilted her head.

"What do you say, Captain?"

CHAPTER 22

MAY 23RD, 1668

Henri wiped his forearm across the sweat beading on his brow. Though the days were getting longer, it was almost dark now, and the humid air still clung to the day's heat. The light changed from golden daylight to peachy sunset on his hands as he finished up securing the lines. It was the *Siren*'s last night in Kadling Kay, and many crew members were off enjoying the luxuries of shore leave. Henri had spent his own free time exploring the markets with Fox, since Robin had been occupied keeping his brother out of trouble as he bought a few things to restock the infirmary.

Henri huffed in exasperation. Not only had David monopolized the only shore leave Henri and Robin were likely to get for weeks, but according to Robin, David had also spent the entire time on dry land trying to convince Robin to "escape while they had the chance."

Henri retied the last knot. Then retied it again. Even though he and Robin had made up, the mood was still awkward between them with the stress of keeping their relationship secret from David.

Henri didn't like it, but Robin had asked for some time, and Henri was willing to give him that grace. Deep down, he still harbored a little irrational bead of anxiety that Robin would leave him after all. If not for his family, then for the prospect of a peaceful life. But Henri told himself to trust Robin. He had to believe their love was strong enough to keep them together.

"Here..."

Henri turned at the sound of Robin's gentle voice to find the captive sailors, including David, gathered near the opposite rail with knapsacks slung on their backs. Robin was with them, talking quietly with David. Captain Rowan must've decided it was time to release the captives.

The bead of anxiety jumped up to lodge in Henri's throat.

No. Robin wasn't going with them. Even if he'd decided to leave, he would never do so without saying goodbye. And besides, he didn't have any belongings with him, only a few folded and sealed papers clutched in his hands. Henri couldn't hear what else Robin was saying, but David looked displeased. Robin tried to give him the papers, but he pushed them away.

Rowan and Logan chose that moment to appear on deck. Rowan's coat fluttered behind him in the breeze that kicked up off the harbor. The brim of Logan's hat drooped in the humidity. They strode over to the group, Logan half a step behind the captain.

"You're free to go," Rowan said without preamble, stopping before the assembled group. "You will be paid for your service thus far and are welcome to stay on as full crew members if you wish. But I will no longer keep you here against your will." Logan began passing out coins from a bag. Only a few weeks' wages, but enough to last till they found another ship, if they didn't drink it away first.

"We already subtly put out word that you were our captives. So you shouldn't have any trouble on our account. However..." His tone shifted, and one or two of the sailors backed up a step. "I urge you to keep anything you've seen here to yourselves. I cannot guarantee how the Deep Water Demon might react if he hears our secrets being whispered through the taverns."

Logan finished handing out the coins, and the sailors hastily disembarked before Rowan could change his mind, leaving only David behind. Rowan raised an eyebrow.

"I would have thought you'd be the most eager to leave our humble vessel, Beckett."

David blanched at the continued refusal of all of them to call him *Master* Beckett. "I'm not leaving until you release my brother!" He seemed to be trying for an air of confidence, maybe even intimidation, but he just sounded like a petulant child. Henri sidled closer, ready to help if there was trouble. Robin's brother or not, he was perfectly willing to throw David off the ship if need be.

"You promised his freedom in exchange for information about Shaw," David said.

"And I *told* you he's free to go. If he is choosing to stay, perhaps you should accept his decision." Rowan's gaze flicked to Henri, then Robin. "You can deal with this, can't you?"

"Yes, Captain," Robin said. Rowan turned on his heel and disappeared back belowdecks with Logan trailing him.

David whirled on his older brother. "We're going," he demanded. Henri half expected him to stomp his foot.

"*You're* going," Robin said firmly. "I'm staying right here. I already told you. Take the letters and—"

"But why?" David shouted, startling some seagulls from the dock pilings. "Why do you insist on staying here?"

Robin's gaze slid to Henri, then away. Henri's breath caught. Was he finally going to tell him?

"I've built a life here," Robin began, squeezing David's arm. "I have friends, and I need to tell you—"

"How can these people be your friends?" David interrupted him, knocking his hand away. He was yelling again. "I'm not leaving you here to throw your life away with a bunch of deviants and murderers! If you won't go, neither will I. I'll wait till you come to your senses!" He stomped away belowdecks, slamming the hatch behind him.

Robin pinched the bridge of his nose, taking a few deep breaths until Henri made it to his side. When Robin felt Henri's hand on his shoulder, he looked up and smiled ruefully.

"You okay?" Henri asked, his voice low.

Robin sighed, leaning in to Henri's touch like he was an anchor. "I tried to tell him."

"I know." Despite the fact it would drive a wedge between them forever, he'd tried. The ball of anxiety, worn smooth by weeks of Henri worrying at it, retreated. Warmth spread through his chest.

"I better go after him before he causes more trouble."

Henri leaned in and pecked Robin on the cheek. "Meet you in our room later?"

"Yeah."

Robin trotted away after his wayward brother.

. . .

By the time Henri had finished up his duties for the night and gave himself a quick scrub to get rid of the day's sweat, Robin was already back in their room. As Henri entered, he looked up from where he was lounging on their bed, long legs stretched out.

"Welcome back." He rested the penny romance they'd both been reading open on his chest and smiled. Gods, that smile. For the first time since their fight, Henri felt heat kindling low in his gut. He crossed the room in two quick strides and knelt one knee on the end of the bed. Robin's breath caught, hazel eyes watching him as he crawled up the bed and brushed the penny novel aside.

"What are you doing?" Robin asked quietly. They hadn't been intimate since before the fight. Nothing more than light touches and kisses to sustain them.

Henri didn't answer, just leaned down, thumb smoothing over Robin's cheek, and kissed him. Robin melted immediately, his mouth going soft and pliant. He let out a breathy moan and wrapped his arms around Henri's shoulders, pulling him closer.

"Henri," Robin breathed between kisses. "I need to..." He surrendered to Henri's lips again, but after a few moments pushed him away slightly. "I didn't tell him yet."

Henri rolled onto this side next to Robin. "I figured as much."

Robin faced him. "I really tried. He just yelled and wouldn't let me get a word in." His gaze lowered. "Are you disappointed?"

Oddly, he wasn't. He loved Robin, and as much as Robin keeping him a secret from his family pained Henri, he wanted to save Robin the heartache of rejection too.

"It's okay." His voice was soft, and he pulled Robin to his chest.

"I really tried." Robin's voice wavered on the verge of tears.

"Hey, Robin, listen to me." Henri tilted Robin's chin up so their eyes met. "I'm sorry I got mad. You tried, and there's still time if you want to tell him, but it doesn't matter to me anymore. Just love me. Quietly or loudly. But don't stop, okay?"

Robin's pretty hazel eyes searched Henri's face for a moment. His hand came up to rest against Henri's chest.

"I've made up my mind to tell him, and I wrote letters to my family explaining everything, so I went into town and mailed them after David yelled at me again. So they'll know whether I'm able to tell him or not. I don't want to hide you, and I'm not ashamed of the life we've built together. I even included a sketch of you, in case they decide to be happy for me." He smiled bashfully, ears turning pink against his sandy blond hair. "You know, back then, I never actually expected to find love. I'd prepared myself for more of a 'bachelor for life' scenario."

Henri planted a kiss against Robin's hairline. "Even if you hadn't left, someone would have fallen for you." Who wouldn't love this tall, sweet man?

"Even if they had, I wouldn't have been free to pursue it." Robin's hand trailed up Henri's chest to his shoulder. "I'm glad I found you." He kissed Henri on the mouth. Sweet at first, then growing more insistent. Henri's heartbeat quickened. He caressed down Robin's neck to push one strap of his suspenders from his shoulder. Despite the unease that had settled between them over the last few weeks, Henri had missed this. Feeling Robin's soft body under his hands. Undressing him slowly and making him gasp. The thought that Robin's family would know about him, even know what he looked like, thrilled him. Or maybe it was just the gesture of Robin sending the letters, ensuring he wouldn't hide Henri anymore.

Henri's tongue invaded the warm interior of Robin's mouth, sliding against Robin's tongue as Robin hastily pushed his hands beneath Henri's shirt. Henri rolled on top of him again, one elbow braced beside Robin's shoulder. He rolled his hips forward, smiling into their kiss as Robin gasped. Robin's hand slipped down Henri's hard stomach and beneath the waistband of his pants, to cup his hardening cock.

"Robin? I—What the fuck?"

They both jumped, Henri nearly toppling off the bed, as the door to their room crashed open. Hands grabbed the back of Henri's shirt as he righted himself, trying to yank him away from Robin.

"Davy, stop!" Robin shouted. Henri twisted in David's grasp and managed to shove him hard enough that Henri's shirt ripped in his hands. David stumbled into the opposite wall, murder in his eyes, and Henri braced himself for another charge. But Robin was suddenly between them, shielding Henri's body with his own.

"I said, stop!" Robin yelled. His back was to Henri, standing at the end of their bed while Henri still knelt on the mattress. His chest rose and fell rapidly with panicked breath.

"I'll kill him," David snarled, hands clenched, white-knuckled, at his sides. "Get out of the way, Robin."

"No." Robin held out one arm to ward his brother off. "It's not what it looks like."

A pang of hurt hit Henri's heart, before he realized what it actually must look like to David. David's innocent, misguided brother pinned to the bed beneath a murderous pirate. All Henri could do was stand back and let Robin handle this. If he stepped in, it would look like Robin was under his control. And if David attacked Henri again, he'd have no choice but to defend himself. He didn't want to hurt someone Robin cared about, no matter how much pain that person had caused both of them.

David took a threatening step forward, eyes locked on Henri. He paid his elder brother no heed.

"You low-life, dirty, f—"

The crack of Robin's slap across David's face dropped the room into dead silence. David's head snapped to the side. His hands came up to cradle the already reddening mark on his cheek.

"Don't you dare insult him." Robin's voice was as sharp as his surgical knife, no longer carrying its usual gentleness. It sounded wrong coming from him. He was always so calm, even when faced with broken bones, bleeding wounds, burns, and fevers. Now Robin's shoulders trembled with anger, and Henri could see his palm and fingers reddening from the sting of the slap.

"Listen to me, David, because I'm only going to say this once. I'm never going home with you. I'm in love with Henri. If you can't accept that, I don't want to see you again."

David's eyes widened, hands dropping away from his face in shock.

"That's not true." David's voice shook.

"It is true." Robin reached back to take Henri's hand, tugging him off the bed so they could stand side-by-side, Robin's shoulder slightly in front of Henri's, as if to protect him.

"You're fucking lying." David's eyes filled with tears, whether from the slap or the revelation, Henri couldn't tell.

Robin sighed and pinched the bridge of his nose with the other hand. "Why the hell do you think I ran away from home in the first place, Davy? For fun? It's because I didn't want to be forced to marry a woman." Henri and Robin's fingers threaded together, and Henri squeezed, lending him courage.

"They wouldn't have forced—"

"They betrothed me without telling me! Look how you're acting right now just because the person I love is a man. You don't think it would've been ten times worse if our parents knew? Henri loves me. I don't have to hide myself from him."

A stunned silence settled into the room, broken only by David's hitching breath. His hazel gaze finally slid to Henri, and Henri's breath caught to see such hatred in eyes that looked so much like Robin's.

David spit at their feet and stomped out.

As soon as the door slammed behind him, Robin slumped against Henri's shoulder.

"You okay?"

Robin let out a shaky breath, and they both sank down to sit on the edge of the bed. "I'll be fine."

"You were so brave, love." Henri petted Robin's hair, as Robin leaned further into him.

"He was gonna hit you," Robin sniffled.

"I think I could've handled it."

Robin looked up at him. "It's just...when he started calling you those awful things, I couldn't stand it."

"Thank you for defending me, mon cher." Henri kissed the furrowed patch of skin right between his eyebrows. They sat cuddled up for a few minutes as Robin's sniffles slowly subsided.

"How about we go to sleep? Maybe you'll both feel better in the morning, and you can talk it out."

"Maybe," Robin mumbled.

They changed into loose, comfortable clothes and slipped beneath the covers. The heated mood of earlier was long gone, but Henri was content just to hold Robin. They settled into each other's arms like they were always meant to fit there.

Henri's mind was just starting to drift when Robin said, "Tell me about your family. Are they waiting for you somewhere?"

Like Robin, Henri's family wasn't something he liked to talk about much. Sharing the sad, gory details of their pasts wasn't something most pirates chatted about over a mug of ale and game of dice. But this was Robin, cozily wrapped up in his arms in their bed.

"My parents are both dead." He'd mentioned it in passing to Robin before, but hadn't gone into detail.

"How did they die?"

Henri tried not to think about it too much. On beautiful spring days it still hurt to remember his mother's funeral. The warm sun on his face, cold dirt in his palm. But still, Robin had been so open with him the last few days, it was only fair that Henri did the same.

"Both of them were pirates." He heard a soft intake of breath, but Robin didn't say anything, so he continued. "My maman retired when I was born, and my father would visit every winter with..." Henri cleared his throat. "But when I was a teenager, he stopped coming. Maman got sick. She slowly wasted away over the years and died when I was twenty-one. The last time I saw my father, I was nineteen. He was acting strange, convinced that everyone was out to get him. He was even suspicious of Maman, who could barely walk by that time. He gave me the key he always used to wear around his neck. I wore it for a few years, hoping he would come back or I'd be able to find him." Even now. he could almost feel the warm brass where it used to rest against his chest, and the smooth bit of old leather his father had feverishly insisted should never be parted from the key.

"Why don't you wear it anymore?" Robin asked.

"A little while after I joined the *Siren* crew, I found out he'd died. Wearing the key seemed a bit pointless after that." He didn't even know what it was meant to unlock.

"I'm sorry." Robin hugged Henri closer, one arm around his waist.

"Don't be. My maman was a good and loving mother, and I made peace with my father's death long ago."

"There's no one else? No siblings?"

Henri buried his face in Robin's already bed-mussed hair. "Let's go to sleep. You must be tired."

He wasn't ready to talk about that just yet.

~

May 24th, 1668

At dawn, when the bosun's whistle woke Henri to return to duty and prepare the *Siren* to depart Kadling Kay, he kissed Robin's warm temple and climbed out of bed. Robin mumbled something in his sleep and rolled over, one arm and one leg hanging over the side of the bed. Henri tucked him back in, then pulled on some clean clothes.

It had been five years since his father's death. Henri riffled around his sea chest, and after a minute, drew out a small leather pouch and tipped out its contents. A tarnished brass key on a leather cord fell into his hand, along with a small square of strange, dappled gray leather. He rubbed his thumb over its smooth surface, then slipped the cord over his neck so the key and leather settled against the center of his chest. He tucked it into his shirt before hurrying up onto the deck to help the others catch the tide.

CHAPTER 23

MAY 23RD, 1668

Tentacles crawled silently across the slate roof where Yves perched. The sun had set, his own shadows blending with thickening darkness over the harbor of Kadling Kay. Below, the docks still bustled with light and life, none the wiser to him lurking on the harbor office's roof. There was a nervous energy about the crowd, no doubt due to the presence of two famous pirate ships in their usually peaceful harbor. He couldn't fault the good townsfolk for their wariness. He'd just as soon slaughter them if he had a purpose for it.

As it was, the satiation of his encounter with Rowan in the alleyway had already worn thin. Death sat in his shadow, gnawing at his bones. He thought of going to the *Siren Song*, pinning Rowan to the wall and fucking him till he cried. Not the bed, that seemed too civilized for his current mood. But he knew he hadn't exactly been gentle in the alley, and Rowan would need time to recover. So he did not go to the *Siren* to ease his hunger, but he did watch it.

Finally, he spotted Rowan talking to the group of captive sailors, and they disembarked. He forcefully pulled his gaze away from his husband to track the sailors through the bustle as they made their way down the docks in a little knot and stopped near the building where Yves waited. Rowan had released them, as Yves knew he would. The man he loved would never deign to keep an innocent person captive. Poor, softhearted Rowan, trying to do the right thing. Affection almost dulled the anger still prickling in Yves's guts.

Yves had tried to be merciful, for Rowan's sake, by offering the sailors an opportunity to live. But here they were, free men.

And that was a problem.

He'd already taken care of the witnesses from the alley, now it was time to wrap things up.

Below, the sailors seemed to be discussing what to do next. No doubt they'd try to get work on the next ship heading back to Kefrye. Unfortunately for them, the harbor offices were closed for the night, so they'd have to find one the hard way. They'd never make it there.

Yves slipped down to the alleyway at the side of the building. He could have sent men to take care of this, but if anyone else knew, he couldn't be sure the information wouldn't make its way back to Rowan. So when the group moved away, Yves slipped after them. The crowd parted around him. An unfortunate side effect of the demon nesting within his flesh. People, especially those unused to violence, shied away from him instinctually. His crew had become more used to it, but still treated him with respectful fear. Rowan was the only person who seemed to crave it. He knew what Yves was. Could see his true form, yet still, he loved him.

Yves frowned as he stalked after the small group of sailors who had not noticed him yet. Why did his thoughts keep turning toward Rowan? When the *Siren* had sailed away from the Teeth, Yves had been determined not to follow. Let Rowan make this mistake and come crawling back if he was beaten. Let him face his betrayer alone.

But after all that talk of death and parting, Yves couldn't risk it. He was furious still. His anger a palpable sourness on his tongue. But Rowan was the only person he cared for in this world, and Yves could not lose him.

The sailors had reached darker streets now, the crowd thinning as they neared the end of the docks. Yves stuck to the shadows as they ducked into a side street. Were they looking for a place to stay? Or going to drink away whatever wages Rowan had inevitably given them? Yves couldn't help the prickle of offense at the thought that they would squander his husband's coin and goodwill.

Even if Yves was going to kill them.

He stepped into the mouth of the street and found his prey waiting.

So they had noticed him following after all. They stood arrayed across the width of the lane, four of them, all with knives or lengths of wood they'd found in the alley. Yves carried his dagger and saber, but did not draw them.

"We know you're following us, Demon," one standing in the center said. He tapped the flat of his knife against his palm. "The Ghost Hawk let us go. We've no business with you."

Yves tilted his head. Knew the flickering of the torch on the wall played tricks on their eyes, casting his face into ghoulish shadow.

"No business? I believe our agreement was join, or die."

"We did join!" another hissed. "But he freed us."

"We promised not to tell about anything we saw!" a third said, wide-eyed and shaking. Clearly out of his mind with fear.

Did Rowan really think a flimsy promise of silence was going to keep their secrets? Yves may have kissed him in front of outsiders, but he'd be damned if he'd let that slipup put Rowan in danger.

"You mistake me." Yves stepped forward, spurs clinking softly. He did not draw his blades, but the sailors' grips tightened on their weapons. "A deal with me does not expire. And no other can release you from it. You may have been under the Ghost Hawk's command, but it is me you pledged your deaths to."

Something snapped in them, terror pushing into action. The first one yelled and charged, the others following. Yves caught the first man by the throat, choking off his forward momentum. Death lurked over Yves's shoulder. Yves wanted to sink his teeth in. To devour. But news of corpses with human bite marks would spread fast, and he did not want Rowan to know. He drew his dagger and slashed across the man's stomach. The flesh parted like an amorous mouth, spilling forth ropes of intestine. The man stilled, mouth dropping open in silent shock before he fell, gurgling, and died on the worn cobbles. Someone yelled, but it seemed no one in this remote section of the docks could hear or care.

Yves breathed in the scent of blood like a drug. The rest of the sailors fell upon him, stepping over their dying colleague.

A snarl caught in Yves's teeth as the dark waters rose in him. One of the men stumbled back in fear. Another slashed at Yves's throat, blade whistling a mere breath from his skin. Yves seized him by the shirt and threw him into the wall, where his head cracked against the stones, blood and brain matter splattering in a halo.

Pain prickled through Yves's spine as a board full of old nails cracked across his back. He hissed—not because of the pain, which was almost like a balm to his hunger, and would be gone soon enough anyway—but because the nails had punctured his shoulder, and the blood would ruin his coat.

He whirled, drawing his saber, but the assailant escaped his slash. There were only two left, and seeing that Yves had no reaction to their attack, they turned and fled.

Within a few paces he took the first to the ground, teeth latching onto the back of his neck. The man's scream bounced off the stone walls. Blood burst on Yves's tongue, heady with life and death. The demon's instinct overtook him, and he bit down harder, teeth crunching against vertebrae. Yves twisted, and the man's flailing stilled. Small, animal-like whimpers falling into the puddles on the street. Yves didn't have time to savor his suffering. He left the man paralyzed on the ground and went after the last one, running him down like a wolf with a deer.

His deer dashed around a corner, and Yves followed him into a dark, dead-end alley. The man—just a boy really, he couldn't have been more than twenty—whirled to face him, eyes wide and shifting like a cornered animal.

"Please," he whispered, backing toward the brick wall, holding a small knife out in front of him with both shaking hands. "I swear, I-I won't tell."

Yves couldn't take that risk. The whole situation was his own fault, his poor control that had put Rowan in danger and their relationship on display. Besides, these men had made a deal with a demon, and it had come due.

Yves stalked forward, the light of the torches at his back. His shadow stretched out long into the darkness before him, invisible tentacles writhing around it. The man's eyes flicked down to the shadow that showed Yves's true form, then back up to his face.

"Monster," he breathed.

The demon, as always, rose further to the surface, pleased to be acknowledged. Known.

His shadow touched the tip of the man's boots.

"S-stay back!" The wavering knife pointed at Yves's heart. "I'll kill you. I swear!" Blood dripped from the tip of Yves's saber as he advanced. The threat didn't matter, and the nail holes in his back were already closing up. He didn't care how much blood he spilled, how much pain he caused or experienced. Anything for Rowan.

"Do it," he growled, the tang of blood still clinging to his taste buds. "See how far it gets you."

One shuddering breath, and the man lunged. Yves didn't raise his sword to defend himself and the knife sank deep into his shoulder. He didn't cry out, didn't stumble. The knife scraped his clavicle. The man gasped and stumbled back, leaving the blade in Yves's body.

"You see now, how futile that is," Yves said calmly.

"Please, have mercy."

Yves's long fingers curled around the hilt of the knife and yanked it out, a gout of blood cascading down the front of his jacket.

"Mercy? You were already given mercy, and you ran from it." The man's back hit the bricks. Yves set the blade against his throat. "This, too, is a mercy." He slit his throat, a sickening gurgle bubbling through the wound as the man tried to draw breath, life draining out of his eyes. Yves resheathed the sword and dropped the knife as the body slumped to the ground.

A beautiful calm washed over him. The demon settled: Death curling up in him like a drowsy cat now that he had blood on his hands. Yves drew a lacy handkerchief from his pocket to wipe the blood from his chin. It was soaked too.

"Tsk." He tucked it back into his coat, then lifted the dead man's arm and wiped his mouth on a clean patch of sleeve.

Yves's shoulder wound tingled as it closed. It would be gone before tomorrow. If Yves's body had still been capable of retaining such wounds, he'd be all scar and no flesh by now. His fingers moved to the scratch Rowan had left on his wrist in the alley a few days ago, then to the remains of the wound Rowan's knife had left against his neck. Any other wound would have healed with no trace by now. But these remained livid against the whiteness of his skin where it had peeled away beneath Rowan's nails and parted for his knife.

Any mark Rowan's hands or mouth left on him stayed. Healed as mortal flesh would. Slow. Itchy. Human.

And Yves—both parts of him—had no idea why.

It was as if Yves's body wanted to hold onto the touch of his beloved. To bear the marks of him. Rowan didn't know. He'd never seen Yves injured by any hand but his own, and therefore had never seen the rapid healing of any wound that wasn't immediately fatal.

Yves let him believe it was normal. Rowan liked marking him. Leaving bruises and scratches on Yves's too perfect skin like a signature. He delighted in that small power. That claim. Yves would not dissuade him of it. He cherished it as well. Every small ache reminded him that Rowan loved him.

They were bound together. Inseparable but for the inevitability of Rowan's eventual death. Not even their current anger could keep them apart. Perhaps this was punishment for Yves's hubris in releasing the demon from its underwater prison by taking it into his body. Fate had given him one weakness in the man he loved. One person who could harm him. One person he was human for. Perhaps one day Rowan could kill him, and he wouldn't come back.

The paralyzed man still clung to life by the time Yves retraced his steps, gasping in a small pool of blood that trickled sluggishly from Yves's bite mark. He'd gotten carried away and used teeth after all. He entertained the idea of cutting away the flesh to hide the bite, but some part of him whispered that was cruel, and Rowan would want him to put the man out of his misery quickly. Yves sighed and turned the man over with the toe of his boot, only to be met with pure terror. The face of a man who knew death stood over him, and was unable to do a thing about it. Yves supposed he could still cut away the bite after he'd killed him, but at this point it seemed more trouble than it was worth. Rowan was leaving with the tide at dawn; he'd never learn of this one way or the other.

Unless...Yves's gaze flicked over the carnage on the street, and he sighed with relief. The painter was not among the victims. Perhaps he'd stayed on to be close to his brother despite his hatred of all of them.

Yves drew his saber across the man's throat.

Yves's steps slowed as he neared the docks. The *Siren* sat far removed from the legitimate ships, but it was bright as a beacon in the dark. Figures moved on the deck, too far away for him to tell who they were, and faint strains of music filtered through the night.

Everything in him pulled him toward the little ship. All he wanted was to go to Rowan's cozy room and fall into bed with him. But his feet didn't move. Anger still overwhelmed whatever longing lived in him.

On the surface, he understood why Rowan resisted his control so strongly, even if it put him in danger. Freedom lived in his precious heart. It was what had drawn both Yves's ire and interest from the time they first met. And it was one of the things Yves loved most about him. But damn if it wasn't infuriating. All Yves was trying to do was protect him. To keep him from making a fatal mistake. To keep them together. But Rowan had a problem with that word, 'keep.' He wasn't something that could be caged. Yves knew that well by now, but it did nothing to soothe the incessant itch to be near Rowan always, to protect him from the world.

Rowan was the only person in the world who mattered. And Yves didn't understand Rowan's attachments to his friends. Least of all that woman he'd almost slept with while they were separated, and now insisted on maintaining a friendship with. None of them were worthy of Rowan. To Yves, the only purpose they served was to keep Rowan happy and alive when Yves couldn't be near him.

Yves turned away from the bright spot that was the *Siren Song*, a beacon of warmth while Yves walked all alone in the dark.

Movement caught his eye, and he retreated into the shadows. A man and a woman stood talking in the shadow of a ship a few berths away. The ship hadn't been there when Yves left to stalk the sailors; it must have arrived only recently. By the profile of the hull, he'd guess it to be Kefryean built, and recently damaged by what looked like cannon fire.

The woman put a hand on the man's shoulder, and Yves rolled his eyes. He'd been half hoping for some plot he could sink his teeth into, but it was likely some sailor negotiating personal entertainment for his first night in port. How disappointing.

But it was the woman who held out a small bag heavy with coin. The man shook his head, but with a few more cajoling words Yves couldn't hear, he pocketed it. The woman returned to the ship, and the man retreated up the dock. When he stepped into the light, Yves was surprised to find he recognized him. Robin Beckett. The man who'd bargained away his freedom to Yves in order to escape his family. The man who'd fruitlessly tended Yves's wounds for nearly a year.

Robin loped uneasily up the dock, glancing around to ensure no one saw him. His gaze passed unseeing over the spot Yves waited in the shadows, and the torchlight caught Robin's face more fully.

No. Not Robin at all, but his brother, *Master Painter* David Beckett.

The demon flared up, eager to kill again. David knew of Yves's and Rowan's relationship, and moreover, despised them. Had Rowan freed him after all? Had he sold the information to that woman? Now that he was free, he'd go singing their secrets like a hungry gull the first chance he got.

Yves drew his dagger, jeweled pommel glinting. Rowan wouldn't like this if he found out. Robin was his friend, a valuable part of his crew, and Rowan couldn't stand to see his friends hurt. But better to ask forgiveness than permission. Yves couldn't risk letting David live. He'd do it quickly, with minimal pain. Maybe that would mollify Rowan's inevitable anger.

The toes of Yves's boots touched the light on the dock boards, shadow tentacles questing ahead of his steps into the light. He looked back, wondering whether he'd need to kill the woman too, even though he hadn't gotten a good look at her. It would be harder to kill her on her ship, but Yves would be careful to leave no witnesses. Rowan and Robin need not find out about this at all.

But instead of heading toward the city, David loped back to the *Siren*. Yves paused. David mounted the gangplank and disappeared belowdecks.

CHAPTER 24

MAY 29TH, 1668

The wooden dick hit Nia's leg for what felt like the twentieth time in as many minutes. She wiggled, trying to subtly adjust the straps that encircled her hips and thighs. She couldn't fathom how men dealt with this shit all day, every day. Especially in pants. She felt like she was constantly adjusting herself.

"Something wrong?" Laurent asked. He seemed to be focusing on mincing an absolutely massive pile of garlic, but from his smile, she knew he'd seen at least some of the little adjustment jig she'd been doing every few minutes since she'd gotten dressed this morning.

"Peachy," Nia answered, unable to keep the bitterness from her voice. Laurent went on mincing his garlic, but the smile didn't falter.

"You and the captain seem to be back on good terms."

Nia adjusted again. Truly, she was beginning to understand why men were how they were, and this equipment didn't even include balls. Gods, she couldn't even imagine what it would be like if she had balls.

"We are," she answered after a minute, refocusing on her own task, peeling some slightly mushy carrots.

"Is there romance on the horizon?"

"Not likely," Nia muttered, brushing a pile of carrot peels to the side. Laurent shot her a sympathetic look.

"She told you about Emilie." It was a statement, not a question.

"She told me some." It wasn't that Nia necessarily wanted romance. It would only make her feel worse when she ultimately absconded with her treasure. If she was honest with herself, she was a little peeved that Zanta had agreed to her "only sex" proposal so readily. She understood, really, but that didn't make it better. Gaining her trust would have made finding the treasure easier, but all Nia needed was a short stretch—or several—of uninterrupted access to Zanta's room. She was confident she could accomplish that through sex alone.

So why was she so annoyed?

Laurent's knife scraped across the cutting board. "So are you going to tell me what you've got under your skirt?"

"Why, Laurent, I didn't think you were interested in the contents of women's skirts," Nia quipped, unable to keep a smile from cracking through her annoyed gloom.

Laurent smiled back, wide enough that the deep lines of all his past smiles formed in his cheeks. "Usually you'd be right, but you seem to have something extra going on right now."

Damn, she shouldn't have fidgeted so much.

"You can't tell anyone."

"Oh, my lips are more sealed than the hull of this ship." His eyes sparkled with anticipation.

Nia glanced at the galley door, firmly closed. "Okay, fine."

Laurent set the knife down, awaiting whatever Nia would show him like a kid with his hand out for a sweet. With another glance at the door, Nia quickly lifted her layers of skirts to reveal the velvet straps and the hard wooden cock hanging down between her legs. Laurent whistled, impressed, and crouched down to get a look at it head-on.

"If anyone could change my allegiances, Nia, it's you and that impressive piece." He looked up at her. "Where'd you get it? Do they take commissions?"

"A friend gave it to me." Nia's face warmed. Every time she'd ever internally or externally judged a partner's manhood flashed before her eyes.

"Some friend," Laurent chuckled. "Did he model it after himself?"

"It's a set. The one he modeled after himself is huge," Nia

answered, pleased as if she'd grown it herself. She was starting to understand why some men had such an ego on them.

"I'd love to see that." Laurent's eyes were wide.

"I'm having a little trouble adjusting," Nia admitted sheepishly.

"Well, usually we aren't walking around with a raging hard on between our legs." Laurent laughed. "I'm typically quite soft while chopping garlic."

The door opening interrupted Nia's laugh. Panicked, she threw her skirts back down, accidentally covering Laurent's head in the process. He yelped, fighting his way out just as Zanta stepped into the galley.

"What are you two troublemakers up to?" Zanta eyed them as Laurent scrambled to his feet and smoothed down his curls, looking like a disheveled owl.

"Just rebuckling the princess's shoe," he answered casually. "You know her dedication to impracticality."

"A dedication that rivals your own, I think," Zanta laughed.

"Fair enough. What can we help you with, Captain? Care for a carrot?" Laurent asked. Nia wanted to kick him in the shin.

Zanta cleared her throat, suddenly looking awkward. "I heard Nia wanted to speak to me."

Laurent glanced between them, fighting a knowing smile. "I'll leave you to it, then." He swept out of the room, winking behind Zanta's back as he closed the door. Oh, he was *never* going to shut up about this. She should've denied everything.

"What did you want to talk about?" Zanta asked. Nia shifted from one foot to the other, the wooden dick hitting her thigh like the clapper of a bell. Wearing it was all well and good, but she'd neglected to actually think of a plan of seduction.

Nia cleared her throat—wonderful, that was attractive—then put on her widest, most honeyed smile.

"Have you given any thought to my proposition?" she asked innocently, as if the proposition in question was merely a potential menu for dinner, and not an agreement to sleep together, upon which Nia's entire plan hinged.

Zanta raised one manicured eyebrow. "This is what you pulled me away from my duties for?"

This wasn't going well. Nia had to lay on the charm, convince Zanta to sleep with her. But the galley workbench separated them, with its piles of garlic and carrots. And Nia didn't think she could accomplish anything close to a seductive walk with the extra equipment she was packing.

"Why? Were you doing something important?" Nia leaned forward against the workbench, making sure Zanta had a nice line of sight down the front of her dress.

"Besides captaining the ship? There's only the matter of those mercenaries still after us."

Right, the mercenaries who were trying to kill them. What a cockblock.

"Yet you still came down here to see me," Nia pointed out, hiding the little bit of pathetic hopefulness that slipped into her voice behind a sultry tone.

Zanta moved a few steps closer, and Nia didn't miss how her dark eyes flicked down to Nia's décolletage.

"I did," Zanta agreed.

"And?"

Zanta brushed the back of Nia's hand with her fingertips.

"I've thought about it."

"Aaaand?" Nia's hands itched with impatience to touch her. Their eyes met again.

"I've *been* thinking about it. That night. Touching you." A faint smile played on her lips, and suddenly all Nia could think of was pulling her against the workbench and kissing her until they both drowned in it. Instead, she held her breath.

"I want you to know, I still love Emilie," Zanta said, her fingertips trailing up the inside of Nia's wrist. "But I really can't stop thinking about you, and...did you mean what you said? That it can just be sex?"

Nia's heartbeat stuttered, and she hoped to the gods Zanta couldn't feel it.

"It doesn't have to mean anything."

"Good." Zanta's hand curled around the back of Nia's neck and pulled her into a kiss across the workbench, just like Nia had imagined a moment before. The wooden dick hit the side of the bench with a faint knock. Zanta flinched, releasing her.

"What was that?" She glanced behind her, but the door remained closed.

"Come on." They couldn't do anything out here, where anyone

could walk through the door. And she didn't know whether Laurent would deign to run interference for them, or cackle gleefully as he allowed any or everyone to barge in. Nia grabbed Zanta's hand and pulled her into the pantry. Her lips were on Zanta's the moment the door slammed behind them. Lantern light poured through the door slats, striping gold across Zanta's bare arms, the sides of her neck and cheeks. All the places Nia wanted to kiss. And she did. She backed Zanta against the door, light bending around her curves, and explored every inch of skin with her mouth. Zanta arched into it, a soft gasp escaping her lips even as she clutched Nia closer. Too late, Nia realized she should've used this opportunity to gain entry to the captain's quarters. That was *much* more private than this damn pantry. She'd been so focused on bedding Zanta again she'd forgotten the part about the actual bed.

No matter, it was a process. The longer it took, the more times she'd get to taste Zanta.

Nia tugged at Zanta's hair, tilting her head to gain better access to her neck, her delectable collarbone straight as an arrow. Her skin tasted faintly of sweat and some herbal perfume or oil, the scent pooling in the dip between collarbone and shoulder. Nia dragged her tongue across it, eliciting a soft moan. Zanta's arms came to rest around Nia's waist, pulling her closer. Her thick thigh slotted between Nia's legs, bumping the wooden cock.

They both froze.

"What's this?" Zanta arched a brow, barely visible in the low light. "Did you grow a dick since last time?"

"Why don't you find out for yourself?" Nia purred.

Zanta pressed her thigh a little harder. "Feels like you're happy to see me," she mused.

"Very."

"Have you been walking around with this all day hoping to run into me?"

"I guess skirts are good for something after all." Nia was glad for the low light hiding most of her blush. She'd known if she got her way Zanta would put that little tidbit together, but it was still embarrassing to be caught wanting. Preparing.

Zanta laughed. "I guess so." Her hands trailed down to Nia's hips, her full lips grazing Nia's ear. "Are you going to show me your little secret, Nia?"

Nia's breath caught, for a split second thinking Zanta knew everything. That she was after the treasure. That she—Zanta's thigh rubbed suggestively between her legs again, and Nia snapped back to logic. Zanta was only talking about the dick. Nia's relief came out in a quiet sigh.

"I don't know," Nia teased. "It's not so little. What I've got under there is quite impressive. Masterfully crafted. I'm not entirely sure you can handle it." If she'd worn John's cock, that might have been true, but she'd picked one of the middle ones for today.

Zanta took Nia's chin between her fingers, eyes roving from her flushed face down her body and back up again. Her thumb grazed Nia's lower lip. "If it's as finely crafted as the rest of you, I can't wait to get my hands on it."

She pushed Nia deeper into the pantry, pressing her back to the packed shelves, and kissed down her neck to the swelling tops of her breasts, unfastening the front of her bodice as she went. Nia's breath quickened, Zanta's mouth leaving little burning embers on her skin. Zanta's hands slipped beneath the stiff leaves of Nia's open bodice to frame her waist again, her leg slotting back between Nia's. Nia rocked her hips forward, rutting on Zanta's muscled thigh.

Zanta's lips grazed the skin at the low neck of Nia's chemise. Kissing from one freckled constellation to the next. Nia's nipples hardened beneath the fabric, the friction of Zanta's thigh between her legs sending warm tingles rushing through her. Zanta thumbed one nipple through the fabric, her other hand hitching Nia's leg up around Zanta's hip, gripping her ample buttocks through her skirts.

"Zanta," Nia gasped, rocking forward again, the cock trapped between their bellies. Even with the layers of skirt, she could get off just by grinding on Zanta's thigh like this. But Zanta had other ideas. She pulled open the ribbon at the neck of Nia's chemise to expose the rosy buds of her nipples. Nia arched encouragingly toward her mouth, and Zanta suckled at her breast.

A little whimper of a moan escaped Nia's lips as tingles shot through her body, her hips continuously grinding. Zanta met her movements. She hitched up Nia's skirt, fingers finding the first velvet strap banding Nia's thigh.

"You came prepared," Zanta murmured between her breasts. Then, realizing what she'd said, jerked back to look up into Nia's face. "Wait. Did you...Is this what was in the package from Logan?"

"I didn't conjure it out of thin air." Nia laughed at the bafflement that stole across Zanta's expression. Where else would she have gotten it? She'd come onto this ship with nothing but the box and the clothes on her back.

"But he...I mean, he looks so..." Another realization dawned. "Did you fuck Logan Crowder?"

Nia giggled again. Despite being second in command to one of the most notorious pirates in the Islands, Logan did indeed look like he'd never used his cock for anything especially interesting. It was part of his appeal, really. Nia never could resist training up an innocent man. Corrupting him just enough to get the job done while still being wide-eyed and malleable.

Zanta wasn't like that. She knew herself, and she definitely knew what she was doing.

"I may have," Nia admitted, hoping it wouldn't put Zanta off.

Zanta peered at Nia's skirts, concentrated bafflement on her face as if she could see through the layers of fabric to the appendage beneath. "Does that mean it's his..."

Nia laughed again. "No, no. I chose one of the others for today."

"Others?"

"There are four." Eventually she'd have to admit to Zanta that one of them was John's, in case she wasn't partial to him.

"Four!" Zanta laughed, hand tugging on the strap. "You get up to a lot of mischief, don't you."

"Not as much as a *literal pirate*," Nia huffed.

"Oh, you don't yet know the level of mischief I can get up to." Zanta trapped her gaze, eyes sparkling, as she lowered slowly to her knees. Her hand slipped up the back of Nia's thigh, coming to rest on the bottom curve of her ass. "Turn around."

Nia did, and nearly yelped when Zanta hiked her skirts up around her waist. Then actually did yelp when Zanta discovered she wasn't wearing anything but the strap underneath, and nipped her ass cheek.

"What are you—" A shiver raced up Nia's spine as Zanta's breath wafted hot against her exposed skin. Zanta pulled her hips back so she had to bend forward, bracing against a shelf laden with jars of preserved vegetables. Zanta wasted no time. Zanta gently separated Nia's cheeks to gain better access. Her tongue found Nia's clit, licking into Nia's wetness.

Nia gasped, clutching the shelf tighter as heat pooled low in her abdomen. Nia may have been the one planning this, but Zanta knew damn well how to please a woman. Nia had a hard time believing it had been—how long did Zanta say?—five years since she'd slept with a woman. Her skills certainly hadn't gone rusty in that time.

A particularly expert flick had Nia rutting her hips back, moaning against the jars. A pantry, even well-kept as it was, wasn't the most dignified place to get eaten out. But, well, it was far from the worst place Nia had ever fucked either. She closed her eyes. Focused on the heated pleasure quickly building toward a crescendo.

Zanta hummed, pleased, her tongue dipping shallowly into Nia's entrance before resuming its delicious drag against Nia's clit.

"Zanta..." Nia moaned. Wetness dripped down her thighs. Zanta hummed again in response and redoubled her efforts, reaching a pattern and speed that had Nia breathless, breasts heaving, hips rolling back of their own volition.

"Zanta...Zanta..." She didn't care if anyone happened to hear. What business was it of theirs where their captain took her pleasure? She had nothing to be ashamed of. Not yet.

Nia tasted metal. She'd bit down on the little brass bar that held the shelves' contents during rough seas. It felt cold on her lips, pressing down on her tongue. It did nothing but turn her moans of Zanta's name wordless as pleasure gushed through her like a flash flood. With one final shudder, one more rut against Zanta's face, she cried out, the bar digging into her mouth like a bit, and came.

Zanta's hands tightened on her, digging into pliant flesh, but she did not slow her pace as euphoria had Nia's eyes rolling back. Zanta lapped up the juices gushing against her mouth and kept on till the aftershocks began to ramp up and Nia's knees threatened to give out.

Nia released the bar, metal tang still coating her tongue, and reached back to tap the side of Zanta's head.

"Stop, stop," she gasped. Zanta pulled back, and Nia whirled to face her, almost sinking to the floor on quivering legs. Zanta stood, catching her around the waist.

Zanta blinked at her with those wide brown eyes, Nia's wetness slicking her lips, her chin, running shiny streaks down the planes of her throat...

"Why'd you stop me?" Zanta's tongue darted out to taste Nia on her lips. Gods, had there ever been a woman as rawly sexy as her? Nia had never met one.

"You can't just keep going till I'm a quivering heap," Nia said between heavy breaths. She didn't miss the gleam that entered Zanta's eye. The defiance that said, *why not?*

Zanta leaned forward, bringing her face close to Nia's. "What if I like you that way? You'd make quite the attractive heap."

"I have to preserve *some* energy for you," Nia laughed. "How am I to ravish you among these lovely sacks of potatoes if my legs no longer have feeling?"

Zanta grinned, the wetness on her cheeks shining against the bands of light. It was almost a relief, teasing like this. Grinning, laughing in an interlude to pleasure. Nia was a natural flirt, but finding partners at the inn, bedding them and never seeing them again, lacked a certain intimate joy. No matter the flirtatious giggles at the beginning, most strangers turned serious once sex was imminent, and while that was satisfying, well, it wasn't *this*.

The quivering in Nia's legs lessened, her breath evening out. She reached out to grasp Zanta's chin, fingers on one side, thumb on the other, and drew her closer till she could smell her own sweetness on Zanta's skin.

"We'll see who's a heap when I'm done with you."

A silly thing to say, but Zanta's pupils dilated, her breath hitching ever so slightly. Nia kissed her, relishing the taste of her own release on Zanta's tongue. Her skirts rustled as she leaned closer. Zanta tugged at the ties, and before long, Nia shed the layers and stood in only her chemise, open over her breasts. The wooden cock peeked out beneath the hem.

She'd always thought men looked silly wearing only a shirt with their dicks hanging out like a little turtle head poking out from its shell, and suffered a flash of self-consciousness. But Zanta gasped upon seeing it.

"A fine specimen indeed." Her hand closed around it like Nia could feel it. Like she was imagining it inside her. Nia reached down to adjust the straps so it stood at attention. Zanta remained fully clothed. That wouldn't do.

Need pushed away the last of Nia's hazy afterglow. A need to touch every inch of Zanta's warm skin. To burrow into her. To make her call Nia's name and keep her coming back again and again.

Nia stripped away Zanta's shirt, her lips following the departure of fabric. Beneath, Zanta's breasts were bound in a bandeau, swelling over the top edge of the fabric with every breath. Nia tugged it down around her waist, mouthing at the velvety swell. Her tongue finally found a pert nipple.

Zanta gasped, fingers tightening in the straps at Nia's waist. Her head tilted forward, face shadowed by the puff of her hair.

Nia pressed her back against the shelves, one hand slipping to the waist of Zanta's trousers.

"Take these off," Nia ordered, slurring a bit, her tongue occupied by nipple. Zanta fumbled with the fastenings, breath harsh, and shucked them off. Nia wasted no time finding the wetness beneath soft black curls. Her fingers circled Zanta's clit, drawing forth a soft moan. Zanta's chest arched further into Nia's attentive mouth. The sound seemed to linger in Nia's ears, ringing through her mind and filling her with determination to hear more, to give this gorgeous, strong woman even more pleasure than she'd given Nia.

Nia pressed closer, crowding Zanta as her fingers worked. The wooden dick brushed Zanta's inner thigh, and she shuddered. Nia rubbed it between her legs, gently at first, before breeching her folds to rub over her clit and entrance.

"Nia." Zanta grabbed Nia by the back of the neck, pulling her head up and kissing her hard.

Nia hitched Zanta's leg up around her hip, bare foot propped on the edge of a crate.

"Do you want me to fuck you, Zanta? Open you up on this stranger's cock?" She pressed the head to Zanta's entrance, angling her hips. Nia had selected one of the others, not John or Logan. And she didn't know who it might be modeled after, if anyone. Maybe it was the Deep Water Demon himself, wouldn't that be exciting.

Zanta clutched at the shelf behind for support, her dark eyes half lidded as she gazed down at Nia, long eyelashes brushing her cheeks.

"Please..." Her voice was husky with lust.

"Please what, sweet? Tell me."

"Fuck me. Fill me up with that beautiful cock."

Nia angled Zanta's hips forward, bracing one of her feet on the shelf behind Zanta and hoping it was as sturdy as it looked. She pressed forward, watching Zanta's eyes roll back as she breached her. Zanta's lips parted in silence.

Nia absorbed Zanta's reactions hungrily, slowly entering inch by inch, careful not to go too fast, knowing that a dick made of wood was much more difficult to accommodate than one of flesh and blood.

"You okay?" Nia asked, low in Zanta's ear.

"Yes. Move, please." Each word came out in short pants. Breathless but no less demanding. Nia resolved to tease her just a bit, stopping only halfway in before pulling back as slowly as possible.

Zanta whined. Impatient and needy. Nia could almost feel her body tightening around the wooden cock, trying to draw her in. She bit her lip, resisting the urge to give in to Zanta's every desire. Instead she resorted to slow, shallow thrusts, building pleasure gradually. Zanta tried to move her hips to take Nia in deeper but couldn't manage it from that angle.

She laved kisses across Zanta's throat, loving the way her pulse fluttered against her lips. How her breath shallowed with every thrust. Zanta's fingers dug into her bare shoulder.

But the control was wearing her down. With Zanta's weight half on her thighs, her muscles were starting to tire. And that wouldn't do, not till she left Zanta a quivering, satisfied heap on the floor, as she'd promised.

Nia pulled out, barely giving Zanta a moment to breathe, let alone complain, before she flipped her around and reentered her in one swift stroke. Zanta cried out in surprised pleasure, clutching at the shelves for stability. Nia framed her waist with her hands, holding her in place and fucking into her. As she watched Zanta's tight, wet heat close around the cock, she began to think of it as her own.

The bare expanse of Zanta's back flexed, still striped in warm gold light from the slats in the pantry door. She was the most beautiful woman Nia had ever slept with. Her figure a perfect hourglass beneath Nia's hands. She marveled at the sight of the wooden cock disappearing into Zanta, at the wetness coating her thighs and smearing Nia's front.

Zanta's moans filled the small space, her hips rocking back in time with Nia's thrusts. She was losing herself, body trembling. Nia knew this was just sex. They'd agreed on it, but right now it felt like Zanta was all hers. She buried her fingers in Zanta's hair, about to pull her up and kiss her neck and whisper sweet nothings in her ear.

"Em...oh, Em..." Zanta moaned.

Em. Emilie. Nia's hips stuttered, something unnamable slicing through her enjoyment, cutting off the possessiveness that was taking root in her. Zanta didn't seem to notice the falter or what she'd said, too lost in whatever fantasy played out in her head.

Right. It was just sex. Zanta could imagine whomever she wanted while Nia fucked her. It was none of Nia's business, as long as she got what she wanted in the end. Her treasure.

Nia revitalized her rhythm with renewed vigor, racing to the finish line as Zanta's moans reached a crescendo and she finally tipped over the edge. Nia imagined her clenching around the wooden cock, riding the wave of pleasure till her limbs trembled.

They slumped to the floor, bodies nestled together like a pair of spoons, Nia still seated inside. Nia gathered Zanta against her chest, kissing the little sweaty curls of hair that stuck to her skin and waiting for the last wave of pleasure to pass.

Zanta looked at her, a lazy smile on her lips. "Now look, we're both a heap."

Nia laughed and hoped it didn't sound hollow, pushing down the hurt that still curdled in her gut.

"So we are. But do me the courtesy of fucking me on a bed next time, and I'll really show you bliss."

Zanta's breath caught, pupils widening. With one last kiss on Zanta's brow, Nia unseated the wooden cock. They dressed each other with shaky limbs, tucking the dick into Nia's deep skirt pocket and giggling when they inevitably tripped over hems and stockings. Nia's hurt ebbed under Zanta's easy smile.

Laurent glanced up as they exited the pantry.

"Oh good, you're done. Could you fetch me some onions on your way out? They're in that basket there."

Zanta's ears reddened comically, but she retrieved the onions and handed them over like some sort of peace offering. Laurent, for his part, accepted them graciously with only a stray wink thrown in Nia's direction when Zanta's back was turned.

"I should get going," Zanta said, straightening her clothes and shooting one last smile over her shoulder to Nia. "I'll see you later?"

Nia nodded, and the captain slipped out the door.

CHAPTER 25

JUNE 1ST, 1668

"I'm boooored!" Fox hung upside down over the edge of Rowan's bed, unbound hair brushing the floor as Rowan flicked shaving soap into a little dish on the mantel. The *Siren* had been patrolling the shipping lanes north of Kadling Kay for at least a week—though Fox really hadn't been keeping track—and absolutely nothing had happened. They'd let ship after ship go by without stealing so much as a copper. And still no sign of Splinter Zanta or the *Monsoon*.

Rowan ignored him, dragging the straight razor across his jaw, but Nephele chirred from her brass perch in the corner.

"That's right!" Fox exclaimed as if the surly hawk had made his point for him. "Why are we just sitting here watching all that treasure sail past?"

Rowan finally glanced at him through the mirror, one eye tired blue and the other empty jade. "We're waiting for Zanta," he said matter-of-factly.

"But how long are we going to wait?" Fox drummed his heels on the mattress, fully aware he was acting like a spoiled toddler, and not giving a single fuck about it. It would do Rowan good to be annoyed at something other than Captain Demon these days.

"Till we find her!" Rowan snapped.

Oop, a little too much. Fox reeled in the brattiness a bit. "Can't we at least snag a prize while we're out here?" He let his arms fall to the floor beside his head, his spine popping rather loudly. Sleeping in the same bed as restless Rowan had turned out to be a battlefield, and Fox had all sorts of kinks in his joints from contorting himself to avoid the occasional flailing limb. It wasn't the most restful sleep he'd ever gotten—certainly nothing compared to being snuggled up in Gaël's arms—but it was a lot better than sleeping by himself. At least if he was getting elbowed in the liver, he knew he wasn't alone.

Besides, Rowan had good reason to be stressed and snappish. Fox had heard the fight between Rowan and the Demon back at the Teeth, and Rowan hadn't worn his wedding ring since. The two had met up before Kadling Kay, but the Demon had left that encounter with blood running down his shirt and Rowan had sported suspiciously finger-shaped bruises on his neck for a few days after. The whole crew was tiptoeing around the topic, whispering when neither Logan nor Rowan were around. They were all used to the harebrained schemes Rowan cooked up, but those usually ended with plunder and full bellies. Moreover, the crew loved Rowan, and worried about him. There had been talk that this fight between the two captains would result in all of them getting kicked off Illusion and worse, making an enemy of the Deep Water Demon.

Fox had told Rowan all of this of course. Whispered it in the dark after they climbed into bed. Rowan had pinched his cheek and told him not to worry, but that was becoming more and more difficult the longer this went on.

"If we snag a prize while we're out here, we might miss the *Monsoon*," Rowan said.

Fox was having an uncharacteristically hard time reading whether Rowan was so determined to warn Zanta because of their friendship, his need to defeat Shaw, or his stubbornness in doing the exact opposite of whatever Captain Demon wanted him to do.

"Well the *Kraken* could—"

"We are *not* relying on the *Kraken*!" Rowan growled. They hadn't seen the warship since Kadling Kay anyway. It was possible the Demon had gotten bored of playing chase with his husband and gone back to pirating. And that was another thing: this situation with Shaw and Zanta could go on for weeks, months, maybe into next season, and if they didn't take any prizes, how were they supposed to eat?

Appalling, that it had come down to Fox of all people to point out the economic unviability of a plan, but needs must.

The door banging open saved him from having to point this out.

"We've got a problem, Captain!" Henri said, slightly out of breath. He barely acknowledged Fox's presence, even though he was half clothed, and not the half Henri would've preferred either. It was common knowledge among the crew—another thing to gossip about—that Fox was spending an awful lot of time in the captain's quarters these days. Henri, of course, knew the real reason for it, and had other things on his mind.

Rowan sighed and mumbled something about not being able to get a good shave in, while wiping the last of the soap off his chin. Fox himself hadn't shaved in several days and had been relieving his boredom by rubbing his scratchy cheeks on his friends' faces like a scruffy cat. Most of them had been largely unperturbed, but David had given him a look that could've peeled tar off the hull when he did it to Robin.

"What is it?" Rowan asked.

Maybe the *Kraken* was back. Maybe they'd spotted the *Monsoon* and they would be back to pirating in no time. But Henri said, "Spotted a ship not far off. We thought it would pass us by like the others but it's heading right for us."

Rowan's attention sharpened. "Any idea who it is?"

Fox remained upside down as Rowan buckled on his leather pauldron and weapons.

"It's got lots of guns but no military insignia. Logan thinks he recognizes it from the docks at Kadling Kay."

"Shit, maybe Shaw found us first." Rowan stepped over the threshold and turned back to Fox. "Well? You were bored; get a move on."

"Aye, Captain." Fox saluted upside down and somersaulted onto the floor, righting himself in time to see Rowan roll his eye, a slight smile tugging the corner of his lips.

By the time Fox sprinted out onto deck, still buckling on his sword belt, the other ship was within range. He squinted at it, a three-masted galleon like the *Siren*, though a bit bigger by Fox's estimate. She flew no flags, not even a hailing signal, yet she was heading straight toward them at speed. This would be an attack then. Fox's stomach tightened with anticipation. They hadn't had a proper fight since the *Sweet Lettie*, and that had been hideously short. Despite the playful nature of his complaints to Rowan, without someone to fight, or Gaël to fuck, Fox really was bored out of his mind.

This resolved one problem at least. Fox bounded up the stairs to where Rowan and Logan presided on the quarterdeck and bounced on the balls of his feet, unable to contain his excitement.

"Please tell me we get to fight 'em!"

Logan looked up from switching out his wooden hand for the steel hook he kept on his belt. "Well, they're not friendly, we know that much."

The *Siren* hadn't moved, but all stood in readiness, from the tops of the masts to the cannons below deck, waiting for the enemy to come to them.

Rowan lowered the spyglass from his eye. "Definitely former Kefryean. It's called the *Marigold*. I don't see Shaw though."

"Would you even recognize him? It's been nine years; spite will have aged him." Logan finished tightening the hook's straps around his wrist.

"I'd recognize him." Rowan grimaced, scars puckering his cheek.

Of course he would. Shaw was Rowan's first love, and first heartbreak. The betrayer who'd cost Rowan the lives of half his original crew. The reason Rowan had still been looking for crew members when he stumbled on Fox getting the crap beat out of him in the back streets of Wave Harbor. Fox had been thinking about that night a lot lately. He'd probably be dead if Rowan hadn't shoved a gun in the attacker's face. But what would've happened if Rowan had accepted Fox's ill-advised advances that night? Would Fox still be a part of this crew today, or would he have moved on? Would he ever have reunited with Gaël?

The boom of a cannon startled Fox from his thought spiral, quickly followed by a sharp blast from Rowan's whistle. The signal to fire. He looked almost as giddy as Fox felt for some action. The *Siren* rocked under them as they returned fire, and Rowan piped several more orders to get the *Siren* under sail. The sails unfurled with a snap, and Fox inhaled the gunpowder-scented air.

The *Siren* swooped closer to the *Marigold*, and unloaded a volley of cannon fire into her side. Fox dashed for the stairs, eager to get in on the action, only to be waylaid by Logan's hook snagging his belt loop.

"Hey!" Fox yelped.

Logan reeled him back, placing a hand on top of Fox's head to keep his attention. Fox nuzzled into it like a pampered cat, and Logan rolled his eyes. Fox really had to get a hold of himself. He was becoming so touch-starved in just a few short weeks without Gaël that any touch was almost overwhelming. Logan turned Fox's head, redirected his focus to Rowan issuing orders on the other side of the deck, a manic glint in his eye.

"Stick to him like glue." Logan's voice was quiet, serious, and some of Fox's giddiness dampened beneath it.

"You don't have to tell me." Fox pouted. Rowan had always been a whirlwind fighter, a natural chaos, but after losing his eye and subsequently half his vision, he'd become more like a rogue typhoon. A bit unbalanced, but just as chaotic. Logan had tasked Fox and Gaël to guard his blind side. Now it seemed that task fell solely on Fox.

Logan raised an eyebrow. The two ships were close now, a constant barrage of cannon fire thundering between them, either missing altogether or not doing a great deal of damage. It was clear both captains intended to board the other, and this fight would come down to hand-to-hand combat.

"He's a bit off these days," Logan gritted out. "You've noticed."

Fox nodded. "It's the fight with the Demon."

"Not much we can do about that. So don't let him do anything too rash. At least not more than usual."

"Aye." Fox probably wasn't the best person for that particular job. Especially now when the tips of his fingers were itching with pent up energy. He did dumb things all the time and often roped the others in as well. Last winter, Logan had had to stitch the right pocket of all his pants closed after Fox and Henri devised a game of slipping little trinkets—acorns, buttons, bits of cheese, and the like—into them, which Logan could not retrieve with his wooden hand. He would have to ask someone—usually Rowan, holding back laughter—or take off his pants entirely to remove the stowaway objects.

Personally, Fox thought it an overreaction.

That was why Fox was probably—no, definitely—the last person Logan should ask to keep their captain from being reckless. Then again, if he and Rowan were going to get into trouble, they were probably the best two to get themselves back out of it.

Logan eyed him wearily. "You're thinking about my pockets, aren't you?"

"What? No!" Fox sputtered. He knew he was easy to read, but Logan could be scarily canny sometimes.

Rowan issued orders in the form of short whistle blasts, the crew following his every command as the two ships hurtled toward each other. Logan's hand on Fox's head wrapped them in a lone pocket of calm amidst the ordered chaos.

"Fox, focus. If this is Shaw's ship, Rowan won't be in his rational mind. Don't let Rowan kill him. We need information."

Fox clamped down on the energy humming through his veins and managed a solemn nod. He didn't point out that he had no idea what Shaw looked like and therefore could not prevent Rowan from revenge-murdering him over regular-murdering anyone else. He'd deal with that when they got to it.

Rowan whistled another signal, and Fox braced as the *Siren* swung about and came to a halt mere feet from the side of the other ship. A maneuver only Rowan would have the balls to execute. Cannon fire fell quiet on both sides, smoke hanging in the air between the ships as both crews readied for a fight.

"Shit," Logan swore under his breath. He pushed Fox toward Rowan, who whistled the signal to board even as he grabbed a rope and readied to swing across. Armed sailors on the other side tossed grappling hooks toward the *Siren*.

Fox caught up just as Rowan stepped up onto the rail, faded black coat flapping in the wind. He caught the back of Rowan's bandolier.

"You're not going without me!"

"Come on then, nanny." Rowan blinked. Frowned. Then lifted his eyepatch and winked. He hauled Fox up on the rail with him.

"Don't get into trouble!" Logan shouted, as pirates swung over the water to clash with the sailors on the *Marigold*'s deck.

"Do you know who you're talking to?" Rowan shouted back with a grin. He wrapped one arm around Fox's waist and leapt off the rail. Fox yelped and barely managed to clutch onto Rowan before they crashed into the thick of the fighting on the *Marigold*'s deck. Fox stumbled, rolled, and righted himself just as a huge sailor barreled toward them. Fox's cutlass barely cleared its sheath. The sailor swung a massive wooden club, and Fox ducked as the crack of Rowan's pistol deafened all three of them. Crimson bloomed on the sailor's chest, and he went down to his knees. The club caught Fox on the back of the knee, bruising but not debilitating, and he kicked the sailor to the ground before whirling on Rowan.

"Bitch! That was *right* in my ear!"

Rowan shouted something that Fox definitely could not hear over the ringing. He smacked the side of his head as if trying to dislodge water. Abandoning the need for words, Rowan signaled for him to follow, and they cut across the deck. Sound slowly washed back into Fox's consciousness as they fought through the crowd, no doubt searching for Shaw. Fox stayed on Rowan's blind side.

Who exactly were these people? They'd attacked without warning, but so far there'd been no sign of Shaw, unless he was the man Rowan was currently skewering with his cutlass. Were they just pirate hunters? Privateers?

A sailor lunged past him, managing to nick Rowan's arm with the tip of a knife before Fox kicked him to the ground and stomped his hand.

"Get your head out of the clouds!" Rowan barked.

"You punched me in the kidney last night!" Fox whined. This was actually fun. He could tell they'd both sleep like the dead tonight. "I'm injured."

"Oh please!" Rowan whirled to punch someone in the face and followed it up with a stab through the neck. "Sleep in your own damn bed if you're going to complain."

Fox pouted while he kneed a man in the balls, then yelped when that didn't work and the man seized him. "Shit!"

Rowan managed to bowl them both over, and the man screamed and cursed as Fox and Rowan stabbed him in the chest together. Fox helped Rowan up, and Rowan wiped a bit of blood from Fox's ear.

"Maybe I will!" Fox knew Rowan didn't mean it, and neither did he. He hammed up the pout that sprouted on his lips. "You'll miss me."

"With my next shot, maybe."

Fox cackled, and Rowan's expression softened slightly, even as they wove through the fighting, heading for the quarterdeck.

"You know, I haven't heard you laugh like that in a while," Rowan said.

"I'm too tired to laugh. You snore!"

Rowan punched an attacking sailor in the face, and he stumbled back. Rowan and Fox both advanced on him.

"I do not." His nose wrinkled as he seized the sailor by the shirt and dumped him down an open hatch.

"How would you know?"

"Yves would've told me."

Fox snorted.

"What?" Rowan was smiling.

"It's funny thinking of you two having normal marriage problems. Next you'll be arguing about how many children to have."

Rowan smacked him on the arm before lunging past him to slash at a sailor. He grabbed Fox's arm to keep him close.

A small pocket of calm descended. Rowan smiled, genuine and free. "I'm glad you stayed, Fox. What would I do without you?"

The fighting flowed around them, and Fox felt a pleased smile tugging at his lips at Rowan's words. Before joining the crew, Fox had never really belonged anywhere. But he was wanted here, needed here, and he wouldn't trade that for the world.

"C'mon." Rowan tugged Fox's arm, and they darted through a passage that had opened up between the fighting bodies. Fox had thought all along they were heading to the quarterdeck, where whoever led this ship would likely be, but he found himself at the door to the room beneath it instead.

"Guard me," Rowan ordered, his previously jovial expression serious now. Fox turned toward the fighting, alert to anyone who dared come near. Rowan rattled the door handle, but it was locked. He grunted in frustration and backed up till he bumped against Fox. He leveraged one hard kick to the area around the lock. Then another. A few sailors charged at them, drawn by the commotion of Rowan's boot striking the wood. Fox readied his cutlass, but other pirates engaged the advancing sailors before they could make it to him.

In one more kick, the door crashed open. Rowan grabbed Fox's hand and dragged him into the room, slamming the damaged door behind them.

In the sudden quiet, Fox's ears rang with the residue of the earlier gunshot. They were in what looked at first to be an office. A large desk sat in the center, orderly but for what the battle had dislodged. Fox spotted a Kefryean-style cabinet bed built into one wall, lattice-carved wooden doors mostly blocking it off from the rest of the room. This must have been the captain's quarters, then.

"Search for anything that might tell us who these assholes are," Rowan ordered, prowling toward the desk.

Fuck, Fox really wasn't the right person for this job. He remained by the door. "I can't read, remember?"

"Then see if you can find a country symbol or anything like that. Steal some shit if you have time." Rowan was already shuffling through papers on the desk. Outside, gunshots went off amongst the clash of blades. Fox rushed to the wardrobe next to the bed, only to be met with a wall of uniforms as soon as he threw the doors open.

"Uh, Captain?"

Rowan looked up, an immediate understanding coming across his features as he took in the neatly organized row of deep maroon uniform jackets.

"Kefryean, as I thought," Rowan snarled. Fox recalled that Shaw was from Kefrye. But he was a mercenary. Even if his mission was sanctioned by the governor, and by extension the Marran Empire, they wouldn't have given him a uniform or official rank. Besides, these jackets looked too small for a grown man.

"Keep looking," Rowan ordered, turning back to the papers in his hands. After a few more seconds, he swore softly under his breath, eye scanning over a small, unrolled piece in his hands.

"What?" Fox prompted.

"Rowan Faine!"

They both whipped around as the door burst open. Fox dodged around the desk as Rowan shoved the paper into his pocket, along with a few others. The woman who'd shouted lunged into the room, almost skewering Fox with a thin, needlelike sword. Fox slashed at her, and she dodged, trying to get around him to Rowan. She was about their height, middle aged but fit. Her faded red hair was shot through with thick swaths of gray and pulled into a severe bun. She wore the same uniform as the ones in the closet.

"Who the fuck are you?" Rowan snarled, flanking around the other side of the desk to slash at her, severing the maroon and silver aiguillette at her shoulder.

Another sailor rushed through the door. Fox bashed him in the nose with the butt of his sword, shoved him back outside, and slammed the door against the oncoming tide of enemies. He quickly put his back against it.

"The commanding officer of this ship," the woman shot back. She lunged again, light on her feet, obviously a formally trained swordswoman, but even one-eyed, Rowan was a force of nature. He met her next attack with a parry that sent her reeling back, and followed up by drawing his dagger and trapping her blade between both of his own. A body slammed against the other side of the door, juddering it against Fox's back, but he held firm. Were they winning out there? Or had the sailors overwhelmed the *Siren*'s scrappy crew?

The commander grit her teeth, straining against Rowan's superior strength. He forced her back a few steps, toward Fox. He met Rowan's eye for the briefest second as the sailors tried to batter down the door behind him. Rowan forced the commander back another step, and Fox grabbed the back of her jacket, yanking her off balance just enough for Rowan to force her to one knee.

Fox set the edge of his cutlass against her chin, still bracing against the door with his back. Her arms gave way, and Rowan snatched the rapier from her.

"Filthy pirates!" she snarled.

Quiet settled within the room. She squared her shoulders, a silver pin at her lapel glinting. Her deep maroon uniform was Kefryean, no doubt about it. He'd thought those defunct after Marra conquered them, but the silvery crossed claymore and unicorn horn stood in sharp contrast to the pin at her other lapel, the golden sun and laurel of Marra.

"You're the one who attacked us!" Rowan laughed. The gleam of battle had returned to his eye. "Tell me who you are, or my man here will cut your throat."

Fox wasn't sure about all that, but he'd probably do it if Rowan asked. They weren't in much position to carry on a lengthy questioning, what with Fox pulling double duty as both threat and doorstop.

"You will surrender to the might of the Marran Empire," the commander said, so self-assured that for a moment Fox thought maybe they had stumbled into battle with an empire ship after all.

"We won't be surrendering to anyone, clearly," Rowan drawled. His accent always came out more when he was in front of an enemy.

It made him sound insolent and roguish. "Least of all that dogshit empire."

"Have some respect! It's your home!" The commander seemed almost startled at Rowan's hatred, but why should she be? Rowan was a pirate, and the empire had enough gold on his head to buy the *Siren* three times over. Besides, this woman looked Kefryean, and she was old enough to have grown up there before the war. She should hate them as much as Rowan did.

"Being bought for cannon fodder as a child didn't exactly endear *my home* to me." Rowan set the edge of his cutlass against her cheek. A strand of white blond hair fell out of its tie, catching in the edge of his eyepatch. "Now tell me who you are." The blade moved down to an insignia on her chest. "I'm guessing...colonel?"

"Colonel Selby Baird," she said between her teeth.

Why did that sound familiar?

"Baird? As in Malcolm Baird?" There was way too much of a glint in Rowan's eye now. Fox wondered if this was the moment he was supposed to step in and calm him like Logan had said.

Baird's scowl said Rowan's guess was right. That explained it somewhat; Malcolm Baird had been the leader of the coup that ended with Kefrye in Marran hands, in return receiving the governorship of his homeland until his recent death.

Rowan cocked his head. "What's the daughter of the late Kefryean governor doing here? Aren't you basically royalty? You should at least be a general by now."

Baird didn't take the bait. They all knew well enough the Marran Empire didn't let women into their military. The fact that she was still ranked at all was a testament to both her skill and the power her family had held up until her father's death.

"Okay, I'll ask a better question," Rowan said, knuckles whitening on the sword hilt. "What's Shaw's plan?"

Baird twitched. Ah, so they were right—she was working with Shaw. Her jaw jutted stubbornly, and she remained silent.

"Fine, we'll see how you feel after a few nights in the brig." Rowan leaned close, the edge of his cutlass sliding against her cheek. "The guy manning the bilge pump is *very* bad at it. Enjoy."

Baird's face screwed up, as if she was imagining what it would be like in the bowels of a pirate ship, up to her ankles in horrendously smelly brackish water and rat turds. If that didn't get her talking, she was far tougher than Fox.

Then again, they'd have to win this battle and get her over to the *Siren* first.

Something heavy hit the door, and it slammed open. Fox collided face first with the wall as sailors barreled into the room. Rowan shouted something, but Fox couldn't hear it over the sudden deafening ringing in his head. He'd managed to keep his cutlass, and he flipped it around now to slam the blade back through the hole in the door pinning him to the wall. A grunt sounded on the other side, and the pressure on the door let up. Fox stumbled away, whipping his cutlass toward one of the intruders.

Baird had taken the opportunity to lunge for Rowan, and she now had him pinned against the desk, a cut on her cheek streaming blood down into the collar of her uniform. Fox kicked the sailor who'd crashed through the door in the back of the knee, and he went down. He slammed the door into the next sailor's face, barely hearing the crunch of a broken nose over the muffled ringing in his ears.

Fox whirled back, determined to help Rowan. They had to get out of here. His head felt like someone had stuffed it full of Nephele's feathers, and they wouldn't be able to fight off whomever came through that door next.

Rowan was saying something to Baird, his teeth bared in a vicious grin. He reached back and found an inkwell, bringing it around swiftly to smash against the side of Baird's head. It exploded in a shower of glittering crystal, black ink splattering across all of them, mixing with the blood to run in red and black rivulets down Baird's neck. She stumbled to the side, and Rowan kicked her down for good measure.

Rowan grabbed Fox's hand and dragged him out into the chaos on deck again. Fox's mind took an extra moment to process everything, and he stopped just outside the door, refusing to let go of Rowan's hand.

"What?" Rowan reached up to touch a spot on Fox's forehead, sending a jolt of pain straight through Fox's skull. "Shit, you hit your head," Rowan said.

Something shifted; maybe it was movement in the corner of Fox's eye, maybe a change in the sounds of battle. Fox spun, barely catching an axe blow on his cross guard that was meant for his shoulder. The sailor's second axe sliced toward Fox's stomach, and Rowan dragged him out of the way, both of them stumbling. The sailor lunged after them. Rowan whirled to block the next blow, keeping Fox behind him. Fox fought his own spinning head to try to spot anyone else who might be coming at them. He had to protect Rowan long enough to get back to the *Siren*.

The sailor growled, and slashed again, blade whistling past Fox's face as Rowan pushed him out of the way. Fox righted himself with effort only to find the sailor inches from him. Fox couldn't think. His arms felt weak. So he did the only thing his addled brain could cook up. He hauled back and spit into the sailor's eye. The man howled, and Fox took his chance, dodging clumsily to the side and slashing across the man's ribs.

Nephele's screech overhead drew their attention. She wheeled above the two ships before diving between the rigging and attacking the next sailor who came near. Gouging at his face with her talons and beating his head with her wings.

"Atta girl!" Rowan whooped.

Hand in hand, Fox and Rowan had almost made it to the rail through the clash of fighting when Baird caught up with them. The side of her face was flecked with blood and ink, ginger hair falling out of its neat bun.

"Surrender," she snarled.

Rowan took in the battle around them, and Fox realized the pirates were losing. The sailors had beaten them back to the rail just like Rowan and Fox. It was time to cut and run. Hopefully the papers Rowan had stuffed in his pocket would yield whatever information he'd been searching for.

"I don't surrender." Rowan pushed Fox onto a plank connecting the two ships and stepped up behind him, keeping one hand on him so he wouldn't fall. A piercing whistle split the air, the signal to retreat. No doubt Logan was watching them from his place of command on the *Siren*'s quarterdeck. Pirates swarmed back over the gap to their own ship, but Rowan and Fox stayed where they were, staring Baird down.

"Tell Shaw I'm coming for him." Rowan's voice came out low and deadly, sending a shiver up Fox's spine.

"Capture them!" Baird ordered her men.

"What the fuck! Get back here!" Fox flinched at Henri's

panicked voice behind them, and the plank beneath him lurched violently. Rowan grabbed Fox just as their end of the plank dislodged from the *Marigold* and plunged into the water below.

It was like smacking against the wall all over again. Freezing water battered his brain in his skull, and he didn't have time to take a breath before plunging under. In the back of his mind, he knew he needed to kick back to the surface, but the shock to his system had rendered him immobile. He focused on keeping what little breath he had in his lungs. If the two ships drifted closer, he would be crushed or drowned.

Something constricted around his torso, and he fought for a second before realizing it was Rowan's arm. A few moments later, their heads broke the surface, and Fox took a deep, shuddering breath, his instincts kicking back to life.

"Fuck." Fox was able to tread water now, but Rowan still held him. The two ships loomed high on either side like the walls of a narrow canyon. Shouting sounded from above as pirates still scrambled to get back to the *Siren*, pursued by Baird's sailors.

Someone else broke the surface with a gasp, and it took Fox's bruised brain a moment to figure out who it was. His sandy blond hair was plastered against his face. Robin? No, David. He must have been on the plank with them when it collapsed.

What the fuck was he even doing here? Fox couldn't imagine he would've wanted to help. Maybe he regretted his choice to stay and had tried to escape via the plank?

"Captain!" Henri's shout accompanied the splash of a rope ladder landing not far from them.

David floundered, his head ducking back under the water, arms flailing up like he didn't know how to swim. He bobbed up again, sputtering, and sank again. Fuck. He actually didn't know how to swim.

"Grab the ladder," Rowan ordered Fox, releasing him now that he'd regained his faculties. Rowan grabbed David as Fox swam for the ladder. A bullet zinged past Fox, and one of David's flailing hands caught Rowan upside the head.

"Stupid motherfucker," Rowan growled as more bullets rained down around them. Fox heard Henri order pirates to return fire. Fox hauled himself up a few rungs of the ladder, his feet still submerged.

Rowan had managed to get David's head above water, and was struggling to drag him toward the *Siren.*

Irritation flashed through Fox. If David wanted to escape so badly, they should just leave him here. He'd nearly drowned them with his stupidity, and they still might get shot for their trouble trying to save him.

"Up," Rowan ordered David as they finally made it to Fox. A bullet buried itself in the wood inches away, and Fox scurried up toward the rail, grateful as hands caught and dragged him onto the deck. Henri shuffled him behind the crowd battling at the rail as the *Siren* pulled away from the other ship. A few sailors who had made it aboard were swiftly dumped over the side.

David collapsed onto the deck, coughing. Rowan cleared the rail with a murderous glint in his eye as the *Siren* tacked to port.

"You're fucking dead," Rowan growled, dragging David up by the back of his shirt. His tall, lanky frame seemed small and weak as he cowered. Rowan shook him. "Why the fuck did you do that?"

David shook his head, wide eyes riveted to Rowan's furious face. He must've been trying to escape. That was the only reason Fox could think of that he would willingly enter the fray. But then why hadn't he left in Kadling Kay? He'd had his freedom then. If he wanted to take Robin with him, Robin wasn't—

Except there Robin was, standing at the rail like his brother had dragged him there.

Rowan drew his dagger and pressed it to David's stomach. "Talk, or I'll fucking gut you."

Oh, this was the moment Logan had been talking about. Fox grabbed Rowan's hand in a firm grip. It was shaking.

"Don't."

"He could've killed us," Rowan hissed.

Fox glanced at Robin, who stood frozen a few feet away, and Rowan followed his gaze. A few tense seconds ticked by before Rowan sheathed the knife back in his belt with the force he would've used to stab David.

"Get him out of my sight."

Robin rushed forward, helping a still sputtering and terrified David to his feet and leading him away. A single cannon's shot boomed from the *Marigold* but fell short. The sailors were disorganized now, and the *Siren* was the fastest ship on the seas. When she fled, nothing could catch her.

Rowan stomped up to the quarterdeck, where Logan looked like he hadn't drawn a single breath from the time his captain had left the *Siren* till his feet were safely back on deck. Logan caught Rowan's arm.

"Orders, Captain?"

Rowan drew the papers from his pocket, now a soggy, water-logged mess of pulp and ink. He chucked them onto the deck with a curse. "One of those was a letter from Shaw. They've found the *Monsoon*, and they're trying to drive her north toward the Storm Ring."

CHAPTER 26

JUNE 1ST, 1668

"He's definitely concussed, alright." Robin stood up from where he'd been pulling Fox's eyelids back to examine his pupil reflexes. Rowan didn't like the way Fox's responding frown looked a little dazed. He was sure this wasn't the first time Fox had had a concussion in his life—he was always charging headfirst into danger, both figuratively and literally—but the lump that was forming on his forehead looked extremely painful.

"What should we do?" Rowan asked. His frustration and anger at how the fight had gone had barely cooled. His chest still felt tight. A frayed bowstring ready to snap.

It was Henri who had gotten the story out of Robin. He had been working on the injured who had already made it to the infirmary when David came and dragged him out, saying something about escaping. Robin had resisted, and when David stepped onto the plank, Robin had tried to pull him back. He'd slipped, and the plank had dislodged.

Rowan didn't blame Robin for any of it. He couldn't be held responsible for his brother's actions. But Rowan could feel the tension between them now.

Robin glanced around at the few other patients in the infirmary. They hadn't lost anyone, in large part due to Robin's skill, but there were still several crew members injured beyond a simple stitch-up. "I have to get back to my patients. Can you take him for the night,

Captain? He needs to be monitored. You shouldn't let him sleep for at least the next four hours. Then wake him and check him every two hours after that." Robin's voice was tight, clinical. Fox made a distressed noise, and Robin reached over to squeeze his shoulder reassuringly. "Get some cold water from the cistern and keep a compress on that lump. The swelling should go down in a few days."

"Would be a shame to ruin this masterpiece," Fox mumbled, gesturing to his face in a swirling motion.

"Aye," Rowan agreed. "Let's get you out of here, hm? Get some cold on that forehead."

After a moment, Fox lifted his arms like a toddler wanting up. Robin and Rowan both moved to get a shoulder under his arm and help him to his feet. Once there, he swayed a bit, and Robin released him into Rowan's sturdy hold.

"Thanks." Rowan looked up at Robin, and was met with a tight smile. "And I'm...sorry about what happened with David. I shouldn't have threatened him like that, no matter what happened."

Robin nodded, almost resigned. "I understand, Captain. I'll keep a better eye on him."

"That's not...He's still your brother," Rowan said weakly. That fact was probably the only thing that had saved David's life in that moment.

Robin nodded again. One of the patients on a cot groaned. "Let me know if you need anything, Captain."

Rowan knew a dismissal when he heard one. He'd lost some of Robin's trust today, and he knew he would have to earn it back. But not tonight. Tonight he had to take care of Fox.

They left Robin to it, making their slow way back to Rowan's room with Fox tucked close to his side. Once they got there, he remembered he wasn't supposed to let Fox fall asleep, but he tucked him sitting up in bed anyway and quickly fetched a bucket of cold water and a cloth. Finding Fox in exactly the same spot he'd left him when he returned.

Fox sighed when the cold, damp cloth pressed into his skin.

"How are you feeling?" Rowan asked. Fox was being awfully quiet, and that worried Rowan most of all.

"Like I got kicked by a horse," Fox answered, leaning back against the headboard and closing his eyes.

"Hey, hey, none of that. Robin said you have to stay awake." Rowan pulled him back up to sitting.

"Tired though. You punched me in the k'ney," Fox whined.

"I'll entertain you. Should we play cards? Shall I enthrall you with tales of my daring adventures?" Rowan asked, trying to keep his tone light and not let his anxiety over Fox's condition show.

"I was there for most of them, but sure, enthrall me," Fox laughed, then winced and repositioned the cloth against his head.

Rowan settled against the headboard beside him and launched straight into a story about the time, at the age of ten, Logan had convinced half the crew of the *M.W.S. Wolf* he'd seen a mermaid wearing a tricorn hat. The kicker was, Logan had been fully convinced of it himself. Rowan had Fox grinning tiredly by the second sentence, and giggling by the end. So he told another, and another, until it was well into the night and Fox finally asked for a break.

"My head hurts," he whined.

"I know, you can rest in a bit. Doctor's orders."

Fox grimaced. "How much longer?"

"An hour at least."

"Ugh, fine. Tell me about you and the Demon, then. What's going on?"

Rowan hadn't expected this, and he was half tempted to spill Logan's juicy secret just to distract Fox, but quickly dismissed that idea.

"It's nothing."

"Yeah, sure. I'm concussed, not stupid. He had blood on his shirt when he walked off the *Siren*."

"That's..."

"Alright, I'm going to sleep."

"Fox," Rowan said warningly.

"I'm just worried," Fox mumbled.

First Logan, now Fox. Henri had been hinting around his availability *to talk* as well. Served Rowan right for having such good friends, he supposed.

"I'm...not sure where we stand actually," Rowan finally confided. Fox lay his head on Rowan's shoulder. "We had a huge fight. And I gave him the ring back."

Fox shifted to get more comfortable. "I thought you just took it off. Why would you give it back to him? That's basically like saying 'we're done' right?"

"I didn't mean anything by it. I was just mad." Rowan felt stupid for it now. Even weeks later, he still found himself touching his ring finger with his thumb, feeling the spot where the ring was missing.

"Maybe you're the one who's concussed, Captain. You shouldn't have done that."

"Yeah, well, he shouldn't have tried to ship me back to Illusion like he owns me," Rowan grumbled.

Fox yawned. "Look, I get not liking being told what to do. We're pirates; all of us have those sorts of hang ups. But yours seem especially intense."

"You try being owned by the navy from the age of nine."

Fox glanced up at him, lips in a tight line. "Point taken."

"I wasn't expecting an apology, but I wasn't expecting him to be so cold," Rowan sighed.

"And you're both too stubborn to fix it."

"I'm still fucking mad."

Fox nodded sagely. "And the blood on his shirt? The scrapes on your face?"

"Taking our anger out, I guess."

"He didn't hurt you?"

"We hurt each other. It was nothing serious," Rowan grumbled.

Fox took his hand and squeezed, seeming to understand. "You still love him though?"

"Yeah, but I'm starting to think he doesn't feel the same."

"He wouldn't have followed us all the way to Kadling Kay if he didn't."

"You sure about that?"

Fox rolled his eyes and lost himself to another yawn. "I'm sure that you wouldn't fall for someone who didn't care about you, Captain."

But that was where Fox was wrong. Rowan had fallen for a man who couldn't love at all. He'd thought he was the exception, but maybe he was just a temporary aberration. An overwhelming urge to tell Fox the truth of Yves's nature overtook him then. Fox was good with people, good with love. He'd been the one to help Rowan realize he was in love. Maybe he could help with this.

"It's not that simple, Fox. I mean, Yves is—"

A soft snore interrupted him, and Rowan glanced down to find Fox asleep, snuggled into his side. Just as well; Rowan didn't think he'd have believed him anyway. It was close enough to the time Robin had said Fox could sleep, so Rowan grabbed a book from the bedside table and cracked it open. Before long, Fox had his head in Rowan's lap and arms wrapped around his thigh.

Rowan flipped listlessly through the pages, not really absorbing the words. Should he apologize to Yves when they saw each other again? Or wait for an apology that might never come? Rowan could no more fight his nature than Yves could.

Rowan buried his hand in Fox's soft hair, listening carefully to his steady breaths. Rowan had no choice but to stay the course and deal with the fallout with Yves afterward. That was, if Yves still wanted him. If this thing with Shaw was going to come between him and Yves, he might as well make it worth all the trouble. And trouble it would be. Before Baird had burst in on them, Rowan had found an official looking letter that referenced a rendezvous, and not just between Baird and Shaw. But he hadn't been able to read fast enough to find out the details. He could very well be sailing them into a massive trap.

CHAPTER 27

JUNE 21ST, 1668

North. Always north. Nia glanced toward the *Lonesome* on the starboard side, still following at a distance, harrying them. A few days ago, they'd swooped close and got a few shots off as Nia cowered in her room. But it hadn't lasted long enough for the memories to beset her. And when she'd emerged again, they'd fallen back to a safe distance and the *Monsoon*'s course had skewed more northeast than due north. And when Zanta had given orders to head east, to see if they could manage to reach the coast of Talva and hide in some cove, they'd been blocked from that too. The *Monsoon*'s occupants hadn't seen a smidgen of land since leaving Souna's fringe islands behind.

It was almost as if the *Lonesome* was steering them toward some predestined place. Nia couldn't figure out what their purpose was. What she did know, was that for all Zanta and her crew's plans and machinations, they couldn't manage to slip the *Lonesome*'s tail.

If they kept on this course, Nia could no longer deny their eventual destination. Their heading pointed straight toward the Sleeping Isles, and the ring of perpetual storms that guarded it.

The *Lonesome* was chasing her home, whether they knew it or not.

Nia smoothed her palms against her stomach. Her nervous habit of checking for the silver key. She'd debated leaving it hidden in the secret compartment in the dick box for safekeeping. It wouldn't do for Zanta to see it now that they were frequently undressing each other. But decided against it when being without it for a day had almost sent her into a panic. Besides, she'd need it if she ever managed to get into Zanta's room.

Last night though, the *Lonesome* had dropped back even more. Maybe to regroup and confer with the *Marigold*, which they hadn't seen in a while. A pit had opened up beneath Nia's ribs, filled with the reanimated corpses of her anxiety and hope. No ship could pass through the Storm Ring unscathed. The sea around the Sleeping Isles always demanded her price, one Nia was afraid she'd have to pay personally.

And after that, if they survived, she'd have to face her own people again.

"Oi! Nia! Hand me that ball of string, will ya?"

Nia snapped from her thoughts to find Colm hoisting a line of multicolored paper lanterns above her head, his bulk on the rope ladder blocking out some of the sunlight. All around, the deck buzzed with activity. Some pirates set up tables from the mess hall, tuned a Yarenen stringed instrument similar to a fiddle, and decorated. While others trimmed the sails to try to press the advantage the *Lonesome*'s sudden distance had given them.

Tensions had been high ever since the *Lonesome* denied them their intended course, so now that they had a little breathing room, Laurent, Sabriye, and Nia had devised a plan to help the crew let off a little steam.

Tonight they were celebrating the summer solstice, and their captain's birthday.

Nia picked up the string ball in question. "I can't exactly come up there in this!" she called up to Colm. She wore her original peachy pink dress, freshly laundered. It had been drying in the sun all day, fluttering from the rigging along with her underthings for all to see. Now it felt warm and stiff against her skin.

"Got something else under there I should know about?" Colm teased with a wink.

Damn Laurent. He'd been after Colm for weeks. Did he tell him about the wooden dicks? When he finished cooking Zanta's birthday feast, Nia was going to throttle him.

Then again, she couldn't quite blame him for whatever pillow talk came out of his mouth after Colm's dick had loosened it for him.

Nia planted her fists on her hips. "I do not know *what* you are referring to," she said in her best approximation of Madame Durand's sternness. She didn't quite pull it off. "Do you want the string or not?"

A gust of wind kicked up, almost jerking the line of lanterns from Colm's hand. "Yes, yes. Toss it."

Nia did. It sailed right past Colm's thick legs and splashed into the waves.

Colm almost fell off the ladder with giggles until Sabriye's call of "Captain on deck!" interrupted him.

Finally. Sabriye had whisked Zanta away to "get her ready for the party" at midday, and it was nearly dinnertime now. Nia turned, eager, only for words to die in her throat.

Sabriye stepped out of the way, and the deck went silent. Skirts swished around Zanta's legs. The elegant teal dress from the wardrobe hugged her body from well-formed shoulder to generous hip, where an elegant rapier rested, before flaring out around her legs. Some of the embroidery was missing. No doubt semi-precious gems, cut and sold when the pirates had acquired the gown. But it was all the more beautiful for the simplicity.

She took Nia's breath away.

"Well?" Zanta called, long gold earrings tinkling as she moved her head, brushing the elegant column of her neck. "Haven't you ever seen a woman in a dress before?" The silence cracked, as if her words had broken them all from a momentary spell. The preparations took on a frantic pace, rushing to finish before dinner, even as crew members called birthday congratulations and compliments to their captain.

Nia didn't move, still bewitched by the captain's beauty. Her skin heated as Zanta's gaze landed on her.

"Dinner is served!" Laurent burst from below with several other crew members, bearing dish after dish of steaming, fragrant food. Nia really should've been helping him, but Laurent had insisted she pretty herself up for the party instead. He must have managed a moment to do the same, for he wore loose pants, a sleeveless caftan, and kohl and a few artful smears of paint around his eyes. A small cheer went up among the crew as they set the platters on the tables, and Nia was quickly swept away in the tide of hungry pirates.

She ended up seated precariously between Colm and Laurent at a different table entirely from Zanta. Food was served. Delicious as always, and she added her voice to the wash of compliments toward Laurent who smiled and preened and encouraged them all to praise him more.

They all fell into easy chatter between bites of food, and Nia surrendered herself to it, barely even hearing the shameless flirting Colm and Laurent volleyed across her. Her cheeks still felt warm, and she found her gaze drifting again and again to the other table.

Zanta sat easily at the head of the long table, presiding over her crew like a queen. Whenever she spoke, all within earshot turned their heads and listened. They leaned forward to hear the words falling from the lips Nia so desperately yearned to kiss. Nia's mouth practically watered as she imagined crawling beneath the feasting table to indulge in a feast of her own beneath Zanta's skirts.

Deep brown eyes rose to meet hers, and Nia's heart ached and sang with sweet chords of music. Zanta smiled, head tilting, before she looked away. The music continued to ring in Nia's ears until she realized the crew had struck up their instruments. The fiddle-like Yarenen string instrument, a drum, a flute, and something that looked like a pan flute. She shook her head, trying to dislodge the spell Zanta had her under. Why should she lose her head because the woman she was sleeping with, the woman she was *using* to get to her treasure, put on a dress and a little rouge and kohl? Nia wasn't some blushing virgin. She and Zanta had been sleeping together almost every day since Zanta had called Emilie's name in the pantry. She didn't love Nia. They hadn't even spent a night together. Nor, frustratingly, had Nia been allowed into the captain's quarters. It had been all quick and knee-buckling trysts in storerooms and alcoves.

Nia's chest grew tight, ribs embracing her lungs like a crushing cage. She turned to tell Laurent she needed air, only to find him in Colm's lap with his caftan undone, feeding the bigger man bits of food and whispering some rather filthy things in his ear.

"Are you having a good time?"

Nia practically jumped out of her skin at the sultry voice in her own ear. Zanta's warm breath sent goosebumps across her neck. Nia allowed a split second to compose herself.

"That question is better posed to you, birthday girl..." She trailed off, wrinkling her nose with a giggle. "Birthday captain."

"Dance with me." Zanta took her hand, and Nia found herself

being tugged onto a clear section of deck where other pirates already twirled to the lively music, all of them—but for Nia—armed, in case the *Lonesome* decided to take advantage of their celebration.

Zanta spun Nia under her arm, then pulled her close by the waist. Nia almost lost her breath, but there was no time for that. Zanta led her in a series of unfamiliar steps that had them both giggling and tripping over their own feet. Everything passed in a blur, the rest of the crew melding into color and sound until it was only her and Zanta and their bodies moving together, timeless but for the measure of their breath.

Eventually, the riotous music slowed and so did they. Their skirts, pink and blue like the meeting of sunset and sea, swished against each other as they swayed. Zanta's breasts heaved against her bodice.

"I thought you didn't like dresses," Nia said, when she'd caught her breath.

"I never said that. I said they were impractical for a pirate ship."

"The most impractical part is how gorgeous you look," Nia murmured, low so no one else could hear. Not her best line, but she was working with a brain absolutely bathed in horny juices and whatever floral perfume Zanta had dabbed on her neck that was now running with sweat down between her breasts. "You're driving everyone to distraction." She wanted to take Zanta away from their admiring eyes, so that only she could see her like this. Flushed and breathless with drink and dancing. Lips parted as if the next thing she'd say would be a declaration.

Zanta's hand tightened possessively at her waist, as if she could read Nia's every thought. The setting sun cast warm light across her bare collarbones.

"Did I distract you too?" Zanta whispered.

"Terribly. I hardly ate a bite for wanting to feast on you."

Zanta leaned in, so close Nia fumbled the steps, and they came to a halt in the crowd of dancers like a lonely island in a raging sea. Nia wanted to stay like this forever. But the ship bore them on toward the Sleeping Isles and their inevitable separation.

Nia should tell her, come clean about her true motive and beg for her treasure. Beg to stay. Zanta had a good heart; she would understand. Wouldn't she?

Nia's lips parted around the secret. Her heart beat in her throat, persistent and terrifying. *I knew Silver Stroud. His treasure is mine, a part of me. I slept with you to get to it.*

But that wasn't really true, was it?

She swallowed the secret down past her heartbeat, and kissed her. Zanta's lips immediately parted for her, not knowing she kissed a mouthful of lies. Nia melted into her, wanting all of her. All she could get before everything came crashing down.

THEY TRIPPED into Nia's tiny room, music and laughter spilling after them before the door slammed. Nia barely managed to light a candle before Zanta backed further into the room, drawing Nia after her until her heel caught on the hem of her dress and she tumbled onto the small stack of crates against the wall. Nia landed atop her, giggling, their voluminous skirts colliding with a soft *whump*. Her face landed right in Zanta's overspilling cleavage, and she buried it deeper into Zanta's scent, the soft mounds of her breasts squeezing Nia's cheeks with every inhale. Zanta's hands threaded in her hair, and now that they were alone, the truth nipped at the tip of Nia's tongue again. But what could she do? Pop up from between her lover's breasts and say *actually I started sleeping with you because I am trying to steal your treasure, but now I actually like you so please don't throw me overboard?* Zanta would never forgive her. She'd throw Nia off the ship at first opportunity, and Nia would never see Zanta, or Laurent, or her treasure again. Nia had no desire to cut their already short time together even shorter. Nor could she risk giving up the chance to get her pelt back.

So she stamped out the words on her tongue against Zanta's skin, tasted every inch of her. The candle flame wavered, casting their shadows long across the walls. Zanta tugged the pins from Nia's hair till it tumbled down over her face. She dug her fingers against Nia's scalp and brought her face up to capture her lips. Heat purred along Nia's nerves and she accepted Zanta's demanding tongue eagerly. Her knee slotted between Zanta's thighs, and she rocked forward, the volume of skirts a frustrating barrier between them.

"Get me out of this damn dress," Zanta panted, unbuckling her sword. When that clanged to the floor, Nia flipped her onto her stomach, kissing the side of her neck as she frantically unlaced and shucked the shell of stiff fabric from her body. She made quick work of the stays too. When she flipped Zanta onto her back again, intending to dive beneath Zanta's chemise and finally get her mouth on her, Zanta buried her hands back in Nia's hair instead.

"Not so fast."

A needy whine escaped Nia's lips, hyperaware of Zanta's nearness and how much she craved her.

"Let me taste you," she begged, straining against Zanta's hand.

"Tell me something first."

Nia stilled. Did Zanta suspect something? If she did, she had terrible timing. That was the sort of thing you asked *after* you got off. Or maybe it was the perfect time. Right now, if she asked Nia outright, Nia was afraid she wouldn't be able to lie.

"Anything." Nia trailed her lips along the inside of Zanta's knee, gaze rising to meet hers.

Zanta bit her lip. "Why do you want this? Why do you want me?" A slight, self-conscious tremor edged her voice.

Nia frowned. What did a woman like Zanta have to be self-conscious about? She was gorgeous, smart, powerful. If the stories sailors told had even an ounce of truth, Zanta could take a ship on her reputation alone with barely a drop of blood shed. She was dangerous. Feared. But she had a wild joy hidden in her that Nia wanted to taste again. And she'd been kind enough not to abandon Nia when she'd first come aboard.

How much of that could Nia say? Zanta didn't want to hear about her sappy feelings. This was just sex. Wasn't it?

Nia dragged her lips a few inches up Zanta's thigh until Zanta's hand stopped her again.

"Nia."

"You're beautiful," Nia breathed, letting a lazy smile spread her lips like she wanted Zanta to spread her legs. "Let me show you how much I want you, birthday girl."

Something flitted across Zanta's expression, her hand releasing. Nia slid lower.

"You're dangerous," Nia murmured, not breaking eye contact. "You strike fear into any poor sod on these seas."

"But not you?" Zanta raised an eyebrow, but her breath came quickly, her skin hot beneath Nia's mouth.

"Not me." Nia slid the delicate hem of Zanta's chemise up over her hips, and ran her tongue along Zanta's skin till she reached the junction of her thighs. "I know how sweet you really are."

She dove in, desperate to taste her, and couldn't hold back the wanton moan that escaped when she ran her tongue up Zanta's moist slit. Zanta gasped, seeming to forget her questions in favor of arching into Nia's touch. Nia hadn't had more than a few sips of wine with dinner, yet she felt drunk on Zanta's body as the sweetness burst on her taste buds. Truly, she could spend the rest of her life worshipping this woman. But it would end eventually, so she put all that future adoration into this moment.

Nia's tongue moved as if it had a mind of its own, vehemently lapping at Zanta's clit, which swelled in response. Zanta moaned, and Nia's eyelids fluttered with the pleasure of pleasuring. She wasn't usually one to get off on giving pleasure, but with Zanta it was different. Everything else fell away. Zanta's reactions were so intoxicating she found herself unable to think of anything but producing the next one.

She pressed her thumb into Zanta's opening up to the first knuckle, and Zanta bucked against her mouth.

"Please..." Zanta whined. Nia smiled and redoubled her efforts. Licking, sucking, pressing her thumb deeper and feeling the flooded walls of her insides. Some dangerous pirate captain she was, if she could come apart so easily in Nia's hands. She let Zanta's melodious moans envelope her in warm pleasure. She would imprint Zanta's softness on her tongue to taste for the rest of her life.

Zanta's moans built till they drowned out the music still filtering through the walls, and Nia lost herself to them. She feasted upon Zanta's essence till she really did feel drunk on it. Maybe that was the lack of air, but Nia didn't care at all. She'd die with her face in Zanta's softness before she gave up on making her sound like that. She moved her thumb in and out with tantalizing slowness, a direct counteraction to the frenetic movement of her mouth. And suddenly Zanta's thighs clapped shut around her head, and Nia could hear nothing as Zanta's hips pushed deliriously against her tongue, and honey filled Nia's mouth as Zanta came with a cry that transcended even the flesh clamped around her. She kept going, unable to resist bringing Zanta back to the edge before she'd even finished her fall. Burying her face between the velvety petals of Zanta's body and indulging her tongue's every whim until Zanta's legs began to quiver.

In her haze, she felt Zanta's hand on her head, and finally she pried Zanta's legs apart and came up for air. A single drop of liquid dripped off the end of Nia's chin and plopped onto the crates; she licked her lips. Zanta lay in a daze, one leg dropped off the edge of the crates and the other still bent and open. Outside, the party still went on. Nia hoped the crew members Zanta had assigned to keep watch and man the lines had stayed sober in case the *Lonesome* decided to take advantage of their merriment, otherwise the weapons on everyone's belts would be utterly useless.

"Are you still alive up there?" Nia giggled. Zanta's hand fisted in her hair and brought her in for a kiss.

"Very much so," Zanta panted. Her hand moved from Nia's hair to the neck of her bodice. "Take this off."

"I don't wanna get up," Nia groaned. "I wanna lay here with you."

Zanta leaned in close, licking a smear of her own juices from the corner of Nia's lips. "Take it off, then bring your box of dicks over so I can choose one to fuck you with."

Heat flooded Nia all over again. When a woman like Zanta ordered you to do something, you did it. She shucked her dress and underthings off, carefully folding the key and waist chain into the fabric out of Zanta's sight before digging the peach blossom box out from where she'd stashed it. Zanta sat up, and Nia opened it for her like a jeweler presenting gems to a princess. Zanta's eyes went immediately to the one on the far left.

She drew the length of polished wood out of the box. It was thick enough that the fingers of one of Nia's hands could not meet around it. The wood was medium toned, a bit darker than John's actual skin tone, but polished to a high, alluring shine. The smoothly carved veins caught the flickering light as Zanta turned it in her hands. Zanta whistled. "I'd like to meet the man who grew this one!"

"You probably have," Nia mumbled. John and Logan were close, and if Zanta knew the *Siren Song* crew as well as it seemed, it was likely she'd run into the *Kraken's Fury* crew as well.

"What?"

"Nothing." No use having that conversation while wet. She'd save it for another time.

Zanta raised one dark brow. "Well? You can take this one right?"

Both Nia's mouth and pussy watered. She'd been dying to use

this one ever since she laid eyes on it. She still dreamed of the times John had fucked her with the real thing. How it had stretched and filled her more than any other. She nodded hastily, barely able to get her words out past her excitement. "I can take anything you give me, Captain."

"Get on the hammock then."

Zanta threaded the wooden dick through the ring and strapped the velvet bands around her thighs and hips as if she had worn one a hundred times before. She drew Nia over to the swinging hammock, strung to exactly waist height. The wooden cock stood straight and proud between Zanta's legs as she seized Nia by the waist, all her post orgasmic weakness seemingly gone, and kissed her fiercely. Nia crumpled into it immediately, letting her body go pliant, not caring how Zanta planned to fuck her just so long as she did. She wasted no time with further foreplay; she knew Nia was already flooded with need. She pushed Nia's sternum gently till she lay sideways over the hammock. Her back supported by the fabric, but her legs and head hanging over each side.

Nia jolted, almost rolling backward off the hammock as Zanta hoisted Nia's legs over her shoulders and thumbed her slit.

"Fuck. So wet for me." Zanta smirked. "Or is it for whoever this cock really belongs to?"

"For you," Nia breathed. Her head already swam with want. Zanta's fingers found her dripping opening and pushed in. "Zanta, please."

"Please what? Don't I need to prepare you a little for this girth?" Zanta was enjoying having Nia at her mercy a little too much. Toying with her.

"I can—" A gasp as Zanta curled her fingers against Nia's slick walls. "I can take you," she begged.

"I don't know if you can," Zanta purred, aching heat following the movement of her fingers. "You're so tight."

Fuck. Why was she teasing so much? All Nia wanted was to be fucked dumb, and forget everything else. Was that so much to ask?

She pressed her heel to Zanta's back, urging her forward. Zanta clicked her tongue. "I should leave you like this. Maybe that will teach you to behave."

Nia groaned, and Zanta laughed. Her fingers stroked twice more before withdrawing. Nia met her eyes as Zanta brought her slick fingers up to her lips, and sucked.

"Fuck..." Nia moaned.

"You taste like peaches dipped in the sea," Zanta commented. Her hands framed either side of Nia's waist, and Nia had only a moment to draw breath before Zanta plunged into her. She choked on a moan, instantly overwhelmed by the thickness stretching her wide, and clutched onto the hammock's ropes for dear life. Zanta planted both feet on the floor and used the hammock to swing Nia off the cock, the wood coming away with a wet squelch, before burying so deep again Nia saw stars framing Zanta's face.

Nia's head fell back to dangle off the side of the hammock as Zanta set a merciless pace, pulling Nia off the cock completely each time before impaling her on it again and again until Nia was screaming, gasping, crying her name with every thrust. She abandoned herself wholly to Zanta's will.

"You like being stuffed full, do you? Come on my fat cock, Nia." Zanta's laugh of sadistic glee rang in her ears as Zanta pounded into her. The stars behind Nia's eyes burst in a galaxy of pleasure, hot liquid gushing around the cock and making the slide of those carved veins against her insides all the more torturous.

Zanta didn't stop, didn't even seem to realize Nia had come, and the carnal heat was already reaching critical levels once again. Her legs tightened around Zanta's neck, and Zanta's teeth scored her skin. Nia wanted to be closer to her, to hold her, but her mind drowned in lust. A bit of drool dripped from the corner of her mouth but she didn't notice, nor have the presence of mind to wipe it away. What did she care about being pretty right now when Zanta was fucking her so hard she'd be out of commission for a week.

"More...more..."

Zanta's fingers had barely brushed her clit when she came again, her whole body seizing, tightening. The whorls of Zanta's fingers burned themselves into Nia's nerves, and she let go of the ropes, letting her upper body sway upside down with the swing of the hammock, all the blood that wasn't engorging her pussy rushing to her head.

"Zan—" One last slam and the cock buried so deep Nia almost blacked out with the sheer volume inside her. Lightning crackled across her nerves, and Zanta held her through it all, filling her to the brim.

It was too soon when Zanta finally withdrew. Nia hadn't come down, and her pussy clenched around the emptiness. Buckles clinked, the hammock dipped, and suddenly Nia was being pulled fully into the hammock on top of Zanta's warm body. Aftershocks quaked Nia's entire being. Zanta's muscled thigh found its way between her legs, and Nia mindlessly ground against it, smearing juices across sweat slick skin. She smothered her cries against Zanta's breasts as she rode out her aftershocks till she was finally spent.

"What a good girl you are, getting off with just my leg," Zanta cooed, petting Nia's sweat-darkened hair. Nia shuddered, but didn't answer, so Zanta kissed her instead. Long and slow till Nia's body relaxed against her. When they pulled back, Zanta just gazed at her. She caressed Nia's cheekbone with her thumb. "What beautiful eyes you have," she murmured.

It was Zanta who had beautiful eyes, brown with a golden sheen, and so deep Nia wanted to fall into them. But she didn't say it. Zanta was allowed to say such things. From her it meant nothing. But Nia was afraid her heart would perch on her tongue for Zanta to see if she voiced all the feelings roiling in her right now. She hid her face between Zanta's breasts. Slowly coming down from the high of multiple orgasms. She couldn't really breathe.

If she suffocated, she suffocated. She'd die happy.

They lapsed into silence. Nia counted the minutes by Zanta's heartbeat. Wishing she could keep time with it forever.

All too soon, reality crept back in.

Zanta picked up the cock and strap from where it had been discarded beside them in the hammock. She twiddled it between her fingers. "So who's this one modeled after? Someone else I know?" She stopped playing and groaned. "Please don't say Rowan. I don't wanna know *this* is what I missed out on."

Right. This was casual for her. Just sex. Nia forced her feelings down and resurrected happy, carefree Nia. She tilted to look at her, chin on her sternum. "Who's Rowan?" She assumed someone close to Logan or John, but she'd never met any of the other pirates on their crews, and neither of them had offered any information either.

"The Ghost Hawk, Captain of the *Siren Song*."

"Oh. You fucked him?" Jealousy flared, unwarranted, considering they were discussing all the men Nia had fucked before this.

"Almost. I was trying to get over...Well, he was one of many rebounds after Emilie."

One of many rebounds, like Nia. That's all she was too, no more than an extended fling. She blinked slowly, letting Zanta's fingers teasing out the knots in her hair untangle the dark thoughts as well.

"Well, it's not him. But you may have met him. It's modeled after John Hakon."

Zanta dropped the dick like it had suddenly turned into a venomous snake. It lodged itself between her body and the side of the hammock. "John Hakon? The Demon's first mate?"

"The very same," Nia giggled, melancholy actually falling away with Zanta's cute reaction. "Why? Not fond of him?"

Zanta grimaced. "He's so stern."

"Not when you get him going." She usually wouldn't fuck and tell, especially to another bedmate, but teasing Zanta proved irresistible. "He carved all the dicks actually. He's quite talented with his hands."

Zanta groaned, but an incredulous smile tugged at her mouth. "I just used the Beast of Whitestone Reef's cock to fuck you," she lamented. There was a beat of silence, then, "I suppose you've had the real thing?"

"I have." If Zanta could still be openly in love with her late fiancée while sleeping with Nia, she could very well hear about Nia's many escapades.

"Have you fucked anyone else I know?" Zanta teased. "The Demon himself, perhaps?"

Nia laughed. "No, even I wouldn't go that far. But most of my conquests are seafaring types, so it's entirely possible we've climbed the same mast before."

"Tell me a name."

Nia thought for a moment, searching for the most famous, most scandalous name in her past who Zanta might know, and finally settled on, "Admiral Fabrice Gouin."

Zanta's mouth dropped open, her fingers stopping their soothing journey through Nia's knotted hair. "Fabrice Gouin? The Governor of Nanad?"

"He wasn't governor back then," Nia grumbled.

"Why on earth would you do that?" Zanta's tone wasn't judgmental, simply astounded and maybe a little awestruck.

"Well I didn't mean to! He caught John with my skirts up in his office, and well...it was the only way to distract him enough to get away."

"The governor—"

"*Future* governor!"

"—caught you...Why were you fucking a pirate war criminal in the gov—I mean admiral's—office?"

"John is not a war criminal," Nia huffed. She didn't know why she felt the need to defend him. He'd been a perfect gentleman to her when he wasn't fucking her against the glass walls of greenhouses and persuading her to steal things from uptight lords and government officials. "He had a very good reason for killing all those people."

"What—No, we're getting off topic. Why were you tupping him in the office?"

"We were stealing something and got carried away," Nia said innocently.

"You're unbelievable. Come here." She was grinning as she caught Nia in a kiss. It carried Nia away on a current of bliss for several minutes till Zanta broke away and settled back down. "I hope John didn't let you do all the dirty work yourself," she grumbled.

Now it was Nia's turn to grin. "I assure you, he had his fingers up that man like a puppet on carnival day."

CHAPTER 28

JULY 3RD, 1668

"Hold this."

Henri sighed against the cold metal of the infirmary bench, but nonetheless held his hand up for Robin to place some inexplicable medical implement in. His fingers closed around the smooth metal and glass without looking, much preferring to remain in his current position with his forehead resting against the worktop.

"Am I boring you?" The clink of glass and sound of pouring liquid accompanied Robin's amused voice.

"Unbearably," Henri groaned. He'd come down hoping to get a good cuddle in before his shift, only to find his boyfriend deep in some concocting process that couldn't be interrupted. Instead of going back up to the deck, Henri had accepted his fate as designated things-holder until it was time for him to report for duty.

"Why don't you go read or something?" More clinking, a pungent smell wafted over, and Henri's nose wrinkled.

"I wanna spend time with you," he grumbled. Even though they'd made up weeks ago, and had really only been fighting for a short time in the first place, Henri hadn't been able to get enough of his boyfriend. He felt clingy, barely able to think about anything but Robin when they were away from each other. And when they were together, he wanted to share everything. It didn't help that so much of Robin's free time was still taken up with making sure David stayed out of trouble and away from Rowan, who still had a short fuse about the almost-drowning situation.

"Poor baby," Robin cooed. A faint thump sounded on the worktop, and Robin's fingertips caressed the exposed back of Henri's neck, trailing comfort. Henri's hair beads clacked against the metal counter as he turned his head. Robin petted him as he focused on the task at hand. Henri let his mind wander for a moment, enjoying the casual intimacy of Robin's touch.

"I had a sister, once."

Robin's fingers stilled where he'd been absently playing with Henri's hair beads. Robin set the glass vial he'd been examining down beside the other items cluttering his workspace.

"Had?" There was a quiet wariness in Robin's voice. Since their reconciliation, they'd started talking more about their pasts, their families. Robin told Henri about how he'd almost been caught kissing another boy in the library his first year of university. Henri told Robin how Maman had scolded him and the baker's boys till they cried when they ate all the honeycomb in the bakery pantry and got the worst tummy aches of their young lives.

He and Robin had laughed, listened with sympathy, and comforted. Robin told him about running away. How it had felt like drowning, his whole future cut off at the roots he'd so carefully tended. Henri had told Robin about Maman's death. How it had been slow. Henri had cared for her for years, and by the end, she was a husk of the woman she'd once been.

But Henri hadn't told him about *this*. He'd never told anyone about it.

"She died," Henri said. Robin's fingers were on the little clay bead his sister had made him. After that first winter playing together on their father's ship. She'd found clay somewhere, and borrowed paint from a crew member, and decorated the bead with little swirls like waves and a border of uneven triangles. She'd worn it on a ribbon around her neck all summer, till she could gleefully present it to him the moment he stepped onto the ship as the first blustery winds of winter blew.

The paint was hopelessly faded now. Just a few chips of blue and red remained. The clay was cracked, and he'd already glued it back together twice.

Robin's large hand smoothed Henri's hair away from his forehead.

"How did she die?"

Henri scuffed his bare foot against the floorboards.

"I don't know actually. She was my half sister, older by a few years. And we didn't even meet until I was eight. She lived on our father's ship, so I only got to see her when they wintered in port." Robin's hand continued its strokes against his forehead, soothing away the little sparks of grief that threatened. "Maman didn't like her. She wouldn't let her stay in our flat above the bakery. And they didn't always make it back to our port before winter." He'd never really understood why his kind, loving mother didn't want his sister to stay with them. Surely living above the bakery would have been better than the cold ship? He'd offered, even begged, to give up his own bed for his new sister. But his sister had never set foot off that ship for as long as he'd known her.

"They stopped visiting when I was fourteen or fifteen. I wanted to go find them but Maman got sick and..." Henri took a shuddering breath. He shouldn't have brought this up now, when Robin was busy, and it was only a few minutes till Henri had to report on deck. But when Robin had started fiddling with the bead, he couldn't stop the flood of memories.

"Take your time," Robin said quietly. He brushed his sheaf of wheaten hair out of his eyes, almost long enough now to gather into a tiny tail.

"My father came back a year or two before Maman died. To say goodbye, I think. But my sister wasn't with him. When I asked where she was, he just said 'she's gone' and left."

Robin's soothing hand stilled. "Gone? Not dead, but gone?"

Henri nodded.

"So couldn't she still be alive?"

"He looked so..." Henri shook his head, trying to dislodge the memory of his father's sunken cheeks and haunted eyes. "He wasn't in his right mind. Grief was eating him up."

Robin nodded, thoughtful.

"But for a while there, after I joined the *Siren*, I'd look for her in every port. Just in case." He sighed, feeling silly about it now. "I don't know if I was really looking. I was probably just trying to make myself feel better."

The aft bell clanged twice, the signal for the afternoon shift change. Henri sat up, offering the metal and glass tube-like item in his hand back to Robin. Robin cupped his hands around Henri's, his hazel gaze soft and inviting.

"Thank you for telling me, Henri."

Henri nodded. His shoulders felt lighter, as if some weight he didn't even know he was carrying was now shared between them. Robin leaned over the table to kiss the tip of his nose. The aft bell rang again, reminding Henri of his duties.

"What was her name? Your sister?"

"Nianthe."

Henri's footsteps were the only sound in the halls of the *Siren* as he made his way up toward the deck. They'd wasted days evading the *Marigold*, only to realize Colonel Baird hadn't followed them at all. Rowan had puzzled over this as they turned north, intent to catch up to the *Monsoon*, wherever she might be, only to realize Baird had had the same idea. The two ships exchanged a couple volleys of cannon fire from a distance before Rowan ordered them to pull back. Henri didn't know the exact plan, but they now followed the *Marigold* north, just barely keeping her in their sights. Rowan didn't seem all that happy about it, but if they wanted to find Zanta quick, what better way than to hunt the hunter?

Between Rowan's sour mood and chasing the mercenaries for weeks on end, tension hung over the crew like an executioner's blade. There were pockets of joviality here and there. Fox was back to his usual bubbly self after recovering from his concussion, and if he was a little extra clingy with his friends, none of them actually minded it. There were murmurs from some that they should turn tail and go back to proper pirating. No one would say it out loud though; they all knew once their captain set his mind on something, he would see it through to the end. And they still held him in enough esteem to trust his leadership.

The bigger problem with morale was—

"Hey, you!"

Henri flinched at the voice, so like Robin's, but with anger and bitterness threaded through. He kept walking, hoping that ignoring

David would discourage him from whatever rude thing he was going to say. But David stomped up and blocked his way before Henri could escape. The stagnant, musty smell of bilge water wafted off him, and Henri wrinkled his nose. He was in no mood for this, and he tried to push past without too much aggression, but that only let David push him back.

"What do you want?" Henri asked wearily. Rowan really shouldn't have allowed him the option to stay back in Kadling Kay.

"I want you to stay away from my brother," David retorted, chest puffed out and fists balled like that would intimidate Henri into obeying.

"This again? Stop wasting both our time." Henri tried to push past again. He was already late for his shift, and didn't have time to entertain David's bigoted arguments.

David shoved him. They were similar in height, but Henri had years of pirating behind him, and David was a painter. Henri didn't even stumble.

"You're just itching to stay on bilge duty, huh? Let me pass, or I'll drag you to the captain myself."

David's face screwed up in disgust. He seemed incapable of getting along with anyone on the ship, least of all Henri. How could two brothers have such different temperaments? Robin seemed to have gotten all the gentleness and caring in the family, and he'd ended up becoming a pirate.

"Just stay away from Robin! This is your last warning. Leave him, or you'll regret it," David snarled.

Henri wasn't an aggressive person by nature, but this was getting irritating. He stepped back into David's personal space, not to push past this time.

"And what are you gonna do? You're stuck on this ship till the captain lets you leave. The only people here who care whether you live or die are Robin and me, and I only care because I don't want Robin to get hurt." He crowded even closer, looming over David in a way he hoped was intimidating. "Don't you dare do anything that will cause Robin pain."

David's expression hardened further. "I'm bringing him home, whether he wants to go or not."

Footsteps sounded overhead and Henri pushed away. He didn't

have time for this. There was nothing David could do if Robin didn't want to leave.

"Good luck with that, 'cause I'm not letting him go."

CHAPTER 29

JULY 16TH, 1668

Nia's fingers tapped a staccato rhythm on the wall boards she leaned against. The *Monsoon* was already too far north. Too close to the Sleeping Isles for Nia's comfort. In a day or two the Storm Ring would come into view on the horizon, and Zanta would have to make the decision to veer west toward Kefrye and the Marran Empire, or east to try to squeeze through the Storm Gap, a dangerously thin stretch of sea between the edge of the Storm Ring and Nanad's rocky coast.

Soon they'd have to do something. Soon *she* would have to do something.

Nia glanced down the empty hall. It was late, lookouts had been posted, and most of the crew had retired to their quarters to either sleep, or drink and play cards. But Zanta was nowhere to be seen. There had been no answer when Nia knocked on her door. No doubt she was holed up somewhere with Sabriye and the lieutenants making plans. Nia wanted to beg her not to try the Storm Gap. It would give them a higher chance of escaping their pursuers, but Nia had seen what those storms did to ships. One false move and they'd be dashed on the rocks in a second.

Zanta was a risk taker, but she also cared about her crew. Nia didn't know which route she would deem the better option, but Nia was determined to talk her into going west if they could.

What she really wanted was to sail straight into the storms and come out the other side to home. There was a trick to navigating the weather safely. Stroud had discovered it, but he'd never revealed it to Nia, and without it none of them would survive that journey.

Besides, home had never really been home in the first place.

Nia straightened as booted footsteps sounded down the corridor. Zanta appeared, looking harried, slight bags under her eyes, but beautiful. Nia's heart fluttered concerningly at the sight of her.

"Zanta, I need to talk to you about—" Zanta crushed her lips in a deep kiss, and all thoughts instantly fled. She melted into it, her arms coming to rest around Zanta's shoulders. The uncertainty of their situation faded momentarily into the background in Zanta's arms. The fact that they could die if the mercenaries caught up, and if that didn't happen, if Nia succeeded in finding her treasure, she'd leave, and never see Zanta again. All that talk could wait, this time was as precious and urgent as anything she'd meant to say.

They stumbled down the hall, Nia's lips tracing the line of Zanta's beautiful neck. Zanta's back thumped against the door to the captain's quarters, and Nia moved one of her hands from Zanta's waist to fumble with the handle. Finally, finally she would be allowed into the inner sanctum of the captain's quarters. She'd fuck Zanta into a stupor, then when the captain fell asleep she'd look for her treasure.

Zanta moaned, tilting her head back against the door to give Nia's mouth better access. Her pulse fluttered against Nia's lips, and her warm scent enveloped Nia's senses. Intoxicating. Nia pulled the handle, but their collective weight held it closed. Zanta's head snapped forward. She pushed Nia away, and a flicker of panic sparked in Nia's gut. Had she come to her senses?

But no, Zanta's brown eyes were hungry. She pushed Nia into the alcove next to her door, and dragged the heavy curtains closed behind them. Lantern light spilled through moth-eaten holes in the fabric, dappling their flushed skin.

Zanta attacked Nia's lips, pushing her up against the shelf that served as an altar. The statue of the entwined serpents rocked with the force of it, but neither of them paid it any mind. Nia's lips parted readily for Zanta's tongue, tasting like the ginger candies she liked so much.

Nia's ass was forced back against the edge of the shelf, and she braced her hand against the surface. The scattered offerings dug into her palm. No food, they didn't want to attract vermin, instead the shelf was heaped with trinkets. Coins and shells and cheap pieces of jewelry from market stalls. Nia silently promised to make an offering of that broach she'd been gifted her last day in Roseforte as an apology for defiling the Serpents' sanctum. It seemed a fitting offering, the last gift she'd received before finally returning to the sea. Maybe the Serpents would protect them from the storms to come.

Zanta's mouth pressed along her cheek and down her jaw, sending tingles racing over her skin. She gripped Zanta's waist and hauled her closer, grinding their hips together.

"Zanta, your room is right there, could we—"

The captain groaned against her neck but didn't answer. Nia had no choice but to surrender to the heat of her mouth. She barely had the presence of mind to wonder what had brought all this on, but all thought fled when Zanta hitched Nia's leg up, hand delving beneath her skirts.

"No dick today?" Zanta chuckled against her skin.

"Just you and me."

Zanta's hand slipped along the back of her thigh and sank into her heat.

"Fuck," Nia gasped, hips twitching into Zanta's touch, the serpent statue rocking on its plinth with her movement. She had to get it together. They were only days away from the Storm Ring, and she was running out of time to gain entry to Zanta's room. As amazing as bedding Zanta was, Nia had to keep her eyes on her goal.

"Zanta." Nia rocked her hips onto Zanta's fingers again, fighting to keep the pleasure from clouding her judgement. "You promised to fuck me in a bed."

"Being worshipped on an altar isn't good enough?" Zanta teased.

That did sound good. A clandestine liaison behind a curtain where anyone could stumble upon them. The little beads of light dappling Zanta's bare shoulders. Offerings tumbling at their feet. Juices running over Zanta's fingers.

No. No. She had to stay focused. She grabbed Zanta's stubborn chin and raised her face. Zanta's gaze locked onto Nia's mouth, brown eyes darker in the gloom.

"I want to take my time with you," Nia whispered. "I want to taste every bit of you until you're a puddle in the sheets." The more she wore Zanta out, the more likely she'd fall asleep so Nia could search the room.

And she'd have a great amount of fun doing it.

A quiet huff escaped Zanta's lips. Her fingers withdrew, and she let Nia's leg drop. Slowly, she took Nia's hand from her face.

"Come on." She threw open the curtain and tugged Nia the few steps to her door. Nia's heart stuttered. After years, her freedom was close at hand. All she had to do was find it.

The faint smell of incense clung to the corners of the room, an oil lamp already lit on the low table. Nia quickly scanned the room, but it looked much the same as before. Floor cushions scattered around the low table, the chair that looked like a throne when Zanta sat on it —now tucked away in the corner—and cushions and blankets piled high on the bed, inviting in the lamp glow. Nia let triumph wash over her for the briefest moment before she dragged Zanta to her. Her treasure didn't matter right now. The talk about the Storm Ring could wait till morning. Only Zanta mattered. The two of them. Together.

Nia pressed her palms to the small of Zanta's back, wanting her close. Their noses brushed, Zanta's shallow breath puffing against Nia's lips. Expectant.

Nia drew back slightly to look at her. Lips parted and wanting. Thick, dark lashes framing shining eyes.

The only way she could've been more beautiful was if she loved Nia back.

No. Nia almost shook her head. She'd not allow that to breach this moment. Not when this was likely to be one of the last times she'd have Zanta like this.

She kissed her so forcefully they stumbled to the bed. Zanta's heels hit the carved wood base and she sprawled onto the mattress, gazing up at Nia. Nia felt like she could fall into those eyes, like diving into the depths of the sea where sunlight barely reached. She wanted to be enveloped in them, enveloped in *her*. To indulge in every taste of her for the last time.

Nia dropped to her knees and removed Zanta's boots, fingers trailing reverently up her ankles, unlacing the sides of her leather pants, lips trailing over the soft skin as each inch was revealed. Before long, the leather was in a heap on the floor, and Zanta was nearly bare before her. Zanta propped herself up on her elbows, shivering as Nia trailed kisses up her inner thigh.

"Kiss my lips instead," Zanta said breathlessly, and the mood shifted. No longer were they stealing moments of intense pleasure in closets and corners. They were a pair of lovers luxuriating in each other. At least for now.

Nia leaned over her, pressing her into the mattress and taking her lips. Zanta's mouth parted greedily for her tongue. She threaded her fingers through Nia's hair, holding her there, and Nia let herself get lost in it. Let herself imagine that they were in love, and that she could stay forever. She caressed the curves of Zanta's body. Reverent. Memorizing.

Zanta made a small, sweet sound against her lips when Nia's thumb brushed her nipple through the bandeau. It sounded like music. Like the sun rising over a calm sea, and Nia never wanted to forget it. Slowly, she removed Zanta's bandeau and underwear until she lay completely bare.

If someone had told Nia this woman was a queen, a goddess, she would believe it without question. Every inch of her was perfection, from her kiss-bitten lips to the little scars that littered her body from years of pirating. Nia leaned back for a better view, tracing any patch of skin that caught her eye. She skimmed the edge of one soft breast, down a few small but jagged scars along her ribs, and over the delicate scales of her tattoo.

Zanta squirmed, color high in her cheeks.

"So beautiful," Nia whispered. Her fingers continued their leisurely journey over the landscape of Zanta's body. "I can't believe I get to see you like this."

A small, mischievous smile quirked Zanta's lips before she seized Nia and flipped her onto her back.

"Are you the only one who gets such privileges?" Nia stared at her for a moment, half mesmerized before she realized she was still fully clothed.

Nia hooked her legs around Zanta's hips and spread her arms out against the cushions.

"Unwrap me then."

Zanta fell upon her like a starving woman, undoing the fastenings of Nia's bodice, tugging the laces of her stays, unwrapping every layer of Nia's dress one by one until she lay naked as the day she was born in the open shell of her gown. Zanta caressed the curve of her waist, where the tiny silver key hung on its chain.

Fuck. She hadn't been expecting this, so she hadn't taken it off. Panic flared. Would Zanta know it was the key to the chest? Was this the moment she discovered Nia had been lying to her?

No. She couldn't. Nia needed her one last time.

Zanta's fingertips traced the delicate chain, found the clasp, and undid it. The chain too, fell to the bed. Why *would* she recognize it? It was a key just like any other, and Nia had absconded with it before Zanta ever set foot on the *Silverfin*. Zanta probably thought nothing of it.

The dress and the key ended up on the floor as Zanta flipped Nia onto her stomach. She swished Nia's hair to the side and trailed light kisses down the back of her neck, murmuring how it looked like flames. Nia shivered as Zanta's lips continued their journey down her spine, then paused at the spot to the left of it, just above her hip. Nia's muscles tensed. She knew what Zanta saw, the scar where Stroud had cut her. Deliberate. A perfect square where flesh had lifted away. Zanta's breath pooled in the hollows of her back, unfelt by the deadened scar tissue. Nia could practically feel the question on the tip of Zanta's tongue, the concerned tilt to her brows. She willed that question to remain unspoken. To let her keep another secret.

Pressure on the scar, not sensation. Zanta had kissed it, an acknowledgment without prying. She moved lower, hands cupping the curve of Nia's ass.

Every nerve in her was alive to Zanta's touch. Her breath.

Heat pooled in Nia's core. Fire licking her skin from the inside wherever Zanta touched. Nia had never been in love before. She'd had flings, infatuations. But nothing ever felt like this; pleasure never came from such a deep well of longing like it did with Zanta. If Nia hadn't needed to find her treasure, she'd never have let it get this far. She'd have fled before feelings ever reared their ugly heads.

Zanta's attentions reached the ample swell of her ass. She groaned appreciatively as Nia's back arched in anticipation. Nia wanted to watch her, to drink in every moment of her, but her mind went blank when Zanta nudged her legs apart and plunged her tongue into Nia's primed heat. Nia gasped as a rush of flame enveloped her. It shouldn't feel this good. It shouldn't make her want to sob, but she was suddenly holding back tears, teeth clenching around words that would rip their tenuous relationship apart.

Zanta's tongue moved, hands gripping her ass cheeks, and Nia cried out. The woman wasn't much of a talker but damn, she could use her tongue. Nia pressed her face to the cushions, muffling her moans as Zanta took her apart, body and heart, little by little. Zanta hummed against her, and even that shook her apart in the most terribly delicious way. She clutched at the sheets and let the fire wash over her and settle in her chest.

When had her plan of seduction for the sake of her treasure turned into this? Why had she let herself catch feelings?

Pleasure and guilt and love warred in her as Zanta's expert tongue brought her closer to the pinnacle. If she fell, she was afraid she'd blurt out everything she'd been holding inside, not only her secret motives, but the feelings neither of them wanted.

"Fuck..." Nia moaned into the pillow, silk soft against her lips. She wished it was Zanta's skin. She wished Zanta would stop the truth from spilling out. Fire curled around her spine, and her mind blanked out as she reached the peak, and fell.

She didn't have time to catch her breath before Zanta's mouth left her. Nia's hips twitched back to chase the sensation, but Zanta flipped her onto her back.

"Zanta..." It wasn't the right time, but Nia couldn't stop herself. Zanta stopped her instead, climbing into her lap, cum-soaked mouth crashing into liar's lips. Zanta's eyes smoldered like coals, and she moaned, wanton and needy as she devoured all Nia's unspoken secrets. All Nia's unwanted love.

Zanta grabbed Nia's wrist and brought her hand to her pussy. No words passed between them, only fervorous kissing. Zanta lowered herself, trapping Nia's hand between her pulsing heat and Nia's leg. Nia ground her palm up against Zanta's clit, producing a moan that shot straight to her core. She repeated the action, curling her fingers up to circle the soaked entrance. Zanta whimpered, tongue lapping into Nia's mouth. One hand came up to cup Nia's cheek, the other taking a wandering journey down the mounds and planes of her bare body.

There was nothing else but this. No mercenaries trying to kill them. No storms on the horizon. No secrets between them.

Zanta pressed down onto Nia's waiting fingers, moaning into Nia's mouth, and began to rock. Her own hand found Nia's pussy once again, deft fingers eagerly circling her clit. Zanta rocked faster, movements fevered and fast, fucking herself on Nia's dainty fingers. She was stunning, coming apart through Nia's touch. A magnificent surrender.

Lightning crackled from Zanta's fingertips, searing through Nia's nerves. She tried to focus on Zanta's pleasure, on the hot tightness clenching her fingers, the swollen bud rubbing the heel of her palm, but her mind was hazy with the honey ginger taste of Zanta's moans, the silk of her body. Bit by bit, she lost herself to their mutual pleasure, until finally, with one last stuttering roll, Zanta cried out her name. Nia saw stars, her name passed from Zanta's lips to hers, the last catalyst for her own orgasm to tumble her off the edge into a haze of pleasure. Zanta rode her fingers for another moment, desperate, whiny. Her skin prickled with goosebumps as she shuddered again, clenching so deliciously around Nia that she could feel Zanta's pulse racing through her fingertips.

Nia wanted to continue, to give Zanta as much pleasure as possible. Not only to exhaust her, but to imprint Nia's fingerprints into her core. To give her everything, because she couldn't give her the truth.

Zanta sighed against her lips. Grinding once more on her slick palm before collapsing to the mattress beside her. Eyes closed, long lashes resting like feathers against her cheeks, she pulled Nia to her. Not kissing, just shared breath, and comfort. A warm glow cradled them close among the sumptuous blankets and cushions, and Nia had almost dozed off when Zanta spoke.

"What was it you wanted to talk about?" Her voice was slurred, sleepy.

The glow dimmed, shadowed by the outside world. This was Nia's chance to come clean. To spill everything and beg Zanta to turn west away from the storms, even if it meant facing the mercenaries head-on. Her heart clenched so hard, she was sure Zanta could hear it crumbling. She couldn't do it. She couldn't bring herself to shatter this illusion. Nia petted Zanta's hair, soothing. "It's late. We can talk tomorrow."

One brown eye cracked open. "You'll stay, won't you?" She snuggled closer into Nia's side. The crumbling pebbles of Nia's heart disintegrated into dust, only held together by Zanta's contented embrace.

She wasn't asking her to stay forever. She didn't know Nia planned to leave. She just wanted a warm body in her bed.

Nia dropped a kiss on top of her fluffy, sex-frizzed hair. "Of course."

Zanta sighed, snuggled into Nia's chest, and slept.

CHAPTER 30

FIVE YEARS AGO - MAY 1ST, 1663

"Where is it?" Silver Stroud howled, hurling objects off the ornately carved shelves in his quarters. Zanta closed the door quietly and locked it behind her. The tantrums and strange behavior had become more frequent the past few months, and the crew was taking notice. It wouldn't do for one of them to walk in on this.

"Where's what?" Emilie shouted, then ducked as an expensive spyglass flew at her, lens shattering as it hit the wall.

Zanta stepped closer. Stroud hadn't noticed her yet, but Emilie's gaze cut toward her, warning her to stay back. Emilie always tried to placate their captain during his *episodes*, but Zanta had lost her patience for him long ago. She wished they could just lock him in and let him sweat it out alone. But Emilie was too kind for her own good, whether or not anyone but Zanta could see that. She wanted to help Stroud, even though it was clear in times like these that there was no reasoning with a madman.

Even as talk of mutiny rumbled through the crew.

A brass navigation instrument crashed to the floor among a flurry of charts.

"What are you looking for?" Emilie repeated, trying to exude an air of calm, though she looked frightened. She wasn't equipped for this. Neither of them were. But Stroud had appointed Emilie first mate after the previous one had absconded in Kefrye with a sackful of valuables. They'd muddled through so far, but this was the worst episode yet. Worse than Stroud's insistence on sailing so close to the Storm Ring without proper supplies. Or his accusations about other crew members stealing from him. Worse than his rants about his missing daughter, who Zanta was no longer sure had ever existed.

"My eye!" Stroud wailed, whirling on them. "My green eye! I'm ready to use it now. There's no other option."

Eye? What the fuck was he talking about? He had two perfectly good eyes in his head, and neither of them were green.

"That greenish marble?" Emilie asked, her false, soothing voice edged with strain. "You lost it in a dice game, remember? You said it was useless."

Stroud stilled, a brass chart divider in one hand, its pointed tines quivering with the shaking of his body.

"Lost?" His eyes were wide and crazed. A shiver ran down Zanta's spine. This was not the man she knew. Not the captain she'd served under for almost three years. There was only madness in those eyes.

"No. No. It can't be lost," Stroud muttered. "How will I find her if I can't see her? How will I find my little girl? My Nianthe?"

Nianthe, Stroud's missing daughter who Zanta suspected was just a figment of his imagination, or long dead. No one on the current crew had been with Stroud back when she'd supposedly gone missing. There was no proof on board the *Silverfin* that she'd ever existed.

"You'll find her some other way," Emilie soothed, holding one hand out, placatingly. They all stared at each other for a moment, the destruction of Stroud's tantrum scattered around them. Zanta took a tentative step toward Emilie, thinking it was over.

Stroud's crazed eyes sliced toward her. He brandished the divider in her direction.

"You. You must know where my eye is. I need it!" This last part was almost a scream, his face turning red beneath his silver beard.

"It's gone," Zanta hissed. She had no idea if what Emilie had said was true or just designed to calm Stroud's rage, but she could hear the other crew members outside. They could surely hear everything. Even if Emilie and Zanta managed to calm him, they would have a mutiny on their hands after this.

"It can't be gone!" Stroud screamed, hysterical, his voice reaching a fever pitch. "I'm ready to use it now! I can find her!" He raised the divider, but this time it was pointed toward himself. Emilie and Zanta both surged forward as Stroud stabbed the prongs into his left eye with a desperate wail.

"Stop!" Emilie shouted. She grabbed his arm, and he tried to shake her off, gouging the instrument deeper and popping the eye out of its socket with a sickening squelch.

"Stop..." This time it was a plea. Tears streamed down Emilie's face. She cared for him. They both did.

Zanta tackled Stroud, and all three of them collided with the shelves. The ornate wood splintered and broke under their weight, sending them crashing to the ground amongst an avalanche of charts, instruments, and artifacts. Stroud's elbow struck Zanta's temple, and her vision went blurry for a moment. Emilie screamed and Zanta tried to scrabble toward her despite the fuzziness in her head. Her fingers slipped on something wet.

When Zanta's vision cleared, her heart went cold.

Stroud pinned Emilie to the boards, knees digging into her chest. Emilie bucked, but Stroud was bigger, stronger. He raised his arm, the bloodstained divider glinting in his hand.

"No!" Zanta lunged forward, grabbing the first thing she could find, a large splinter of wood. Stroud struck, stabbing the sharp prongs of the instrument into Emilie's throat just as Zanta reached them.

An anguished snarl ripped from Zanta's chest, and she drove the sharp splinter into Stroud's back, between his ribs and into his heart. A killing blow, just as he'd taught her.

A shocked exhalation was the only sound that escaped him before his body toppled to the side among the debris of his madness.

Zanta scrambled over him, knees and hands slipping in the gathering pool of blood.

"Emilie..." Her beloved's name escaped her lips in a sob as she knelt beside her. Emilie's cornflower blue eyes met hers, light fading fast. Her pale fingers fluttered uselessly over the spot where the divider tines pierced her throat.

"Emilie...honey..." Zanta's bloodstained hand cupped Emilie's cheek.

Emilie exhaled shakily, as if trying to speak, but blood gurgled up around the tines and at the corners of her lips. A single tear clung to her pale blond lashes, but she did not look away from

Zanta's face as she breathed her last and the light faded from her eyes.

Grief, dark and desperate, coiled through Zanta's chest, dragging her down into its lonely embrace. She looked back into Emilie's now lifeless eyes and sobbed, repeating her name over and over as if to call her back from the icy depths of the underworld.

It did not take long for the crew to break the door down. They found Zanta soaked in the blood of her captain and her lover, clutching Emilie's body close. It was too late for them. And it was too late for Zanta. The grief in her had already hardened to something vast and all consuming. She was born anew from the blood that coated her skin. She'd killed the killer of her love. Driven a piece of his own ship through his heart.

She was reborn as Splinter Zanta, captain of the *Silverfin*.

July 16th, 1668

Zanta slept, her breath deep and her skin warm beneath the light blankets. Nia watched her for some time, holding back from touching so as not to risk waking her. She'd fallen asleep without first donning her silk hair wrap that Nia had seen her wear sometimes when urgent business took her away from morning routines. The little braids at her temple fell across her face where she lay with her cheek pressed to the pillow. One of the bright glass beads had become trapped under her cheek and would leave a mark when she woke. Nia's fingers itched to free it, but she had things to do.

When Nia was sure Zanta would not wake easily, she carefully extracted herself from the warm, sex-disheveled bed. Her limbs felt heavy with satiation, and she wanted nothing more than to crawl back in. To kiss Zanta's lips, gather her up, and succumb to sleep.

Well, almost nothing.

Nia could not let her feelings cause her to forget her purpose, both aboard the *Monsoon* and in Zanta's bed. The true reason she had decided to seduce Zanta in the first place.

Her treasure hid somewhere in this room, and she had to find it.

Nia retrieved her chemise from the floor to cover her nakedness. She could not search Zanta's room in the same state of undress she'd just lain with her.

Guilt pricked at Nia's heart as she knelt in front of the first cabinet at the side of the room and eased it open. Zanta had been nothing but kind to her, and here she was rifling through her possessions as she slept.

The chest was not within the first cabinet, nor the second. She rifled through their contents, knocked softly against the bottoms and backs of the cabinets, and dug her fingers into knots, searching for hidden compartments. She found nothing but papers and books, navigational tools, trinkets, and clothes. All the normal possessions of a life at sea.

The hinges of the fourth cabinet squeaked as she opened it. She froze, only her head turning to look at Zanta's slumbering form. Zanta sighed and rolled over onto her back, one hand dangling off the edge of the bed.

Nia waited for her to open her eyes. To find Nia elbows-deep in her belongings. But Zanta's eyes remained closed.

Fuck, Nia would have to be quicker. Her heart fluttered nervously in her chest. It *had* to be here. She would have died weeks ago if the treasure wasn't on this ship, and she'd searched every other place but this room.

She crossed the room to the cabinets on the other side, stepping over the piles of clothes they'd left in their haste to feel each other. The next cabinet did not squeak, but Nia gasped when she saw what lay within. Tucked amongst a bundle of blankets was a tin bucket, full to the brim with brass keys. What did Zanta need with all these keys? Why were there so many? Nia picked one off the top of the pile, turning it over in the dull light. Was Zanta searching for a key to open the chest? But they were the wrong size. Nothing like the tiny silver key Nia kept around her waist. The key to her freedom.

Behind her, Zanta moaned. A low, pained sound, and Nia almost dropped the key. But when she looked, Zanta was still asleep, a frown on her face.

Was she having a nightmare? Nia replaced the key, careful not to make a sound, and moved on to the next cabinet.

And the next.

And the next.

Nothing. How could there be nothing?

Nia sat back on her heels, dumbfounded. Her heart clenched. It had to be here; this was the only place it could be. The only place close enough, safe enough...

Was there a secret compartment below the floorboards? No, she'd searched the room beneath this and didn't think there'd be space for a compartment deep enough for the chest.

Nia stood, her eyes roaming the room, searching for another place large enough. It was iron, and heavy; it would not be hidden anywhere high up.

On the bed, Zanta moaned again, her head turning fitfully on the pillow. But she still did not wake.

The bed. It was low, but built into the structure of the room so that one long side rested beneath the windows, the other enclosed by carved panels in the Yarenen style, all arabesque and geometry.

If the floor below was hollow, it would be enough to accommodate the chest beneath.

Nia's breath caught. Why had she not seen it sooner? All she'd done was waste time looking in the obvious places. She hurried over to the bed, almost tripping on her discarded dress. She knelt by the bedside, breath shallow, almost face-to-face with Zanta. If she leaned forward a little, she would be able to kiss Zanta's fingers.

Instead, she felt around the edges of the panel, searching for a catch or gap. Her fingertips met the barest sliver of a hidden metal hinge.

Nia's heart leapt. It was here. It had to be. She searched the other side of the panel and found a catch. The panel popped open.

Silently, carefully, she peered into the space beneath the bed. Two chests lay in the dark. One wooden, no doubt the *Monsoon*'s coffers. And the other...

Nia's heart fluttered, and she reached out, her fingertips meeting the familiar iron filigree.

A heartbeat aside from her own thrummed through her. The rhythm and life of the seas, of her people. Calling to her. Bidding her to come home. Tears pricked behind Nia's eyes, and she had to fight down the urge to drag the chest from its hiding place and immediately abscond with it.

Was the pelt within the chest whole? Or was the square that had been cut to keep her from escaping still separate from it?

Zanta's fingers twitched, only inches from her face, and Nia flinched. She forced herself to think rationally. She'd have to drag the chest out to open the lid, which would inevitably wake up Zanta.

And what if the pelt wasn't whole? She'd still be stuck on this ship, and Zanta would know her secret.

Zanta whimpered, and Nia forced her hand away from the iron chest. Tears streaked down Zanta's beautiful face, dark eyelashes damp. Her breath was no longer even, but came in hitching pants.

"Please..." Her voice was desperate, her body wracked with the throes of her nightmare. Sweat prickling her skin. "Don't..."

Nia's heart skipped several beats. What was she dreaming of that distressed her so?

She looked back to the chest. Her treasure. Her freedom. She should take it and flee. When would she ever get a chance like this again?

"Don't..." Nia knew that Zanta's pleading word was not directed at her, but it struck her all the same. Her heart clenched, and before she could think about what she was doing, she eased the secret panel closed and climbed back onto the bed.

"Zanta." She kept her voice gentle, so as to not startle her. She cupped Zanta's cheek, intending to wipe her tears, but Zanta thrashed and knocked her hand away.

"Zanta," Nia repeated more firmly. "Wake up." She shook Zanta's shoulder, touch still gentle despite her growing concern.

Zanta inhaled sharply, body shuddering, eyes moving back and forth frantically beneath her lids.

"Wake up. You're safe. You're—"

Zanta woke with a gasp, eyes wild. For a moment it seemed she didn't know where she was and fought against Nia's hold.

"It's okay. You're safe."

Brown eyes lit on Nia, widening in recognition. Her struggles abated, but her breath still came in short, terrified gasps. She grabbed Nia's hand in both of hers and held it to her chest. Nia felt her heartbeat against her sternum, as frantic as a bird fighting a storm.

They just stared at each other for a few moments, until slowly, Zanta's breathing began to ease, and the tight grip on Nia's hand loosened.

"You were having a nightmare," Nia soothed. "It's over now. I'm here." She raised their clasped hands to kiss the back of Zanta's fingers. Zanta still said nothing, just closed her tearful eyes and took a few deep, steadying breaths.

When she opened them again, their gentle depths held a sorrow not dulled by time. "Thank you."

Nia kissed her fingers again and brought their clasped hands to her own heart. "What were you dreaming about?"

Zanta searched her face, no doubt trying to parse whether she should reveal the dream's contents. It was one thing to share her bed with a woman she barely knew. It was quite another to share something so personal as the disturbed inner workings of her sleeping mind.

Finally, she sighed and lay back against the pillows.

"I dreamed of the night I killed Silver Stroud."

Nausea curdled in Nia's stomach. Was this the truth? Or did Zanta somehow suspect Nia's connection to Stroud? Had she been truly sleeping and dreaming? Or was she awake to witness Nia's search?

No, the tear stains were still on her cheeks, distress plain on her features.

"It haunts you," she said.

"It was not what I would have chosen."

Nia frowned. She had no love lost for her father. He was the direct cause of her mother's death and all the misery of her childhood. But all the stories of his death painted Zanta as a vicious mutineer.

"What happened, truly?" Nia asked quietly. "I have heard all the stories, but considering I do not see a bloody splinter hung as a trophy above your bed, maybe the stories are wrong."

"There was no mutiny. At least none led by me. He was..." She took a deep, shuddering breath, her eyes lowering to their clasped hands. "The mood aboard the *Silverfin* had been bad for some time. We hadn't taken any prizes in a long time, yet we sailed all over the Islands, and the crew was growing restless and discontent."

"Why?" Nia prompted. "Why sail if not to plunder?"

"He was looking for someone, his daughter."

Nia sucked in a breath. He'd still been looking for her? A confusion of feelings stirred in her. Should she be pleased that her father had searched for her? Or disgusted that her captor had hunted her? Had he done it out of love? Or so he could get his treasure hunter back?

"His daughter?" she asked, trying to keep the overwhelming interest from her tone.

"He said she was lost, but would not say whether she was drowned or kidnapped or what had happened to her. And not one of the crew had ever seen her. Some said she must have been a figment of his imagination."

"His imagination?" Nia frowned. "Why would they think that?"

Zanta sighed. "By the end he was raving mad. He could not say whether she was a child or as old as me. The former first mate stole from him, so Stroud became paranoid that the rest of us were stealing from him too. But really he'd just gambled away all our money after finding solace at the bottom of a bottle. Then finally he lost this trinket that he was convinced would help him find her. He flew into a rage and..." Zanta's story trailed off, and she met Nia's eyes again. "Emilie tried to stop him from hurting himself, and he murdered her. I killed him trying to save her."

Nia's heart hammered in her chest, her mind reeling. So this was the truth. Her father had not succumbed to a brash mutiny, but madness. All because of her. Because she had run away. She bit her lip hard as the realization struck her, the truth of her identity threatening to burst past her lips.

Zanta's fiancée was dead because of Nia.

"I'm sorry." It was all her fault, even her father's death. If she had not run away from the *Silverfin*...

"I'm sorry if I frightened you," Zanta said, interrupting Nia's guilty thoughts.

"It was nothing." Nia's belly still rolled with nausea. Conflicting feelings churning like a whirlpool. "I was worried for you."

How could she ever confess the truth now? It would hurt Zanta too much to learn that the woman who now shared her bed—even if there was no deeper feeling in it on her part—was the one responsible for her fiancée's death. Better to let her think Nia was just a treasure-seeking thief.

"I'm fine," Zanta murmured. "It was a long time ago."

"I'm...so sorry." Nia barely kept the ragged tears from her voice, guilt eating her alive.

"She was the love of my life," Zanta said wistfully.

Her words shouldn't have stung. But their barb pierced Nia's aching heart.

Zanta had not slept with another woman in five years. Had kept that one last piece of loyalty to her lover. And by some cruel twist of fate, it was Nia who had broken it.

"I am sorry you lost her. I am a poor substitute." She released Zanta's hand and began to gather her clothes.

"Nia, I didn't mean—"

"It's quite alright," Nia interrupted, pulling on her skirt and scooping the rest of her clothes from the floor, the key cold as a knife against her arm. "I'm glad your nightmare has passed. I'll go back to my own bed and let you sleep."

"Nia, wait—"

But she was already out the door, rushing past the alcove they'd so recently dallied in, toward her own lonely room.

What was she thinking? She had to leave this place. Take her treasure and go. And though this had always been her plan, she'd been content to linger until now. She could not share Zanta's bed or endure her casual affections any longer. Not when Nia now knew the whole truth, and Zanta knew none of it.

At the next opportunity to flee, Nia would find her way back into Zanta's chambers, and abscond with her treasure.

CHAPTER 31

JULY 17TH, 1668

Yves's anger was a bruise that never healed, yellowing and receding only to be prodded back to life by his own pride. He felt the ache of it as the hailing flag ran up the mast, and he waited to see if the *Siren* would respond.

After sating death in Kadling Kay, Yves had tried to sail away. Tried to leave Rowan to his own mistakes. But it didn't stick. After only a few days, it became too much. He'd had no choice but to find him. The demon's instincts had urged him north. Rowan's presence somewhere in the sea ahead of them tugging at the dark waters in him like a moon to the tides.

Did Rowan know the sway he held over Yves? How thoughts of Rowan consumed him utterly? Yves thought not. Rowan was just a man after all. He did not see how he brought the only light into Yves's dark world.

Finally, after weeks of sailing, the skull-and-wings of Rowan's insignia had snapped on the horizon, and Yves had known his instincts had not led him astray. The *Siren* sailed slowly, and at first Yves had worried Rowan had run into trouble, but as the *Kraken* gained on the smaller ship, he spotted the prey Rowan had in his sights.

Now Yves held his breath, waiting for the little ship ahead to either respond or flee. He wouldn't blame Rowan if he wanted nothing to do with him anymore. The *Kraken* would never be able to catch the *Siren* if Rowan decided to run away. For once, he was at the mercy of Rowan's whims, and he hated it.

"Are you gonna hold your breath till you pass out?" Doe appeared beside him, her presence as his first mate somewhat more motherly than John's, but no less sarcastic. What curse had befallen Yves that he was fated to always have a first mate who challenged him but was too competent to get rid of?

"He wouldn't refuse me," Yves said darkly, exhaling as he saw the *Siren* run up the flag that meant they could meet. The distance between the two ships closed quickly, and now that seeing Rowan again was inevitable, Yves's anger flared once again.

"I don't know what kind of fucked up game you two are playing, Captain, but if you keep going like this he'll leave you."

"None of your business," Yves growled. She didn't have to tell him. He knew. The incorporeal tentacles at his back twitched in annoyance. His worry for Rowan's safety grew with each day they drew closer to the Sleeping Isles, and with it, his anger over the fact that Rowan seemed to possess not a scrap of self-preservation. With each moment, Yves felt his control slipping into the dark depths of the water below.

Before, his mind had been harmonious. Hounded by death, yes, but one with the demon. But for the past few days, the demon had been pushing to the surface more and more, fighting for dominance. Was it his separation from Rowan that had it chomping at the bit? Or the nearness to the place it was imprisoned? The dark waters were rising, growing more powerful. Too large for the human part of Yves to contain, as if it would burst through his skin.

"Should we ready a boat for you, Captain?" Doe asked, unperturbed by Yves's foul mood. The *Siren* was within range now, but he could see them preparing a boat already.

"No need. It seems that my husband is coming to us."

Rowan arrived with storm clouds around his head. "Make it quick," he snapped as soon as he stepped onto the deck, leaving behind the crew members who'd rowed in the boat. He wasn't wearing his eyepatch. "The more time you waste the more likely we are to lose them."

Yves's chest tightened. They hadn't exactly been kind to each other the last few times they'd met, but this was openly hostile. His pride prodded anger back to the surface.

"We have something to discuss."

"Well? Spit it out, then."

Fury engulfed him, burning away the tenderness that had been slumbering beneath. The demon gnashed its teeth, ready to sink them into Rowan's flesh. Rowan smirked as Yves grabbed his wrist and dragged him into the stateroom. The door slammed behind them, and Yves pushed Rowan against the table, chairs clattering to the floor.

"Obstinate wretch," Yves hissed, seizing Rowan's face in one hand, squeezing, feeling Rowan's teeth through his cheeks. "I am trying to protect you."

Fuck, it felt good to touch him again. So fragile. So beautiful and tenuous with all his mortal imperfections. Yves wanted to destroy him. His mouth watered for it.

Rowan slapped his hand away. "Funny, protecting me looks an awful lot like hurting me," he snarled, working his sore jaw from side to side. Yves backed off half a step.

Had he actually hurt him? They'd always played rough, and Rowan never seemed to mind.

"Rowan—"

"No. Fucking listen to me. I did well enough before you came along, and I'm doing fine now. You weren't there when that ship out there attacked, yet here I am hale and whole. I don't *need* your protection and you won't convince me to abandon course. So either shut up or stop following me!"

Yves's resolve hardened. The demon's darkness surged to the forefront of his mind like a flash flood. Those fuckers had attacked *their* beloved. Rowan's considerable skill was of no consequence. Forget the danger the mercenaries posed, he and the demon couldn't let Rowan go any further. They had to prevent him from going near the Sleeping Isles and the Storm Ring, for his own good.

His tentacles writhed around him, darkening the room. Rowan seemed unphased, scars standing out livid and red against his face.

"You can't follow her into the Storm Ring. It's madness. You won't survive."

Rowan's laugh was shallow and cutting. "If my survival means so much to you, maybe you should help me instead of being a dick."

"I won't let you go." Yves's voice deepened with the demon's echoes, the ancient evil that lived inside him and wanted nothing more than to devour this man. To protect him from everything but itself.

The demon loved Rowan in a possessive, hungry way. The same way it had once hungered for the ships passing through its waters and dragged them down to depths unknown. Somewhere at the bottom of the sea there was a cave so dark only the pinprick lights of the demon's tentacles had ever illuminated it. And no being of land or sea dared venture there. Its rocks were littered with the rotting corpses of ships, treasure spilling from their rended bowels. The bones of humans and all manner of creatures, unbleached by sunlight, wore away in the deep currents.

The demon had dreamed, rather wistfully, of taking Rowan's body there when he inevitably succumbed to death. It wanted to curl around him like a tomb, and watch his beloved face decay. It would embrace his bones for eternity. A treasure to surpass all treasures that had come before.

It *was* love. The only love Yves had to give.

He stepped into Rowan's space again, ready to kiss or throttle him. He hadn't yet decided which.

"You. Cannot. Go. There." The demon's shadowy waters pressed close to the inside of his skin, flooded the space between his ribs. Something akin to panic edged its anger; Yves didn't want to know what could make such an ancient being afraid.

Rowan crossed his arms, unflinching at the evil that lurked inside his husband, unafraid of the danger that awaited him in the Sleeping Isles. That hard jade eye flayed Yves open, as if it could see straight to his drowned soul.

Rowan had told him once that he was terrifying. That had been before Rowan donned the jade eye and saw Yves's true nature. Yet he still kissed him, still let Yves take him to bed. Now he stood steadfast against him.

"Give me a good reason," Rowan said.

It was like the demon took over, brine on his tongue and the deep voice of that ancient creature pushing all the way to the surface. "The Storm Ring will cut you down like the frail creature you are." He could see Rowan's temper flare, and swallowed down what he really wanted to say: *Do not make me drag your body back out of the depths when the storms shatter you. Do not leave me alone.*

Yves seized Rowan by the back of the neck, dragging him forward so their faces were a mere breath away. Rowan shoved futilely against his chest, but he didn't budge. Rowan couldn't outmatch Yves for strength.

"This time, I will keep you," the demon growled. Briny water practically dripped from his lips. What would Rowan do if Yves kissed him right now, with not a stitch of humanity left on the surface? What would he do if Yves chained him to the bed and ravaged him till he couldn't even think of escape? Would his love finally fall away like his terror? Would Yves keep him in body, but lose his heart?

He fought the demon for control, trying to force himself back to the surface and give Rowan at least some of the gentleness he deserved. But the demon retained its steadfast control of his body, the tentacles lashing out to grip Rowan's ankle, his waist.

"Let. Me. Go." Rowan grit his teeth through every word.

"Not until you listen." Yves thought himself above begging, but his soul felt like it was drowning in his and the demon's shared desperation.

"I'm done listening to you." Faster than Yves could conjure his next words, Rowan drew the jeweled dagger from Yves's belt and stabbed it up through Yves's arm. The tip emerged from the top of Yves's bicep, slick and glittering as a newly cut ruby. The demon crashed back down into the deep recesses of Yves's body with a howl, tentacles recoiling. Yves's hand went slack. Rowan slipped out of his grip.

Contrary to rumor, Yves could still feel pain. It raced across his nerves now, hot and icy at once. It no longer carried the same potency as when he was young and mortal, for nothing could come of it now. He would die, or not, and he'd come back before the day was out. It made him reckless with himself and others. He cared little for their pain, and even less for his own.

They could not be reckless with this one precious mortal they'd bound themselves to.

This, *this* was a wound from his beloved's hand. And though pain lanced through him and blood dripped onto the table's surface like scattered garnets, it was nothing compared to his heart stuttering as

Rowan slipped from his arms and made it to the door in a few quick strides.

"Rowan." Yves sagged against the edge of the table, wrenching the dagger out and letting it clatter to the floor. Blood flowed freely down his arm, staining the expensive lace of his sleeve. Rowan paused at the doorway. The briefest flash of concern furrowing his brow before his resolve hardened again. He turned, and fled.

Now that hurt.

CHAPTER 32

JULY 19TH, 1668

A dark, flickering bank of clouds cut the horizon edge to edge, the air crackling with unseen energy that made the hair on Zanta's arms stand on end. She didn't know which direction to focus on first. Which danger was escapable, and which would cut them down. Was it the two mercenary ships that had driven them to the edge of the map, and trapped them in a choice between a battle against man and a battle against the elements? Or was it the storm itself, so massive that it seemed to swallow the entire sea and charge the air with lightning and the scent of rain?

Or was it that she'd fucked up royally with Nia?

Zanta collapsed the spyglass she'd been using to torture herself with the futility of their situation. Her eyes found Nia instead. She was down on the main deck, helping Laurent and Colm prepare for the storm. Zanta had ordered the crew to prepare for anything, so half of them secured the ship against the storm, and half readied for battle.

The bright banner of Nia's hair had escaped its pins and now whipped around her face with the threat of the storm. It drew Zanta's gaze like a call to war. Zanta hadn't meant to tell her the details of Emilie's death. But when she'd woken up from that horrible nightmare, adrenaline rushing through her veins and tears on her cheeks, and found Nia there to comfort her, she hadn't been able to hold back. She'd told Nia everything. And the expression on Nia's face had been horrible. She'd looked sick, and Zanta didn't know why.

Or, she didn't want to think about why.

They were just casually hooking up, right? No matter how Zanta felt about it, about Nia, that had been their agreement. She was under no illusions that Nia planned to stay on the *Monsoon* long term. Their relationship—whatever it was—had an end date, and she'd thought she was fine with it. If they got through this, Nia would surely leave. But Nia's words the other night stung.

I am a poor substitute.

Nia wasn't a substitute at all. She might be the only woman Zanta had slept with since Emilie's death, but Zanta wasn't looking to replace one with the other. They shared certain superficial similarities. Fair skin and hair, freckles on cute button noses. But there the similarities ended. Emilie had been calm, one could even say stoic, most of the time. She'd let nothing out, and hoarded her joy, her softness, for private moments only. Zanta had loved her strength, had loved that she was the only person who had been allowed to see the soft underbelly of Emilie's soul.

Nia was Emilie inside out. She let her joy out into the world where it could flit from person to person like a butterfly, sharing lightheartedness with whomever it touched. But she hoarded her stormy feelings for private moments, a space Zanta had only just begun to see the cracks of. She'd seen a bit of it after the battle, when she found Nia crying in the wardrobe. And the other night, when she left Zanta's room in a gloomy cloud before Zanta could say something like, *you're nothing alike, but I care for you*, that could've either fixed everything or made it so much worse.

That would have been bad enough, if Nia stayed mad at her. If she'd cut off their arrangement or sulked or shown *any* outward sign that she was upset. But she didn't. The next morning she'd gone back to her usual bubbly self, and treated Zanta like nothing happened. And that was somehow worse.

Distant thunder echoed from the dark bank of clouds. Zanta turned her eyes to the storm ahead, and a minute later a pair of arms wrapped around her waist. Nia's lips found the nape of her neck, ghosting across her skin over the stiff collar of her jacket.

This was worse, because Nia's mood had no cracks. And that meant Zanta's feelings were unreciprocated. She didn't matter to Nia beyond pleasure, perhaps friendship, and she tried to tell herself she had to be content with that while it lasted.

Before she could say anything, Nia slipped around to stand by her side, hands trailing over her waist. Nia's hair whipped toward the encroaching ships at their back, but she raised her chin toward the darkness lurking in the opposite direction.

"That's the Storm Ring." There was no question in her voice.

"Looks like it."

Nia dragged her eyes away from the clouds and met Zanta's gaze. "We can't go through it. We have to turn back. Fight our way out if we need to."

This sternness was unlike her. Was she afraid?

"Did you forget that it's two against one?" Zanta didn't mean to sound derisive, but her nerves were frayed to threads. They had made one last bid for freedom a few days before, and been beaten back again when the *Marigold* finally caught up to its companion. Now she faced an impossible choice: turn and fight to the end, or take her chances with the storm. A choice she still hadn't had the courage to make.

If the *Monsoon* slowed to try and avoid the storm, both mercenary ships would fall on them like a pack of wolves. Zanta and her crew had managed to escape them once before. But after weeks of little scrimmages which had worn down both the crew and the ship, unable to make land and rest or resupply, Zanta wasn't confident they could win or even escape. But if they kept running, they'd plunge headfirst into a storm so deadly no ship had survived it. None but the *Silverfin*.

A shout rang out from the crow's nest, followed instantaneously by the boom of a cannon and the rumble of thunder. The *Lonesome* swooped within range, its companion not far behind. *Shit.* The mercenaries' trap snapped shut, paralyzing Zanta with indecision. They could turn and face the mercenaries who wanted them dead. Or sail into the endless and ancient storm that wanted nothing, but might kill them anyway.

"Zanta!" Nia's fingers dug into her cheeks, forcing Zanta to meet her eyes, so green and bright in the gray darkness that threatened them. "We can't face the storm. Trust me, we—" The percussion of more cannon fire interrupted her, one shot crashing through the glass windows of Zanta's bedchamber below them. The *Monsoon* shuddered, her sails snapping as the storm's edges seized them.

They could still fight free. But Zanta wouldn't be able to pull the same stunt she had before. It would be a head-on fight while also battling the edge of the storm that even now dragged them closer.

A pirate scrambled down from the rigging and bounded up to her. "Message from the lookout, Captain. Spotted two more ships behind the others. Couldn't see the flags, but one is a warship. They're gaining fast."

Fuck. The Serpents certainly weren't looking out for her today. The *Monsoon* was outnumbered four to one. If that warship caught them, they were done for.

"Captain, what are your orders?" Sabriye appeared at their side. The press of the crew's attention smothered Zanta like a waterlogged blanket. She'd always prided herself on her leadership. Her quick and decisive actions. But now...

Now, whatever she chose would be wrong. If they fought, they'd die. If they weathered the storm, they'd die. And the consequences of both would rest solely on Zanta's shoulders.

Nia's warm fingers threaded through hers, and Zanta straightened her back, imagining a rod of iron securing her spine. Strong. Unbreakable. The wind whipped her coattails around her legs as it dragged the *Monsoon* closer to the encroaching clouds.

"We weather the storm." Uncertainty wavered in her voice, but only Nia and Sabriye heard it before the wind snatched it away. Zanta squeezed Nia's hand once before she strode to the quarterdeck rail and called, clear and certain, "Stay the course!"

There was no way around it. No edge. No clear section of sky in the distance. The storm was inevitable, but this fight wasn't. They had no choice but to be swallowed by the storm. She couldn't let her crew and ship be weakened by battle first.

Several crew members paled, or made warding signs. She circled her serpent tattoo with shaking fingers. A habitual gesture, no real intention or prayer behind it, but it brought her comfort.

She took a deep, steadying breath and began issuing orders. The crew jumped to obey. They trusted her to lead them through.

She hoped against hope that trust was not misplaced.

~

"FUCK. FUCK. SHIT. NO, NONONONO." Rowan slammed the spyglass closed and pinched the bridge of his nose. The *Monsoon*, pursued by the two mercenary ships, had just sailed directly into a massive wall of storms. He could no longer see any sign of any of them, and the *Siren* was on course for the same fate.

He'd managed to catch up, but not enough. The *Monsoon* hadn't spotted the *Siren* and *Kraken*, or had mistaken them for more enemies. Rowan had dispatched Nephele with a message tied to her leg, assuring Zanta allies were close at hand. They could fight the mercenaries together. The *Siren* and *Monsoon* might stand a chance, but with the *Kraken* on their side—as Rowan hoped it was—they'd shred those bastards to nothing but splinters. But the wind had buffeted Nephele down again and again until she was too exhausted to continue and Rowan had to bring her inside, cradling her like a baby.

Now the *Monsoon* was gone. If Rowan hadn't hung back to meet with Yves when he hailed him, he might have caught up in time. But his heart had stupidly wanted to give his husband one last chance, and to be reassured he had Rowan's back no matter what.

That hadn't happened, but the *Kraken* still followed in their wake.

Rowan swept his gaze over his crew, then to the *Kraken* not far behind, contemplating his choices. There was little chance they would be able to avoid the storm now. The wind was already strong, the atmosphere charged with danger. It was now a matter of following the *Monsoon* or not. On the other side of the storm—if there indeed was another side—they'd still need help. Rowan had no choice but to go. And where Rowan went, Yves would follow. Wouldn't he?

Yves had warned against this. He seemed so sure that Rowan would not survive. And maybe he was right. Maybe by this time tomorrow, Rowan, his crew, and his beloved ship would be nothing but fish food drifting beneath the sea. But it wasn't anger or obstinance that spurred him on now. A deep feeling tugged at his gut that he had to help Zanta, and they would come out on the other side of this.

Rowan stepped up to the rail of the quarterdeck, feeling the nervous energy of the crew like fingers on his skin. Their eyes raked over him, some pleading, some alive with the prospect of testing their might against the forces of nature.

"That is where we are going," Rowan announced, pointing to the ominous clouds before them. "There's no avoiding it now." The currents already had them; the storm would catch them one way or another. Better to meet it head-on. "If you're the praying type, best get it out of the way now. You'll have no time when we're in the thick of it." Below, crew members bowed their heads, or touched serpent tattoos. Some men had one god; some had many.

Rowan had no god but luck, no faith but his crew. And it was the strength of their backs and their will that would see them through this.

PART 3
THE STORM

CHAPTER 33

UNKNOWN DATE, 1668

Zanta sputtered as a massive wave crested over the side of the *Monsoon*. Salt water flooded her nose and mouth and stung the myriad of little cuts on her cheeks. The force of it pushed her back a few steps, and she had barely regained her footing when another wave slapped her. The lifeline tugging at her waist kept her from being swept overboard.

As soon as the *Monsoon* had plunged into the storm, Zanta knew they were fucked. There was no end to it. A slate gray ceiling of clouds hung low over the water as far as she could see, as if the whole world had been consumed. Lightning flickered constantly between the dark roiling folds, and forked down toward tumultuous waves.

They'd battled for hours, losing sight of the *Lonesome* and *Marigold* as night darkened their world. There was no navigation. All her crew could do was hunker down and try to keep the ship from capsizing. They had no sense of direction, no ability to steer beyond making sure the mountainous waves didn't catch them broadside.

Zanta struggled to keep her footing, leaning heavily against the mast for support, and surveyed the crew in flashes of lightning. Exhaustion hung from the limbs of every last one like dragging seaweed, but they fought valiantly on against the forces of nature. In all Zanta's years at sea, she'd never seen a storm like this. It raged like it had a personal vendetta against them, tossing the ship from wave to wave like a cat with a bug.

How long had they been in it? It had to be past midnight already. Would Zanta live long enough to see a clear morning? Would there even be a clear morning to see?

The *Monsoon* crested another wave and plunged down the other side. For one weightless moment, they were floating. The roar of the waves was like a beast trying to swallow them whole. The next wave loomed ahead, craggy with white foam that shone like a predator's teeth in the dark.

A crack cut through the storm, one rung of the mainsail finally losing its battle with the driving wind and snapping free. The weight of the wooden beam popped lower rungs free and dragged a web of rope and torn yellow sail with it. All Zanta could do was watch in horror as it trailed broken ropes like death ribbons. Shouts rang through the night, and the rest seemed like it happened so slowly, in between flickers of lightning, that time almost stood still.

Sabriye lunged toward the falling beams. The tangle of wood and sail hit the deck with a deafening crash, splintering the boards. Ropes whipped down after, catching Colm from his place at the wheel, and knocking him to the ground.

"Fuck!" Zanta bolted as the wheel spun out of control, and the *Monsoon* heeled sharply, abandoned to the whims of the storm. Sabriye got there first, leaping over the fallen yard and lunging for the out of control wheel.

The wheel spokes cracked across Sabriye's hand and her face twisted in a rictus of pain as the wave bore down on them. But she reached again anyway, desperately trying to get the ship back under control.

It was too late. The next wave pounced on them, and the *Monsoon* met it sideways instead of head-on.

"Sab—" The deck pitched, as the swell of the wave lifted it. Zanta grabbed for the first solid thing she could find, the capstan with its winding anchor chain. Around her, the crew's shouts echoed. Some managed to grab the mast, ropes, rails, anything solid. The deck tilted to a steep angle, seawater rushing over the starboard rail to consume them all. A man slid past her toward the yawning maw of the sea and Zanta reached for him, missed, and watched the sea swallow him, the snapped safety line trailing him like the rope of a noose.

Another body slid down the deck and crashed into her, knocking the breath from her lungs and almost making her release the links of the anchor chain. It was Laurent. Blessedly still clinging to life. He said nothing, just clutched onto her with wild eyes as the ship rolled and plunged them into the water with a great groan of timbers.

The frigid water almost snatched her last breath from her as silence enveloped them, the underwater world almost peaceful. The storm didn't exist here, but neither did breath or light or warmth. A scream built up behind Zanta's sealed lips. But if she let it out, she knew seawater would invade her lungs, and it would all be over. She squeezed her eyes shut. Not that it made much of a difference to the utter darkness. All that existed was the hard metal of the chain against her palm, and Laurent's arms and legs squeezing her.

She hadn't gotten a good breath before, and her lungs were already screaming, heaving against the spars of her ribs. Old breath desperate to escape and be replaced with the crushing pressure of water.

Should she let go? Take Laurent and try to swim for the surface? She wasn't sure she could. The cold locked her muscles in place, and she didn't know which way was up, not with the entire ship tumbling through the wave. All she could do was hold on.

Sound crashed back into her world. The pounding of waves, the persistent beating of rain. She dragged in a deep, ragged breath before she even opened her eyes. Air, not seawater, filled her lungs.

She opened her eyes, half expecting another impact, but none came. The *Monsoon* sat upright at the bottom of a valley between waves. The wave that had rolled them retreating, the next closing in, blocking out the flickering sky.

Move, move. Do something. Her freezing fingers unlocked from the chain, mind lit up with a thousand details at once. The main mast was gone, snapped off with the impact of the water. Her crew, those who'd held on, whose lifelines remained intact, scrambled to their feet. Up on the quarterdeck, the wheel whipped violently with no one there to hold it.

No one there.

No Colm. No Sabriye.

"Fuck!" Zanta dragged Laurent to his feet. "Pull the lines." The storm almost swallowed her voice, but those who heard, obeyed. Hand over hand, they dragged in the waterlogged ropes that were pulled taut over the side, dragging their macabre burdens behind the ship. Zanta caught the out of control wheel, fought to steer them into the next wave so they wouldn't roll again. She did not see the crew pull their comrades from the water. But she heard them. Retching up seawater when their knees hit the deck. And she heard the silence too. The silence of the drowned.

"Colm!" Laurent tugged the taut lifeline secured to the base of the wheel, but he couldn't manage it, not by himself. Zanta wrestled the wheel to port trying to get the *Monsoon* back on track before the next wave.

"Captain! Help me!" Laurent had one foot braced on the shattered rail, desperately hauling at the rope.

"Kinda busy," Zanta gritted out. Every muscle ached, blisters forming where she gripped the wheel spokes.

"Captain!" Desperation cracked Laurent's voice, and she knew Colm was drowning or already dead on the other end of the line. One of her beloved crew members, under her care and protection. But she couldn't go to them.

"He'll die!" Laurent sobbed.

"We'll *all* die if we roll again!" Zanta snapped, guilt twisting her guts. Someone else would come soon, wouldn't they? Someone else would help him when she couldn't.

Wind whipped stinging rain into her face as she finally wrestled the ship to face the wave head-on, just as it began to roll beneath the bow. She locked her gaze dead ahead, clutching onto this one bit of control that remained to her, and blocking out everything else. Laurent's cries of frustration and fear as he tried to save his friend. Drowned corpses scattered across the deck. Sabriye missing. Worry over Nia below deck. One mast gone, and the other split. She would deal with it all later. After she sailed them out of this storm.

CHAPTER 34

UNKNOWN DATE, 1668

Salt water surged through Yves's veins, lightning and thunder crackling up his bones as the storm thrashed the *Kraken's Fury*. He stood on the deck of his beloved ship, letting the rain slick his skin and soak his fine clothes as Doe barked orders and his crew fought for their lives against this onslaught of nature.

It had been so long since Yves had killed. So long since the demon could slake its thirst on either blood or Rowan's supple body. Death had its claws in his stomach, and he was ravenous.

When Rowan had foolishly sailed into the storm under some misguided sense of friendship for Splinter Zanta, Yves had no choice but to follow. He cared little for the safety of his own crew beyond their ability to serve him. Protecting Rowan remained his only goal. He hadn't expected a strange calm, almost relief, to envelop him as soon as the first drops of rain iced his skin.

But the tension inside him still held, even grew, with every league the *Kraken* ate up between them and the Sleeping Isles. Demon shadow pressed against the inside of his skin, wrapped every bone and filled him so completely he felt the dark waters might split him open like an overripe fruit and consume the world.

What would happen if the demon took over completely? Would the human part of Yves finally be consumed, and cease to exist entirely? Yves didn't know. And if the demon knew, it kept it from him somehow. Perhaps this had always been its plan. Perhaps it had driven his obsession with Rowan and allowed love to weaken him enough to overpower his will. It was a strange feeling, this paranoia toward a creature that lived within him, whose thoughts and feelings twined so closely with his own that they might as well be his, if not for their inhumanity.

Once Yves had thought them harmonious, one being, but the further north they sailed, the more the demon manifested. A few times in the past few days he'd caught crew members, even Doe, looking at him with a perplexed expression. As if they'd caught a glimpse of his true form, the tentacles lurking in the shadows.

So he let the wind and rain lash him. Luxuriated in the raw power of the sea, the fear it elicited in the mortals on his crew. It was intoxicating, exhilarating. Death sent white waves to snap at their heels, toying with them before it intended to swallow them whole. But Yves had his own prey in mind, and he would not allow his crew to flounder before he saw Rowan and the *Siren* safely through. He could not lose him, the anchor to his last shreds of humanity. The light breaking through deep water, allowing life to grow.

There was no light here. The *Siren* was quick, but strength was needed to weather a storm like this. Yves could barely make it out in the distance. The long, plaintive call of Rowan's bosun's whistle broke the night between crashes of deafening thunder. The only way Yves knew his beloved still lived. He clung to that sound like the call of a siren, ignoring any other calls that might try to catch his ear. It tugged at his heart and drew him onward like a leash.

The *Siren* hurtled over the peak of a wave, disappearing from Yves's sight. A chill overcame him. No. He could not lose sight of Rowan. His hand raised of its own accord, like the demon had done it, trying to take hold of the storm and bend it to their whims. It let out a frustrated growl through his mouth when his human body failed to grasp control of the waves.

Yves barked orders, his words cutting the storm like a blade. Had the crew noticed yet, that the sea did not reach out to snatch them from the deck? That the howling wind and waves and rain had not deigned to kill a single one of them in the endless hours of battling the storm? Perhaps not. The storm might not obey him, but it could sense his wrath, and decided to spare his vessel.

His crew obeyed, exhausted and hollow-eyed, but when the *Kraken* crested the wave, the *Siren* was gone.

No. No. *No.* NO. Yves whipped around, eyes searching the storm. Ears pricked for the telltale whistle. But the *Kraken* was alone in the churn of unquiet sea. And all at once that calm, that sense of belonging in the storm, disappeared.

Rowan couldn't be gone. Yves, the demon, both of them would feel if he'd been swallowed up by the sea. Every nerve in them was alive with the crashing of waves, the rain driving into dark water. They would *know*.

The demon surged up like bile, and Yves doubled over, biting back a pained cry. The storm's cacophony snapped into something like a song. Every crack of thunder, a beat of his cold, incomplete heart. Every destructive wave, a surge of salty blood in his veins. The beat of the rain on his skin felt like an embrace.

Dark water coated his tongue and threatened to spill out of his mouth. And this time, he did not fight it down. Did not cling to humanity. He had to protect Rowan, and if he couldn't, there was no point in resisting the demon's undertow.

CHAPTER 35

UNKNOWN DATE, 1668

The *Kraken* hurtled into the bowl between two massive waves, its snapping tentacled flag disappearing behind the wall of water as if swallowed up by the sea itself. Rowan caught his breath and held it, eye trained on the spot the *Kraken* had vanished. Waiting. Hoping that it would reemerge. Bolts of lightning sliced the air in quick succession, highlighting every drop of driving rain, every crag of the waves. But the *Kraken* did not reappear.

Wind snatched away the breath Rowan held, and before he could draw another, lightning forked overhead, narrowly missing the *Siren*'s main mast. Rowan had no choice but to plunge back into the fray. Rain lashed his face as he sprinted down the deck to help a knot of crew members haul in a line. At the front of his mind, worry over Yves and his crew burned. He knew Yves would not stay dead if the *Kraken* succumbed to the storm. But that didn't mean he couldn't be lost. It didn't mean the loss of his ship and crew wouldn't affect him and the other survivors, if there were any.

Stupid. He shouldn't have done this. Yves was right. They were all going to die.

The sodden rope burned as it slipped through his palms. Rowan caught it again, gritting his teeth, his bootheels sliding across the slick deck. He could not think of Yves now. All he could do was fight the storm and survive, so Yves had someone to return to if all else was lost.

Time slowed and stretched, every moment saturated with freezing rain, crashing waves, and the flicker of lightning. All the lanterns had gone out, snuffed by wind and rain, and between the flashes of lightning, the ship plunged into oppressive darkness, careening blindly through the waves.

THE *SIREN*'s crew battled through the storm. Not even a sliver of light peaked through the clouds to tell him whether it was day or night. All was darkness, endless hours, maybe days, until he could no longer feel time slipping past. Rowan's body sagged with fatigue, wet clothes dragging at his limbs, but even that felt like a distant thing. He did not know how long it had been since the *Kraken* had disappeared.

Rowan found himself missing the stars, the sun, though they wouldn't have been able to navigate by them even if he could see them. It was all they could do to keep the ship heading straight into the waves, and they had no idea where they were or how close they might be to a shore or the edge of the storm, if there was one.

"Rowan!"

He whipped around at the sound of Logan's shout from the quarterdeck, wiped rivulets of rain and sea spray from his eye and squinted through the dark. Lightning flickered, illuminating the quarterdeck and Logan. His real hand clutched one spoke of the wheel, he and two other crew members braced bodily against it to keep the ship from turning broadside into the waves. The silvery steel hook gleamed at the end of his other arm, pointed toward the bow of the ship, his face a rictus of fear. Rowan followed Logan's direction to the bow and beyond. Darkness obscured the sea again for a brief, terrifying moment until another bolt of lightning threaded the low clouds and two spires of ghostly rock loomed up in front of them like pale fingers reaching out of the sea, waves crashing almost to their jagged, towering peaks.

And the *Siren* was heading right toward them.

Rowan froze, his heart stilling in his chest, and it felt like everything else stopped with him. As if the world itself shared his terror. With the next flash of lightning, everything came into sharp focus.

"Turn! Turn!" But there was no time. The *Siren* hurtled onward, and if they tried to turn, the waves would smash them broadside into the rocks. He sprinted toward the quarterdeck, his mind racing ahead with the image of the rocks seared behind his eyes. He took the steps two at a time and skidded to a halt beside Logan, a plan half formed and on the tip of his tongue.

"Steer between the rocks!" Rowan shouted. Logan's eyes widened, then his jaw clenched in determination.

"Help me." Along with the other crew members, they grabbed the spokes of the wheel, struggling against the pull of the waves on the rudder as the *Siren* careened inevitably toward their doom. Millimeter by millimeter they turned the wheel, as the rocks loomed closer in the flashes of lightning.

"Brace!" Logan shouted, as Rowan fumbled with the bosun's whistle around his neck and brought it to his lips. He blew the order to brace as hard as he could, the whistle's sharp sound barely piercing the storm's onslaught. But some of the crew braced and held, pulling their companions down with them.

The next flash brought the rocks into sharp relief against the dark night, looming high above them. Rowan went to his knees, still bracing the wheel against his shoulder, and dragged Logan down with him, hugging him against his chest. Logan's soaked blond curls pressed to Rowan's chin, his huffing breath against Rowan's neck the only warmth in the storm.

Another flash and the *Siren* crested the swell of a massive wave, slowing as the bow slipped between the spires. They would make it. Gods, they had to.

Darkness shrouded whatever fate would meet them on the other side.

With a horrible grinding sound like bones macerated between a sea monster's teeth, the *Siren* struck first one spire, then the other and lurched to a halt. Rowan's shoulder slammed bruisingly against the wheel. A scream pierced the storm's roar, cut off by the sickening thud of a body hitting the deck.

The wave dropped out from under them, and they became weightless for a heart-stopping moment as the *Siren* dropped, the sides of the ship scraping down the jagged rock faces that held them on both sides. Logan whimpered low in his throat, hook dug into the column of the wheel and the other arm wrapped tight around Rowan's back. The *Siren*'s fall shuddered to a stop, stuck fast between the two spires of rock.

For the first time in what felt like days, the *Siren* was still. Rowan lifted his head tentatively, sure that at any moment the sides would give way, and they'd fall to their deaths into the hungry sea below.

Another massive wave just like the one that had wedged them broke upon the stern, crashing over the quarterdeck and almost washing Logan out of Rowan's arms. They clutched each other tighter until the wave fell away.

When Rowan released him, Logan sprawled to the deck. Shaking. Then turned over and heaved up bile onto the already slick wood.

"What the fuck. Are we..." Logan's lank hair hung over his face.

But they couldn't afford this moment of weakness. Rowan clambered shakily to his feet and tugged Logan up after him. A smaller wave broke on the hull, causing the *Siren* to shudder. They both rushed to the rail.

The dark sea churned far below, white caps silvered by lightning. The *Siren* was wedged over fifty feet high above it.

"Fuck." Rowan ran a hand down his face. A hysterical laugh bubbled up his throat, his knees going watery. He clutched the rail to keep himself upright.

They were stuck, and only a wave of epic proportions was going to unstick them, but they were alive for now. Would they be able to weather the storm like this? And what would happen if the storm quieted and they were still stuck here, far above the sea?

"Captain!" Henri's shout pulled Rowan and Logan away from the rail and down the stairs to the main deck, where the crew was picking themselves up. Henri was down on one knee next to a fallen crew member, his fingers pressed to the woman's neck.

"She fell from the rigging," Henri said when they stopped beside him. He shook his head. "Dead." His brown eyes looked haunted, and Rowan was sure he was thinking this could have been his fate more than a year ago, when he'd fallen from the rigging and broken his leg. He removed his fingers from the woman's lack of pulse and closed her staring eyes. If there had once been blood around the body, the storm had already washed it away. Rowan allowed himself a brief flash of grief for his fallen crew member. Her name was Marta. Even if Rowan wasn't as close with some of the crew, they were his family and his responsibility.

"Take her below, and help Robin," Rowan ordered, trying to keep his voice steady. Henri nodded and, with the help of another crew member, picked up the body. The rest of the crew began to gather around, muttering amongst themselves.

"We're stuck for now." Rowan addressed them, his tired voice accompanied by the crack of the rudder whipping back and forth in the wind. His gaze roved over them, soaked, haggard, exhausted. How many had he lost? How many were dead because of his foolishness?

He swallowed, throat feeling raw. He had to lead, now. He had to make sure no one else would be lost. They'd worked hard through the storm to keep the *Siren* afloat, and now there was nothing to do but wait. He pointed to knots of crew members in turn. "You, clear the debris, and do as much as you can to secure the ship and cargo. Prioritize food and fresh water over anything else. You, attend the injured, bring them to the infirmary, and make a list of casualties." His heart clenched at the thought of yet another list of names to bring home to Illusion. Crew who depended on him who'd been swept away or killed in the storm. He tried to shake it off as he pointed to the last group, the men and women who'd worked harder, and took more risk than all the rest in the rigging. "Get some rest while you can. Everyone, stay to the center of the ship as much as possible. I don't know how secure we are but we have no choice but to wait and hope the storm moves away."

They all nodded solemnly and went about their tasks, limbs heavy, picking carefully across the deck like any stray movement would send them all plummeting to their deaths. Rowan stood still for a few breaths. Until he felt a warm presence at his side.

"This is gonna make for one hell of a 'glad we're alive' party later," Fox quipped when Rowan looked at him. Dark bags clung under his eyes. He was as exhausted as the rest of them, but his chip-toothed smile still brightened the darkness.

Rowan felt himself smiling back, even as he said, "Well, the night is still young."

Fox shrugged, rain dripping down his sharp chin. "Don't speak that into existence, Captain. We'll live to get fucked another day." He winked, and Rowan rolled his eye.

"Go check the damage on the sides and report back."

"Aye, Captain." Fox sauntered off, as if he wasn't going to check just how fucked they were. The *Siren* scraping down the jagged rocks under its own weight had sounded bad. But was it bad enough to compromise the hull? If a rogue wave didn't dislodge them sometime before the storm's end, they'd have a hell of a time unsticking the *Siren* from its current perch without having to worry about holes.

He told himself there was no use worrying about it until Fox came back with answers. So he forced the thoughts and plans to the back of his mind to join his worries over the fate of the *Kraken* and her immortal captain. He managed to drag himself back up to the quarterdeck, where Logan was attempting to hold the wheel steady as the rudder whipped around at the mercy of the wind and waves still battering them. Rowan's body moved automatically, grabbing a coil of rope and helping Logan lash the wheel so the rudder sat as flush with the back of the ship as they could get it. When they were done, Logan sank heavily on the deck, rubbing the stump of his wrist.

"You okay?" Rowan asked.

Logan looked up at him, hazel eyes dark and shadowed by his sodden golden curls. "Just sore," he replied nonchalantly, but winced.

"Let me see." Rowan knelt and gently took Logan's arm. "Has your hand been hurting?" He knew Logan still got ghostly pains in his missing hand, like Rowan did with his eye. Sometimes it helped if Logan could watch someone else rub the false hand, as if it tricked his mind into easing the soreness of muscle and tendon that was no longer there.

"No, it's..." Rowan pushed Logan's sodden sleeve up his arm to see his wrist red and raw beneath the leather straps that secured the hook's base to his wrist. Logan sighed. "The padding on the straps fell off a while ago." The wet leather had been chafing his skin for who knew how long. And the skin beneath was raw to the point of bleeding.

"Go below and get some ointment and bandages from Robin. Then go rest."

Logan looked almost ashamed. "No, it's okay. You need me here."

"I do. Gods know I do, but you're hurt, and I don't want it to get infected. Go rest. I'll wake you up in a few hours. I can handle everything else for now."

Logan opened his mouth to protest again, then seemed to think better of it. His lips thinned to a line, and he nodded. Rowan helped him up and sent him on his way below to the infirmary.

The rain lessened slightly, a small reprieve even as the wind still snapped at the lines and waves still battered the hull. Fox emerged from below, cast around looking for him, then made his way up to the quarterdeck. His usual boundless energy was nowhere to be found.

"How bad?" Rowan asked when Fox mounted the top step.

"It's—" Fox flinched as a crack of thunder interrupted him, then started fidgeting with the braided leather bracelet he always wore these days. "It's not great but not as bad as it could be. I couldn't find any holes in the hull but some of the gun hatches and port holes got scraped clean off." He tugged gently at the bracelet. "Not gonna lie, Captain, I think a few of the boards are only an inch or two away from breaking." As if to illustrate his point, the ship groaned. The entire crew froze in their tracks, waiting to see if the sides would give way and plunge them into the sea below. But she held fast, faithful as always. Rowan pressed a palm to the wheel column, silently thanking his ship for seeing him through this far. He didn't even want to think about what might happen if they couldn't get her unstuck.

His gaze swept over the ship. They'd taken on water, lost cargo, and supplies, and the bowsprit was cracked from the repeated impact with the waves, but the masts were intact and so was the hull, for now.

The sails were all furled, but his winged flag still snapped in the wind at the top of the main mast, and he didn't want to risk sending someone up to retrieve it.

Rowan couldn't decide if their situation was dire, or safe for now.

"What's the plan, Captain?" Fox seemed to be past the point of exhaustion now and on to the stage of manic fidgeting, his fingers tripping over the salt-worn bumps of the bracelet as if they were piano keys.

Rowan sighed. "The plan is to rest until either the storm stops, or we're forced to think of a plan." His exhausted mind could only run in circles at this point. "Go to bed. You look about ready to drop dead."

Fox's eyes narrowed. "Are you coming with?"

Rowan shook his head. "I'm staying up to finish the work."

"And will you be resting after that?" Fox chided, sounding like a mix between Logan and a mother.

Rowan shrugged. "Someone has to stay up and keep an eye on things."

"And that someone has to be you?" It was a testament to Fox's exhaustion that he didn't come back with some sort of "with only one eye?" quip.

"It's my ship, Fox. You're all under my care."

"Oh." Fox blinked innocently, rain droplets clinging to his long brown lashes. "And here I thought we were a team."

Rowan sighed and clamped his hands on Fox's shoulders, steering him toward the stairs. "I already promised Logan I'd wake him up in a few hours to take my place. Happy?"

Fox scrunched up his face skeptically, but turned to go. He'd been sneaking into Rowan's room less and less these days, getting used to sleeping alone, but...

"Ah, wait." Rowan pulled him back, realizing Fox was shivering. "Your room must be right under the damage. Take mine."

The chipped-tooth smile replaced Fox's weariness. "Make sure you dry off before you get into bed. I don't want your cold-ass feet waking me up."

"Yes, dear," Rowan soothed. Fox threw him a sly look, then trudged down the stairs. The truth was, Rowan had no intention of sleeping while the storm still raged. He had a duty to watch over his ship and crew, and on top of that, worry over Yves and the *Kraken* gnawed at the pit of his stomach. Or maybe that was the hunger.

He trudged down the steps after Fox and went to help the crew with their tasks, seeking to keep his mind away from bleak thoughts.

ONE BY ONE, Rowan sent the crew to their beds as the storm raged on, until he realized he was the only one left on deck. It had to be getting on toward morning now, but the storm showed no sign of letting up. Nor did the sky lighten. He hunkered down in the lee of the quarterdeck, out of the worst of the wind, and listened to it howl around the airborne sides of the *Siren*, almost sounding melodic to his exhausted mind. His *Siren*, singing him a tragic lullaby. After a while, it lulled him into something like a trance. He tucked his fingers into his armpits for warmth, teeth on the verge of chattering.

Where was the sun? Where was the end to this storm? Or were they going to be trapped like this forever? The whole world was made of darkness now. How much longer could they withstand it?

A new sound threaded through the cacophony of the squall. At first, he thought it was the wind whistling through the rigging, but it cut off, then continued in two long notes. Rowan sat bolt upright, frigid muscles protesting the sudden movement, and listened.

There. Again. So faint he almost thought he was imagining it. A bosun's whistle. The high, sweet sound of humanity among this terrifying symphony of nature.

Rowan clambered up the stairs to the quarterdeck, wind buffeting him as he went, the sodden tails of his coat slapping at his legs. He squinted through the gloom, searching for any sign of another ship on the open sea. What if it was one of the mercenaries? It almost didn't matter. He just needed something, anything, to show that they hadn't sailed straight into the underworld and would be trapped here forever.

He did not let himself hope it was the *Kraken*. Not yet.

Nothing but darkness met his searching gaze, rain driving into his face. He clutched the rail, heart hammering as a wave slapped the stern. Then, cresting a massive wave much too close for comfort, a single blue pinprick split the darkness.

The *Kraken*'s bow light.

Rowan's elation quickly dashed upon the rocks as he realized just how close the *Kraken* was. A bolt of lightning struck the lightning rod on the *Kraken*'s main mast and visibly crackled down the conducting chain into the roiling water, throwing the ship into stark relief. Including the single, unmovable figure standing at the bow. Lightning flashed again, casting the writhing shadows of the demon's tentacles onto the sails.

The *Kraken* hurtled down the other side of the wave, heading straight for the rocks where the *Siren* was trapped.

"Fuck." Rowan scrambled to a hatch in the deck and drew out a lantern, flint, and steel. He opened the shutter just a crack, hoping the wick hadn't fallen victim to the rain, and struck the steel. Sparks flared and died under the storm's onslaught. He struck again. Again. Each spark dying before it could catch. He looked back over his shoulder, but couldn't find the *Kraken*'s blue light.

"Come on," he muttered, striking the flint again, clutching it so hard his fingers ached. It sparked, caught, sputtered. Rowan slammed the shutter closed before the storm could put the tender flame out. He stumbled back to the rail and held the lantern aloft, waiting for the blue light to appear again.

There, at the top of a wave. Rowan flicked the shutter open and closed again, signaling, "stay back" and "rocks" over and over till the *Kraken* disappeared behind another swell. Rowan slumped against the rail. Shaking. Hoping they'd seen his warning. Overhead, the black winged flag snapped, and the storm practically snarled its displeasure at being denied another victim.

Another bolt of lightning flashed overhead, and the *Kraken* reappeared. They'd somehow managed to veer off the collision course with the rocks, and were dragging chains and the aft anchor to slow their speed. The stoic figure at the bow was nowhere to be seen.

A sigh of relief caught in Rowan's throat before a great tearing sounded from the top of the *Siren*'s main mast. The massive flag broke free of its earthly attachments. It twisted on the wind, undulating like a great black serpent. Rowan watched, almost mesmerized by its violent dance. And it felt like the last of his hope was flying away with it. When it would inevitably settle and sink beneath the surface of the sea, despair would settle with it.

Rowan couldn't let that happen. No matter what, he was a fighter, and the flag had been with him almost since the beginning, sewn by his and Logan's own hands. It bore burn marks and patches where cannonballs and bullets had ripped through it. Scars that mirrored his own. A tapestry of all he and the *Siren* and their crew had endured together. He wouldn't let this symbol of his career, the life he'd built for himself and his friends, slip into the night.

A corner of the flag whipped past his face, and he lunged after it, boots clumsy and slipping on the slick deck. It twisted out of his grasp. Taunting. He lunged again and missed, crashing face down onto the sodden boards.

Suddenly, all the hours of being awake in the pounding rain caught up with him, and he stayed down, turning over onto his back to watch his flag disappear into the endless storm.

"Fuck!" he screamed, and even that was carried off by the wind. He lacked the strength to get up, freezing rain streaming down his face. If a few tears mingled with the rain, well, no one was there to see it. Thunder boomed like the sky itself would tumble down upon his head. Rowan's body began to shiver, and he knew he should go wake Logan to keep watch in his place. But fatigue kept him rooted to the spot. He wished Yves was here. All he wanted was to curl up in Yves's warm embrace and sleep till the storm blew itself out, even if that took a lifetime.

Rowan wanted to close his eyes, but he kept his gaze trained on the low ceiling of clouds above him, seeing in his mind's eye that stoic figure on the *Kraken*'s bow with shadows writhing behind it. Why was the demon manifesting like that? So obvious even blocked by Rowan's eyepatch. Fear clamped around Rowan's gut. Had the demon taken over? Had Rowan lost his last chance to forgive, and be forgiven?

And if Yves hadn't been consumed, was he worried about Rowan or still mad? The stretch of roiling sea between them felt like an uncrossable chasm. Rowan had succumbed to Yves's loveless seduction time and time again, until it became too much. He'd stabbed Yves, and even knowing it wouldn't kill him, guilt ate at him, and loneliness held him down like a loveless fuck.

Did Yves still love him? Or had Rowan gone back to being his breakable human plaything?

Hopelessness yawned in the bottom of his chest, yet some part of him still reached out for Yves. Clung to the love they'd shared. As if his yearning would draw Yves to him across the chasm of the water.

A wave smacked the hull, causing the *Siren* to shudder and groan. Rowan pressed his palms to the deck, feeling the shockwaves through the wood and willing the timbers to hold strong. More water washed over the rail, and Rowan struggled to his knees, but could only watch listlessly as a third massive wave rushed toward him. He squeezed his eyes shut, bracing for impact. The wave crashed over him, almost sweeping him away, and when it passed, he sat there shivering, head down with salt water dripping into his eyes.

Something shifted in the atmosphere. A lull in the storm? A sound only half heard? Rowan raised his head to face whatever it was head-on.

Yves stepped over the rail as another wave broke over the back of the ship, haloing him in silvered droplets as lightning flashed overhead. The *Siren*'s black flag trailed from his shoulders like a cape, twisted around the shadow tentacles that writhed behind him. In a long charcoal coat with pearls at the collar, he was a picture of contrasts. Onyx hair and alabaster skin. He was not a demon, but a god born of this ferocious sea. A force of nature greater than any storm. It felt right to be here, kneeling before him in supplication. A mere mortal before an unfathomable god.

Yves's booted feet settled on the deck, the flag still trailing over the rail. The wind snatched Rowan's gasp away into the night, sharp air caressing his lips like a lover's bite. Yves's face was twisted in a rictus of rage, or pain. His eyes completely black, consumed by the demon. Inhuman and terrifying. He stared at Rowan as if looking through him, and for a few seconds Rowan thought Yves didn't recognize him again. If this reunion was to be a reckoning, if Yves and the demon wanted to devour him for good, would Rowan fight or let himself be consumed?

Yet the instant their eyes met, the inhuman pain fell away, stars returning to the black voids in Yves's eye sockets. He returned Rowan's pleading gaze with emotion so raw Rowan could see it even through the godly guise.

Yves's coral lips parted, his ruby wedding ring glinting like blood on his finger as he reached out. He took one step in Rowan's direction. He said something, words lost to the storm.

The thrall over Rowan snapped. He lurched to his feet, fatigue falling away, but Yves was already sprinting across the slick deck. He crashed into Rowan's arms just as thunder cracked above them. Rowan didn't care if Yves was still angry. Nor did he care about his own residual resentment. He only wanted to hold Yves and know he was here. Yves had come for him, and love must still live between them.

Yves's arms enclosed him tightly, almost squeezing the breath from his lungs. Lips moving against his neck, forming words Rowan couldn't hear. But neither of them let go.

Finally, Yves pulled back. He framed Rowan's scarred face between his hands, drinking in the sight of him. Rowan was sure he looked like a drowned rat, nothing compared to Yves's beauty. Even soaking wet, he was godly.

Yves drew a deep breath, and it was as if he'd inhaled the wind itself. The storm fell to a quiet lull, and Yves spoke, his deep voice rumbling like thunder. "I thought I'd lost you. I shouldn't...I'm sorry. Please..."

Forgive me was lost to the wind and waves.

Rowan searched Yves's expression, earnestness mixed with anticipation of heartbreak.

"You abandoned the *Kraken.*" Rowan's voice sounded rough from shouting over the storm. How had he even gotten here? Had he swam all this way? Even with the demon's strength, he should have been lost to the undertow.

"I needed to see you with my own eyes. I needed to know you were safe."

Yves drew Rowan to his chest, tucking Rowan's head into his neck and holding him there until everything faded away but the galloping pound of Yves's heart. Had he really been so worried? So frightened? Rowan's hands fisted in the back of Yves's sodden, ridiculously expensive coat, and something cracked open in him. Hope. All the love that he had tried to keep buried the last few weeks. All the tenderness beaten into submission by his own anger and Yves's behavior. It flooded to the surface, more powerful than the storm still thrashing around them.

Rowan raised his face to look at his beloved, haloed by lightning. Where a fully-human body would be cold from submergence in the sea, Yves's hands scorched Rowan's skin, chasing away his chills. Warmth kindled in his chest, his sluggish and hopeless heart beating faster. He needed to know.

Rowan leaned forward, eyes fluttering closed. Thunder rumbled, drowning out the small, surprised noise Yves made as Rowan captured his lips. His long fingers weaved into Rowan's soaked hair, hanging lank around his ears. Rowan's tongue slipped into his hot mouth, the kiss deepening, warmth spreading through him as if he was drinking it away from Yves's body.

Wind whipped the flag up in a cyclone, twisting the sodden fabric around their entwined bodies as the tentacles enclosed them too. Yves's lips moved hungrily against his, the kiss growing more fevered and possessive. One of the tentacles cradled the small of Rowan's back, anchoring them.

For a moment, anxiety spiked. Despite Yves's tender words, this would be just like last time. Loveless. Pleasure without substance. Hot tears pricked in the corners of his eyes, and Yves pulled back, holding him at arm's length by the shoulders, black eyes wide and wanting.

"I missed kissing you," Rowan croaked, barely loud enough to be heard over the howling wind. "We didn't...You didn't...You haven't kissed me in so long."

Yves's expression crumpled, softness seeping in through destruction. "I'm sorry I was so brutal with you, darling." His fingers tightened, then loosened on Rowan's shoulders, like he was holding back from crushing him in another embrace. "I shouldn't have taken my anger out on you. I should have been in control."

Rowan's breath caught. He didn't know what to say. It hadn't just been Yves's anger that fueled their unloving, desperate couplings in the hallway and alley. Rowan had been just as guilty of using Yves, even if he was the one at a disadvantage.

Yves's tender, hopeful expression warred with the terrifying countenance of the demon. He was waiting for Rowan to speak, to deny him. Rowan removed Yves's hand from his shoulder, and Yves drew in a sharp breath, the wind dying with it for just a second. But instead of leaving, Rowan stepped closer into his arms.

The wind howled through the closing distance of their bodies like a jubilant song. Yves cupped Rowan's face between his scorching hands again, tracing the crossed scars with his thumb and searching Rowan's expression like he couldn't believe Rowan still wanted him. Rowan had no words to give to what he felt, but a small, tentative smile curved his lips. Yves fell upon him like a starving man, kissing his jaw, his neck, tasting the salt spray clinging to his cold skin. Rowan tilted his head back. The rain no longer felt like cold needles, but cleansing waters that would wash away the last of his anger. Yves twitched the collar of Rowan's shirt aside, mouth traveling across his collarbone to the hollow of his throat. The tentacle tightened around his waist possessively.

"I missed you." Yves's words came as hot and desperate as his kisses. "I'll do whatever you want. I'll follow you to the ends of the earth. Just say you still want me. Say you still love me."

Shock sliced through Rowan like lightning, and his voice came out timid. "You still want my love? I'm not back to being your plaything?"

Yves jerked back. "You were never just a plaything," he said vehemently, cupping Rowan's face again. His eyebrows pulled together. "You must know that you are the only person in the world I love."

The only person in the world he was capable of loving. Rowan still didn't understand it. But whether it was fate, or the demon had simply decided Rowan was his, it didn't matter.

Yves's fingers tightened in Rowan's hair at his silence. His expression was stricken, and Rowan's heart squeezed painfully.

"Rowan, please tell me you never doubted the depths of my love."

He was so earnest. Rowan swallowed, and shook his head, but Yves sensed the hesitation in it.

Yves sank to his knees, hands trailing from Rowan's face and down his arms to grasp both of his hands. He gazed up at Rowan with pure adoration, pure contrition. Stars that didn't exist in this stormy sky reflected in his eyes.

"I know I am selfish. I am cruel. And I've not treated you as you deserve. But I will do anything, give anything, to make you happy." He flung an arm out to sea where the *Kraken* fought the waves. "If we cannot save the *Siren*, I will give you the *Kraken's Fury*."

Rowan searched his face and found only honesty there. Yves would give him anything he desired, even his most treasured possession. But he could never accept it.

"If we cannot save the *Siren*"—his voice only wavered slightly—"you will steal the next fastest ship in the Islands for me."

A wry smile played at the corners of Yves's lips. "Anything you desire shall be yours. I will obey your every word, enact your every whim."

Rowan's thumb caressed the curve of Yves's lips. He drew Yves to standing again. "Anything?"

"Yes."

"Then kiss me more. Make love to me properly."

Surprise flitted across Yves's face. "You do not have to offer me this," he said seriously.

But Rowan wanted to. He wanted Yves to love him properly for the first time in months.

He captured Yves's lips in a tender kiss. And when he pulled back, Yves's expression had settled into a familiar hunger. He took Rowan's chin between thumb and forefinger and tilted it up so that droplets of rain slid down his cheeks like tears. Their lips met again. Tenderly at first, then growing in hunger. Rowan melted into it, his heartbeat quickening with every breath they shared.

The tip of the tentacle at his back slipped beneath the hem of his shirt. Cold, barely-there flesh sending a shiver up his spine in contrast with how Yves's human touch warmed him. Rowan released a small, pleased sound, which seemed to spur both Yves and the tentacles on. He backed Rowan against the wheel, still lashed in position. Rowan's back arched, giving the tentacle room to explore further, his hips canting against Yves's body. His cock engorged as Yves's hot mouth moved across his scars and down his throat. Yves's teeth nipped at his chilled skin, his other hand trailed down Rowan's body to cup his hardening manhood.

"Shall I bring you to your bedchamber or are you eager to have me here?" Yves's voice trembled through his body like thunder. Rowan's heart thrilled at it, and he tried to drag Yves closer by the front of his coat, but they were already pressed together. He growled in impatience and tugged open the buttons at Yves's collar.

"Very well, then." A smile edged Yves's voice now. The flag wrapped around them like a living thing as Yves dragged him down to the deck. He laid him on his back on a spread-out corner of the flag, and wasted no time in rucking up Rowan's soaked shirt and kissing the exposed flesh of his chest. As his tongue roved over Rowan's peaked nipples, the tentacles crawled across the deck like mist, solidifying into dark blue flesh speckled with light.

One of the tentacles coiled around his wrist, holding it to the deck. Yves's lips moved down over Rowan's ribs to his stomach. He arched his back into the touch. Wanting more, needing everything. Yves stroked a thumb up Rowan's shaft through his pants. Rain pooled in Rowan's navel and Yves licked it away. Pleasure rippled up Rowan's spine, and he wanted to close his eyes, to savor it, but he was mesmerized by the dark, lightning-threaded clouds and the rain falling down on them. He blinked, trying to keep his head as Yves mouthed his cock over the sodden fabric, slowly loosening the ties of his britches. Rowan's hips bucked involuntarily, chasing the pressure of Yves's glorious mouth.

"Yves," he gasped. The suckers left little puckered kisses as the tentacle coiled further beneath his sleeve. Yves tugged down the waistband of Rowan's britches and undergarments, his tongue swirling around Rowan's sensitive cockhead, cold rain dripping from his hair down Rowan's shaft.

Rowan gasped, the duality of hot and cold sending his mind swimming. His body moved without his direct order, and before he knew it, Yves was beneath him instead, thin waist trapped between Rowan's thighs. Yves's black hair spread out around his head like a dark halo, melding with the flag beneath him. He gazed up at Rowan's half-undressed and needy form with shining eyes.

Rowan rutted down on Yves's hardening cock, and Yves grabbed him, long-fingered hands framing Rowan's waist.

"You're beautiful." It sounded like a confession.

Rowan leaned low over him, lips brushing his. "When you first stepped foot on this deck in the rain..." He ran his hands up under Yves's silken shirt, relishing the burning skin. "I thought you looked like a god. You are the most beautiful, most terrible thing I've ever seen."

The tentacles writhed, and the obsidian of his eyes seemed to darken further. The demon seemed pleased at being named a god by their beloved.

"Who says I am not a god?" The echoes of the demon's voice curled through the storm like the waves below.

"Shall I get on my knees in worship of you?"

Yves smiled. "You already are."

Rowan kissed him, hips rutting against him and a moan between them. "Shall I pray to you then? Beg for your mercy?"

Yves ground up against his buttocks. "All my mercy is yours to command."

It felt like a promise as much as the earlier apologies had. Yves's hands slipped from Rowan's waist to his hips, thumb once again skimming the rim of Rowan's pink cockhead, and Rowan forgot everything but his touch. Rowan's body shuddered, and he continued lavishing open-mouthed kisses over Yves's wet skin, slowly undressing him from his fine clothes. A pleased rumble vibrated beneath his lips.

Rowan had long ago given up trying to separate the reactions of demon and man. They were often the same, but sometimes the separation was obvious. Now, they both wanted to ravish Rowan with Yves's inhumanly beautiful body. But Yves held them back, basking in Rowan's attention. Letting Rowan take what he willed.

Rowan stripped off his own coat, and Yves sat up to let Rowan tear the pearl-studded brocade from his shoulders as well. The fine sleeve beneath was stained with a streak of fresh blood, and Rowan suddenly remembered he'd stabbed him last time they were together. He touched the spot tentatively, but Yves didn't so much as flinch.

Rowan made to pull his own linen shirt over his head but Yves stopped him with one hand on his.

"You'll freeze."

"You will keep me warm." Rowan dug his fingers into the shiny strands of Yves's hair and kissed him as a pair of tentacles quested up Rowan's thighs. One wrapped lightly around his cock and the other slipped beneath his clothes. He moaned as a sucker suckled at his leaking tip.

Yves wrapped his arms around Rowan's waist and flipped him onto his back again. He ripped his own silk shirt off and pillowed it beneath Rowan's head. The stab wound glistened on his skin, not stitched, not even bandaged. A thin trail of blood snaked down his pale arm, diluted by the rain.

But it was what swung free from Yves's neck that caught Rowan's attention.

A thin silver chain hung down to his chest, threaded through a simple silver ring studded with tiny sapphires and emeralds. Rowan's wedding ring that he had so angrily pressed into Yves's palm all those weeks ago. The chain it hung from was the same as the one Rowan had wondered about during their encounter in the hallway. Yves had been wearing the ring all this time. Even when they were so angry with each other, he'd kept this part of Rowan close. Like a widower pining after a dead husband.

Rowan fought the sudden urge to reach out and snatch it back. He felt like crying. Like apologizing again and again for how he'd treated Yves too. But Yves seemed not to notice. He pulled Rowan's boots off and dragged his britches and undergarments down his legs until he was only in his shirt and soaked wool stockings on the rain-washed deck.

Cold air hit Rowan's exposed skin, and he shivered. But tentacles crept over his stomach and chest, leaving warm trails of liquid in their wake and sucking searing marks into his flesh. Two tentacles cuffed his wrists again, gently holding them to the deck beside his head.

Yves picked up one of Rowan's legs, eyes meeting as his lips trailed up Rowan's stocking-clad calf to his knee, then past the garter, releasing it deftly with his fingers as his mouth traveled Rowan's inner thigh. A tentacle tip slipped under the stocking and stripped it from his leg. Then did the same to the other leg.

Rowan couldn't tear his gaze away from Yves's beauty, seen only through flashes illuminating the night. His pale skin shone like marble, pink coral lips parted for his tongue to taste the rain and precum dripping from Rowan's cock. One tentacle laved liquid over

Rowan's puckered hole, then on Yves's fingers. Blue light pulsed in tandem with their heartbeats from the tentacles' myriad of speckles like the storm-choked stars above.

"Please..." Rowan whined, sure his voice could not be heard over the lashing storm. Yves's slick fingers pressed past his entrance. It was easy, like the tentacle's warm liquid had already primed him. Yves's tongue swirled around Rowan's tip, then his beautiful lips closed over it, hot mouth sinking deliciously down over Rowan's shaft. Rowan's hips bucked up off the deck as Yves's long tongue wrapped around him and tentacle suckers lipped at his nipples. Yves hollowed his cheeks and bobbed down. He added a second finger, its tattoo of a knucklebone disappearing into Rowan. If the *Siren* was truly lost, Rowan would get a tattoo to match.

Yves's fingertips circled Rowan's prostate, and stars burst at the corners of his vision, not the result of his magical eye, but entirely the pleasure of Yves's heat around him, his fingers opening Rowan up with practiced ease.

This was not the hurried fuck in a foreign alley, but care. Worship. Reverence. A terrifying sea god on his knees for the pleasure of his beloved. The one thing keeping him tethered to humanity.

Yves slipped his third finger in, ruby wedding ring pressing cold against Rowan's rim, showing Rowan's claim over him even as Yves claimed him with deft fingers and cunning mouth. Rowan's fists clenched, shame washing over him as he found no ring of his own on his finger.

His gaze turned skyward in absolution, raindrops plinking off his eyepatch as a moan tore from him, his cock hitting the back of Yves's throat.

He couldn't stand it anymore. He needed Yves inside him. Needed to be filled with his love and look him in the eyes.

"I need you," he gasped. Yves didn't need begging; he'd already spent all his mercy on holding back thus far. He removed his fingers and released Rowan's cock with a pop, exposing it to the cold lash of rain. He prowled up Rowan's body, muscles flowing beneath marble skin. He released his cock from his trousers, a great white pillar veined with pulsing blood. One hand trailed up Rowan's leg.

"Rowan," he growled, the demon's echoes deepening his voice till it seemed part of the storm itself. Rain dripped from his hair onto Rowan's face. More droplets in the storm washing their anger and hurt away. Yves's eyes roiled like smoke, like the clouds above and waves below, vacillating between pure demonic obsidian and human emotion. "I cannot hold back. I need..." His warm, huffing breaths ghosted across Rowan's face. Heavy cock pressing to Rowan's entrance, barely restrained.

Rowan freed one hand from the tentacles and reached up to grab the ring swinging from Yves's neck like a beacon.

"Give me my ring and claim me as yours again."

Yves's stormy eyes settled into humanity, dark irises full of yearning. They were both still for a moment, rain sluicing down their entwined bodies as the waves battered the ship. Yves ripped the chain from around his neck, delicate silver links breaking. The emeralds and sapphires of Rowan's ring glittered in the bioluminescent light like a band of calm sea. At the same time, a tentacle slithered around the curve of Yves's hip to wrap in a spiral around the pillar of his cock.

Yves took Rowan's raised hand, kissing his palm, and slid the ring home.

"I am yours," Rowan breathed.

All at once the demon crashed back to the forefront, darkness overtaking Yves's eyes like a tidal wave. He forced Rowan's hand back to the deck, their fingers lacing together.

"I love you," Yves growled. The last shred of his control, his humanity, snapped. Lightning crackled through the clouds, suspending raindrops like diamonds in the air around them as Yves thrust, his tentacle-coiled cock penetrating Rowan up to the hilt.

Wind snatched Rowan's cry away as it whipped the winged flag around them in a twisting dance. Lightning raced through Rowan's nerves, and his back arched to meet Yves's next deep thrust. Yves's lips crashed into his, swallowing his moan like nectar before it could be carried off by the storm. The flag twisted and caught and settled around them like a shroud.

Rowan's legs locked around Yves's hips as his thrusts grew more frenzied and brutal. No longer fueled by anger, but raw passion. Pure love.

The ridges of the tentacle around Yves's girthy cock stretched him to the brink of destruction, pounding every part of his insides as the rain pounded the stormy sea. Yves moaned, deep and guttural between their lips, lost to the bliss of his beloved's sweet and yielding insides.

Their hearts beat as one, blood thundering through their veins, stronger than any tide. Rowan's fingers tightened on Yves's, and his moans became nothing but soundless cries, lost in the euphoria of loving again.

"Ro—" Yves choked, his teeth digging hard into Rowan's bottom lip, crashing him back into reality as the *Siren* shuddered with the battery of waves. He couldn't feel his fingers, nor his toes, but warmth gushed through him as Yves spilled first. He felt it leak between the ribbing of the tentacle and overflow. Yves's thrusts slowed. One breath. Two. His cock softened within the confines of the tentacle. Then Rowan kissed him, and he engorged again. Harder and girthier than before.

The top of a wave broke over the stern, engulfing them in salt water, but it did nothing to dampen the heat between them. Yves's lips dragged down Rowan's skin, teeth scoring his collarbone. He gathered Rowan close, holding tight as another wave crashed over them. For just a moment, they were submerged in the dark water. Locked together with the roar of the turbulent sea in their ears. Then the wave spent itself across the deck, and Rowan gasped for air as they emerged. His legs tightened around Yves's hips, drawing him deeper, the tentacle ridges making a sucking sound inside his flesh.

"Hang on tight to me," Yves said in his ear. Rowan clung to his shoulders. With one arm and a tentacle wrapped around Rowan's waist, Yves stood, still lodged deep in Rowan's guts. In a few long strides, Rowan's back hit the mizzenmast. Yves groaned as he captured Rowan's lips again, mouth moving hungrily. His fingertips dug into Rowan's bare thigh, his other arm still locked around his waist, supporting his entire weight.

Rowan had never been more grateful for Yves's demon strength. His fingernails dug into Yves's perfect, bleeding skin as Yves pulled back and slammed in. Then again, setting a savage pace. The mixture of Yves's cum and the tentacle's juices squelched out with every thrust, and ran down the curve of his buttcheek. Only to be washed away by the driving rain that ran down his body in rivers.

Rowan broke the kiss, head tilting back against the groaning wood of the mast. Yves's hot breath huffed against his throat and with every thrust, every rumble of thunder, his sanity slipped away more and more, giving way to unimaginable rapture. Every bolt of lightning that flickered through the clouds laced his veins, and when one of the tentacles wrapped around his throbbing cock, he tumbled over the edge into a churning sea of bliss. An agonized cry tore from him, and he clutched Yves desperately to keep himself anchored to sanity as he came across his wet stomach.

"Rowan," Yves groaned, his mouth open and hot on Rowan's throat. The storm reached a howling crescendo, and in a few more thrusts, Yves came for a second time.

Silence.

For a moment, Rowan thought he'd lost his hearing with the force of his orgasm. Yves sank to his knees, cradling Rowan's limp body against the base of the mast. The tentacle uncoiled from his softening cock, becoming only shadow once again, and leaving them connected only by human flesh.

Slowly, Rowan caught his breath and, mind still hazed in afterglow, realized the rain no longer stung his skin, and the rumble of thunder grew more distant with every breath.

His eyes lifted to find orange dawn creeping across the sky, chasing the black clouds further out to sea. Mist, pink as a maiden's blush, hung all around their entwined bodies, soothing the rain's sting. Yet lightning still flickered in the glow, the accompanying rumble now as low and comforting as a heartbeat.

When his gaze found Yves, he was watching him with dark, yet human eyes.

"I love you," Rowan said, still out of breath. Yves smiled and kissed him, and didn't let go until Rowan was gasping and wondering if Yves would take him again in this liminal rosy mist.

All at once his body felt heavy, the hours of fighting the storm finally catching up with him. He leaned forward, resting their foreheads together as Yves combed his messy hair back from his face with his fingers.

"Are you alright, darling? Was I too rough on you?" Worry tinged his voice.

"I'm fine, just need sleep." Now that he was safe and sated, Rowan's eyelids drooped.

"I'll take you to bed then." Yves disengaged from their embrace and left him propped against the mizzenmast as he went about gathering their scattered clothing. Rowan blinked slowly, trying to stay awake. Further out to sea, the *Kraken's Fury* rolled on unquiet waves. Rowan pressed a hand to the *Siren*'s deck, silently hoping they would be able to get her back to the sea without catastrophe.

Yves returned with a bundle of Rowan's clothes in hand. "Your trousers and a stocking got swept away in the wave." He handed over Rowan's coat. Once Rowan had managed to struggle into it, Yves pulled on his own shirt and helped him slowly to his feet.

The storm grew more and more distant, sharp salt and lightning replaced by the particular ozone scent of the open sea after a squall—wet wood, rope, and stone.

Was it over? Or had they sailed just close enough to the edge for a reprieve? Rowan's mind couldn't struggle close enough to consciousness to care. The *Siren*'s flag lay coiled like a discarded serpent skin on the deck. Safe.

Rowan accepted Yves's offered arm, caring nothing for the warm dribbles of liquid that tracked down his inner thighs. But after a few steps, his legs wavered. Without a word, Yves bent and picked him up, cradling Rowan's exhausted, shivering body against his chest. They descended the quarterdeck stairs and headed belowdecks. Rowan bid them stop at Logan's door, and made Yves set him back on his feet. He rapped on the door, and waited to hear the stirrings of bedclothes on the other side.

"Time for your watch," Rowan called, and heard a sleepy mumble of, "Aye, I'm up," from the other side. In truth, it was far past time for Logan's watch, and the others would be waking with the morning light, but someone had to keep watch over the *Siren*'s precarious position.

Yves didn't wait for further confirmation of the first mate's wakefulness. He tugged Rowan down the hall toward the captain's quarters.

It wasn't until they'd made it to his door, Yves's hand already turning the knob, that Rowan remembered Fox. He tugged Yves's arm.

"Wait, there's something—" But the door swung open, and Yves strode over the threshold. His dark gaze sped straight to the form slumbering peacefully bundled under Rowan's blankets.

"Who the *fuck* is in your bed," Yves growled, the demon echoing in his voice. Outside, a crack of thunder boomed closer than the retreating storm.

Fox stirred, the quilt slipping from his shoulder to expose freckled skin. He must have been too exhausted to find dry clothes. Damn him. It looked like he'd simply crawled out of his wet clothes and directly into Rowan's bed, leaving a trail of sodden garments puddling on the floor in his wake.

A low rumble reverberated through the room, and at first Rowan thought it was thunder again, but the sound emanated from his husband. Yves lunged, eyes pitch black and murderous, as if he would seize Fox and break him right there.

"Yves!"

Yves's body stilled, as if commanded by some inexplicable force. He let out another growl, shadows writhing at his back and hands balled into fists at his sides. His teeth ground together so hard Rowan could almost hear it.

Finally, Fox sat up. Possibly the slowest anyone had *ever* sat up. Or it was Rowan's impending horror that slowed time so that the blanket seemed to ripple down Fox's chest, Rowan chanting *don't be naked don't be naked* over and over in his head with every inch of skin that was revealed. Fox, seemingly unaware of the danger, rubbed his eyes as the blanket fell away and the windows backlit him with rosy light.

Fox was, of course, as naked as the day he was born.

Oh gods, Rowan's luck had finally abandoned him. Why did he have to be naked and make this situation so much more incriminating?

As Fox rubbed sleep from his eyes, Yves lunged again. Fox's eyes flew wide, finally registering the situation. He seized a pillow and swung, nearly walloping Yves in the face, but Rowan caught Yves's arm and yanked him back. Fox stared at them wide-eyed, his cheek creased by heavy sleep as Rowan pried Yves's fist open and threaded their fingers together. Fox still held his pillow weapon up, ready to fight or flee. Thankfully, in his sleepiness, he hadn't gone for the knife Rowan kept under his pillow.

"Did you miss topping so much you had to take this temptress into your bed? Or is this revenge?" Yves said. Rowan expected anger, and it was there on the surface, but something else lurked deeper. Something Yves himself was unlikely to confront. Grief.

"It's not like that," Rowan said quietly. He grabbed Yves's chin and forced him to look away from the other man in his husband's bed. Forced him to look Rowan in the eye. "He's been sleeping here. *Just* sleeping. Because he is lonely with Gaël gone. Nothing untoward happened. I promise."

Yves's eyes flickered to human, then to demon obsidian and back again. But he kept them locked on Rowan. Where their fingers were laced together, his hand trembled.

And Rowan realized suddenly that he'd *never* seen Yves's demon side while wearing his eyepatch, but it was here now, fighting for dominance. And it had been perfectly visible out on deck as the storm raged around them.

"Get out," Yves growled at Fox. Fox's wide green gaze flicked between the two captains, unaware of the inhuman echoes in Yves's voice or the shadows that threatened to snuff out the morning light suffusing the room. Slowly, he put the pillow down and climbed out of bed, heedless of his nakedness. Keeping an eye on Yves, he crossed to an open chest and drew out an emerald green dressing gown Yves had left some time ago. Yves's nostrils flared in indignation as Fox settled it around his shoulders, not bothering to cinch it closed, and breezed from the room like a courtesan leaving the royal marriage bed.

As soon as the door closed behind him, Yves began to shake. Rowan reached up to cup the side of his face, but Yves squeezed his eyes shut, slowly sinking to his knees on the damp rug. His shaking hands clutched Rowan's shirt as he pressed his forehead to Rowan's stomach.

"I swear it's the truth. I would never betray you." Rowan tried to sink down beside him, but Yves's hold only tightened.

Yves's breath came shallow, like he was swallowing back sobs and trying to contain the demon at the same time.

"Yves?"

When his eyes opened, they were fully human again.

"I—" Another shallow, aching breath. And Rowan knew, beyond any doubt, the true depths of Yves's love for him.

"I love you, Yves. I only want you." He caressed Yves's sodden hair, wishing he could smooth the anguished lines from his brow.

When Yves's voice came, it was shaky. "I told you my mercy was yours to command. That includes mercy for little freckled temptresses with perky asses." He paused, then kissed Rowan's palm. "If you say it is the truth, then I believe you. Just...don't go."

Rowan frowned, trying to puzzle through what he meant. Did Yves think he would leave him? Or was he using this to guilt Rowan into giving up on his pursuit of Zanta? He opened his mouth to protest. To say he could go wherever he pleased, and Yves's apologies changed nothing about the course he had chosen, but Yves interrupted him.

"Please, Rowan. I thought I'd lost you. You can't go without me." His voice was desperate, almost broken. "I don't care if you slept with him or not. I just need you to be mine."

Any uncertainty that may have lingered at the bottom of Rowan's heart drained away. He sank to his knees, gathering Yves to him. He kissed him again. "I won't leave you behind."

He would drag Yves and the demon both kicking and screaming into death with him if that was what Yves wanted.

CHAPTER 36

UNKNOWN DATE, 1668

"Zanta?" A gentle voice caressed her ears where there used to be snapping timbers, screams, and the rage of the storm. Now, only an eerie silence and that familiar voice reached her. The voice, usually brash and laughing, now soft.

"Zanta." Fingers against hers, prying them from their death grip on the wheel. "It's over."

Zanta blinked, blisters ripping as her hands separated from the wooden spokes.

"Gods, your hands are freezing!" Finally, Zanta's gaze focused on Nia. Disheveled, bruised, but alive and warm. She took Zanta's freezing hands between hers, thumbs rubbing across her skin. Behind her, the sky blushed as if embarrassed for its tantrum, the sea calm as a sleeping child beneath it.

Her mind snapped into focus. They'd sailed through the storm. They were alive.

"Colm, Laurent, are they...How many dead?" Her voice came out harsh with salt.

Nia's bright green eyes were dim, exhausted. "Colm and Laurent are alive. I don't know how many crew...I..." Her gaze drifted past Zanta.

"What?" The storm still raged in the distance, lightning forking down like a cage. But Zanta paid no attention to it. Three crew members were hauling up a rope that still dragged behind the ship.

"It's the last lifeline," Nia said quietly. "It's..."

But Zanta knew who it was. The only person it could be. Because if Sabriye was alive, she would've already been by Zanta's side.

She broke away from Nia as they finally pulled the body onto the deck. Zanta froze in her tracks, unable to approach as they turned the body over to face the now gentle sky.

Sabriye's face had a pale, bloodless cast to it. Her dark hair sticking to it like wounds. Brown eyes open and staring, reflecting the strange pink light. She'd drowned before bruises could form, but her hands—those hands that had worked beside Zanta for years, that had patted her back and wiped her tears and punched her arm when she made a bad joke—were clawed like a hawk's talons, every finger broken from the impact of the wheel spokes when she'd tried to get the ship under control.

Zanta knew it was her, but it didn't look like her. It looked like a drowned corpse. Not Sabriye at all. Not her best friend.

All at once the horror of the last hours caught up with her, and her legs gave out, knees hitting the deck and shooting bone-deep pain up her legs. Nia was by her side in a second, but Zanta couldn't look away from those sightless eyes. The crew members gently turned Sabriye on her side, as if she was sleeping. Seawater dribbled from her open mouth, and her eyes stared directly at Zanta, no longer filled with the light of the sky. Just empty.

Zanta was underwater again. No breath left in her lungs. All sounds muffled. She felt her vocal cords straining and knew grief was pouring out of her like coughed up seawater. Nia held her, trying to comfort her. The others dealt with the bodies while all Zanta could do was scream.

CHAPTER 37

UNKNOWN DATE, 1668

It was not the bright afternoon light that woke Rowan from his deathlike slumber, but the sheer stillness of the ship. He was used to falling asleep and waking up to the gentle rock of the *Siren* traversing the waves. So at first, when his consciousness surfaced enough to be at least halfawake, he imagined himself back on Illusion. But no, even in Illusion's manor house with its fine feather bed and softest linens money could buy, Rowan often slept in his cabin aboard the *Siren*. And besides, he could hear the familiar creak of her timbers around him.

Rowan's eyes fluttered open, and he found himself staring at waves of light reflecting off the water onto the ceiling. He'd managed to extricate himself from Yves's embrace sometime during the night, as he often did. Now he lay on his back with the blankets kicked down around his knees and one leg flung over Yves's legs. His fitful posture took up most of the bed, and he glanced over to find Yves slumbering peacefully on his side in the small sliver that remained. One hand was tucked beneath the pillow to keep sleep-Rowan from flinging it, and the other pressed down against Rowan's chest, whether to keep Rowan's fitful sleep at bay or feel Rowan's heartbeat, he didn't know.

Rowan tried to keep his breathing slow and even so as to not disturb him. There was nothing of the demon in him now. Thick, dark eyelashes rested against pale cheekbones, and pink lips slightly parted around sleeping breaths. Yves always looked fully human when he slept, and as much as Rowan loved every part of him, including the inhuman parts, he relished these moments too. Moments when Yves was at peace, and Rowan could imagine them growing old together.

Every inhale brought Yves's scent to his nose, but there was something new to it now. Something electric and watery mixed in with his usual scent of salt, sex, and whatever cologne was most fashionable at the time. It was as if he'd wrapped the storm around himself like a cloak, ozone and rain and death all woven into one.

Lost in these thoughts, he brushed the backs of his fingers over Yves's lips. Yves blinked awake.

"I didn't mean to wake you," Rowan said softly.

"You woke me approximately six times with your thrashing." Yves's voice was deep and grumbly with sleep, but held an ocean of affection. The shadows unfurled from his back, dampening some of the afternoon light, but did not stir further.

What did stir, was Yves's cock against Rowan's leg.

Yves's hand wandered down to grab Rowan's waist, tugging him closer so he could nuzzle into Rowan's neck.

"You sleep like an unruly toddler, you know. I'm surprised that little minx of yours isn't absolutely covered in bruises from your battering." He feathered kisses over the tender skin between Rowan's neck and shoulder.

"He's not a minx. He's Fox," Rowan protested, nonetheless enjoying the attention.

"A minx is not the same as a mink, darling." Yves's hand roamed across Rowan's waist, and up the inner thigh of the leg still flung over him. "His skin would not be as pretty decorating the collars of my coats."

"I know *that.*" Rowan tried to wiggle out of his grip, but not very hard. "I just mean Fox is Fox. He's just like that."

Yves sighed almost contentedly, seeming not to care anymore that he'd found a naked man in his husband's bed just a few hours ago.

"Look, Yves, about last ni—" Rowan's apology cut off as Yves kissed him. He surrendered to it, Yves's mouth moving warm and sweet as honey against his. When Yves pulled away, he smoothed Rowan's still-damp hair back from his forehead.

"Don't speak of it again, darling. We should only look forward."

Forward, toward Zanta and Shaw. But first he had to...He sat up, suddenly remembering the reason he'd woken up in the first place. The *Siren* was stuck, and now that the storm was over, they had no way to get it down, and no way to know when or if the storm would come back. He clambered off the end of the bed before Yves could seduce him further, but as soon as his feet hit the cold floor, his knees went weak.

"Shit." He grabbed the edge of the bedframe to steady himself. In the bliss of finally waking up on the right side of Yves's temper, he'd almost forgotten the other events of the night. Every muscle from his neck down to his feet ached with the long, cold hours of battling the storm. Especially his lower back, which cramped with the sweet ache almost akin to longing that usually followed a night with his husband.

Yves nudged Rowan's hand with his foot. "Come back to bed. The *Siren* isn't going anywhere."

"That's the problem." Rowan pushed off the bedframe and crossed the rug unsteadily. It was bad enough for his balance that the *Siren* was now stationary, but to add muscle soreness on top of that? It was a wonder he made it to his destination. He steadied himself against the wall and drew a fresh pair of breeches from the same trunk Fox had kidnapped Yves's dressing gown last night. Yves likely wouldn't be getting that back. The hem was probably dragging across the deck behind Fox even now, and he would probably make some argument about how it "brought out his eyes"—everything seemed to—or that he was owed it as restitution for the emotional damage of being kicked out of bed naked by a jealous pirate captain—not the first time *that* had happened—and honestly? Rowan was inclined to let him keep it. He knew Fox would reach new heights of androgynous rakishness in it, and gods help Gaël when he returned to that.

"Need help with those?"

Rowan blinked, realizing he'd just been staring at the breeches in his hand for long enough for Yves to sneak up on him. He contemplated the wad of fabric for another moment, trying to muster up the strength to lift his foot and attempt to put them on.

Yves's arms wrapped around his waist, lips meeting the back of Rowan's shoulder.

"Come back to bed."

"I have things to do." But he allowed himself to lean back into Yves's chest for just a moment.

"Then perhaps a skirt is better suited for your sudden frailty?"

"And give you unfettered access to my nethers? Not a chance." Even now Yves's massive cock rested, half hard, against Rowan's naked buttocks. A threat, and a promise.

Yves sighed, as if his entire life was one long chore and he didn't even have a bit of dick to look forward to at the end of it.

"Let me help you, then," he said sullenly. Rowan might have even imagined he was pouting. "Lean on me."

A DAMP BREEZE caressed Rowan's face as he finally stepped out onto the eerily still deck of the *Siren Song*. The air still smelled of rain, but the pink mist had mostly cleared away with the sun's ascent. A few gray clouds scuttled high in the pale sky, not quite threatening another storm. Thunder rumbled in the distance, darkness hanging over the horizon.

Having gotten used to some of the soreness, Rowan strode across the deck between the few crew members who weren't still abed. They milled around uselessly, having precious little to do with the ship stuck high above the water's surface.

"Captain!" Logan waved to him from the rail near one of the rock spires. His fingers curled into his palm when he spotted Yves walking behind Rowan. His mouth thinned to a line, partly hidden by the shade of his hat. Ignoring that for now, Rowan joined him at the rail. Logan ignored Yves's presence altogether.

"Are you feeling alright? Did you get enough sleep? You really should have woken me earlier."

"I'm fine. I probably got more sleep than you." Rowan waved off his concerns, hoping Logan hadn't noticed how gingerly he'd walked over.

Logan's gaze flicked to Yves, the disapproval in his expression deepening. "Somehow I doubt that."

Gods, at some point Rowan would have to explain he and Yves had made up, but he was too weary for it right now.

"So how are we going to get our trusty *Siren* out of this mess?" Rowan asked with forced cheerfulness.

Logan grimaced, then returned to what he'd been doing. Which Rowan now saw was a tally of the damages incurred, written in Logan's shaky handwriting.

"Honestly, short of dismantling the entire ship, I can't really think of anything," Logan said grimly.

Rowan's gaze swept over the damage. In the daylight, it looked even worse than it had last night. That few foot drop had gouged the *Siren*'s well-maintained sides, leaving only a few inches of board and a spray of foot-long splinters trapped between the ship and the pale rock. Rowan reached out and tentatively touched the rock, as if the little pressure from his hand would dislodge the *Siren* and send all of them plummeting to their deaths.

"How far down do the scrapes go?" The rock was cold beneath his touch, and he followed the line of it up to the top of the spire, which tapered almost to a point twenty feet above the top of the mainmast.

"Hard to tell," Logan said. "I tried knocking from the inside and managed to see a bit through one of the damaged gunports. If I had to guess, I don't think any especially weak points would be below the waterline."

That wasn't as bad as it could've been. "So if we get her unstuck, and don't incur any further damage in the process, we might sail out of here?"

"That's a big if, Captain. If we have to go back through the storm, the damaged bits definitely won't hold."

But ideas already fired through Rowan's mind. Logan let him indulge in the lofty heights of fantasy for a few moments before bringing him back to solid ground.

"Even if we can get it unstuck, the fall..."

"We'll use ropes and winches and lower it down," Rowan said.

"I...We can look, but do you really think we have enough rope to support the whole ship? And what would we use as ballast?"

Damn and bless Logan for being the perpetual voice of reason. He'd kept Rowan out of many a scrape in their sixteen years of sailing together, but if Rowan wasn't able to go off on a harebrained scheme to save his own ship, what hope was there? And on top of that, if the *Monsoon* and the mercenaries had survived the storm, Zanta was still in imminent danger.

"The *Kraken* should still be nearby. We have extra supplies and —" Yves was interrupted by a long whistle from below the ship. "Speaking of." He strode up the quarterdeck steps with Rowan and Logan hot on his heels. From this vantage point, Rowan could see the two spires of rock that held them were part of a cluster of pale, jagged rocks that stretched up toward the sky like needles scraping the clouds. Only open sea surrounded them, no sign of land or other ships besides the *Kraken* anywhere on the horizon. They peered over the stern rail to find one of the *Kraken*'s landing boats bobbing calmly on the waves with several crew members gazing up at them.

"Lo!" Doe called, raising a hand in greeting. "How're you faring up there?" The weak sun sparkled off the debris-strewn water beneath the boat. The *Kraken* remained anchored a safe distance from the perilous rocks.

"Could be better!" Logan called back.

"Drop down a ladder!"

Rowan didn't know if they had a rope ladder long enough. After some searching, they managed to secure a few together and drop one end over the stern. Doe made quick work of the climb, though the breeze swayed her like a trapeze artist beneath the ship. When she made it to the rail, Yves helped her onto the deck like a gentleman. The other two *Kraken* crew members stayed behind on the boat.

"Glad to see you're okay, Captains, Mr. Crowder." She tipped her hat to them with a grin, then looked around at the ship and its rocky prison. "Quite a predicament we've found ourselves in. What's the plan?"

The four of them hunkered down in the center of the ship in the long shadow of one of the spires. Doe told them the state of the ship as she'd seen it from below. The *Siren* wasn't as high up as Rowan had originally thought now that the water wasn't taken up with producing massive waves. Still, there was a good twenty to thirty feet between the hull and the water's surface. The two spires weren't much thicker at the base. But what held the *Siren* aloft besides the rock trapping the sides were two small ledges that had stopped their downward trajectory in the first place.

They tossed around ideas, sent crew members to take stock of supplies. And with every idea that was brought up and shot down, Rowan lost a little bit more hope. The *Siren*'s deck was cool and damp beneath his legs, scoured clean by the storm. It was wrong that she should be so still. In the decade since Rowan had first staged a mutiny and become her captain, he'd only had to dry dock her once. And it had broken his heart. This was so much worse, because this time he didn't know if he would ever get her back into the sea. He picked at a pebble wedged between the boards by his knee.

"The way I see it, our only option is to chip away the rock and hope the ropes hold," Doe said, expanding on the tenth iteration of a harebrained plan.

"The water is shallow here," Yves cut in. "Even if we have enough rope, chain, and tackle, I don't know if the *Kraken* can get close enough to serve as ballast."

"Even if it all works out, it might take a damn long time to chip away the rock," Logan said. Nods around the circle as they all contemplated. "Rowan? What do you think?" Logan finally asked.

As the captain and owner of the *Siren Song*, he had final say. The plan was to dismantle the *Siren*'s rigging to salvage as much rope as possible. Then run rope and chain as securely as possible beneath the hull and secure it above their heads to the rocks on either side, then to the *Kraken*. After that, they'd carefully chip away the rock and possibly grease the sides until the *Siren* was free. The free weight would inevitably drag the *Kraken* closer, but they were hoping the larger ship's weight would slow the fall enough to save the *Siren*.

It was absolutely stupid. None of them were engineers, or even really good enough at mathematics to know if they had enough supplies to accomplish it. On top of that, the whole operation would take days, maybe even weeks.

Weeks they didn't have, because when they'd all foolishly sailed into that storm, Shaw's ship and the *Marigold* had already been hot on the *Monsoon*'s tail. Assuming they'd survived, Zanta and her crew might be fighting for their lives or already dead. And then Shaw would come after Rowan and find the *Siren* and crew stuck like gristle between teeth, just waiting to be plucked out.

They still had one seaworthy ship. The *Kraken*. They could go after Zanta now and intervene before it was too late.

In the end, it was a choice between his ship, the only home he'd had for the last ten years, which ultimately was just an object, only wood and metal and sailcloth. Or his friend, whose life could not be replaced once it was snatched away.

Not to mention, if Zanta really did hold the secret to the Sleeping Isles, how many countless lives would be lost if Shaw was allowed to gain that knowledge?

"Rowan?" Logan's voice was soft. They were all looking at him, and he knew by the sympathy on their faces that his expression must look as bleak as it felt.

"That plan will take too long." He kept his voice slow and measured, betraying none of the panic he felt at the thought of abandoning the *Siren*. "If Zanta and her crew survived, they're in danger. We'll take the *Kraken* and deal with that, then circle back and see if we can save the *Siren*. We'll leave crew and supplies here to get started on the plan while we're gone."

"You're going with the *Kraken*?" Logan asked. "Surely Captain Yves can handle Shaw."

"I got us into this mess, and I'll see it through." Besides, he'd promised Yves they wouldn't be parted again.

Silence prevailed, but for the susurration of waves far below. Then Yves rose gracefully to his feet. "You heard the man. We've no time to waste." He offered a hand to help Rowan to his feet.

THEY ROUSED THE CREW QUICKLY, divvying up who would go and who would stay. Extra supplies were ferried from the *Kraken* to the *Siren* to last a month, in case they were late or failed to return at all. Fox, Henri, and Robin all climbed down the swaying ladder. They left the injured with the *Siren*, but traded the *Kraken*'s doctor—who'd suffered a broken ankle during the storm—for Robin, who would be more equipped to triage battle injuries. Rowan had a feeling he would need Robin by his side for what was to come. He needed all his friends with him.

Even David was already tucked safely on the *Kraken* where Rowan and Robin could keep an eye on him.

As the second to last boat rowed toward the *Kraken*, Rowan closed his eyes and leaned back against the mizzenmast in the same spot he'd gotten fucked last night. He didn't dwell on that now. The curve of the wood pressed into this back, a calm and reassuring presence. He listened to the creak of the timbers, the wind whistling through the lines, and missed the sound of waves slapping against the sides. The *Siren* spoke to him, that haunting, calling song that had driven him to great lengths to become her captain, and now he was leaving her and his crew behind.

He inhaled the sharp, salty air through his nose and out through his mouth, then opened his eyes. Logan stood at his side with a rucksack slung over his back.

"What are you doing?" Rowan asked. They'd agreed Logan would stay behind to oversee everything. He was Rowan's second in command, and besides, Rowan didn't want him in the inevitable fight if he could help it.

"Doe agreed to take command of the *Siren* so I could come with you. The whole rope and pulley thing was her idea anyway."

"But the crew don't know her. And..."

"And she's got two working hands?" Logan finished for him.

Sometimes, Rowan hated it when Logan knew exactly what he was thinking. But he knew Logan well too. Knew that stubborn look on his face and how he hated to be coddled. Rowan understood the feeling. He was doing the exact thing Yves had tried to do to him.

"And the *Siren* is your home," Rowan finished lamely.

Logan's eyebrows drew together in a scowl. "*You're* my home, idiot. You think I'd be here, let alone a pirate, if it weren't for you?" He stomped away toward the rope ladder muttering "dumbass" and "dimwit" under his breath.

Thoroughly told off, Rowan took in one last look at his ship—coils of extra rope and chain dotting the deck, and his crew up on the yards dismantling the rigging—then followed after his first mate.

CHAPTER 38

UNKNOWN DATE, 1668

Zanta let her mind wander as her fingers traced down Nia's back, lingering on the strange square scar which marred the otherwise perfect peachy landscape. It was still strange to have Nia in her bed. Strange, but not unpleasant. Despite their current circumstances and the danger ever looming on the horizon, a peace had settled in her, one that she hadn't felt since before Emilie's death. One she hadn't felt touching anyone else. They still hadn't reconciled the fight they'd had before sailing into the storm. But it seemed distant now, unimportant in light of what they currently faced. Zanta couldn't let herself think too deeply about their relationship any more than she let herself dwell on the lives lost in the storm.

As long as she kept touching Nia, nothing else could be wrong.

Nia sighed in her sleep. Midday sunlight streamed through the broken windows, but they'd all taken to snatching little moments of rest whenever they could. Despite the peace Nia's presence brought, today Zanta couldn't sleep, not when the *Monsoon*'s masts were broken, and a full third of her crew were either dead, critically injured, or missing.

Including Sabriye.

Zanta closed her eyes, and rested her cheek against Nia's warm shoulder. She'd failed to protect them. She'd made the decision to sail into that storm, and had it even been the right one? Her best friend was dead, and the *Monsoon* was adrift, with nothing to do but wait like a sitting duck for either friend or foe to find them.

For two days, the *Monsoon* had drifted, at the mercy of the currents pulling them further and further north. Zanta had doubled the around-the-clock watch. If the mercenaries found them, Zanta wanted her crew to be ready to fight to the end. Because now, they couldn't run.

Her fingers continued their swirling trail over Nia's skin, trying to lull herself to sleep so she could at least get an hour of rest before it was her turn to go on watch.

No sooner had her eyes drifted closed than the door to her cabin banged open. Zanta sat bolt upright, nerves going taut, but it was just Laurent. Nia didn't wake, only shifted in her sleep and sighed. The woman really didn't have any sense of urgency or self-preservation when she was naked.

"What is it?" Zanta whispered, drawing the blanket up to cover Nia's exposed skin. Her gaze wandered to the hall behind Laurent, half expecting Sabriye. But the hallway remained empty. Sabriye was gone. She'd never burst into Zanta's rooms with bad or good news again.

Shit. It had been two days since Sabriye was swept over the side, and Zanta still expected her to just show up again like nothing had ever happened.

"We spotted a ship," Laurent said. His curly black hair was mussed, dark circles under his eyes from endless hours sitting by Colm's side in the infirmary, on top of his other duties. Colm's ribs and several other bones had broken with the impact of the sail rung, and he'd nearly drowned after being swept over the side. But he would survive. Many others wouldn't. Hadn't.

Double shit. "I'll be right there. I'm letting you off watch early; go back to Colm."

Laurent nodded grimly, closing the door behind him.

"Nia." Zanta leaned low over her and kissed the nape of her neck. Nia stirred.

"Hm?"

"Wake up and get dressed." Zanta climbed over her, and began gathering her clothes. Nia sat up, propped on one arm. Her red curls stuck out wild around her head.

"They spotted a ship." Zanta pulled on her boots and strapped on her sword belt. "Stay here, and if there's trouble, hide."

Nia's light green eyes went wide, and she nodded. Zanta was almost out the door when Nia caught up with her, still naked and warm with sleep.

"Be safe." She tucked one of Zanta's braids back from her forehead and kissed her.

Trepidation bloomed in Zanta's chest as the huge warship sped toward them. She'd done all she could. Roused and armed the crew. Checked on Nia, then waited. The cannons were primed, weapons gripped in sweaty hands.

It had to be the same warship the lookout had seen before the storm. Now it had come to claim its prize.

The hours ticked by, and the ship loomed closer and closer until faint details began to resolve. Afternoon light glinted off something shiny on the bow, and she shaded her eyes against the glare. Then a wave caught the hull just right for the glare to dim and reveal what it hid. A massive kraken figurehead, studded with colored glass, the tentacles wrapping the front of the ship and trailing along its sides. She recognized it instantly. The *Kraken's Fury*, the infamous warship of the Deep Water Demon.

Zanta's first instinct was to flee. If the demon and his crew meant them harm, there was little chance of winning. But the *Monsoon* was dead in the water. She took a deep breath, wishing Sabriye was here to strategize with her.

But the Demon was Rowan's man, wasn't he? She and Rowan were acquaintances, probably even friends by now, and if the Demon had any loyalty to his lover, maybe Zanta could use that to ensure her crew's safety. Who knew? Maybe he'd even deign to tow them to shore if she begged hard enough.

"Run up the colors!" she ordered. The idle crew ran to do her bidding, and despite the *Monsoon*'s stagnant position, there was enough of a breeze to snap her flag out nice and proud when they attached it to the top of the half-missing mast.

In response, blue sails emblazoned with a kraken dropped down over the nondescript white ones, and the tentacled flag climbed to the top of the main mast. No going back now. Zanta's fingers encircled the spot on her opposite forearm where the serpent resided. Hoping for the best. She didn't know whether to be frightened or grateful that it was the most notorious pirate captain on the seas that had found her in this vulnerable state instead of the mercenaries. She didn't want to spare a thought for how or why the Deep Water Demon was here.

Her crew shifted nervously around her, waiting to see what would happen. As the *Kraken* drew closer, Zanta sucked in a breath and held it.

Just as the pressure in her lungs began to grow uncomfortable, the massive ship slowed, and a familiar blond head popped up over the terrifying kraken figurehead.

"Zanta!"

Her breath escaped in a relieved rush. It was the Ghost Hawk, peering one-eyed down at her. Today wouldn't be the day she died after all.

HENRI PINCHED ROBIN'S CHEEK, watching affectionately how it grew pink beneath his fingers before releasing him. Robin swatted his hand away lightly.

"You're sure you don't want help?" Henri asked.

Robin was in the process of packing up medical supplies to take over to the *Monsoon*. Though it was taking longer than necessary, because he was no longer familiar with the *Kraken*'s infirmary. Robin waved him off.

"The captain said he wanted you on deck. You better go." Two amber glass bottles clinked together as Robin shooed him again. "Go. Go. You're distracting me."

"Fine." They'd found the *Monsoon* crippled in the water two days after leaving the *Siren*. From a distance, it had looked like a wreck. No masts, no sails, no movement. The only sign anyone at all had survived were the dark mourning ribbons tied to the rails. If someone was left to mourn, that meant someone was alive. Now the splinter heart flag fluttered on the broken mast. But with damage like that, there were bound to be casualties, and Rowan had ordered them to prepare for the worst as they carefully maneuvered the ships to float side-by-side.

A bump that was unmistakably the gangplank being positioned

sounded overhead. Henri rushed up to the deck, but not before Robin managed to pinch him on the buttcheek.

"Revenge for the cheek pinch!" Robin called after his retreating form.

Henri made it onto the deck just as Rowan stepped onto the gangplank, and he fell in step behind Logan. The *Kraken*'s crew looked on from their stations, and Captain Demon stood with his hands spread imperiously on the quarterdeck rail. Aloof as always. Henri was honestly a little surprised he'd agreed to this. It was unfortunately common knowledge among the crews that Rowan and Zanta had kissed that winter they had first left Illusion and Rowan lost his eye. Rowan and the Demon had had a brief, yet loud, shouting match then makeup session about it the summer after. So, like children whose parents were fighting, no one on Illusion had brought it up since. Even when it became clear that Rowan and Zanta intended to continue their friendship. The Demon must have been jealous, angry even, but he'd still followed Rowan on this disastrous mission anyway. Though some of them had noticed Rowan limping around the day after the storm, clearly not from an actual injury.

Maybe aloofness was the safest for all of them.

Henri's boots thumped on the wide gangplank as he crossed over to the *Monsoon*. He heard Logan gasp softly, and looked up.

The damage was much worse than they'd thought. Both masts were broken off and lost somewhere in the storm, along with the yellow sails Henri had always found cheerful. Not a scrap of sailcloth remained, only rubble pushed hastily to the rails and bits of rope swaying in the breeze like cobwebs.

Captain Zanta, with her hair tied back in a green scarf and her clothes rumpled, looked as exhausted as the rest of her crew, which numbered about half its usual size. Henri wondered how many of the rest nursed injuries below deck, and how many were dead or missing.

He stepped onto deck as Rowan wrapped Captain Zanta in a short embrace that the Demon surely wouldn't like.

"Are you well?" Rowan asked when they broke apart. "What am I saying? Of course you're not. How many did you lose?" It may have been blunt, but that was Rowan's way.

Zanta gave an exhausted sort of smile. "A third of the crew, including my first mate. Not to mention our masts are gone and most of our supplies spoiled. I'm sure glad you showed up, and not those asshole mercs."

Rowan's grimace matched her own. "About that...We have a lot to discuss."

Zanta's brown eyes swept over the small contingent of *Siren Song* crew that had followed him aboard, then to the *Kraken* behind him.

"Please tell me the *Siren* wasn't lost as well."

"She's in a bit of a bind at the moment. But better off than you, I think," Rowan said, as Robin hurried down the gangplank. "I brought the doctor."

Relief washed over Zanta's weary face, and she looked like she could have kissed Robin when he stepped onto deck with his bag of medical supplies.

She motioned to a skinny fellow with a slight hook nose. "Laurent, show Dr. Beckett below will you?"

Robin squeezed Henri's hand in passing as he followed the man belowdecks.

"We have a lot to discuss about that Marran shit who's been following you," Rowan said.

"They're more than just pirate hunters, aren't they." Zanta said quietly.

"Afraid so." He glanced around at the listless ship. "Let Logan and the rest help with cleanup. We need to talk in private."

Zanta glanced around as well, as if looking for someone, then nodded. Rowan drew her over to the gangplank, speaking quietly but not yet moving to board the *Kraken*.

Left to their own devices, the crews of the *Siren* and *Monsoon* stood around for a moment before Logan said, "Well, we best do as the captains say. There's spoiled food? Let's dispose of it before it starts stinking. We have enough food stores to share." The *Monsoon* crew seemed to startle out of a daze at Logan's brisk tone, but nonetheless got to work.

Logan motioned to Henri to follow him, then turned to one of the *Monsoon* crew members. "Show us the food."

The man nodded and led them toward the door Robin had disappeared through moments before. When they were a few yards away, it opened, and a woman emerged, red-gold hair gleaming in the sunlight. Her skirt caught on a splintered board. She yanked it free, and when she looked up, her freckled face and green eyes struck

Henri with the strangest sense of déjà vu. For a moment, it overwhelmed him, and he stared at her dumbly until Logan exclaimed,

"Nia!"

Henri blinked, coming out of his stupor of memories of those long-ago winters and that little frizzle-haired girl who'd nonetheless been taller than him. It had been eighteen years between then and now. She was all grown up, and so was he.

Nia made a small sound of delight, and dashed over to hug Logan. How did they know each other? Henri forced his mouth to close as they stepped apart and Logan grasped her by the elbows.

"I'm so glad you're alright! When I heard Roseforte got sacked, I was so worried!" Logan exclaimed.

Roseforte? That's where she'd been? This whole time she'd been...so close?

"As you can see I've been whisked away by dashing pirates," Nia giggled, too cheerful for the circumstances. "I'm quite well and..." Her eyes finally landed on Henri, standing just past Logan's shoulder, and her smile faltered. Henri realized he'd been staring. Maybe she didn't recognize him.

"N-Nia..." he managed.

A myriad of expressions flicked across her face in quick succession. Confusion, shock, and finally recognition. The smile spread across her face once more, wider than before. Much wider than it had ever been when they were children and there was a perpetual snow cloud hanging over her head.

She disengaged herself from Logan and took a tentative step toward Henri. When she spoke, her voice was so quiet, so hopeful. "Are you Henri? Henri Wells?"

Henri found himself unable to speak, having wasted his only words on her name. But he nodded. Nia's seafoam eyes instantly brimmed with tears, and she launched herself into his arms so hard he stumbled back with the force of it. Her arms wrapped around his waist and his around her shoulders, and suddenly there were hot tears spilling down both their cheeks. Absurdly, it struck him how much shorter she was than him now that they were both grown. He'd almost expected her to still tower over him.

Henri was half aware of everyone staring at them, yet he still allowed himself to bury his face into the poof of hair on top of her head.

"I thought you were dead," Henri sobbed. "He told me you were gone."

"Oh!" Nia pulled back to look up into his face. She dashed the tears away from her cheeks, but they kept falling anyway. "I looked for you after I escaped, but I-I couldn't remember what town you lived in." She smiled sadly. "I'm so sorry. I should have tried harder to find you."

Henri didn't quite know what to say to that. In the silence someone cleared their throat. They both looked over to where Logan, and the rest of the combined crews, were staring at their unexpected display.

"How do you two know each other?" Logan asked tightly. Henri couldn't imagine what they were all thinking. Nia stepped out of Henri's embrace, but kept a grip on his little and ring fingers as if they were still children.

Nia smiled again through her tears.

"Henri is my little brother."

NIA COULDN'T SEEM to let go of Henri's fingers. She felt like a kid again, leading her newfound half brother around the *Silverfin*, with only the bleak winter sun shining through the portholes to light their way. After she'd finally escaped their father, she'd searched and searched for him, but she'd just been a kid last time their father had let her see Henri, and she hadn't known the name of the town he lived in, only that it was somewhere on the western coast of Talva.

And eventually, she'd found herself at the Swan Inn. A temporary position. A room in the attic. She told herself she'd continue the search once she earned some money. She asked around. She listened for any word of him or Silver Stroud. And then, news had come that Stroud had been killed, and such a weight had lifted from her that she worried she might float away. She didn't have to run away anymore. She could have a life for herself.

Until the sickness of being separated from her pelt claimed her, she would live.

So yes, she didn't want to let go of her brother. The one person who had shown her kindness after her mother's death. If she did, they might be separated again.

Henri is my little brother.

She'd said it with pride, out loud for all to hear. More than a few gasps had met her statement, and color had risen to Logan's cheeks.

Oh. Oh no. She'd been carrying on with him and John for ages, and all this time he'd been on the same crew as her long lost brother. If she'd known they were friends, she might not have slept with them.

"You don't look much alike," a freckled, feminine pirate quipped, breaking the shock that seemed to hold them all in situ.

"I take more after my mother than our father," Henri rumbled. Gods, he was tall now. She'd barely recognized him at first, but his wide sparkly eyes and the beads in his locs had given him away. She'd made one of those beads, an amateur clay thing she'd daubed with paint. He still wore it.

"Nia?"

They all turned to find Zanta and a blond man with an eyepatch walking over from where they'd witnessed the whole thing. A massive warship loomed behind them. Nia didn't let go of Henri's fingers.

The blond man's head twitched back ever so slightly when his eye landed on Nia, as if startled. She didn't know him, right? Surely she'd recognize such a striking face.

He lifted a burnished leather eyepatch from his right eye and squinted at her a moment, brow furrowing, then resettled it.

Nia's fingers tightened around Henri's. The fake eye beneath the patch had not been a normal glass one, painted to look natural, but a milky seafoam green.

The same color as her eyes.

The same color as her mother's eyes.

"Where did you get that?" she blurted. Her skin suddenly turned cold, and she had to fight down the panicked feeling of being back on the *Silverfin*. Was she going crazy? Or was that the small stone orb that her father had taken from her mother after her death?

The blond man's gaze flicked from Nia's and Henri's hands clasped together, then to Zanta, who was also staring at him in shock.

"What, my eye? It was—"

"It belonged to my father," Nia interrupted.

The man tilted his head. "And who is your father?"

"Wells Stroud," Henri answered.

Both Zanta and the blond man flinched.

"Come with us," the blond said.

They crossed the gangplank onto the huge warship with its towering blue sails and intimidating tentacled flag. A shiver rattled down her spine as she realized what ship it was. The *Kraken's Fury*. John's ship, but more than that, the ship of the Deep Water Demon.

A fine man like John wouldn't work for someone who was all bad, would he? She tried to push down all the fear that threatened to bubble up when she stepped foot on that infamous deck. Henri took her hand again, squeezing reassuringly. She followed him, Zanta, Logan, and the blond man who could only be the Ghost Hawk down a hallway to a large set of doors. The Ghost Hawk didn't bother knocking, just opened the door and ushered them all inside.

A tall, dark-haired man sat in a wingback chair before a cold fireplace. He looked up when they entered, smooth brow furrowing at the intrusion.

"Rowan, what—" His dark gaze slid past the others straight to Nia. He tilted his head, eyes sparking with interest. Their eyes met and he nodded once in acknowledgment, as if her true nature were plain to his eyes only, and he'd dubbed them the same.

Nia jerked back, almost yanking her hand from Henri's gasp. Her heart pounded hard against her ribs. Instinctual, animal panic overtaking rational thought.

The man's body unfolded from the chair. He didn't break eye contact, and she couldn't look away. Snared like prey.

He didn't look any different than the average man, perhaps more beautiful, but every instinct told her he was a predator of the deep waters. The kind that would snap someone like her up without a second thought. Every part of her recoiled from him.

"So," the Ghost Hawk said, and the man's eyes snapped to him, expression softening, "now that we're all here, we should all get on the same page."

They settled around a long table with a map of the Islands embedded in the wood. Nia kept as far away from the man—the Deep Water Demon, he must be—as possible, and sat with Logan, Henri, and Zanta between them.

Nia clutched Henri's hand under the table, her other tracing the mother-of-pearl outline of the Sleeping Isles.

The Demon sat at the head of the table and folded his hands on its surface. But it was the Ghost Hawk who spoke.

"Now, I believe introductions are in order. I'm Rowan, captain of the *Siren Song*, and this is—"

"She knows who I am," the Demon cut in.

Captain Rowan rolled his eye, but continued. "You seem to know Logan and Henri already. Tell me how that is..."

His sentence trailed off, prompting her to introduce herself.

"Nia. I, ah..." She looked from Zanta to Logan to Henri, pointedly avoiding the Demon. But when she looked back to Captain Rowan, he seemed to recognize her name.

"Nia," he said slowly. "You're the one who Logan—"

"Got information about Cyrus from last year," Logan interrupted quickly. A look passed between the two men. So he was hiding the fact that she, Logan, and John had slept together. Maybe that was for the best.

"And Henri is your half brother?" Captain Rowan prompted.

"Yes..."

"And your father was Silver Stroud?"

Her gut curdled. "Yes."

Silence met this statement for a few long moments.

Captain Rowan turned to Henri. "And you didn't feel the need to share this all these years? Especially when we're being hunted down because of him?"

Shame flickered briefly across Henri's face. "It's not exactly something I'm proud of," he grumbled.

"You don't have the same surname as Stroud," Logan pointed out.

"My maman wanted to protect me from his reputation so they agreed to use his first name instead. Everyone called him Silver anyway. Not many people knew him as Wells Stroud."

Zanta stared at Nia as if she'd seen a ghost. "So his daughter was real after all," she said quietly. "You're Nianthe."

Nia nodded, not quite able to meet her eyes. She shouldn't have hid it from Zanta, especially after they'd started sleeping together. But her father had hurt Zanta so badly, and Nia didn't know if the blossoming feelings between them could survive that association.

Captain Rowan nodded solemnly, as if several threads were connecting in his mind. He touched tentative fingers to his eyepatch, then removed it. "And you say my eye belonged to him?"

The sight of that familiar green orb sitting in this stranger's eye socket almost took Nia's breath away. "It belonged to my mother first. She kept it in a necklace, and when she died, he *took* it." She managed to force the words past the lump forming in her throat. There was more to it. The orb was one of the Eyes of the Sea, an artifact the people of the Sleeping Isles treasured. But her mother had never been allowed to wear it as Captain Rowan did now, not after she'd betrayed her people by falling for an outsider.

But how much could she tell them? Both Captain Rowan and the Demon had reacted to her, but how much did they really suspect? Not even Henri knew what she really was.

"I remember Stroud losing that thing gambling," Zanta said, her tone tightly controlled. "He was distraught about it. Said there was no way he'd find his daughter without it."

Captain Rowan pinched the bridge of his nose. He muttered something that sounded like "Fucking Fox" which Nia could not even begin to interpret.

"So this is what David meant when he said Shaw suspected I had something of Stroud's," Rowan said after he'd recovered from his bout of annoyance.

"Who's Shaw?" Zanta asked.

"Warrick Shaw, the man who's been hunting us both." Rowan quickly explained the situation they collectively found themselves in. The Marran Empire's imminent invasion of the Sleeping Isles had sent this Kefryean mercenary, Shaw, after both Zanta and Rowan for their supposed possession of artifacts once belonging to Silver Stroud. Stroud was famous for being one of the only outsiders to have explored those elusive islands and supposedly befriended the people there. And when he was alive, he was rumored to hold the secrets to conquering them.

Nia knew the truth. Her father had shipwrecked on the outer Sleeping Isles, and her mother had found him. He wooed her to the point that she willingly gave him her pelt. At least that's what her mother had told her. But when he found out she was pregnant with his child, he left and took the pelt with him. Only to return years later when Nia's mother was already on the verge of death from the absence of her pelt. When she'd died, he'd taken Nia, both pelts, and all the treasures he could get his hands on, and fled.

Nia didn't know where the other treasures had ended up, but the iron chest, and the Eye of the Sea, those must be the treasures Shaw sought. Aside from the people of the Sleeping Isles, no one but Nia knew the true nature of these treasures. The chest contained her pelt. And the Eye, if used correctly, could see the truth beneath the truth.

She couldn't say any of this, though surely Rowan knew the power contained in the stone resting in his eye socket. She kept quiet as the others discussed it. She didn't like how the Demon still watched her.

What manner of creature was he? Surely no friend. When the others stopped talking, would he expose her secret?

She had to get her pelt and get out. She had to warn her people of what was coming. But the pelt was still locked away under Zanta's bed. Nia had the key around her waist at this very moment, and if the pelt was whole, she could flee...

"Henri," Zanta blurted, grabbing his arm so hard he flinched. "Did your father ever give you a key?"

Fuck. Zanta still hadn't put it together. Even knowing Nia was Stroud's daughter, she didn't understand the depth of the secrets Nia kept from her.

"Y-yes," Henri said, startled.

Zanta jumped to her feet, beautifully carved wooden chair scraping across the floor. "A brass key with square teeth?"

What? That wasn't...

Henri just looked bewildered. "Yeah." He pulled a cord from the front of his shirt, a tarnished brass key and a square of supple gray pelt swinging from it.

Nia jolted, barely keeping herself from snatching that piece of herself from his hands.

Zanta found she couldn't breathe properly. The key was right there, right in front of her. Exactly how she remembered it. But what if it too wasn't the key she sought? Stroud had been unstable toward the end, and it was entirely possible he gave the wrong key to his son.

And what if it was the right one? Was she ready to have the object of her misery and fascination revealed at last? Her mind wheeled through all the revelations that had just crossed this table.

Nia had a half brother, and they were both children of Zanta's late captain, Silver Stroud. Nia was the fabled Nianthe, the loss of whom had eventually driven Stroud to madness. To killing Emilie.

To Zanta killing him. If Nia had stayed with her father, would any of that have happened? Would Emilie be alive even now?

No, Zanta couldn't go down that path. If Nia had run from her own father, it would have been for a good reason. She was not to blame for the actions of a madman.

Oh gods, Zanta had killed Nia's father. Her gaze sliced to the other woman, staring at the key in Henri's hand like she'd seen a ghost. Her usual bubbly confidence was pushed to the background, replaced by a sort of fidgety energy. She met Zanta's eyes only briefly and quickly looked away. Did she think Zanta was angry with her for keeping her parentage a secret? Was she angry with Zanta for the long ago killing of her father? Or would she thank her?

"I'll go get the chest." Zanta couldn't stay in this room anymore. She needed to be back on her own ship, her own turf. "I think it's about time to find out why we're being hunted."

She made it all the way to the *Monsoon* before Nia caught up with her. Nia didn't say anything, so neither did Zanta. They made their way in silence down to Zanta's quarters, where they'd been naked in bed together only a few hours ago. Something had irreversibly shifted between them now. Truths were out in the open, and Zanta didn't know if they would be able to come together through the tangled web their lives had become.

Though she could feel Nia's presence at her back, Zanta didn't hesitate to take the chest from its hiding place. It felt strange to reveal the small iron box after it had resided under her bed in secret for the last five years. But she didn't want any secrets between them now.

Zanta stared at it a moment, running her hands over the lid as she had so many times before. But this time felt different. This time she had hope.

She hoisted it into her arms and found Nia standing in the doorway as if they were back to where they'd been weeks ago, and she needed permission to come in. Nia's eyes rose to meet hers. Startling light green just like Rowan's fake eye.

"I'm sorry," Nia said, her voice little more than a whisper. "I should've told you before. I-I should have told you."

A few steps brought Zanta to her side, the iron chest between them.

"I understand why you didn't." She did understand, even if

confusion and hurt still roiled through her. "I'm sorry I killed your father."

Nia chuckled mirthlessly. "He was never really a father to me."

Zanta nodded, and Nia's gaze fell to the iron chest. "I'm sorry," she said again, and it felt like it was for something else. But Nia didn't explain further. She stepped out of the doorway, and they silently made their way back up to the debris-strewn deck.

Rowan, the Demon, and their small contingent of *Siren* crew members stood at the center of the deck. Zanta set the chest at their feet.

"So this is what Shaw wanted from you?" Rowan asked, nudging it with his boot. The eyepatch was back over his eye, but he flipped it up to squint at the chest as if that would help him see more clearly, then glanced at Nia. It was incredibly eerie to see that green stone in his eye socket when Stroud had been so obsessed with not being able to "use it" for whatever it was he'd thought it was supposed to do.

"What's in it?" Fox asked.

"I guess we'll find out." Zanta held out her hand for the key. Henri hesitated, and Zanta suddenly realized that he too had known all along that she was the killer of his father. After the chest was opened, she owed him an apology.

The key was just as Zanta remembered, from the size down to the angular brass teeth. It was strung on a cord along with a strange square of gray leather. Henri rubbed a thumb over the square, reluctant to let it go. Then pressed it into Zanta's offered palm.

As soon as the warm brass hit her skin, Zanta knew it was the one. Her heartbeat stuttered, then began to race as she knelt beside the chest. Nia knelt beside her, breath coming shallow and quick, like she was on the verge of tears.

They would have a proper talk after this, Zanta promised silently.

Zanta held her breath as she pushed aside a bit of iron filigree and inserted the key into the keyhole beneath. It slid in easily, and Nia's breath hitched. She was hyperaware of the other woman by her side. In this pivotal moment, the moment she'd been working toward since she drove that piece of the *Silverfin* through Silver Stroud's heart. Since he'd killed Emilie. All she could do was hope it had all been worth it.

She hesitated for just a moment, her fingers warming the metal.

Zanta didn't know if she was ready to find out what the chest contained. What had been so important that it had driven Stroud to madness? That it had cost Emilie her life? That Shaw would now hunt her across the seas for it?

"Zanta?" Nia's voice was quiet, almost reverent. Zanta looked over at her. Her cheeks were pink, lips slightly parted in anticipation. But she wasn't looking back at Zanta, her eyes were riveted to the chest.

The lock gave no resistance as Zanta turned the key. The mechanism within clicked.

She reached for the iron lid, but it didn't budge when she tried to raise it.

"No," she breathed. She pushed harder. Then pried. Maybe it was just stuck. Rusted shut after being at sea for years and years. There had to be a way to open it. This was the key. It had to be. This was...

A small piece of the filigree popped open beneath her fingers, revealing a second, smaller keyhole.

No. It couldn't be. She'd prodded and pried every inch of this box before, and this piece had never moved. This was supposed to be over. She was supposed to move on.

Nia leapt to her feet, fumbling with her clothes, hands shaking. But whatever she was looking for wasn't forthcoming, and she began frantically stripping her clothes off right there on deck.

"What the fuck..."

Nia's blouse fluttered to the deck. She unlaced her stays and pulled down her skirt, revealing a thin silver chain around her waist. And from that chain hung a tiny silver key.

What on earth? How had Zanta not noticed that before? How...

Nia failed to unclasp the key from the chain with shaking hands, so she simply ripped it off. She fell back to her knees in only her underthings and slid the key into the secondary lock. There was no hesitation; she twisted it.

The lid clicked open just a crack.

They both reached for the lid at the same time, and the disused hinges squealed as they opened it together. Zanta's heart beat out of her chest.

Folded within the confines of the chest was a sheaf of gray

leather, lightly speckled. Zanta frowned in confusion. This couldn't be it. Maybe Silver Stroud's treasure was beneath...

Nia let out a sob, and reached out a trembling hand. Her fingertips touched the leather so gently as if she couldn't believe what she was seeing. Zanta had the sense that she was witnessing something private. Sacred.

Before she could say anything, Nia snatched the sheaf of leather and the brass key with its square of matching leather attached. It came alive in her hands, rippling like silk as it unfolded. Then Nia was sprinting across the deck on bare feet. She reached the rail.

"Nia!"

Zanta's shout didn't slow her. She didn't even look back. She leaped over the side of the ship, her elated laugh turning into a joyous bark as she spun in midair, wrapping the pelt around her naked body and transforming.

It was not Nia's body that entered the water, but a sleek gray seal. It disappeared beneath the waves with barely a splash.

They all stood stunned for a moment, unable to comprehend what they'd just witnessed.

Then Zanta's feet were moving. She, Henri, and Logan reached the rail just in time to see the seal leap out of the water, jewel-like droplets flicking from her tail fins. Her discarded underthings floating beside the hull.

All Zanta could do was stare open-mouthed as she disappeared from view.

That seal was Nia. And Nia was...Zanta couldn't wrap her head around it. Didn't have the words for it. Nia was...

She was gone.

"We have to go after her!" Henri shouted. He looked ready to strip off his boots and jump in if they didn't immediately agree. Zanta felt the same urge rise up in her. Nia would come back, wouldn't she? Was she even in her right mind in that form? Zanta's mind felt full and empty at once, trying desperately to grasp the situation. She stared at the spot Nia had disappeared, not even ripples remained to mark her passage.

"Rowan." Henri whirled, searching out his captain. "We're going after her. Right?"

"I—What is she?" Rowan seemed as stunned as the rest of them, but the Demon remained calm as ever. As if he'd been expecting this.

He rested a hand on Rowan's shoulder, and Rowan's mouth snapped shut, some of the tension releasing from his shoulders.

"She is a Selkie, and of course we are going after her." The Demon's tone brooked no argument. His word, final.

Henri froze, blinking in surprise. Even Zanta knew the Deep Water Demon was not one for sentiment. Zanta had always wondered what a man like Rowan saw in him. The Demon was a man of violence, a man who never did anything unless it benefited him.

No one moved. The Demon tilted his head.

"Well?"

A stunned veil lifted from them all. The *Kraken* crew members rushed to prepare their ship to sail, but Zanta remained frozen. Her heart felt like it had replaced the pelt, locked in the iron box. She wanted to go after Nia more than anything, but the *Monsoon*, her beloved home, was too broken.

Rowan appeared at her side. "It will take too long if we have to tow the *Monsoon*," he said, sympathetic lines marring his brow.

"I know." But she couldn't abandon it, not for anything. Not even hopelessness. Not even Nia. She couldn't meet Rowan's eye.

"You want to come with us to find her though."

"I can't leave the *Monsoon* to drift. I'll never find it again." Like she was adrift, caught between her life and the woman she cared for above all else.

Rowan grimaced, and she remembered that he'd left the *Siren* behind. For her.

"We'll tow you to the next rock spire and secure the *Monsoon*. After that, you can come with us or...we'll come back for you if we can."

Zanta nodded, and Rowan squeezed her shoulder reassuringly. "We'll find her."

She shouldn't rely on his kindness. She couldn't trust whatever motive the Demon had for agreeing to this so readily. But she had no choice.

Her feet carried her back to the iron chest, the driving force behind the last five years of her life. Now empty. She had wanted Emilie's death to mean something, even though in the back of her mind she always knew that whatever the chest contained, it wouldn't be enough.

The chest was not empty. Zanta picked up a battered leather journal from where it sat alone at the bottom of the chest, and felt Henri lingering at her elbow. She thrust the journal at him, leather grain smooth against her fingertips.

"Here. It must've been your father's." The man she'd killed.

Henri didn't reach for it. "Keep it. I don't want to know."

She tucked it close to her chest. "I'm sorry."

"It doesn't matter. As long as we find Nia. Nothing else matters." Someone called him from the *Kraken*, and he was gone.

Zanta looked down at the empty chest. Silver Stroud had always said it would bring his daughter back to him. But it had taken her away from Zanta, just as it had taken Emilie.

Zanta passed her hands over the worn leather, the cover's corners curled up with brine, the silver clasp tarnished. It protested as she undid it, the spine creaking as she opened the journal of the man she'd murdered.

CHAPTER 39

UNKNOWN DATE, 1668

The amber glass bottles clinked as Henri stowed the last of them in the apothecary cabinets. He hoped he'd done it right. He wasn't familiar with how the *Kraken*'s stores were organized, and his mind was elsewhere, swimming through the currents with Nia. It had been days since he'd seen her transform with his own eyes, and among all the jumbled thoughts tumbling through him, one that kept repeating over and over till it carried a heavy coating of guilt and hurt along with it was, *Why didn't she tell me?*

It was such a stupid thing to think. He knew it was. But he couldn't shake it. He and Nia hadn't seen each other since they were kids, and ultimately they'd only spent a few winters together. There were so many reasons she shouldn't or couldn't have told him. They were both just children, and he'd loved their father, and their father had probably sworn her to secrecy. He'd been a worse man than Henri had realized back then. But still, if Nia had told Henri the truth, he would've tried to help, even if he was just a kid.

Stupid, that he was hung up on that when Nia was missing, the *Siren* was stuck, and they were likely still being hunted by Rowan's evil ex. Not to mention Robin was still treating the injured pirates from the *Monsoon*, who'd been moved to the *Kraken*.

As if summoned by Henri's thoughts, the apothecary door swung open, and Robin stumbled through from the infirmary proper. He leaned heavily against the countertop, head down, blond hair hanging lank over his eyes.

"You're done?" Henri reached across the counter to take his hand, but it remained firmly pressed to the cold stone surface. "Robin?" Worry edged out the tumult of other feelings. He smoothed a thumb over the back of Robin's white knuckles, searching. Exhaustion shrouded every line of his body, and when he finally looked up after the third stroke of Henri's thumb, shadows clung beneath his eyes. He looked so wrung out, Henri's heart clenched in response.

"Robin?" he asked again. Robin's eyes locked onto him, looked through him. Henri let go and rounded the counter. He smoothed the wheat blond hair back from Robin's forehead, and Robin startled, as if just realizing Henri was there.

"I couldn't. I—" He swallowed roughly, then his expression crumpled.

"There were so many I couldn't save." He collapsed into Henri's arms, shoulders shaking.

A whole new wave of guilt assailed Henri as he wrapped Robin in a tight embrace. Robin had always been strong in his own quiet way. He took care of everyone on the ship with minimal fuss. He'd saved so many of their lives more times than Henri could recall. He handled horrific injuries with competence and grace, and he'd sometimes looked a bit haunted, but he'd never *cracked* like this.

While Henri had been dealing with the treasure and Nia reappearing and disappearing in his life, Robin had been working tirelessly to save lives with very little sleep since the storm. And apparently lost quite a few of them.

"Shh, shh, Robin, you're okay."

Robin pressed his face to Henri's skin, tears sliding down Henri's neck into the collar of his shirt. Robin's body shook, but not with sobs. He was too exhausted for that. Henri guided him to sit on a chair in the corner and knelt on the floor in front of him, still holding him. He pressed Robin's face tighter into his neck, his other arm squeezing him, grounding him until he cried himself out. It didn't take long. The tears slowed, his breathing evened out, and Henri was just beginning to think he'd cried himself to sleep when Robin spoke.

"I'm sorry."

"It's okay." Henri stroked his hair. "Whatever you're sorry for, it's okay."

"I couldn't save all of them." Robin's breath hitched. His arms hung heavy around Henri's waist.

"You tried your best, Robin. You saved as many as you could." He knew it was an empty platitude in the grand scheme of things. Robin had always been harder on himself than necessary. Every death of someone under his care weighed as heavily as if the entire sea pressed down on him. With three crews to take care of, he'd been working nearly around the clock, and it all piled up.

"You're the best doctor I've ever met," Henri whispered. Robin's body stiffened for a moment, then relaxed.

"I'm so tired."

"Let's get you to bed." He kissed the side of Robin's head, then guided him to his feet. After a few dragging steps, Henri lifted him, one arm around his back and the other beneath his legs. Robin didn't even protest like he usually would, he just laid his head on Henri's shoulder.

When they made it to their room a few doors down from the infirmary, Henri sat him down on the thin bed. Robin clung to him.

"I'm right here." Henri planted another kiss on his ear, and Robin released him. Henri removed Robin's boots and socks, then moved to pull off his shirt and replace it with one of Henri's own large, soft nightshirts. He stripped off Robin's trousers, letting the shirt's folds fall over Robin's hips. Robin surrendered to Henri's attentions, once again retreating within. He stared through Henri as he changed himself into nightclothes too.

Henri crawled into bed, then when Robin made no move to join him, pulled him down into his arms. Robin settled on his front between Henri's legs, head on Henri's stomach. Henri closed his eyes and buried his fingers in Robin's hair, trying to still all the thoughts swirling through his head. Outside their little pocket of darkness, the ship still stirred with the activities of settling into night. Henri remembered he'd skipped dinner, but he had no desire to move from this spot.

After a long while, Robin shifted.

"Your stomach is growling."

"Sorry."

More silence, Henri hoped Robin was relaxing into sleep.

"I can't sleep."

"You're exhausted, mon cher." He stroked Robin's cheek. It felt more hollow than its usual round fullness.

"I keep..." He swallowed, throat bobbing against Henri's stomach.

"Do you want to talk about it?"

"I just want to sleep, but my brain won't be quiet."

Henri knew the feeling. They dropped into silence again, listening to each other's breathing and footsteps on the deck above.

"I'm sorry," Robin whispered. He sounded on the verge of tears again.

"About what?"

"About Nia...You must be hurting, but I'm making things all about myself." They'd barely talked in days, Robin either busy in the infirmary, or snatching a moment of sleep.

"We can talk about it tomorrow."

Robin sighed into his touch.

"Do you want something to help you sleep?" Henri felt Robin nod.

He shifted out from under him, murmured he would be right back, and padded barefoot back to the infirmary's storeroom. He lit the lamp and grabbed the vial of mild sleeping draught off the shelf, then paused, frowning. The spot next to the draught was empty. He could've sworn he'd restocked the essence of poppy after Robin had taken the old bottle for the *Monsoon*'s patients.

Henri shook his head. He was distracted by everything with Nia. Maybe he hadn't restocked it after all. He'd get to it tomorrow. Henri made his way back to Robin.

CHAPTER 40

UNKNOWN DATE, 1668

Her name is Gwyneth.

Zanta ran her finger over the dry ink, faded in the afternoon sun. Even if it wouldn't help them, the name beneath her fingers felt like a balm. A tenuous string tethering her to Nia. The name of Nia's mother.

It had taken two days before Zanta finally started reading Stroud's journal. Even if it might contain information that could lead them to Nia, she hadn't had the time or the energy. She spent the first day preparing the *Monsoon* for abandonment, packing up everything of value and reassuring the crew as the *Kraken* towed them north, looking for a place to leave Zanta's beloved ship.

They'd found a spot on the second day. A tall spire with a collar of sand and a deep reef in which to anchor. Her injured crew members were already safely aboard the *Kraken*. All that remained was to transfer the goods and the rest of her crew, and leave the *Monsoon* behind.

Easier said than done. Zanta managed to stay her tears till she was alone.

So it was on the third day, the *Kraken* with three diminished crews of pirates aboard and weaving between the spires, that Zanta finally cracked the journal open.

I am being called north,

the first line read in Stroud's steady hand.

Father always told me stories of the Sleeping Isles, but no one knows if they are true. I want to know. I believe there is something for me there. The riches of ten thousand wrecked ships. A secret island I can rule as my own. The glory of discovery. So many have tried and failed to reach them. So many great men have lost their lives to the ring of storms, or whatever lies beyond it. But I am not like those men.

So he'd gone looking for the Sleeping Isles. He'd risked his crew, his ship, for what? Words told in a child's bedtime story. Everyone in the Islands knew that to sail to the Sleeping Isles was as good as sailing to your death. The Nanadie said it was the mouth to the underworld. The Talvans did not speak of it, lest evil come upon them. Kefryeans purported monsters lived there. Yarenens said it was where La's serpentine head rested. No matter which story might be true, one fact remained. If you sailed into the storms, you didn't come back.

But Silver Stroud had. He wrote of his first attempt to break through, and how the storm had spit them back out north of Nanad relatively unscathed.

Yasmina says I am a fool with a death wish. But the Silverfin is not badly damaged, and we only lost a few men. We lived. Why else would we come away with our lives if we were not meant to try again?

Zanta recognized the fanaticism that had eventually turned to madness. He'd always been as changeable as the weather. Prone to flights of fancy and wont to follow whatever idea flitted across his mind. Zanta read on.

I am alone. We tried again, and I think this time we succeeded. This place does not look like any shore I know. Mist clings everywhere, and the sea is broken by a forest of rock. Are these the Sleeping Isles?

I went overboard in the storm, and I do not know if the Silverfin or Yasmina and the rest of the crew survived. Maybe it is only me who was meant to reach this fabled place. I washed ashore at the base of one of the stone trees, and all I have with me is my journal, pen, and ink. It was wrapped in oilcloth in my pocket. It's a wonder it all survived. Yet more proof I was meant to come here.

He stayed on that rock spire for several days, starving, and then:

Her name is Gwyneth. She swam up to my rock and saved my life. I was delirious with hunger and thirst, and at first mistook her for a seal. I do not know how she managed to get me to this new island. But I am here now, in a little house carved into the side of a cliff overlooking a pebble beach and tide pools.

And then the next entry.

Gwyneth is beautiful. Her eyes are as green as sea foam and her hair is brown and lush. She lives on this tiny island alone, I think. She speaks a language shockingly similar to those I heard in old plays when father used to take me to festivals in the town square. We have been able to communicate in simple words, but it is hard to parse. Perhaps I will teach her my language.

She does not speak about her people. Maybe there are none. Maybe she is a castaway like me.

I stepped outside while she was sleeping and looked at

the stars. It is strange being this far north, but I think I know where I am.

Zanta jumped to her feet. Stroud had recorded the coordinates of Gwyneth's island. Maybe Nia wouldn't be going there. Maybe Gwyneth was not her mother. But it was something. It was a place to start.

HENRI TRIED to distract himself by counting all the knots currently twisting up his stomach. It felt like there was a complex enough tangle of guts in there to rerig the *Monsoon* twice over. Nia was gone. Just as he'd found her again, she'd disappeared. She'd wrapped herself in a cloak of the same gray leather he'd worn around his neck for years, jumped over the side of the ship, and *transformed*.

He stopped walking in the middle of the hallway, and touched his chest where the key and piece of leather had once rested. He'd had a piece of her with him all this time and not realized it. If he'd known...But knowing wouldn't have changed anything, would it? It would not have helped him find her faster.

"Henri?" Logan's soft voice broke into his spiraling thoughts. "You alright?"

It had been days of carefully navigating the strange seascape of the Sleeping Isles. Days of quick little meetings between the core group. The three captains, Logan, and him, all cooped up in the Demon's lavish stateroom going over insufficient charts and whatever new bits of information Splinter Zanta had gleaned from Stroud's journal. His father's journal.

She'd offered it to him of course. As Silver Stroud's son, Henri had more of a right to read those words than Stroud's onetime subordinate and murderer. But Henri couldn't bring himself to read it. What if there was something about him in there? What if the already tenuous feelings he had for Wells Stroud as his father were shattered by his father's innermost thoughts inked out in black and white?

Besides, Henri was such a tangle that he didn't think he could parse the words and do what must be done. Teasing out useful information and discarding the rest. So he'd let Zanta have it, and she seemed grateful for it.

"Henri?"

Right, Logan. Logan, who had barely talked to him in days, and kept darting nervous glances at him. Now, Logan just looked worried. Henri couldn't help the self-deprecating chuckle that escaped him. Nianthe, the only family he had left in the world, was gone, and he didn't know what to do about it.

"No, I don't think I'm alright."

Logan set a hand on his arm, right over where his serpent tattoo was covered by his sleeve.

"We'll find her. She's still..." Logan trailed off, no doubt realizing that his platitudes were empty. They could chase her all they wanted. But they didn't even know if she was still in her right mind in that...form. They didn't know anything. They wouldn't even be able to tell her apart from any other seal they might encounter.

Henri swallowed around the tightness in his throat. Logan's hand squeezed.

"We'll find her," Logan repeated. He looked just as stricken as Henri felt, and Henri suddenly remembered how Logan and Nia had greeted each other like old friends.

"You knew her, didn't you? How? I mean—" He cut himself off as Logan's face went red enough to rival the Demon's rubies. "What is it?"

"I, ah...I do know her." Logan rubbed the back of his neck, avoiding eye contact.

"How? You barely leave the *Siren*."

Logan said nothing. He seemed to be attempting to disappear through sheer force of will.

"Logan?"

Logan hauled in a deep breath. "Don't be mad."

If Logan, of all people, was asking him not to be mad, he didn't know what could possibly come out of his mouth next. Henri just crossed his arms.

"Um, remember when I went to Roseforte a while ago?"

Henri frowned. "When you were looking for Cyrus, or when you and John got information on the *Trinity*?" Why was Logan acting so strangely?

"Both? Um...Me and John...She was our informant both times." He blinked very hard, then his eyes rose to meet Henri's. "And we slept with her."

"You—" All the knots tightened into a ball of anger, heavy in his stomach. He grabbed Logan's arm in a tight grip. "What the fuck do you mean 'we' slept with her? Both of you?"

"Yeah." Logan's gaze held steady, even as shame laced his voice.

"What the fuck, Logan!" This seemed to be the only thing he could say. His mind reeled. Logan, one of his closest friends, and John, the Demon's stern second in command, had both...He didn't know which was worse, to be honest. And he did not want to think of it.

"In our defense, we didn't know she was your sister. I didn't even know you *had* a sister," Logan offered up weakly.

That hit Henri like a slap, and he released Logan's arm. Of course Logan didn't know he had a sister. He hadn't told anyone, because he'd thought her dead, and it was better to leave the dead to memory where they belonged. On top of that, he hadn't seen Nia since they were children. He had no right to her besides their shared blood. He knew the child she was, not the woman she had become, and he had no right to brotherly righteousness or anger at Logan for sleeping with a stranger.

The knot of anger loosened, just enough to get his fingers in. Henri slumped against the wall of the corridor. Leaned his head back and closed his eyes.

"Sorry," Logan said.

Henri dragged a hand over his mouth. Let out a long exhale. "It's fine, Logan, really. As long as you treated her well, I have no right to be mad at you." From the way Nia ran into Logan's arms earlier, and what he knew of Logan personally, he was sure that was the case.

John, on the other hand...

"Wait." Henri reached out to clutch Logan's forearms again. "When you said you...I mean...both? At the same..." He really didn't want to know, but the stuttering words were out of his mouth before he could stop them.

Logan turned even redder. "Do you really want to know?"

"No!" Henri released him in horror. "But I mean, are you and John...?"

Redder still, as if all the blood in Logan's whole body had pushed to the surface of his cheeks.

"We're, ah, hooking up?"

Well, fuck. Henri had not seen that coming. Logan was such an innocent figure in his mind. Someone dependable and solid and soft. Not really the type of guy Henri thought would have a casual affair with the man who had caused his hand to be amputated. To be honest, Henri had thought Logan a virgin.

"And you're okay with that?" Henri asked carefully. If John was taking advantage of him, Henri didn't know what he'd do. Probably get the crew together and hunt John down.

The blush on Logan's cheeks was slowly receding. "Why wouldn't I be?"

"Well, okay then. As long as you're happy." As soon as the others found out, they'd interrogate it out of him. No juicy detail could elude Fox once he got a whiff of gossip. Logan reached up to pat Henri's shoulder with his wooden hand, a faint smile touching his lips.

"Don't worry too much, big guy."

The door at the end of the hall banged open, and Splinter Zanta dashed past them, skidded to a halt, and doubled back to grab Henri's arm.

"What's going on?" Logan asked.

Zanta held up Stroud's journal, her finger marking a page. "I think I've found us a heading."

CHAPTER 41

UNKNOWN DATE, 1668

Pale stone spires crowded in on every side like a petrified forest, the blue waves beneath the *Kraken* a stark contrast to the constant flickering of lightning as they left the Storm Ring further and further behind. Zanta paused her skimming of Stroud's journal to watch the *Kraken* pass under an arch of stone that barely cleared the top of the mainmast. It would have been near impossible to navigate these waters even in the more agile *Monsoon* or *Siren,* but they were stuck with the *Kraken,* a cannon instead of a bow. At least they were afloat—that was more than could be said for either of the others right now. Between the Demon and Rowan, however, they managed to find clear passage time and again as they picked their way toward the destination Zanta had read about.

They hadn't seen another living soul apart from gulls and fish since they'd passed through the Storm Ring. Wreckage floated everywhere, but there was no way to know if it belonged to the mercenaries, was pieces of the *Monsoon* that had broken off in the storm, or remained from some long ago tragedy. If they were still being hunted, it would be almost impossible to spot another ship until it was right on top of them.

Even if the mercenaries had perished, Zanta knew now that they were not alone in the Sleeping Isles. She'd spent the last few days doing nothing but scouring the sporadic entries in the journal for any detail that might help them find Nia, and learned that Nia was not the only one of her kind here. These islands were home to a society of Selkies, hidden away for centuries by the Storm Ring. Zanta flinched at every splash, every glisten on the water, expecting a hoard of seal people to rise up out of the sea and surround them, but what turned her stomach more were Stroud's own words.

I fear that Yasmina and the others perished in the storm. I have been on this island for gods know how long. I should've dated these entries, but I do not know what day it is or how long I have been here. If the Silverfin is still afloat, wouldn't they have found me by now?

I have taught Gwyneth some of my language, and she has taught me some of hers. The two are not so different as I first thought. I have been here long enough that we can communicate more easily now.

Then later.

Last night I woke up and Gwyneth was gone. For a moment, I thought I'd dreamed her. But I ventured out to the beach and I saw her in the water. She was naked. Hair streaming down her back, skin pale in the moonlight. I wanted to call out, but I could not. She wrapped herself in something that looked like an animal skin, and suddenly it was not a woman standing there but a gray seal slipping into the waves. I waited all night for her to return, but she didn't. I am alone again.

Several pages of hasty sketches followed. A small dwelling carved into the side of a cliff. The shoreline. Shells. The vague strokes of a woman's face that was probably Gwyneth, and a more detailed face that looked like a female version of Henri and was labeled, *Yasmina*.

Gwyneth has returned and she is not alone. There was another seal with her. Another creature like her, who turned into an old woman when she took off the seal pelt. Gwyneth led her up the beach by the arm, with the gray pelts draped over their shoulders.

The woman is blind, but she looked at me as if she could see me. Her eyes are two stone marbles. The right one is light green, like Gwyneth's eyes. The left is pitch black, like onyx. She yelled at Gwyneth in their strange language and I managed to catch some of it. Gwyneth later told me she should not have saved my life. They kill outsiders, to keep themselves safe.

There must be people here, on the other islands. I will ask Gwyneth about it, if I can.

A green stone eye? It had to be the same one Rowan had. Nia had said that her father stole it after her mother died, so it must be.

The blind woman banished me from the house, but Gwyneth led me to a cave down the beach. I asked her all my questions. She said she was forbidden to tell me these things. She shouldn't have brought me here. But I took her hands in mine and thanked her for saving my life, and told her my ship was surely sunk and my crew was dead. And she was the only thing I had in all the world.

She told me everything.

This island, small as it is, is called Seer's Isle. There are many other islands. She wouldn't name them all or tell me where they were. Her people are called Selkies. They have both a human form, and a form that is like a seal. There has not been a living human here in hundreds of years.

The old woman is something called a Seer, and Gwyneth is her apprentice and caretaker. The strange stone eyes are handed down from seer to seer and allow them to see beyond our world. They are the Eyes of the Sea. The green one is called Truth and the black one is called Fate.

It is truly fate that has brought me here. If the Selkies have riches like this entrusted to an old woman all alone on a remote island, what must their kings and warriors have?

Zanta's stomach curdled. When she'd known Silver Stroud, he'd already been humbled by the loss of his daughter, but his words on this page hinted at the ego that had always been front and center in his personality. These words said that he thought he had a right to whatever treasures he could manage to snatch from the Selkies. Zanta was a pirate herself, dozens of pirates surrounded her on this ship, yet she had a code, and that code did not include robbing an isolated people of their cultural treasures. She doubted Stroud had intended to use diplomacy to get what he wanted.

She skimmed over more drawings and found a series of short entries spaced far apart, among some ragged edges of torn-out pages.

Gwyneth and I are in love.

Gwyneth is pregnant.

Several pages of detailed drawings of a woman's face with smudges of green in her eyes accompanied notes about Selkies and their culture and the Isles. She resembled Nia only in the way her eyes scrunched up with her smile.

Yasmina and the crew live! The Silverfin is battered but sailable. They thought me dead, and have been looking for a way back through the Storm Ring. The old woman screeched curses at us, but there is nothing she can do. I am going to sail out of here and find the treasures of the Sleeping Isles.

I asked Gwyneth to come with me, though I didn't tell

her my plans. I could conquer this place, and become king among them given enough men and supplies. And she could be my queen. Our child will be the prince of the Selkies. Perhaps Yasmina will agree to be mine too.

Zanta stared at the page for a long while, sickened. Then flipped to the next entry.

I overheard Gwyneth and the old woman talking and found the secret to getting through the Storm Ring. A Selkie pelt, freely given, is the key to tame the storms.

Zanta clamped a hand over her mouth and read on.

Gwyneth will not leave Seer's Isle. I thought it would be best to bring her with me, but she is stubborn. I will have to find some other way.

I have the pelt, but I do not have Gwyneth or my unborn child. They remain behind. The Selkies found us. Warriors arrived in boats, and in their seal forms, at dawn, and we fled on the Silverfin, but not before I convinced Gwyneth to give me her pelt.

It is a thing of beauty, and it will tame the storms.

She flipped to the middle of the journal, finding several more jagged edges where pages used to be. Had Stroud torn them out himself or had someone else gotten their hands on the journal? She flipped further, and found more missing pages and then:

He stole from me. The bastard. The last piece of Gywneth is gone.

Zanta remembered not long before Emilie had become Stroud's

first mate, her predecessor had absconded with their takings for the season. Had he stolen other things too? And had Nia's mother's pelt been among them?

Zanta nearly jumped out of her skin as a large hand landed on her shoulder. She slammed the book closed and blinked away building tears before looking up to find Henri.

"Anything helpful?" he asked. They'd not talked further about the journal or Stroud or Nia in the days of navigating the forest of rocks.

Zanta shook her head. What could she tell him? That his father was a monster who had abandoned his pregnant lover and planned to conquer her people? She understood what had happened now, and little things about where they were, but there was nothing that would help them find Nia or navigate these treacherous waters.

"The captains are meeting." Henri released her shoulder and cocked his thumb toward the *Kraken*'s stateroom. She tucked the journal into her waistband and followed him in.

The Demon, as always, lounged at the head of the table, boots propped on the shiny surface, legs crossed like he had not a care in the world. While the rest of them looked stressed and disheveled, his onyx hair remained perfectly arranged, his elegant clothes clean, and his skin flawless. Beside him, Rowan had taken off his eyepatch to redo his ponytail, clothes rumpled from the wind. Together they looked like a scrappy mutt and a well-bred hunting hound. But even a hound was a dog, no matter the riches heaped upon it.

Next to Rowan sat his first mate, Logan, Fox sitting on the other side wearing a very elegant green robe over tight pants with laces up the sides. Henri settled into the chair next to him, leaving the space on the Demon's left to Zanta. Like Zanta, the Demon was currently without a first mate, but while his had been left behind to deal with the *Siren*, Zanta's was dead.

She couldn't think of that now. She had to stay focused on the matter at hand. There would be time to grieve if they survived this.

She settled into the chair, leaning away from the Demon's shiny boots. Today's spurs were silver, etched with such fine scrollwork one would only be able to see it if one were kissing his boots or dying at his feet.

"Anything helpful in the journal?" Rowan asked, tying off his hair but not replacing the eyepatch. The blank green eye was unnerving now that she looked at it dead-on, like it could see every part of her. But then again, if it was the same eye the old seer had had in Stroud's journals, maybe it could.

Zanta resisted the urge to cover herself. "Your eye's magical. That's what it said." She hadn't meant it to come out accusatory, but her voice held an edge she couldn't shake.

Rowan blinked. "Did it now?" Logan, Fox, and Henri seemed nervous, the Demon's sharp gaze fixed on her.

Zanta retrieved the journal from her waistband and stabbed at the cover with her finger. "Stroud shipwrecked here almost thirty years ago. He met some Selkies just like Nia, and one of those Selkies was a seer. Her eyes had been plucked out and replaced with two stones. One green, called Truth, and the other black, Fate." She wouldn't tell them about Nia's parentage, how Stroud had cruelly used her mother and tossed them both aside. It was too personal. Zanta herself felt like she shouldn't know.

Rowan's fingertips touched the skin under his eye gently. "Truth...I see."

"You don't deny it's magical?" Zanta asked pointedly. She'd half expected him to; it wasn't the sort of thing he'd want spread around. Especially if it was the artifact Shaw hunted for.

A cocky grin twitched at the corners of his mouth. "I'll admit I've been...seeing things here and there since I started wearing it." He and Yves shared a look Zanta couldn't decipher.

"What kinds of things?" Fox asked eagerly.

"Well for starters, when we met Nia, she was all shimmery."

"Shimmery?" Henri frowned.

"Like caustic reflections, light reflecting off water. And then I remembered I saw the same shimmers around the chest back in—" He cut a glance at the Demon, then cleared his throat. "In your quarters aboard the *Monsoon* back in Wave Harbor." He pointedly did not look at his husband again as the Demon glared at them both.

"Nia's pelt," Zanta breathed.

"I'd assume so." Rowan nodded thoughtfully. "I think the eye, Truth, let me see a hint of her true form."

"That's amazing!" Fox bounced in his seat like a child shown a magic trick. "I can't believe I gave you a magical eye. You owe me a raise, I think."

"Next prize we take you can have first dibs on anything interesting," Rowan said indulgently.

"How come you didn't tell us about this, Captain?" Logan asked, his voice low, as if masking a hint of hurt.

Rowan shrugged. "Robin said minor visual hallucinations were possible with the loss of an eye, just like your hand pains. I didn't think much of it."

"You were having *hallucinations* and didn't tell—"

"I don't see how this is helpful to the matter at hand," the Demon interrupted Logan, earning himself a glare. He turned to Zanta. "Was there anything else of use in the book?"

"The Sleeping Isles are full of Selkies, like Nia, and they don't like intruders. We have to try to get out as soon as we find her."

"And how do we do that?" Henri piped up. "I don't think we'll survive the Storm Ring a second time. Especially with the *Siren* damaged."

"There's a way..." She trailed off, realizing that the way involved Nia freely giving her pelt. Was that why they'd been so damaged despite having the pelt on board? It was stolen? What if Nia didn't want to go with them? If she told these pirates, especially the Demon, that Nia was the key to their escape, it could put her in danger.

"Well? We await at your leisure," the Demon purred, all sarcastic gallantry.

Zanta took a deep breath. She couldn't very well keep this information to herself now that she'd said there was a way. Rowan wasn't one to be cruel. He'd stop the Demon from gaining the pelt by nefarious means, wouldn't he?

"A Selkie pelt, freely given, is necessary to weather the storms." But what if Nia didn't want to return with them? What if she wanted to stay here, with her people?

The Demon rolled his eyes, muttering something that sounded like "typical" under his breath.

Henri raised his eyebrows. "But both Nia and the pelt were on the *Monsoon*, and it's wrecked more than the *Kraken* and *Siren* put together."

A pang gripped Zanta's heart. Her ship, her home, was gone, probably for good. Her best friend was gone. If Nia had confessed earlier and gotten her pelt back, would Sabriye still be alive? Would they even now be leaving this place on the *Monsoon*?

She wished Nia had trusted her.

"It wasn't freely given," Logan said. "Stroud stole it, right?"

Zanta nodded.

"So she'll have to come with us. That was the plan already." Henri seemed unsure of his own words.

Before Zanta could answer, there was a thump from outside as if someone had run into the door. Everyone but the Demon sat up straight, hands going to weapons. The Demon lazily set his feet on the floor, spurs clinking. A few seconds later the door wrenched open, and Laurent rushed through, stopping short when he found all three captains staring at him.

"What's happened?" Zanta demanded.

"Land. We've spotted actual land."

CHAPTER 42

UNKNOWN DATE, 1668

Zanta rushed out on deck with the others hot on her heels in time to see a small island appear between two spires. It was the same pale stone, cliffs reaching up to the bruised sky, and crowned by windswept trees. The way was clear, as if the forest of rock had opened up the way just for them.

"Is that the one?" Henri asked at her side.

"I don't know." The journal had described an island like this, but she didn't see a cove and a pebble beach, nor a dwelling carved into the cliffs. If this wasn't it, would they just keep searching? The Sleeping Isles were an archipelago. Gods only knew how many of these islands were contained within the Storm Ring. And what if she'd been wrong? What if Nia wasn't going back to Seer's Isle after all?

"I think it is." Rowan gazed at the island, sans eyepatch. "There's something..." He shook his head and squinted harder. "I think we should check it out."

Upon his word, the Demon signaled to his crew, and they jumped to do his bidding, staying on course for the island and preparing landing boats, should they be required.

The *Kraken* maneuvered carefully between the rocks, spotters at every rail to call out pitfalls that might be lurking beneath the water to gouge out the ship's guts. As they neared the island, more and more wreckage bobbed in the waves, pieces of wood and rope, bodies.

Zanta worried her lip between her teeth, willing her searching gaze not to find any corpse with a face she knew. The *Kraken* banked to port around the edge of the island, still too far away to pick out much detail on the shore.

As they rounded a jutting cliff, a small cove opened up before them, bracketed by tall spires, the water light and too shallow for the massive ship to approach any further. Smashed upon the rocks, the corpse of another ship languished. Its insides lay exposed to the waves, pale sails floating beneath the surface like giant white jellyfish. Rope-tangled corpses bobbed in the surf. Drowned. Or dashed on the rocks. Zanta caught her breath as she read the lettering on the smashed-up side. *Mar—* The *Marigold*, dead in the water with its crew strewn about like any other flotsam.

"There! A survivor!" Logan pointed to a lone figure huddled in the corner of a torn open room at the stern.

They prepared a boat, and several crew members rowed out to rescue the last survivor of the *Marigold*. A woman. She shivered in her soaked uniform as she stepped aboard the *Kraken*.

"Baird," Rowan growled. She squared her shoulders when she saw him, though the shivering undercut her show of defiance.

"Ghost Hawk," she said.

"Are you the only survivor?"

Baird's posture deflated a little. She pressed her pale lips into a line. "Yes."

"Where is the *Lonesome*?"

She shook her head, and Rowan stepped toward her, all threat and menace. They stared at each other for a moment.

"Take her below," he ordered Logan. "Give her dry clothes, food, water. Then throw her in the brig. We'll see how ready she is to talk when she realizes her life is in our hands."

"Zanta, is that..." Henri grabbed Zanta's shoulder as their captive was led away. Zanta's gaze finally slipped past the wreckage to the interior of the cove. A pebble beach ringed in cliffs and...Zanta frantically flipped to a page of sketches in the journal and held it up against the backdrop. Henri's eyes widened.

The charcoal lines matched the stone exactly. An ornate little dwelling carved directly into the side of the cliff. They'd found it. The Seer's Isle.

. . .

"I THINK I should go by myself." Zanta stood at the rail of the *Kraken*, facing off against the other two captains and their crew. They'd anchored as close to the entrance of the cove as depth would allow, far enough away from the wreckage of the *Marigold* that the floating bodies weren't constantly bumping against the hull.

"You can't go by yourself." Rowan crossed his arms. He looked like he had a fierce headache coming on. Whether that was due to her stubbornness or whatever the magical eye was showing him, Zanta couldn't say. "What if the *Lonesome* is lurking around somewhere? Or hostile Selkies?"

Fair. Zanta knew she was being irrational, but the tug in her gut told her this was something she had to do alone. If Nia was there, she might be frightened. If Nia wasn't there...Zanta needed to be able to deal with it alone.

"If Nia's there, I don't want to scare her with a bunch of pirates she doesn't know," Zanta argued. Rowan grimaced and the Demon remained silent. He probably didn't care one way or the other whether Zanta found Nia or got attacked by whomever might be lurking on the island.

"Here, then." Logan handed her a pressed paper tube that smelled vaguely sulfuric. "Use this flare if you need us." Zanta nodded and tucked it into the bag where she'd also stowed the journal and a set of clothes for Nia.

"Logan, you can't just—" But Zanta didn't hear the rest of Rowan's scolding. She swung her leg over the rail and climbed down to the waiting rowboat.

SMALL, choppy waves slapped the sides of the boat as Zanta rowed through the cove. Distant thunder rumbled behind her, and she inhaled the scent of salt through her nose, hoping the Storm Ring wouldn't deign to reach this far into the interior of the Sleeping Isles again. What manner of thing was the Storm Ring? It couldn't be a natural phenomenon. Had the Selkies created it somehow to protect themselves?

Zanta's arms began to ache as the *Kraken* receded, and she was alone in the cove. Small bits of debris bumped against the sides of the boat, and she hoped no bodies floated nearby. She knew Rowan and the others would be watching her, and felt slightly guilty that she'd denied Henri the opportunity to come with her and search for his sister. But this was something she had to do alone, so she put her head down and rowed.

She didn't dare glance to shore till she was almost there. Zanta twisted in her seat and scanned the pebbly beach, empty but for the waterlogged corpse of a mercenary and bits of the *Marigold*. The little dwelling in the cliff hung higher than a person's height, whatever stairs or ladder used to reach it now washed away or collapsed. Had Nia come here and found a way up to her old home? Had she even made it here at all?

The waves grew choppier the closer Zanta rowed to shore, becoming white and foamy and coughing up all manner of flotsam to roll against the white pebbles. There, under an overhanging bit of rock, the barest flash of orange.

Zanta was out of the boat in a second, splashing down into waist high water and dragging the boat only far enough to beach it in the shallows. She ran, heart in her throat, salt spray splashing around her legs as she scrambled up the beach, pebbles shifting beneath her water-filled boots. It had to be Nia, it had to. Please.

"Nia!" Zanta slipped and almost fell on the pebbles but kept going. Whatever was under the overhang didn't move or respond to her call.

Salt air burned down Zanta's throat, already tight with tears. She neared the depression in the rock, and the orange smudge solidified into a spill of hair like a flame. Nia lay on her side, facing away from the beach. Naked but for the gray pelt which draped over her body and cast a shimmer like water on the rock above.

"Nia!" *Gods, please let her be alive. Please let her not be drowned like all the others.*

Nia stirred, and sat up just as Zanta skidded to her knees and threw her arms around Nia's warm, bare shoulders. Nia yelped and shoved her away. Zanta sprawled on the pebbles.

"Z-Zanta?" Nia's voice was tentative, green eyes so wide they seemed to contain the entirety of the restless sea. "Oh gods, it's you!"

"It's me."

Nia grabbed her hand and held it to her cheek. "I...How did you find me?"

All Zanta wanted to do was drown in her warmth. She pressed

her hand tighter to Nia's cheek instead, savoring the real living person beneath her palm.

"I read Stroud's journal. I'm sorry. It was the only way to find you."

Nia's lips parted around silence. Zanta's other hand fisted in the cold pebbles beneath their knees. She wanted to kiss her, fill that wordless mouth with confessions. But she held back, unsure if she was wanted here.

Nia turned her face away, leaving Zanta's palm cold. "You know everything, then." She clutched the pelt tighter around herself like armor.

"I know enough, Nia—"

"I'm sorry," Nia blurted, voice quavering. Zanta's heart sank. This was it. Nia was going to tell her she wasn't going back. "I should've told you earlier. I should've stopped you from sailing into the Storm Ring. If I had, maybe Sabriye and the others would still be alive. We're being hunted because of me." The last word came out roughened, as if she had to force it past her teeth.

"You could've told me." Zanta's voice was gentle, not accusing, but Nia shrank further into herself.

"I was afraid that..." Her voice broke.

"Why did you run? Once you had your pelt back, why did you leave?"

"I was finally free."

"I wouldn't have hurt you, Nia. I wouldn't have kept you like Stroud did." She must know that. She must understand how deeply Zanta cared for her. But how could she, when Zanta had kept her feelings so closely guarded all this time?

Nia bit her lip, still unable to meet Zanta's eyes. "I didn't know that at the beginning and then...we started sleeping together, so..." She trailed off and realization struck Zanta like lightning.

Besides, you have something I want. That's what Nia had said to her that first day.

Zanta's heart tossed in the waves, as cracked and broken as the wreckage. No. It couldn't be. Zanta knew they'd agreed not to get feelings involved, but this...

"Did you only sleep with me to gain access to your pelt?" She barely got the words out around what felt like a shard of the *Marigold*'s wreck in her throat.

Nia's head snapped up, rivulets of fiery hair blowing across her face. Her wide green eyes finally met Zanta's. "Please don't hate me."

She couldn't. Even when her heart was breaking against the rocks, she couldn't hate Nia, because she understood. The pelt was a vital part of her, and if it were Zanta, she'd have done anything to get it back. Zanta's hand snapped out, dragging Nia to her over the slippery pebbles and wrapping her into a tight embrace. Nia's body shuddered, but she let go of her pelt and threaded her arms around Zanta's waist in return.

Fuck. Could she hear the way Zanta's heart was cracking apart?

"I understand." She staved off a sob by burying her face in Nia's hair. Nia was alive, and that's all that mattered. Zanta's feelings didn't come into the equation. She could be content with this.

Nia pulled away, and Zanta's stomach clenched in panic before she realized Nia's hands were still on her, smoothing away Zanta's tears. "Don't cry. I'm sorry. I tricked you, and then I let my feelings get in the way of your crew's safety. I was afraid I'd lose you, that you'd hate me."

Zanta's brow furrowed. "Lose me?"

Nia nodded, not meeting her eyes again. "I'm sorry. I know we decided it was just sex but...I let myself fall for you. I didn't want it to end, even if you were just using me to feel close to Emilie again."

Zanta's mouth opened, but no sound came out. Nia had feelings for her? Nia wanted more than their arrangement?

She surged forward and kissed Nia's worry-bitten lips, a delirious smile on her face. A small noise escaped Nia, but she surrendered to the kiss readily, her hands fisting in Zanta's soaked shirt like she would float away.

"You're not a replacement for her," Zanta said breathlessly when they broke apart. "I care for you all on your own. You're joyful and beautiful, and I never want to let you go again. I want to know everything about you. I never want to wake up without you in my arms."

A disbelieving laugh bubbled up from Nia's lips, and she kissed Zanta until the sound of waves and thunder faded into the background and Zanta's head spun with giddiness.

Nia loved her back.

Zanta lay her back against the pebble beach in their little alcove away from prying eyes, bare but for the shimmering Selkie pelt beneath her, and kissed down her neck, collarbone, between her lovely freckled breasts until she reached the junction of Nia's thighs. They parted easily with a sigh, and a deeper exhale when Zanta's tongue found her sweet center. Overripe peaches and sweet sea air. Zanta tasted her until she trembled. Pleasure like thunder shaking her apart.

When they were done, Zanta took Nia's head into her lap, Nia still bare but for the pelt, and Zanta still fully dressed in waterlogged coat, boots, weapons. She combed her fingers through the flames of Nia's hair, and asked her.

Nia told her everything, truth after truth spilling out like they'd been living at the tip of her tongue ready to leap the whole time. She told her about Stroud and her mother. About Stroud absconding with her mother's pelt, and how over the next decade her mother slowly withered away without that vital piece of her. How the other Selkies shunned them for being tainted with outsider blood.

She told how Stroud returned to their side because the pelt had begun to dull, and witnessed her mother's last breaths. How he'd taken Nia and the green stone eye and brought them into the human world with him. He'd given Nia her dead mother's pelt for comfort, but kept Nia's under lock and key so she couldn't run. She only got to take on her Selkie form when he needed her to dive down and retrieve treasure for him, and even then, he'd cut a small piece to keep with him so she could never escape.

She told Zanta everything Zanta had read in the journal and more, without the screen of Stroud's delusions of grandeur. Zanta thought Nia must hate Stroud, her own flesh and blood, her own father, for the things he'd done, but Nia said it all with such wistful sadness, as if she didn't know whether it had happened to her or someone else. As if she didn't know whether to love or hate the father who had been both caretaker and jailer.

"It's been ten years since I got up the courage to escape without my pelt, and I've been waiting to die since." She smiled sadly, leaning into Zanta's caressing hand. "I guess it's because I'm half human that I've lasted this long."

"But you're okay now that you have it back, right?" She couldn't lose Nia again. Couldn't bear to watch her slowly wither away like stone beneath waves.

"I think so. There hasn't been a Selkie and human child since before the Storm Ring. I'm not sure how things would affect me."

Zanta let out a relieved breath and they lapsed into comfortable silence, until Zanta asked, "Are you coming back with me?"

Nia gazed at the ornate little dwelling in the cliff where she must've grown up till Stroud kidnapped her. Despite its run-down state, it was pretty. The front held three arched windows, with intricate lattice carved right from the stone to allow air and light, but block out the worst of the sea. To the side, a small arched doorway led into the dark interior. "I came to this beach because I wanted to see my home again. But there's nothing for me here. My mother is gone, and my own people didn't want me even when I was an innocent child. I doubt I'd be welcome now that I've grown up in the outside world." The wistfulness clung to her voice like the sigh of the wind against the jagged cliffs.

"Do you want to try?" She could repair the *Monsoon* and take Nia anywhere she wanted to go. As long as they were together.

Nia shook her head and sat up. "If the *Lonesome* is still out there, we need to do something about it. Or at least warn the Selkies about what's coming, but..." She took a deep breath, then exhaled slowly like she was feeding it to the wind. "It's best they never know I was here."

They finally picked themselves up off the beach. The others would be getting restless by now, wondering where Zanta was. She handed Nia the bundle of clothes—the striped trousers and a shirt, not a dress—that she'd packed. Nia grimaced as she pulled the ugly striped trousers out.

"I can't go back in my natural Selkie state?" Nia teased. "I'll race you to the ship."

"Like you said before, that ass might cause a riot. Then where would we be?"

CHAPTER 43

UNKNOWN DATE, 1668

Henri and Logan practically bowled Nia over with hugs as soon as she stepped foot on the *Kraken*. Henri dropping a kiss on the top of Nia's head and Logan smooching her cheek. She'd probably have to tell Logan it was over between them, now that she and Zanta were together. But that was a conversation for another time. The giddiness of her feelings being returned was enough to carry her through anything. Her sorrow over never being able to truly return home, guilt over the deaths of Zanta's crew and the wreck of the *Monsoon*. A slight regret that she'd likely never have the chance to get double-teamed by Logan and John again. None of it could touch this euphoria.

Until the Demon's shadow darkened her path.

"We have much to discuss." His manner was inscrutable, deep voice echoing in her brain so much it ached behind her eyes. She'd wondered about him in the days she'd spent swimming home in her Selkie form. The idea of him creeping through the watery shadows like a ghost haunted her. So ominous that a few times she'd become convinced he'd transformed into whatever true form lurked beneath that flawless skin, and was coming to devour her whole or drag her into the depths.

Nia took an involuntary step back, bumping into Henri's chest. She opened her mouth but couldn't speak, as if he'd stolen her voice and all her sense.

Zanta's hand found hers. "She's tired. I'll take her to rest." She made to tug Nia away.

"We should really talk strategy," Captain Rowan cut in, placating. Truth winking in his eye socket, somehow soothing Nia's nerves. Nia's mother had always been vague about how the stone worked. After Nia's father left, the Selkies had stripped her mother of her role as a seer's apprentice. But the old seer had died before a new one could be found and trained. Gwenyth had been allowed to stay on Seer's Isle only because no other place wanted her, but she was banned from ever using Truth for herself, or imparting any wisdom she had learned as an apprentice.

Did the eye show the viewer the truths of the world? Or make it so they could never lie?

"I promise we'll make it short. But I'm sure all of us would rather get out of here before the Selkies or Shaw find us, and like it or not, Nia is part of that conversation."

Zanta shot Nia a sympathetic look. "Fine, let's talk."

They met in the Demon's private chambers. Unease threaded through Nia's nerves, but she had Zanta at her side, and Henri and Logan too. They would protect her from whatever the Demon was.

"We should anchor here for the night," Captain Rowan began, plopping into the seat at the head of the table, and waving the Demon to the right-hand seat when he glowered at him. The rest of them settled in around the table. "We want to get out of here as soon as possible. The *Marigold* is clearly lost with all hands, but the *Lonesome* and Shaw could still be out there. In the morning we should leave and find the *Siren* again, before Shaw manages to find us."

"What about the Selkies?" Henri piped up. "We can't leave Shaw here to do whatever he wants to them."

"That's true. We came all this way to warn Zanta, but now more lives are at stake," Logan agreed. Nia graced them both with a grateful smile.

"The Selkies are more than capable of—" Captain Rowan's hand on the Demon's arm silenced him.

"In that case, our two options are to warn the Selkies, which will be met with hostility. Or take the fight to Shaw, wherever he may be." Captain Rowan turned to skewer Zanta and Nia with his piercing blue and green gaze. "What do you think?"

Zanta seemed to be waiting for Nia to say something. When she didn't, Zanta said, "We have that woman from the *Marigold* in the brig. We need to question her before we do anything else."

Captain Rowan glanced at the Demon, and received a slight nod. "Agreed, then. We'll find out what Baird knows and go from there."

"There is still the small matter of the Storm Ring," the Demon cut in. His black eyes found the bundle of pelt in Nia's arms, and she shivered. "If what the journal says is true, we need a Selkie pelt, freely given, to cross back through." He leaned toward her over the table. "The Selkie is returning with us, I assume?"

"Lay off the intimidation," Zanta hissed, at the same time Henri said, "Don't speak to her like that." A silence settled over the table. The Demon sat back in his chair.

"My apologies. The question still stands. Are you returning with us, dear Selkie? Will you lend us your power, and save us all from our inevitable watery graves?"

Nia still couldn't speak. She felt like she'd swallowed lungfuls of seawater. A Selkie pelt could protect them in the storm? Was that why her father had taken her mother's pelt, and later, her?

Zanta placed a reassuring hand between her shoulder blades, and Nia managed to squeak out a, "Yes, I'm coming back with you."

Captain Rowan graced her with an encouraging smile. "Only one problem remains. If we're able to get the *Siren* unstuck, we'll have two ships, and only one Selkie to stave off the storms." He cocked his head at her. "Does the freely given pelt calm the storms, or only extend protection over the vessel that carries it?"

They were all looking at her now. Expecting answers she didn't know. Zanta's hand rubbed circles on her back, and Logan gave her a nod.

"I-I don't know."

"It's no matter." The Demon took up Captain Rowan's hand, and placed a gallant kiss on his fingers. "The *Siren* shall carry our Selkie savior. Me and mine shall weather the storms on our own. In the meantime, it's obvious that Shaw will want the pelt if he finds us, or vice versa. We should secure it somewhere for safekeeping."

Nia sprang to her feet, ready to flee. She wouldn't give up her pelt again. Not to anyone. Least of all to this...this *evil creature*.

"Absolutely not," Zanta growled.

"If Shaw finds us, he will know instantly Nia is a Selkie if she has it on her. And he will use the pelt to control her," the Demon said. "It would be better in a safe hiding place."

"We're leaving." Zanta grabbed Nia by the arm and led her out into the hall, and Captain Rowan hurried after them.

"Zanta." She whirled on him, dragging Nia with her, and the captain held up his hands placatingly. "I'm not here to argue his case. I came to talk to you about what we should do with the *Monsoon*."

Zanta nodded wearily, then planted a kiss on Nia's cheek. "Let Henri or Logan take you to find some food, hm?" Nia nodded, and Zanta disappeared with the other captain, leaving Nia unsure of what to do. She was exhausted, having swum for days to reach Seer's Isle, only to find nothing and no one there. She didn't know what she'd expected, to be honest. But the Seer's Isle being abandoned was just another in a long line of worries vying for her attention.

She leaned against the wall of the corridor and closed her eyes, breathing slowly and deliberately, trying to get her emotions under control.

A few breaths later, she choked on a sinister feeling. The Demon caught her by the arm as she turned to flee, grip so tight she thought her bones might crumble to dust. She froze immediately, as his evil aura enveloped her. So oppressive she felt like she'd swum too deep. He dragged her into the nearest room, and clamped his other hand over her mouth as she heard Henri and Logan pass by outside.

"We must hide your pelt," he growled in the language of the Selkies, removing his silencing hand. It took Nia an agonizing moment to parse through what he had said. She'd almost forgotten the language of her people after so long away with no other Selkie to speak to. How did this awful creature know it? It sounded foul from his mouth when the last voice that had spoken it to her was her mother's. "Like Rowan said, we don't know if the mercenaries survived the storms. We can't let them have it."

She remained frozen, expecting him to take her pelt from her, but he didn't, the stipulation of *freely given* hanging over their heads.

"It will be safe with me," Nia managed to say, the language of her childhood feeling foreign on her unpracticed tongue. Was that a flicker of movement in the shadows behind him? Or were her eyes playing tricks?

"It won't; you know it won't. Don't you want to protect your people?"

Her heart hammered. "What do you know about my people?" she hissed.

He didn't answer. Instead he said, "You know what I am."

"I don't," she protested. He was the kind of monster inked on maps to warn people to stay away. The kind of monster Selkie mothers warned their children about before their first ventures out to sea. No, she didn't know exactly what he was, but she knew he was something dark and unknowable in human form.

The Demon smirked. "You know enough to know I'm the most dangerous person on this ship—"

"All the more reason not to let you have it!" Nia snapped.

"All the more reason to let me *protect you*." The Demon shook her, her back thumping against the wall. She clutched her pelt tighter, unable to keep from cowering. He sighed and released her, but didn't move away. "You don't trust me, nor should you, but you trust Logan and your brother and Splinter Zanta, do you not?" She nodded warily. "*They* all trust Captain Rowan. He is a good man. I am not doing any of this out of the goodness of my heart, but because *he* desires it. I will defend you and your pelt because *he* wishes me to. And he would never breach his friends' trust, nor take away your freedom."

"I..." Nia clutched her pelt tighter. It was a pretty speech for a monster. But even if this man had just been a man, he was still the most brutal pirate out there. He couldn't be trusted.

The Demon leaned into her line of sight, and Nia would've called his expression earnest if she believed him capable of such an emotion.

"You don't want to be controlled again," he said in a low voice. "You don't want to lose yourself again. I can understand that. I've lost myself more times than I can count. You look at us, and see the same type of people as your father. But we've come all this way, fought and braved the storms to warn your beloved captain. We won't turn our backs now that the danger is near."

She finally met his eyes, searching for something human in them, something she could trust. And found only darkness.

When she said nothing, he took half a step back. "I give you my word I will return it to you before we reach the Storm Ring."

And somehow, she believed him.

CHAPTER 44

UNKNOWN DATE, 1668

The pelt was soft and cool beneath Yves's hands, and he had to force the demon part of him to let it go, to tuck it in the safe behind the painting in his parlor. He ran his fingers over it one last time, the human part of him feeling something akin to guilt as he caressed the skin of a creature that was not Rowan. It shimmered over his fingers and the walls of the safe. More mesmerizing than gold or jewels. It was just as the demon remembered from days long past.

The demon's thoughts dominated their consciousness more and more. It remembered more than Yves's human mind could hold. It had dredged up a language they'd never spoken with this human mouth before. That same mouth salivated at the thought of devouring this Selkie, as it had so many of her ancestors. They hadn't tasted Selkie flesh in so long, not since they had ruled beneath the sea. Not since the betrayal.

The door clicking open forced the demon's thoughts deeper into the recesses of their mind, and Yves found Rowan at his side.

"Yves..." His voice was stern. "Please tell me you convinced Nia. Please tell me you did not *steal* her pelt." But he wasn't looking at Yves; his eyes were fixed on the pelt's shimmer. He reached out as if to caress it, but grabbed Yves's hand and drew it away instead.

"I convinced her," Yves answered truthfully. For once he'd been able to speak earnestly with someone other than Rowan, though he'd fought the demon's instincts the whole way. More than ever, the demon pressed on the inside of his skin like it was trying to get out. He knew the Selkie was terrified of him, some ancient animal instinct steering her on the path to survival.

He locked the safe and replaced the painting over it. Some frivolous seascape, but it was better than the portrait of the late commander of this ship. Now that he and Rowan were reunited, he'd have to convince the painter to take up their portrait again. Yves tucked the key into its hidden compartment behind the carvings adorning the mantel. A place only he and Rowan and the first mates knew.

"You will give it back," Rowan said, half order, half hopeful.

Yves reached out to comb his fingers through Rowan's fine blond hair. "As you command."

Rowan's eye roll was interrupted by a knock on the door. At their call, the cook from the *Monsoon* entered, carrying a tray of food.

"Was told you eat privately," he said, placing the food on the dining table.

Rowan smiled as the scent of warm spices wafted through the room. "It smells divine. If you ever tire of Zanta's crew, we'd be happy to have you on the *Siren*."

"Ah, well. I usually don't say no to a handsome face, but I owe a great deal of loyalty to my captain. So I'll have to turn you down."

Yves's jealousy flared like a ravenous beast, barely feeling the placating hand Rowan rested on his wrist without even looking. Rowan squeezed once, as if to say *be good*, then crossed the room toward the food. "You haven't been cooking for the whole crew all by yourself, right? You have help?" Yves's own cooks were quite good, but nothing compared to this man's art.

The cook paused on the threshold. "The *Kraken*'s cooks have been quite accommodating, and I enlisted another young man to assist as well. Would be a handsome fellow if his attitude wasn't so sour. Now, if you'll excuse me, I have to get back."

Rowan nodded, and the cook slipped out the door.

The two captains ate and drank their fill, and soon, no morsel was left on the plates. Yves stood from the table and drew Rowan over to the armchairs in front of the unlit fireplace, above which hung the boring seascape and its concealed treasure. He lowered himself into one of the chairs and drew Rowan into his lap. Before Rowan could protest, Yves tugged the tie from his hair, letting the white-gold strands fall around his ears.

"Undressing me already?" Rowan mumbled, amused.

Yves combed his long fingers through his husband's hair. "I just like touching you."

Rowan winced as Yves's fingers caught a knot. He moved on from combing to rubbing small circles into the base of Rowan's skull with his thumb. He'd observed how stiffly Rowan was moving and wanted to soothe his aches away.

"You realize we still have to interrogate Colonel Baird tonight," Rowan grumbled.

"No use being tense before you even enter the room. Let me take care of you for an hour, at least," Yves cajoled him. "Take your shirt off."

"I hardly think it's time for..." Rowan's words trailed off when faced with an elegantly arched brow. He rolled his eye and lifted the shirt up around his shoulders to expose his back. "This is as much as you're getting, you heathen."

"Turn."

Sighing, Rowan settled with his back to Yves's chest, then let out a moan as Yves's fingers pinched the muscle between his shoulder and neck. Since losing his eye, Rowan had a bad habit of tilting his head to regain equilibrium, and Yves knew it wreaked havoc on his neck and shoulders.

Yves kept his fingers moving, digging knots out of his husband's muscles, and relishing the half-agonized moans each stroke elicited from that delicious mouth. Later. He had to at least wait to seduce till Rowan was no longer suffering. The wound in Yves's arm twinged with each movement, but it only served as a reminder day after day that he needed to be better, for Rowan.

"You shouldn't let it get this bad," Yves complained after a particularly stubborn knot broke under his thumbs.

Rowan glanced at Yves out of the corner of his eye. "As if you'd allow anyone else to touch me like this."

Yves's thumbs pressed another bone-tingling line up the back of his neck, releasing a moan that went straight to Yves's cock. "Not if you moan like that," Yves whispered in his ear.

"Well, then there's no help for it."

A few more strokes drew pleased noises from Rowan's lips. "Perhaps Robin," Yves mused. "He is a doctor, and afraid enough not to cross me."

Rowan snorted. "Yeah, I'll let you pitch that idea. 'Please rub my husband while I'm away.' I'm sure that will go over well."

Yves chuckled. With one last stroke of his thumbs, he left off massaging and wrapped his arms around Rowan's chest instead, leaning in to kiss the side of his neck.

It didn't elicit the reaction Yves had been hoping for. Instead, Rowan yawned.

"Tired, darling? Shall we retire to the bedroom? The interrogation can wait until tomorrow, I'm sure." It was barely dark out, yet exhaustion crawled through Yves's blood as well.

Rowan didn't answer. Yves tilted Rowan's face toward him with gentle fingers, and found him already deeply asleep. Curious, even in exhaustion Rowan didn't usually fall asleep right away. But it had been an eventful few days, they could pick up where they'd left off in the morning when they were well rested.

He lifted Rowan into his arms, and managed a few steps. But his limbs felt sluggish. He couldn't be that tired, could he? Another step. He stumbled over the edge of the rug and flopped heavily into the other armchair.

Something is wrong. The demon's voice followed him into the deep waters of sleep.

THE STARS SEEMED DIFFERENT HERE. Fox couldn't put his finger on why. He tilted his head back as the *Kraken*'s deck lanterns went out one by one. Everyone but the watchmen had retired below hours ago, and they didn't want to draw the attention of whomever, or whatever, might be lurking in these unknown waters. Fox wasn't the superstitious sort, except when it suited him, but between the Storm Ring, the rock spires, and the mist that crept out of nowhere, even he had to admit there was an eerie feel about the place.

Not to mention that woman Nia was, in fact, a Selkie. And Rowan apparently had a magical eye.

They'd taken refuge outside a cove next to the tiny island they'd found Nia on. A concave cliff with a small house carved into its light stone created the cove, but formations of those rock spires dotted the entrance and the sea as far as the eye could see. A few of the Talvan and Nanadie crew members had been muttering about some legend about gates to the underworld since they'd emerged on the other side of the storms. The Demon had looked faintly amused by that, which to be honest made the whole thing more eerie. But at the end of the day, the spot was as defensible a position as they were likely to find.

The last of the lanterns went out, the other watchmen—a few from each crew—whispering to each other nervously at their posts. Fox yawned, waiting for his eyes to adjust to the pitch blackness. The stars really were strange here. They weren't brighter or rearranged or anything so obvious as that. But more...significant? Like those familiar little specks of light could reach down and change the course of his life if they wanted.

He didn't know whether to be unsettled or comforted.

"If you can hear me, get us out of this safe. Get me back to Gaël," Fox murmured quietly.

"Fox?"

At first, Fox couldn't tell who it was in the dark, till he spotted Robin's mop of blond hair and the canvas apron tied around his waist. His face was shadowed, but he held a cup and bowl in his hands.

"You didn't eat dinner." His voice sounded strange, but Fox couldn't figure out why. Maybe it was the spooky atmosphere. Everything felt strange here.

"I'm not hungry," Fox mumbled. He couldn't see the other watchmen in the dark, but their whispers had all gone quiet.

"Still, you should eat." Robin held the bowl and cup out, piled high with a mishmash of provisions from the three combined ships. Fox took them, and the faceless Robin nodded.

He retreated before Fox could say goodnight. Odd, but Robin had been so exhausted lately, taking care of everyone. He was probably eager to fall into bed.

The food wasn't hot anymore, but Fox tucked in anyway, the unfamiliar spices tickling his tongue. That cook from the *Monsoon* was a magician. Fox had only intended to take a few bites, but soon enough he was shoving the last spoonful into his mouth and washing it down with watered-down ale. He patted his tummy, satisfied, thinking it felt a bit squishier than usual now that he wasn't getting regular exercise by pouncing on Gaël at every opportunity.

Darkness tucked close around him, a warm blanket to lull him.

He wanted to sleep. He was as exhausted as the rest of them. But he'd volunteered for watch instead. With Rowan and the Demon sharing a bed again, Fox hadn't been sleeping well, even when he climbed in with Logan or created a blanket cocoon for himself right between Henri and Robin, like he was their kid. Sitting up here with nothing to do but think wasn't much better than anxiously tossing and turning, but at least he had a purpose. At least he could look at the stars.

Time slipped away, as it always did on watch. Until he couldn't tell whether it had been fifteen minutes or several hours. His eyelids grew heavy, and he lay back against the base of the bowsprit, intent on figuring out the stars to keep himself awake. After a while, he heard movement in the dark, no doubt another watchman shifting positions. The time between blinks lengthened. The stars seemed to be dancing, so close it was like they had alighted on the crow's nest and in the water, coming to dance with him.

CHAPTER 45

UNKNOWN DATE, 1668

A cold icicle of metal at her throat and hard wood under her sore back roused Zanta from the deepest sleep of her life. Weak morning light slipped its fingers into her eyes, blinding. She winced, trying to sit up and finding her hands bound in rope. She huffed and fell back to the deck as the icicle pressed tighter to her skin, trying to get her bearings. Last night she and Nia had turned in early after dinner, cuddled up on the little pallet that smelled faintly musty. She'd been exhausted, slipping quickly into the dark embrace of sleep before Nia had even finished saying good night.

Nia. Where was she? Zanta sat bolt upright, heedless of the icy edge of the saber nicking her skin.

"Watch it," the saber-holder growled. Crashing and shouting rang somewhere in the distance, muffled by the ship's thick boards, and Zanta shook her head frantically, trying to dislodge the strange grogginess that clung to her like seaweed.

Had Rowan and the Demon betrayed her? Her eyes focused on an unfamiliar face at the other end of the saber. He didn't look like a pirate. It had to be Shaw's men. The *Lonesome* must have survived the storm and found them.

Zanta surged to her feet, heedless of the threat as the sword nicked her collarbone. Her limbs felt like bags of sand, but she managed to make it two steps across the *Kraken*'s main deck before two men tackled her, smashing her shoulder against the unforgiving wood. More crashes sounded from below. The *Kraken*'s main deck swarmed with mercenaries, and she managed to kick one of them in the gut before another pushed her head against the deck with his knee. In her narrowed line of sight, a door banged open and Laurent dashed through, only to be caught by mercenaries and hauled back through it. But not before he spotted her. His desperate cry of "Captain!" stirring more shouts from below.

Her crew was alive, at least. Their throats hadn't been slashed in their sleep. She hauled in a deep breath through her nose, refusing to close her eyes, as she knew the ghosts of Sabriye and her dead crew members lingered in the darkness behind her eyelids.

"Zanta..." Nia's voice somewhere out of her line of sight made Zanta's body go rigid.

"Behave and we won't hurt her," the man trapping Zanta said, and she managed the barest nod. The knee lifted away from her face, and they hauled her unsteadily to her feet.

"Let me go!" Nia struggled against her bonds near the port rail. One of the mercenaries smacked her.

A surge of energy tightened Zanta's heavy limbs, and she lurched forward, only to be caught again. It was no use. Zanta tried to get her bearings once again, hoping she could find a way out of this.

The rock spires cast stripes of shadow and light over the perpetual mist. The *Kraken's Fury* still sat at anchor at the mouth of the cove, the wreckage of the *Marigold* clinging brokenly to the rocks. Masts from what she assumed was the *Lonesome* jutted from somewhere below the *Kraken*'s port rail. The ship was shorter, smaller. But they had the *Kraken* pinned with them on one side and shallow waters on the other. Even if the pirates managed to regain control of the *Kraken*, they'd have to fight their way out.

The lookouts were nowhere to be seen. Were they with the rest of the crew below? Or had something more nefarious happened? Some of the fight went out of her as she realized how truly fucked they were.

Before her mind could register that fact more deeply, the quarterdeck door banged open, emitting more mercenaries. Two escorted a struggling Rowan, his chin bruised and hands bound in rope. Then four more dragged the Demon into the light, unconscious body bound hand and foot in iron shackles and a deep bruise already forming at his temple like one of them had cracked him across the head with a blunt object. Both of them were fully dressed, as if they'd fallen asleep unexpectedly, and Rowan seemed just as sluggish as Zanta felt, though based on the bruising, they'd both put up a hell of a fight. What was wrong with them all? Was it some magic of the Seer's Isle that kept them in thrall? Or something more intentional?

The mercs dragged them to the rail, dumping the unconscious Demon at the feet of a man who could only be Warrick Shaw. Rowan flinched as the Demon's skull struck the deck. But Zanta had eyes only for the enemy.

He was well dressed in the Kefryean style, a light shirt beneath a heavily embroidered vest, and a matching pleated Kefryean skirt that reached the tops of his boots mid-calf. He couldn't have yet reached thirty, but the bald dome of his head glistened with sweat over a luxuriously curled brown mustache. He certainly looked the part of a former nobleman turned mercenary. Zanta had to assume he'd been handsomer back when Rowan had slept with him.

But there was something else. Zanta squinted at him, the light hurting her tired eyes. Where had she seen him before?

"Ah, you're all here," Shaw said nonchalantly, as if they had arrived late to a dinner party instead of being dragged from their beds and tied up. Zanta thought his manner a bit too easy. Sure, Shaw and his men had managed to subdue three of the most infamous pirate captains and their crews without bloodshed—Zanta was beginning to think they'd been drugged—but pirates were nothing if not unpredictable. Especially when one of the captives was the Deep Water Demon, even unconscious. Zanta wouldn't have been so calm if she was in Shaw's shoes.

"What do you want?" Rowan growled. His face twisted into a disgusted grimace, the crossed scars puckering his cheek. Nia shifted closer to Zanta, away from the others. Zanta wished she could put her arm around her.

Shaw ignored the question. His eyes swept over them again. "Where's little Logan? I assume he became your first mate after me? Get him." This last was directed toward one of his men. Then, to another, "Wake the Demon up."

That seemed like a bad idea to Zanta, but who was she to stop an enemy from making a mistake?

The merc in question swallowed nervously, and made a sign

against evil, running his middle finger down the bridge of his nose. Then he reeled back and kicked the Demon right in the gut.

Rowan jerked against his restraints as his husband doubled up, coughing. But when he opened his black eyes, a chill engulfed the ship. His gaze speared Shaw directly, and he maintained eye contact as he slowly rose to his knees, but no further, his progress arrested by a sword tip at his throat.

The first merc returned, pulling Logan by the arm. The skin around the first mate's eye shone purple beneath the mop of gold hair. When he saw Shaw, a strangely amused expression passed over his face. Building in intensity until his lips were pressed together to hold something in. By the time they deposited him next to Rowan, his shoulders were shaking, and he couldn't hold it in anymore. He burst out laughing. It rang out over the water for a few moments before he visibly forced it down.

"Sorry, sorry," he gasped. "It's just..." Another short fit of near-hysterical giggles. He leaned against Rowan's shoulder. "He's bald now."

Rowan snorted. Shaw's face, or rather his whole head, turned red.

"You are not so unmarred yourself," Shaw growled. "Tell me, was it your captain's mistakes that cost you your hand? Or was it your own naiveté?"

That silenced the last snickers of laughter. Their expressions sobered. Shaw stepped forward, grabbing Rowan's jaw and turning his face to show the scarred side. The Demon hissed, lurching to his feet, chains rattling, only to be dragged back and subdued by four men. Rowan cut him a glance, and Zanta had the feeling that it was only Rowan's silent communication that placated him for now.

"Tsk, you used to be so pretty," Shaw said to Rowan. "See what a life of crime gets you?"

"As if it's much better to betray your country to the empire," Rowan scoffed, jerking out of Shaw's grasp. "Besides, you didn't seem so concerned about my pretty face when you tried to have me killed."

"Well, we won't have a repeat performance of that if you cooperate. This doesn't have to get ugly."

"Too late, you're already here," Logan mumbled.

Shaw's expression shuttered. "Tie him to the rail." Two mercenaries jumped to do his bidding, dragging Logan over, and lashing his arms to the rail so that he sat on deck with his arms straight out to each side. They didn't bother to divest him of his wooden hand. Logan jerked against the ropes, then frantically began bending the wooden fingers against the rail until only his middle finger remained upright. He mirrored the gesture with his real hand, staring Shaw down.

Shaw nodded at the mercenary, who punched Logan straight in the face. They were getting to him, his bald head still flushed as red as could be.

"It's clear to me you'll continue to be obstinate," Shaw said. His gaze raked over Rowan's face, then moved on to the Demon, then Zanta, with Nia huddling at her side.

"You haven't even told us what you want," Zanta chimed in, trying to keep her voice neutral. They all knew what he wanted, or at least they had a pretty good hunch. But they had to play dumb. Deny everything. If Shaw got his hands on what he was looking for, it wouldn't be good for Nia or her people.

"You're the girl who killed Silver Stroud," Shaw said, as if murdering her mentor, and the subsequent years of successful pirating, were all a girlish fluke.

"I am Splinter Zanta, yeah."

"Are you in possession of Stroud's treasure?"

She raised her chin. "No."

"I see." He signaled to someone on the *Lonesome*, who dragged a group of trussed up captives onto the quarterdeck. Instantly recognizable as last night's watchmen.

"Fox!" Rowan shouted, jerking against the mercenaries holding him. Logan struggled too, though he couldn't crane his head back enough to see the captives.

Shaw's eyebrows rose. All seven captives, three from the *Kraken*, and two each from the *Monsoon* and *Siren*, including that little spitfire Fox, were intricately tied and gagged. The thin rope secured their arms behind their backs, then looped over their shoulders and twisted down their sternums almost like harnesses. How had all of them been captured without raising the alarm? Zanta didn't know about the *Kraken* crew members, but she trusted the men she'd set on watch, and she knew Rowan and Fox were close. They wouldn't have betrayed their captains.

"You see, I have the upper hand in all aspects," Shaw said coolly.

"Your crews are in custody. I have all the hostages I need to compel you to give me what I want. I still know you, Rowan. I know you care for your crew. Now, here's how it's going to go. You're going to give me Silver Stroud's treasure, or I'm going to drop your people off the side one by one until you do."

Zanta sucked in a breath as one of the men from the *Kraken* was dragged to the rail. Rowan glanced at the Demon out of the corner of his eye. The Demon remained unmoved. Not even a hint of concern for the fact that one of his men was about to die. The man, to his credit, just closed his eyes and took a deep breath.

How could the Demon—totally devoid of human emotion as far as Zanta could tell—inspire enough loyalty that a man would drown for him without a sound of protest?

Nia's shoulder touched Zanta's. She was shaking, her eyes trained on the man who was about to die for the sake of her secrets.

A flicker of surprise passed over Shaw's face. "I've never known you to be cold, Rowan."

"You've never known me," Rowan replied flatly. "If you have qualms about killing a man in cold blood, don't do it. You could walk away right now."

Shaw threw his head back and laughed. The sound bounced off the pillars of stone surrounding them. Ominous even in the growing daylight.

"Oh, but I do know you." Shaw ran his hand over Rowan's hair. The Demon tensed, but Rowan waved him off. "I know how stubborn you are. Well, fine. Maybe the ladies will be easier to break." He gestured to the mercenaries. "Take her."

Before his words could penetrate Zanta's skull, they ripped Nia from her side. The hostages on the *Lonesome* were dragged back out of sight.

"No!" Too late, Zanta realized her visceral reaction played right into Shaw's hands. This is what he'd been looking for, a sign of connection. A reaction that would show Nia was a better hostage. Someone who mattered to her personally. Then again, Nia and Zanta had been dragged from the same bed. Shaw would've already known they were close.

No use hiding it now. Zanta jerked against the ropes and restraining hands as Shaw's lackeys wrapped Nia in chains, and attached a round of chain shot to her ankles. Nia's mouth had thinned to a tight line. She elbowed one of the mercenaries in the ribs, earning herself a punch to the gut. She doubled over, coughing, and they finished binding her, then lifted her onto a plank that jutted out from the *Kraken*'s side.

"Let her go, motherfucker!" Logan thrashed against the ropes binding him to the rail beside the plank. Nia glanced over her shoulder from Logan to Zanta, holding fast to her nerves. "T-take me instead." Logan didn't look at Nia. His eyes were trained earnestly on Shaw.

"Logan," Rowan hissed, a rebuke and warning.

"Thank you for volunteering. Though I don't think I need you just yet." Shaw stepped up beside the plank, partially blocking Logan from view. He drew his sword and tapped it against the chains around Nia's legs. Her body stiffened, head lowering to stare at the misty water beneath her feet.

"You know," Shaw said almost conversationally. "I've been searching for the two of you for a while. I didn't expect you to make it so easy for me by finding each other first. Let alone leading me to the very place we needed to be."

"As if you didn't drive us here on purpose," Zanta spat. "Tell us what you're really after."

"I told you, Stroud's treasure."

"What does a few coins have to do with any of this?" She knew exactly how it was connected. Did Shaw know what the treasure really contained? If he did, did he plan to use the pelt, the journal, and the eye to infiltrate the Sleeping Isles? All she could do was deny, deny, deny. Shaw didn't know the pelt belonged to Nia, or he wouldn't be using her as a bargaining chip.

If he knew, that knowledge might save Nia's life, but he would use it against her people. It wasn't Zanta's secret to tell. It wasn't her choice to make. And thus far, Nia had remained silent.

"A few coins? No, Stroud's treasure is much more than that." Shaw pulled a small sheaf of papers from his vest and held it up. They were weathered, ripped along one edge, and scrawled with faded lettering Zanta had come to know intimately.

The missing pages of Stroud's journal. She forced recognition away from her expression, but all at once things clicked into place. Shaw's face was familiar, and if she imagined him younger, and with receding hair on his head instead of on his upper lip...He'd used a different name back then, but now Zanta was sure it was him. Stroud's former first mate. The thief.

"Some time ago, these papers came into my possession," Shaw said, as if he hadn't stolen them and quickened Stroud's descent into madness. "After my failure with you, Rowan, the Marran Empire gave me another chance to prove myself. Stroud's poor first mate got his head bashed in in a tavern brawl, and I was able to talk my way into the position. I meant to set a trap just like I did with you. But something more important came up." The papers fluttered in the breeze. What did they say? What information was Zanta missing that Shaw had? "These are pages from Silver Stroud's personal journal. I thought perhaps they would reveal where the fabled treasure was. And they did, but it is not gold and jewels. It's the key to something far greater. A way to conquer the Sleeping Isles. The old governor never believed me, but the new one sees the brilliance in my plan. You see, the chest contains the rest of this journal, a crystal ball that will show the truth, and the pelt of a creature of legend. The Sleeping Isles are not just a tribal backwater. If they were, one of the empires would have conquered them long ago. No, the people here are Selkies, protected by the sea itself."

Silence dropped over them like a shroud. They'd all known this, yet it stunned them to hear it spoken aloud.

Rowan's bark of laughter broke the tension. "Selkies? *That's* why you hunted us down? Selkies aren't real, you fucking lunatic. Those papers are obviously the ravings of a madman."

He was a good liar. If Zanta hadn't seen Nia transform with her own eyes, she might have believed him.

"I assure you, Selkies are very real. I did not just take Stroud's journal at face value. I have something that proves it all." Shaw snapped his fingers, and a mercenary appeared where the captives had been, holding a bundle of familiar gray speckled leather. For a moment, Zanta thought they'd found Nia's pelt after all, but as it unfurled in the mercenary's hands, she saw it was dull and lifeless, nothing close to the vital and shiny pelt she'd drawn from the chest so many days ago.

Nia made a low sound in her throat that could have been mistaken for pure fear for her life. She was no longer looking down at the water, but straight ahead at the pelt.

"A genuine Selkie pelt," Shaw declared. Nausea rose in Zanta's throat as she remembered one of the last pages she'd read of Stroud's journal.

He stole from me, the bastard. The last piece of Gwyneth is gone.

They were looking at Nia's mother's pelt, the absence of which had slowly killed her over the first decade of Nia's life. Zanta remembered when Emilie's predecessor, who she now knew was Shaw, had absconded one night in a Kefryean port with a great deal of Stroud's valuables. How Stroud had seemed to mourn instead of getting angry. How it had accelerated his distrust of his crew, and spurred on his ultimate descent into madness.

"It's just a seal pelt," Rowan scoffed. "What do they go for these days? A dozen copper tals? Maybe a silver?"

Shaw didn't seem to hear him. His eyes were lit with a fanatical fervor Zanta recognized all too well. "It says here," he continued, waving the papers, "Stroud was in possession of two pelts. One from his dead lover and one from their daughter. And imagine my surprise when I read another page. 'I am a fool. I gambled away my crystal, and it sailed away on a ship called the *Siren Song*. Now I will never find her.'" Shaw raised an eyebrow. "It's here, plain as day. You have the crystal, but you do not seem to have the *Siren Song* anymore. Did you let such a treasure go down with your ship? Or is it here?"

"You're mad." Rowan's face had gone white. "I knew you were a crooked bastard, but you're actually mad. You're going to condemn the people of the Sleeping Isles to war and slaughter at Marra's hands just like you condemned your own people! Just like you condemned *me*! And for what? A fairytale on a few scraps of paper?"

Zanta squeezed her eyes shut, forcing herself to think past the dread that grew through her chest like weeds. They couldn't go on like this. Denying everything Shaw said. Eventually he would snap and plunge Nia into the water. Without her pelt, she was just a human, as capable of drowning as any of them. And then Shaw would move on to the next, and the next, until the captains either handed him the treasure or his men found it.

Whichever it was, Nia was running out of time.

Zanta's eyes snapped open as the sword clanked against Nia's chains again. Nia stood preternaturally still, her gaze riveted to her mother's pelt.

"No more stalling," Shaw said. "I've told you what I want. I've got my men searching your ship. We *will* find what we're looking for. But if you tell me, I might let you live."

"I've heard that before," Rowan sneered. "You know how I respond to dirty deals with the empire."

"I do," Shaw agreed. "Fine then, I guess there are plenty of people on this ship to sacrifice." He prodded Nia in the back with the tip of his sword, and she lurched away from it, down the length of the plank.

"Wait!" Zanta didn't recognize her own voice for a moment. She'd played her hand again, after Rowan had denied it all so vehemently. "I-if we give you what you want, you'll let us go?" Deep down she knew it wasn't likely, but she couldn't just watch Nia drop into the sea and do nothing.

Nia's head whipped around. Her eyes were flat, emotionless. She shook her head.

"Yes," Shaw said. "I am a man of my word."

"Bullshit," Rowan growled. "Zanta, don't—" A mercenary clamped a hand over his mouth.

Tears blurred the scene before her. If she told Shaw where to find it all, Rowan would lose his eye; Nia's people would suffer; Nia herself would be in servitude to Shaw.

But she would be alive.

"I'll give you what you want," Zanta said. She thought she heard Nia's horrified exhalation of "*Zanta*", but she plowed on. "I'm not just Silver Stroud's killer. I'm the daughter he wrote about. The Selkie." Maybe Nia and the others could get away before Shaw found out the truth.

"Are you," Shaw said slowly, eyes narrowing.

"If you let the others go, I'll cooperate." A wave broke against the side of the *Kraken,* sending sea spray up around Nia's bound body. Zanta could buy enough time for her and the others to get away. She wouldn't have her pelt, but Henri and Logan would look after her. And Zanta knew nothing of the Selkies. Shaw would only have the journal to go by. She hoped they never found it in the little gap beneath the floorboards where she'd hidden it.

"And let you lead me into a trap?" Shaw laughed, an unpleasant grating sound. He poked Nia in the back again, and this time she stumbled. Her bare feet slipped on the slick wood. Zanta and Rowan both lurched forward, held back only by the mercenaries. Nia righted herself with great effort, breathing hard and still wobbling as the plank bowed beneath her.

"What do you want from me?" Zanta screamed. The ropes creaked as she strained against them. "I already said—"

"Prove it. Give me the pelt and transform."

Fuck.

Zanta's mind whirled. Could she fake it somehow?

In the misty gaps between the spires, Zanta thought she saw something move. The Selkies come to defend their land? She squinted, but found nothing but the mist rising in tendrils off the water. She refocused, seeking Nia's light green eyes. Full of all the emotion Zanta had been so afraid to interpret before. But now she knew. As they both stood on the *Kraken*'s deck, bound and hopeless, she knew Nia loved her.

They were willing to die for each other.

"Give him nothing," Nia said, so quietly it was almost lost to the waves. But Zanta heard it.

And so did Shaw.

Shaw stabbed her in the back. Not deep, but enough to unbalance her, enough for her to bleed as she lost her footing and plunged into the waiting waves.

CHAPTER 46

UNKNOWN DATE, 1668

Nia didn't have time to scream, so Zanta screamed for her. It filled Rowan's head, horrible and wrenching. And then something else drowned it out.

Boom! Boom! Boom!

The thunder of a full broadside echoed from the mist. Zanta surged forward, finally breaking from the mercenary's hold. She screamed Nia's name again as she made it to the rail, but what could she do? Her arms were still bound.

But someone could do something.

"Yves!"

Yves's dark eyes found him. He'd accepted Rowan's lead silently throughout their ordeal, but now he looked vicious, ready to fight.

"Go!" Rowan shouted. "Get Nia!"

He hesitated only for a second, torn between obeying Rowan and protecting him. With every moment of delay, Rowan imagined Nia sinking deeper beneath the waves. Struggling. Losing breath.

Shouting rang out belowdecks. Their crews had heard the cannon fire. Shaw shouted for his men.

A ball of fire arced toward them, ricocheting off a stone pillar, and crashing to the sea off the *Lonesome*'s bow. Two sets of masts appeared from the mist.

"Go!" Rowan ordered Yves.

Yves broke for the side as fast as the chains allowed.

"Seize him!" Shaw bellowed, even as he discarded his sword and raised a pistol. From his position on the ground, Logan kicked the back of Shaw's knee, and the shot went wide. The bullet caught Yves in the arm as he dove off the end of the plank.

Chaos descended. As clashing sounded from below, Rowan barreled forward into Shaw, hoping to knock him overboard, but only succeeded in landing both of them in a tangled heap in Logan's lap. Rowan managed to disengage himself, and snatched up Shaw's sword. He brought it down with as much force as he could muster on the ropes binding Logan's real hand to the rail. It wedged fast in the wood, and Rowan had to abandon it as Shaw roared to his feet.

More flaming projectiles rained down on the two ships, accompanied by near continuous cannon fire. Were they friend or foe? It didn't matter for now. All that mattered was using the chaos to his advantage.

To Rowan's left, Zanta headbutted a mercenary in the face. He went down, clutching a broken nose, and his cutlass skittered away. The other mercenaries converged on Rowan. Bound and outnumbered, he didn't stand a chance.

The door to below deck burst open, but instead of Rowan or Yves's crew, it was Gaël who charged onto the deck, followed by five crew members who had joined the *Sweet Mercy* all those months ago.

Rowan's heart thudded. He couldn't spare a glance for the attacking ships, but if Gaël was here, he was willing to bet one of them was the *Sweet Mercy*. It didn't matter right now how they'd managed the miracle of being here, how they'd managed to approach undetected, or how Gaël and his men were on board the *Kraken* when the ships were still far away. All that mattered now was that they stood a chance.

Gaël roared a battle cry as the group crashed into the surprised mercenaries. One of Gaël's axes embedded into a merc's jaw. A spray of crimson followed the arc of the blade on its way out. Gaël's eyes darted across the deck, no doubt searching for Fox in the melee.

Rowan reached the broken-nosed man's discarded cutlass. He dug his toe under the cross guard and flipped it up, barely managing to catch it in his bound hands. He stabbed the point between two deck boards and frantically sawed his bindings against the sharp edge.

Not fast enough. A mercenary charged him. Rowan rolled away, kicking the man in the shin, and sprang to his feet just in time to catch a knife stroke on the last strands of rope holding him. Feeling roared back into his hands with a vengeance, needles prickling inside his skin. He backed up a step, clumsily wrenched the sword from between the deck boards, and avoided the merc's next charge with a side step, landing a harsh stroke across the man's hip.

Pirates spilled onto the deck, beating the mercenaries back. Rowan's head whipped around, taking in the situation in a matter of moments. No sign of Yves or Nia yet. Logan had escaped his confinement and now skewered a mercenary's shoulder with his hook and tossed him overboard. His detached wooden hand remained bound to the rail.

But where was Shaw? Where was Zanta?

The attacking ships had edged closer now, still barely visible through the mist. The *Lonesome* weakly returned fire on them, but they were unprepared. Most of their crew had been on the *Kraken* keeping the pirates subdued and searching for Stroud's treasure.

"Rowan!"

He whipped around in time to find a mercenary charging up from his blind side. Thanks to Logan's shout, he managed to catch the swing on his cross guard, steel screaming. When he pushed the man back, and Logan pierced his throat with the sharp tip of his hook, a different scream filled the air.

A hawk's scream.

Nephele's gray silhouette passed in front of the strange sky. Soaring high out of range among the tops of the stone spires. But if she was here, that meant the other ship...

"It's the *Siren*!" Logan whooped, his astonished joy mirroring the lift in Rowan's heart. Last time they'd seen their beloved ship, she'd been hopelessly wedged between two spires high above the water's surface. Yet here she was, coming to their rescue alongside the *Sweet Mercy*, hale and whole. A laugh burst out of him, cut short by a shout from the quarterdeck.

Zanta squared off with Shaw, and she was injured, favoring her right leg.

"Take care of things down here. I'm going after Shaw." The pirates were gaining the upper hand, and Rowan didn't wait for Logan's agreement before he charged for the stairs.

Gaël caught up with him just as he reached the bottom step.

"Where's Fox?" he shouted, frantic.

"The other ship! He's a hostage!"

Gaël's eyes widened only for a second before he whirled.

"You! With me." What was left of his group of *Mercy* crew broke away to follow him through the fray toward the *Lonesome*. Rowan bounded up the stairs.

He didn't give Shaw time to react. He barreled into him, knocking him against the wheel column. Zanta shouted, and Shaw punched Rowan on his blind side, dislodging his eye patch.

The world shifted, disorienting. Suddenly the air came alive with magic only he could see. Shaw's eyes widened. "You—"

They'd both lost their weapons in the tackle. Zanta hobbled toward them, in no condition to fight.

"Your sword!" Rowan held out his hand. He could end this now while he had Shaw trapped against the wheel. Zanta tossed it, and Rowan would've caught it if not for the explosion of a stray projectile colliding with the *Kraken*'s sterncastle, knocking them all off their feet. Zanta cried out as her injured leg hit the deck.

Godsdamnit, John was launching literal fireballs from a fucking *trebuchet*.

Rowan scrambled to his feet, casting about for a weapon. If he hadn't been caught sleeping he'd have at least four knives, and a couple guns on him. But he'd woken up on the floor of Yves's parlor to the sight of Yves getting struck hard in the head with the butt of a rifle.

He spotted Zanta's fallen sword and dove for it. It was getting fucking annoying to constantly have to find new weapons. Shaw caught his legs, bringing him crashing to the deck. He kicked, but Shaw's weight pinned him. He scrambled onto Rowan and drew a pistol from his boot.

It was a tiny thing. The kind of gun designed for assassinations and last resorts. Not enough firepower to blow the back of your head off, but enough to kill at close range. Shaw pressed it to Rowan's forehead.

"You have the crystal eye," Shaw growled. The warm metal imprinted a circle into Rowan's skin.

Rowan couldn't deny it now, it was there in his face, plain as day. Shaw clearly hadn't thought the object described in the journal was an *actual eye* until the moment he'd seen it in Rowan's eye socket.

"Give it to me." The hand that wasn't holding a gun reached for his face, thumb settling against his tear duct like he intended to gouge it out with his bare fingers. Rowan's mind went blank.

No. *No.* Not again. He *couldn't...*

He couldn't give up the one thing that allowed him to truly see Yves.

Before he could react, Shaw wrenched him to his feet. The clamor of Rowan's panicked thoughts had drowned out the sudden eerie silence down on the deck. Even the bombardment seemed to be over. Shaw locked an arm around Rowan's shoulders, and settled the gun barrel against his temple.

And Rowan saw the reason for the silence. No one had won, but a new player had entered the game.

Chains rattled as Yves stepped over the rail of the *Kraken's Fury,* Nia's limp and sodden form slung over his shoulder.

CHAPTER 47

UNKNOWN DATE, 1668

"Nobody move or your captain dies!" Shaw's shout cut the silence, but only some of the fighters looked up. All attention remained riveted to the Demon.

Because he and Nia had been gone too long. It was impossible they could've survived.

Something akin to horror curdled in Zanta's gut as the Demon slowly looked up to where Shaw held his husband hostage. He dropped Nia like she meant nothing, and she crumpled to the deck with an awful, soggy thud. Unmoving.

"Nia!" Zanta croaked. She tried to stand, but blinding pain flared through her hip where Shaw had thrown her against the mizzenmast. She collapsed near the rail.

The Demon stepped over Nia's body. Pirates and mercenaries alike parted before him. Only a few people had seen him go into the water after Nia, but all of them had witnessed him emerge in chains. The iron links dragged across the deck, holding everyone on board under some strange spell. No one moved but him.

The Demon stalked up the steps like a prowling wolf, seawater dripping from his hair, his coat, his fingertips. His eyes gleamed with feral darkness.

Shaw snapped out of it first.

"Stay back!" he barked, pressing the pistol tighter to Rowan's head. "I'll kill him!"

Rowan didn't even flinch. Now that the Demon was back, a calmness had loosened his posture, as if there was no reality in his mind where his husband would let him come to harm. Every line of him held a self-assurance that this was not his day to die.

How could he be so sure? Not even the Demon could stop a bullet.

The Demon's gaze sharpened, but he did not stop his ascent. He didn't even look at Shaw. He had eyes only for his husband. His slow, measured steps thumped on the boards like a heartbeat, accompanied only by the drip of water, the clink of spurs, and the drag of chains.

Shaw stepped back, wrenching Rowan's head back by the hair.

"I said stop!" he ordered, with the voice of a man who was used to being the most powerful in the room.

But he couldn't hold a candle to the power of the Deep Water Demon, and pirates never obeyed.

Shaw jammed the barrel harder against Rowan's skull. Rowan hissed. The Demon's steps faltered.

Why hadn't Shaw shot Rowan yet? Lingering feelings? Or was he afraid the bullet would shatter the crystal eye?

Zanta could've sworn the Demon's eyes darkened, a vicious aura rolling off his soaked body. Her skin prickled in response.

"Stay back!" True fear entered Shaw's voice for the first time. He turned the pistol on the Demon and pulled the trigger.

The Demon's head snapped back, a perfectly round hole blooming in the middle of his forehead as the echoes of the gunshot rang between the stones. Zanta screamed. Below, pirates rushed forward.

Rowan's body jerked, as if it was he who'd been shot. As if his nerves were misfiring, trying to reject the lead violently lodged in his brain. He said his husband's name on an exhale, so quiet Zanta barely heard it, but that was the only thing he said. He did not cry or scream or struggle. He gazed at the Demon with tearless, clear eyes.

Zanta couldn't wrap her head around it. Weeks after the battle at Wave Harbor, she'd been the one to deliver the news to Rowan that the Deep Water Demon was dead, and the sound that had ripped from his chest still haunted her. Now the same man was gunned down right in front of him, and he barely even flinched? Didn't even try to go to his fallen lover's side?

In fact, a small, wicked smile was spreading across his lips.

Because the Demon had not fallen. There was no topple backward down the stairs as a dead man should have. He remained frozen, one foot poised above the second to last step.

Horror crackled up Zanta's spine as the Demon's head slowly tilted forward. Soaked onyx hair fell into his eyes, perfectly framing the bullet hole dead center in his forehead. A trail of crimson gushed down between his brows, mingling with the seawater to drip from his chin.

He was alive. Horribly. Impossibly.

And he was grinning.

Shaw's spent pistol clattered to the deck. He drew a dagger with shaking hands, and pressed a thin line of blood into Rowan's throat. The Demon's black, inhuman gaze finally fixed on the man who held his beloved prisoner. His jaw worked, and then his mouth yawned wide. Seawater and blood poured from his lips, and something metallic pinged to the deck and rolled toward Zanta.

The bullet.

What the *fuck* was he?

Someone on the deck below screamed, and the Demon lunged, snatching Rowan away with one arm, and seizing Shaw by the throat with the other. Shaw drew half a terrified breath before the Demon snapped his neck with a flick of the wrist. Using no more effort than one would use to snap a twig.

The Demon released him, and he crumpled to the deck, as lifeless as a puppet with cut strings. The Demon's attention zeroed in on Rowan, brow furrowing with all the anguish he hadn't shown with a bullet lodged in his brain. The air thickened, choking, but Zanta couldn't look away. The Demon clutched Rowan to his chest, eyes roving over him possessively, and Rowan arched into the embrace. Zanta thought, ridiculously, the Demon was about to bite him. A drop of diluted blood dripped from the tip of his nose to Rowan's parted lips.

The Demon's eyelids fluttered. He bent to kiss the blood away.

A jolt ran through Zanta's body as if she was coming out of a trance. She struggled to her feet, shock and pain making everything slow. The silence was deafening. The only movement...

A choked sob climbed up Zanta's throat. She hobbled to the stairs, left leg dragging. Below, Nia lay sprawled where the Demon had dropped her, soaked red hair like twisted seaweed splayed around her head.

CHAPTER 48

UNKNOWN DATE, 1668

Zanta practically tumbled down the stairs. No one helped her. But she couldn't feel the pain now. Her eyes were trained on Nia's deathly still body, Robin kneeling beside her, frantically pumping her chest. Grief twisted through Zanta, wriggling between her guts and latching onto her bones. Nia couldn't be gone. She'd only just returned to the sea, her true form. Zanta had let her drown for the sake of her secrets.

Zanta fell to her knees in a puddle beside Nia's body, pain lancing through her hip. Robin glanced at her but continued working. He left off compressions and tilted Nia's chin up with gentle, practiced fingers. He pinched her nose and bent down to breathe life back into her still form.

One breath. Two. Nia's chest rose, and Zanta's hope rose with it. She held her own breath, as if denying herself would let Nia live. Hot tears slipped down her cheeks.

Please...please...

After the third breath, Robin sat back. Nia's chest remained still. Robin did not continue compressions.

Zanta tore her gaze away from Nia's deathly pallor.

"She's gone." His voice was gentle. His eyes shone with tears.

"No," It came out choked as grief coiled around her throat. She reached across Nia's body to grab his wrist. "Try again. Please..."

He laid a large hand over hers. "She's been down too long. She was underwater so long..."

No. It wasn't fair. It wasn't right. Would she never feel Nia's warmth beside her again? Bicker with her, or hear her laugh ring out over the waves? Zanta couldn't bear it. Why should the Demon survive to return to his beloved, but not Nia?

Nia was a creature of the sea, but it had killed her. Here, so close to her true home.

Zanta's grief caught on that.

"Her pelt!" She whirled, half stood, and collapsed to the deck again as pain flared up her leg. "Someone get her pelt!"

"Where is it?" Zanta hadn't noticed Logan beside her, silently crying.

"The safe! The Demon's safe!" Last night Nia had confessed to giving the pelt to the Demon, who'd told her that's where it would be. Logan dashed off.

He emerged what felt like an eternity later, clutching Nia's shimmery pelt with his hook arm and dragging Henri with the other hand.

As soon as Henri saw his sister lying there, motionless on the deck, his face crumpled. Robin caught him, and held him as he knelt by her side. His hands trembled violently as he reached out to caress her cheek.

Zanta snatched the pelt from Logan's grasp and laid it carefully over Nia's body. This was their last chance. Their only chance. Henri's grief wouldn't matter if this worked.

Nothing happened.

A sob wracked Zanta's body. She rested her head against Nia's chest. It was like putting her ear to a seashell. All she could hear was the *whoosh* of waves, and her own grief stricken sobs.

"If you come back to me. I'll never set foot on land again," Zanta whispered against the silvery pelt, words broken by hitching breaths. Like Nia, Zanta was born for the sea. Born with salt in her blood. "I'll sail with you forever." Her voice broke on the last word.

And she felt it.

It couldn't be real. This flicker of life. It was only her imagination. Her own pulse. But she felt it.

Zanta sat up, tilted Nia's face to hers, and breathed.

She breathed away every ounce of life she had in her. Nia's lips softly accepted it, and Zanta felt it again, the flutter of a pulse beneath her fingertips. Zanta raked in a shuddering inhale, and breathed for Nia again. The kiss of life, a rebirth from the cold and loving embrace of the sea, who never gave you up once she had you.

But they belonged to each other now.

Nia's body jolted. She turned on her side, and retched up a gout of seawater. Then sucked in a huge, ragged breath.

Fuck. She was alive. Zanta barely let her recover her breath before crushing her in a hug. She'd meant what she said. She would've given anything for Nia to come back to her. As soon as Nia's feet had left the plank, Zanta had wished it was her sinking to the bottom of the sea instead. If only so she wouldn't have to lose another woman she loved.

"Zanta..." Nia croaked, her throat raw with salt water. Zanta shook her head and buried her face deeper into the side of Nia's neck. Nia's arms came around her shakily, and she felt Henri and the others hovering nearby, anxious to make sure Nia was okay. Zanta couldn't bear to release her yet.

"I love you," Zanta hiccuped. "I don't think we said it properly before, but I do."

Nia finally managed to wrestle a bit out of her embrace. She framed Zanta's face between cold, clammy hands, green eyes bright and searching. "Zanta, listen to me. Listen. I love you too, more than anything but...what did you promise to get me back?"

CHAPTER 49

UNKNOWN DATE, 1668

Rowan's mouth moved slowly against Yves's, savoring the taste of him, coppery blood mingling with seawater on their tongues. His fingers dug into the front of Yves's soaked clothes. Yves's arms tightened at his waist.

Yves's shadowy tentacles writhed around them, cutting them off from the outside world. In the back of Rowan's mind, he knew this was bad. Very bad. But he couldn't bring himself to care. They were both alive. Yves's arms were around him. Yves was kissing him.

Rowan's body began to shiver, the reality of witnessing Yves die and resurrect right in front of him chasing the adrenaline away. He'd seen the bullet enter Yves's forehead, his head snapping back with the force of it. At the time, Rowan hadn't been frightened. Deep down, he held the utter belief that Yves would never leave him behind.

"Yves," Rowan murmured into the kiss.

Yves's body trembled now, echoing Rowan's own shiver. He pulled back slightly, hands coming up to thread through the messy strands of Rowan's hair. Rowan met his gaze, the flat darkness of the demon side blacking everything out. There was nothing of Yves's humanity in them; the demon held him together. Yves said nothing, but rested his forehead against Rowan's, the bullet wound pressed to his skin, blood dripping slow and warm down Rowan's face.

A shudder wracked Yves's body.

Rowan pulled back, and without the connection of their bodies, Yves's legs seemed to give out. He crumpled to his knees.

"Yves!" Rowan grabbed him, but he was already stumbling back to his feet. Fumbling. Unsteady. The shadows at his back were fading, the void receding from his eyes.

"Captain." John appeared at Rowan's side. He drew Rowan close, one hand clutching his arm. "Everyone saw," he said, low and stern. Rowan wasn't sure if the demon shadows were visible to everyone now or just him. But it didn't matter. Everyone had seen Yves get shot in the head and not die. Their secret was revealed for all to see.

Yves stumbled again, and both Rowan and John moved to catch him. Yves draped an arm lazily across Rowan's shoulders, chains rattling, head lolling like a drunk.

The deck of the *Kraken* remained utterly silent, but for the quiet sobs of relief from Zanta, clutching Nia's shivering wet form in her arms. Robin and Henri knelt beside them, but the rest of the crew stood dumbstruck, staring at their captains. They hadn't known. Rowan hadn't even told those closest to him. Now the truth was out.

Yves moaned, low and pained.

"Take him to rest," John said quietly. "I'll handle things up here."

Rowan nodded. The crew shifted back as the two captains descended the stairs. Even Logan's eyes were wide with fear and distrust.

Rowan's heart clenched painfully, but he couldn't worry about that now. He dragged Yves into the stateroom and down the hidden stairs to the captain's quarters.

Rowan laid Yves gently on the bed, unable to remove his soaked clothes and boots with the manacles still clamped at his wrists and ankles. Blood seeped sluggishly from the wound but pink scar tissue slowly formed at its edges. Bile rose in Rowan's throat, and he averted his eyes. It didn't matter that he knew Yves couldn't die, the sight of that bullet hole in his head burned itself into Rowan's memory.

"Ro..." Yves's voice came out hoarse from the damage of the bullet traveling down through his brain to the back of his throat. He swallowed, plush lips stained with blood.

"Let me clean you up." Rowan tried to step away. He needed to find something to open the manacles, but Yves caught his wrist, grip weaker than it should have been. Rowan looked back to his face. The wound was a bit smaller now, scar tissue already fading to smooth skin around the edges. It was unnerving to see Yves so weak, so wounded. Rowan hoped he wasn't in much pain. Rowan had never seen him die before. How long did it usually take to heal and bounce back? He knew the first time, when Yves and the demon were newly one, it had taken days for Yves to open his eyes again after drowning. And whenever he'd seen Yves merely injured—usually by Rowan's nails or teeth in the throes of passion—the wounds had healed just as any other person's would. But this, a bullet to the skull, hadn't even killed him for long enough to fall.

Yves's grip tightened, some of his strength beginning to return.

"Kiss me, darling," he slurred, a coy, lazy smile curling his lips. His eyes were glassy. What was he doing? He'd been shot in the head. He was probably in immeasurable pain, yet he was acting like a tipsy youth.

"Are you in pain?" Yves's grip still trapped Rowan's wrist, but he bent low to smooth some strands of hair away from Yves's face.

Yves giggled. *Giggled.* Rowan had never actually heard him giggle before. It was a light and musical sound, like a child full of joy at receiving a sweet.

"I feel..." Yves swallowed again, the damage to his throat slowly knitting back together like the shreds of brain matter.

Oh. His brain. The bullet had traveled right down the middle, and now that the demon had faded into the background, that left Yves to deal with the consequences.

"I f-feel..." Yves blinked, brow furrowing and wrinkling the edges of the wound when he couldn't form the words correctly. The demon void began to spread out from one of his irises, curling across the white of his eye like smoke.

Yves's fingers tightened suddenly. He yanked Rowan down onto the bed and rolled on top of him. The chain hit Rowan's sternum as Yves pinned his wrists to the pillow beside his head.

"Yves, what—" Rowan's protest was cut off as Yves captured his lips in a sloppy kiss. A wanton moan escaped Yves's damaged throat.

For a moment, Rowan let himself give in to Yves's delicious tongue slipping into his mouth, to Yves's body on top of his. Then blood dribbled out of the bullet wound onto his face, Yves's hips rutted against Rowan's thigh, hard cock evident, and Rowan's mind cleared.

Rowan broke the kiss, but Yves was not deterred. His lips moved down over Rowan's neck, nipping his skin playfully.

"Wait..."

Yves's long tongue licked sloppily over the shallow wound from Shaw's knife, and up the side of Rowan's neck to his cheek.

"Stop," Rowan ordered.

Yves stilled, his tongue still flat against the scars on Rowan's cheek. Rowan pushed his shoulder, for once having almost equal strength between them. Yves landed on his back, damp hair splayed out across the pillow. He giggled again and tried to pull Rowan down on top of him.

"Please..." Yves's voice came out breathy and alluring. He licked a speck of blood from his plush lips, thighs falling open invitingly. "Don't you want to fuck me?"

Rowan's thoughts stuttered. Was Yves actually asking him for this? He couldn't deny he'd dreamed of it. Of Yves looking just like this—minus the blood—falling apart beneath him. Begging for him. His long legs wrapping around Rowan's waist. His soft, pliant insides sliding around Rowan's cock.

"Rowan..." Yves whimpered. Gods, he was gorgeous. Even with rivulets of blood on his pale face and a bullet hole in his skull. For once his hair was a mess. *He* was a mess. And he was all the more beautiful for it. Rowan's mind clouded, and he leaned down to capture that begging mouth. Yves moaned into it, needy, the tendons of his wrist flexing against Rowan's palm. Rowan's hips stuttered against him once, then he broke the kiss, pulling back to search Yves's eyes. One shone starry and human, the other as fathomless as the dark depths of the sea.

The sight jolted Rowan back to reality. Yves was injured, not in his right mind. Rowan wanted him, but not like this.

Yves strained against Rowan's hold, trying to recapture their kiss. Rowan covered Yves's mouth with his other hand, pushing Yves's head into the pillow. He leaned down to kiss the little knot of scar tissue in the middle of Yves's forehead, and Yves whimpered behind his hand.

"I can't fuck you, love. Not like this," Rowan said gently. His lips traveled to Yves's hairline, his temple, his cheek. Yves's eyelids fluttered. "It's time to rest now."

Yves's body surged against him, thighs tightening on either side of his hips. But he was still too weak to dislodge Rowan's hold.

After a few moments of struggle, Yves finally relaxed, and Rowan settled down on the bed next to him, removing his hand from Yves's mouth. The seawater from Yves's clothes soaked into Rowan's front, but he drew him close all the same. Yves sighed contentedly, and after a while, turned his head to gaze at Rowan. The pink scar was fading, the void of Yves's demon eye receding again. Rowan stroked his hair, trying to soothe whatever passions still lingered.

Had Yves meant what he said about Rowan fucking him, or was that just the result of the temporary brain damage? They'd been sleeping together for almost two years, and Rowan had never topped. Due to Yves's past, being on the receiving end wasn't something he was comfortable with, and Rowan hadn't ever pushed him on that. Now he wondered if Yves had some desire for it, deep down.

He locked the thoughts away for another time, and they lay side by side for what felt like an hour, listening to the activity throughout the ship and the waves outside the windows. Rowan wondered if John had been able to placate the crew enough that they wouldn't have double mutinies on their hands when Yves resurfaced from his injuries. What worried him most was the betrayal on Logan's face. Fox and Henri would probably feel the same way, but they hadn't been on deck to see it with their own eyes. They were Rowan's closest friends in the world, more like family, and Rowan hated keeping secrets from them. But this hadn't been his secret to tell.

Yves shifted and Rowan realized he'd been drifting off in his own thoughts. He opened his eyes to see Yves on his side, gazing at him with two fully human eyes. Rowan stroked his hair back from his forehead. The skin there was as unblemished as always, the bullet wound fully healed, as if it had never been.

"Are you back?" Rowan asked quietly, almost afraid of the answer.

Yves nodded, not taking his wide, dark eyes from Rowan's face. He leaned close hesitantly, seeming pleased when Rowan didn't pull away, and planted a soft kiss on his lips.

"I'm sorry," Yves said when he pulled away.

"For what?"

"For making you watch me die. For almost letting you get hurt. For..." His brows furrowed in concentration, as if trying to remember what had happened between getting shot and now. "For...acting like a fool."

"We're both fools, remember?" Rowan murmured.

"I never wanted you to see me like that." The words were so reminiscent of their wedding night that Rowan shivered.

~

"I WILL SEE all of you, and love you all the more," he whispered, tucking a strand of onyx hair behind Yves's ear. "You should know that by now."

Logan's hands shook. Nia still lay on the deck, covered by her pelt and bracketed by Zanta and Henri. He wanted to go to her and wrap her in a hug, but it wasn't his place. She'd almost drowned, and she needed the people she loved around her. That wasn't him.

Was it a miracle that she'd survived? Or had her pelt brought her back somehow?

Logan's head whipped around, immediately finding Rowan and the Demon locked in an embrace up on the quarterdeck, Shaw dead at their feet. Dread curdled in his gut. Shaw had shot the Demon in the head. The hole still dripped in his forehead. On top of that, he'd been underwater for almost as long as Nia. How the fuck was he still alive?

The Demon stumbled, Rowan caught him, and John—who had just arrived on the *Sweet Mercy*—rushed up the stairs to help. Rowan dragged the Demon down the stairs and toward the captain's quarters. Dread spiked, spurring Logan after them. He didn't know what he intended to do, but the urge to not allow Rowan to be alone with that monster overwhelmed him. When the pair reached the door, Rowan's one blue eye locked on Logan, then he turned away, disappearing with the Demon.

John stopped Logan in front of the door, the barest flash of relief showing on his face.

"Let me through," Logan said, through gritted teeth. He needed to get to Rowan, protect him from whatever the Demon was.

"Leave them." John squeezed his shoulder. Logan knocked his arm aside, and tried to sidestep him, but John got in his way again. They eyed each other. Either John was taking this in incredible stride, or he'd already known what the Demon was.

"You knew," Logan accused. John grabbed him by the arm and hauled him into the shelter of the quarterdeck wall slightly tucked away from the rest of the stunned crew.

"It was not my secret to tell."

"How long?"

"What?"

"How long have you known he's not human?" The words stuck in Logan's mouth like bitter tar. A few months ago, he wouldn't have been able to wrap his head around this. He would've tried to chalk it up to a misfire of his own perception. But now he'd seen Nia transform into a Selkie before his own eyes, and if something like a Selkie could exist, why not a darker, more insidious creature?

"Since the start of the season," John answered.

So the Demon had kept it even from his closest confidant. "Did Rowan know before today?"

"Since the wedding."

Fuck, Logan had half hoped that Rowan hadn't known, or had just found out, or...something. He didn't want to believe that his best friend would keep something like this from him for over a year. Rowan had known, and John had known, and they'd kept Logan in the dark. That meant John already knew about this when they'd slept together at the Teeth. Somehow that made Logan feel even worse. What else were they keeping from him?

"How did you get here?" Logan asked. He didn't know why. John had saved them. But the *Sweet Mercy* looked practically as new as the day they'd stolen her, while every other ship that had sailed through the Storm Ring was battered and broken. Logan wasn't naturally the suspicious sort, but something about that seemed wrong.

John shrugged. "The Storm Ring seems to be mostly legend and tale. The section we went through was nothing more than a mild squall." He seemed to catch himself, noticing how the rest of the ships were damaged. "Though that doesn't seem to be the case for you."

"No," Logan huffed. "It was the worst storm of my life." But the anomalies of the Storm Ring didn't explain why John had sailed through it in the first place. How had he known they would be here? Logan's eyes caught on the battered navy uniform John always wore. A symbol of the life he had left, a symbol of their enemy.

Logan tried to step away, nausea rising in his throat, but John hauled him into a tight hug. Logan froze, brain stuttering, warring between betrayal and confusion. John had never embraced him like this, just holding him in a completely nonsexual way.

"I'm glad you made it through," John murmured. Then, "We need to keep it together till they get back." He released him, but lingered with his hands on Logan's arms for a moment. Logan searched his expression, finding only determination. No trace of the earlier softness.

CHAPTER 50

UNKNOWN DATE, 1668

Logan swallowed his heart back down as Henri lifted Nia into his arms, Robin helping a limping Zanta to stand as they made their way belowdecks.

"Is that...Nia?" John took a hesitant step forward, and this time it was Logan who stopped him from butting in where they didn't belong.

"What on earth is going on here?" John's usual confidence seemed shaken now, and Logan's heart gave a pathetic little stutter. He cared about Nia, they both did, but had Logan misjudged their dynamic? Did John have stronger feelings for her than he'd let on?

"I could ask you the same thing," Logan said. John's explanation of how and why he was here didn't fully make sense. After learning what Rowan had kept from him...he felt like he didn't know anything anymore.

John opened his mouth as if to reply, but a commotion rose from the deck where pirates and mercenaries who had been fighting moments ago suddenly remembered that fact.

"Oi!" Logan barked, nerves finally snapping. In the absence of the other three captains, it was him and John holding everything together now. "Your leader is dead; lay off!"

The mercenaries froze, adrift without Shaw. John stepped in as pirates from the *Sweet Mercy* arrived, fresh and untainted by battle. "Round up the mercs," he ordered. Pirates from every crew obeyed.

And so did Logan. He didn't want to think. He simply followed the directions of the only captain left on deck, and pushed away all the thoughts that tried to force their way into his brain. He regrouped his crew and took stock of who was left.

Members of Gaël's team started to reappear on the *Lonesome*'s deck after routing what remained of the mercenary crew. The other hostages appeared alongside them, looking battered but whole. Fox was still missing, but Gaël had gone after him. They would be okay if they were together. Right now Logan had to focus on his people aboard the *Kraken*. He had to pick up Rowan's slack.

By the time he got his crew sorted and the pirates rallied to round up the last of the mercenaries, Doe had arrived with the damaged, but sailable, *Siren Song*.

"Looks like you're doing just fine here," Doe exclaimed, taking in the situation at a glance. She ruffled Logan's hair in an overwhelmingly motherly gesture, and all at once Logan missed his own mum terribly. She would've known what to say to help him sort out this jumble of feelings he was patently ignoring. Or maybe she wouldn't. He hadn't seen her since he was nine, and she'd died while he was in the navy. Maybe she wouldn't have been the mother he remembered.

Now this was a whole new spiral. He clamped it down, and graced Doe with a half-hearted smile.

"Tried my best. You got here just in time."

Doe nodded and looked around again, her almost jovial demeanor dampened slightly. "Where are the captains?"

Right, the captains. "Zanta is attending to Nia." He realized Doe wouldn't know who that was. "Her lover, who almost drowned. Rowan and the Demon..." Nausea curdled again, some of the dark thoughts succeeded in bubbling to the surface. He took a deep breath to steady himself. "The Demon is...not human."

Doe's face performed a complex maneuver before settling on an expression of understanding. "Ah."

"What, you knew too? Did everyone know but me?" Logan's voice rose with anxiety, and several nearby crew members looked at them askance.

"I didn't know till you just told me," Doe reassured him. "But back when we were first sailing together, when the crew was full of Talvan sailors who didn't want to follow him, there were rumors. They insisted they'd killed Yves when he first took the ship. Stabbed him right through the neck, and watched him bleed out. And there were times..." Her expression grew distant with memory. "He protected me from them, and there were times when it seemed like a darkness overtook him, and he was stronger than he should've been." Doe refocused on Logan, a gentle smile tugging at the lined corners of her mouth. "So no, Logan, I didn't know. But after everything, it makes sense."

A shout from the bow interrupted Logan's next words. John's men dragged Selby Baird from the knot of captive mercenaries. She'd changed back into her uniform, with its strange mix of Kefryean and Marran insignia. The crossed unicorn horn and claymore of Kefryean nobility sitting right beside the Marran laurel and sun. Despite her days surviving the wreckage of her ship, and night in the brig, she seemed calm and in control. She was Shaw's second in command, commander of the mercenaries in her own right.

Had she escaped before the *Lonesome* arrived? Or had the mercenaries let her out?

Pushing aside their conversation, Logan and Doe hurried over, flanking John. Despite Logan's resentment, John was the only captain they had right now, and they had to present a united front.

John gazed at the woman coolly, taking in the insignia, and what they meant.

"Colonel Selby Baird, I presume."

Baird cocked her head to the side, assessing him right back. John's old navy uniform, with its red replacement sleeve standing out starkly against the black. Her eyebrows rose.

"The Beast, I presume."

Did they know each other? Or was Baird as infamous as John?

"Your leader is dead. Your crew and ship are captured. I think now is the time for you to offer your formal surrender," John said.

Baird's eyes flicked over the three of them, then to all the pirates amassed at their back.

"I don't see any captains to surrender to."

John smiled politely. "Oh, didn't you hear? I've been elevated."

His words were undercut by the door to the captain's quarters opening. Every head whipped around to look, even John's.

"Speak of the Demon," Baird muttered under her breath.

Rowan and the Demon emerged, the Demon looking none the

worse for wear. Logan's heartbeat ratcheted up. There wasn't even a mark where the bullet had penetrated the Demon's skull.

Instead of retreating up to the quarterdeck where he could lord over his ship like the tyrant he was, the Demon stepped onto a shallow crate, just high enough that he could see the faces of all those gathered on the *Kraken*'s deck. Rowan took up a position by his side, and the chains still at the Demon's wrists rattled as Rowan squeezed his hand.

The crowd remained deadly quiet, waiting.

"You all saw what you saw," the Demon began, his voice steady. Not at all like a man who had been drowned and shot and gods knew what else in the last few hours. "Your eyes did not deceive you. I was shot in the head, and I lived." Murmurs broke through the crowd, but not one of them dared challenge him. "The name Deep Water Demon is not just a name. The kraken symbol is not just a symbol. I am not fully human. I am a demon."

The men and women at the front shrank back. The Talvans made their sign against evil, touching eyelids then lips. The Yarenens encircled their serpent tattoos with shaking fingers.

"I handpicked each of you for my crew, not only because of your strength, but your ability to withstand the fear I elicit. You came to me as desperate rogues and refugees. I gave you a home and a purpose. I would ask that you continue to follow me, despite my deception." He splayed his hands in front of him, displaying the manacles that bound him. "I am at your mercy."

Logan held his breath, waiting to see what the *Kraken* crew members would do. None of this was up to him. The Demon had kept his true nature from the men and women who owed him loyalty. Rowan had hidden the fact there was a monster in their midst, even from the people who were like family to him. Logan didn't know what the others would do. But he didn't trust the Demon, and now it seemed like he couldn't trust Rowan either.

Before any of them could answer, an arrow streaked through the air and embedded in the wood between the Demon's feet. Logan whipped around as figures appeared on the clifftops, bare-chested with gray speckled seal pelts over their heads and backs. Two dozen arrows trained on the ships below. A pirate shouted from the rail, and Logan rushed over to see the water around the ships crowded with seals and more warriors armed with spears swarming up the sides.

The Selkies had found them.

THE END

CONTENT WARNINGS

Not all of the items listed are major themes but all are present in some form. I believe in being as thorough as possible in listing content so my readers can make informed decisions about what they read.

General

Brief suicidal ideation, Internalized homophobia and homophobia by estranged family members , Graphic violence, blood, and gore, Murder, Eye mutilation (again, sorry), Stalking by a romantic partner, Traumatic brain injury, Shipwreck(s), Drowning (including descriptions of a drowned corpse), Body horror, Themes of colonialism

~

Sex

Explicit, on-page sex, Bondage, Praise kink, Unnegotiated dom/sub dynamics, Mild blood play, Ye olde sex toys, Lack of aftercare

~

For a fully up to date content warnings page please follow the QR code:

ACKNOWLEDGMENTS

Splinter Heart took a bit longer to write than I'd have liked, thanks in part to accidentally writing *Undefined Tides* in the middle. As I move further into my author career, I am developing something of a routine, or maybe more of a cycle when it comes to drafting, editing, and publishing books. But in the end, it's all up to whatever chaos my brain decides to produce. So let's thank the people who make sense out of the chaos.

As always, my biggest supporters and the people I want to thank the most are my beta readers: Emma, Lacey, and Chris. Thank you for being so excited to see the boys again. My critique partners, Austin and Erin, also gave a lot of awesome feedback. I'd also like to thank my husband, Tom, for his continuing support and willingness to help me with all sorts of author nonsense.

Additionally, a huge and loving thank you to my editor, Kal Morgan, your work on these books is invaluable in making my writing actually readable and publishable. Thank you also to Amphi at Amphi Studios for formatting, and Kelly at Velvet Library for proofreading.

Lastly I'd like to thank the artists that worked on the beautiful art to accompany this book and bring my characters to life. The artist of my author portrait, Gukkhwa (Eunhye Cho). My cover artist, Maria Arteta. Typography, cover design, and interior art by Amphi at Amphi Studio. And map by Isaac Jordan. You were all so wonderful to work with, and seeing my characters and vision come to life under your skilled hands has truly been a dream come true.

ABOUT THE AUTHOR

Briar Belmont

Briar Belmont writes spicy queer romance and fantasy. Her debut novel, *Demon of the Deep*, came out in 2024, followed by *Undefined Tides*. She lives in Minnesota with her husband, dog, and four cats.

Author Portrait by Gukkhwa (Eunhye Cho)

~

instagram.com/briar_belmont

www.ingramcontent.com/pod-product-compliance
Lightning Source LLC
La Vergne TN
LVHW091246150826
845673LV00006B/1334